The Spark

That

Left Us

The Spark That Left Us

K. Brooks
Visit my website at www.thesparkthatleftus.com
Or Follow me on Twitter @sparksthatleft

To the little birdie in my ear,

Who kept me pushing on through

The Spark That Left Us

By K. Brooks

Chapter 1

The Calm Before the Storm

If I had known, that one week was all that was left, maybe I would have paid attention. If I had known, maybe I would have taken a little more time to care.

But I hadn't known, as most of us don't, the path my day, and week would end up taking, a foreign route, bizarre to me, controlled by the forces in a world of which we have no perception, and I had failed to see the big picture, let alone the consequences of anyone else's actions.

But it's always in the details, isn't it? Just those little tattered pieces of information, the love notes to a better time, and a better place, that can hold the key to catching onto the reality of a situation.

It's in the smell of the grass after the rainfall, wafting through the window you didn't remember leaving open, teasing your nostrils with the promise of spring. It's in the click of the clock turning to alarm, as it switches to that God-awful country station you listen to in order to assure you rise from sleep.

It's in the thick scent of coffee brewing in the morning, sticking to the back of your throat, urging you to rise. Never mind that you didn't set the timer, and that you never drink coffee.

I should've known today and the week that followed wouldn't be anything I'd ever experienced. I should have clutched those details to my chest and run with them, analyzed them, and used them to protect myself. They practically screamed at me in that calm, still moment before I had even opened my eyes.

"Um, might be my old age catching up with me... **but** I don't believe you live here," I protested, rubbing sleep from my eyes as I padded into the brightly lit kitchen.

My sister looked up at me from the coffee she was brewing, the machine steaming and spitting, and shot me a dirty look from behind a pair of oversized aviators. Dressed in last night's revelry, complete with torn fishnets, spiked heels and of course, her hangover sunglasses; she looked what only could be described as 'rough'.

"I was downtown. You're closer than Reggie's, and you left your window unlocked. Bad habit you know," she sipped gently at her freshly poured cup and considered me through the steam.

I made a non-committal noise through my nose and reached around her to pour my own. I ignored the fact that her voice had hitched slightly at the mention of Reggie's name, a misstep in a long routine I chose to ignore. I turned to face her, leaning against the counter,

"You want to lecture me on bad habits now, huh? Sneaking in windows, crashing on my couch. Next I turn around, you'll be leaving your clothes and a toothbrush here," I gesture my cup at her, sloshing droplets across the floor.

Our mutual bad habits had been a frequent discussion many times up until now, and I wasn't eager to start it all over again. God knows it would only end in something breaking, someone crying, and a disapproving phone call from Mother. No, thank you. She continued to stare at me, challenging me from behind her dark over-sized lenses.

She drains her cup, and drops it, thudding into the sink.

"You're right, I know. But at least I made the coffee," her face brightened behind the glasses.

I took a sip and grimaced. I remembered now why I didn't drink it.

"Well, best be onward and outward. I am sure Mother will be expecting me to be snug in my bed when she makes the morning rounds," she sashays across the kitchen tile, tottering on the slightly too-high heels, through the adjoining living room and heads for the front door.

Having so skillfully climbed through the window last night, no doubtfully drunk, I questioned whether I should ask her to leave the way she came – if only to get a last parting rise from her. She unlocks the door and strides off down the stairs, wiggling her fingers in a goodbye over her shoulder. As I begin to shut the door behind her, I hear a snort coming from under the bay window and I turn abruptly toward the sound. A tall, dark-clothed man seemed to be snoozing on my couch; feet tucked up and his head on a throw pillow. I pause, turn back to the door and throw it open.

"Forgetting something? I don't want to keep it!"

She turned at my voice and continued walking backwards, putting a hand against her brow to shield her eyes behind the glasses from the hot morning sun. I could feel it beating off the still-wet sidewalk, an unusually hot day for the time of year.

She shrugged, holding her hand to her ear and scrunching up her face. She waved at me once more and was promptly on her way. I huffed, and quietly closed the door. I wish this hadn't been the first time she'd left a bad date on my couch. More than one awkward conversation had occurred in my living room after a vanishing Clara. It had usually resulted in a hurried attempt to abandon ship as quickly as possible, his walk of shame in buttoned dress shirts and crumpled ties. Not to mention the one memorable morning with the one who spent four hours crying out his life story at my kitchen table. The click of the latch seemed to echo through the now-oddly quiet house. I turned back towards the couch, determined to oust this errant Sleeping Beauty, and usher him on his Clara-less way.

Problem was, Sleeping Beauty was gone. Presumably awake, but definitely gone.

Chapter 2

Stranger Things

My lifestyle in no way, shape, or form, indicated that my own strange man would be sleeping on my couch. My sister was clearly an idiot, once again unable to deal with the consequences, and leaving me to pick up the pieces.

The fact that she couldn't have bothered to warn me ahead of time was a sure sign of this. Then again, perhaps if I had been paying attention to my own living room, this could have been addressed sooner. Ideally, before she had run away from my home. More pressing than these thoughts however was where he had gone, and why he was here, and why he was not waiting patiently where I left him for the boot. I cleared my throat.

I then made a cursory pass at looking behind the couch, and under the coffee table. You never know, do you? I slowly moved through the living room towards the kitchen. Passing the small powder room, I toed the door open and with a quick side-eye judged that no one was lurking within. The kitchen was wide open and airy, no one hiding under the butcher block table. I began to turn towards the hall leading to the bedrooms and was promptly stopped by a knife to the throat. It gently pricked the soft hollow above my clavicle and I resisted the urge to gasp. The unwanted house guest placed his other hand on my shoulder and leaned in towards my ear,

"I don't want to hurt you. I'm not here to hurt you, I just need to figure something out," his voice was shaking and I could feel his warm breath on the back of my neck as he paused, waiting for my response.

I nodded slightly, trying desperately to avoid the tip of the knife where it pricked at my throat. The hand on my shoulder moved to my forearm, and forcefully pulled it behind me. Grabbing me by the elbow, he pulled me roughly to the kitchen table and shoved me down into a chair.

He pointed at me with the knife, which wavered in his shaking hand,

"Don't move, just, stay, right there,"

The now-attacker left me then, moving room to room, closing windows and shutting curtains and blinds as he went. Soon, my comfortable home that a short time ago had been warm and bright, progressively became dark and stuffy, the humidity building in the after-rain heat. He peered out the front window, anxiously, still gripping the small knife in his hand. He returned to where I sat, and crouched down to my level. I could see he was sweating profusely, whether from illness or anxiety or the heat, I couldn't tell, but the odd sheen it gave to his strangely bright and reflective eyes in the dark made me assume he was more than completely mad.

Upon closer inspection, he was a little older than I had originally presumed, clocking in at maybe mid-thirties, an unusual choice for Clara, who usually ran with the young bucks that strutted around the clubs, closer to her own age.

What could only be laugh lines creased around his eyes, and were just beginning to form at the corners of his mouth. He certainly wasn't laughing now, but they were there, accusatory in comparison with his behavior. Maybe he wouldn't be so bad, maybe it was all a misunderstanding? Maybe he's actually a fun guy? I realized at this moment that he was also wearing a suit. Not a terribly expensive looking suit and he was missing his tie, but he looked like he belonged in it, no kid playing dress up during a night out on the town.

Trying to look anywhere other than his odd, silvery eyes, I focused on a spot just above his hairline. He continued to study me intensely, not saying a word. I can't say I was scared in this moment, now that the knife was away from my skin, no, not yet. I was more intensely confused, bordering on annoyed by one of my sister's silly friends and whatever bizarre game he was playing. It would be better to figure out what the Hell was going on first, and continue from there, rather than give him the satisfaction of a complete meltdown.

"Have you seen anyone?"

He gestured with the knife, vaguely at the window.

I slowly shook my head, glancing at the window in question and then back to his concerned face,

"I have no idea what you're talking about, my sister was just here, but I am sure there are less menacing ways of discussing this... why are you in my house? Are you friends with Reggie? Are you robbing me? Is someone after you?"

Suddenly the flood gates had opened – my response in the situation, somehow, was to cram as many questions into the shortest amount of time possible. He frowned slightly. Not at me, but at a rattle coming from the back door. It was barely perceptible, a slight twist of the knob and an inward squeezing of the frame, as if someone had gingerly pushed against it to see if it was unlocked. He was up instantly from the floor to the kitchen window, peering between blinds he barely parted. He suddenly threw himself back against the wall, ever so silently, waiting, breath held. I debated whether to scream, attract the attention of whoever was outside, maybe they would break the door down. Maybe they will manage to get to me before he does, cutting off my cries for salvation. I decided against it.

If this man was afraid, of them, whoever they were, who's to say they won't take out their only witness too? They obviously weren't law enforcement, they would've come to the door, nice normal people, announcing their arrival and proclaiming their intent. I've never been on a different side of the law to experience otherwise.

"He's here. It won't be long before he finds a way in," he whispered to me.

Still pressed against the wall next to the window, head precariously close to knocking the clock from its perch, clutching the switchblade he had threatened me with, he seemed more akin to a child, hiding from the boogeyman, than someone I should genuinely be afraid of.

"You know I have no idea who 'he' is right? Or who you are? Or why you're cowering like a baby over there? Just let me go, please? We'll forget this ever happened,"

I leaned forward in my seat, gesturing slowly and calmly, hoping to high heaven he would just leave me here and go about his bizarre business elsewhere. He peered out of the window again, and ducked towards the floor. Almost completely bent double, he scurried towards the back of my chair.

"I'm don't know what to do, ok? I don't know if he'll hurt you too, I barely know what he is,"

I nodded slightly, a hint of crazy evident in his voice. He seemed genuinely terrified, and I debated whether or not I should be just as afraid of his would-be assailant.

"Do you owe him money? Drugs? Just tell me, I can try to help you, maybe?"

And call the cops the second I could get to my phone. I folded my hands in my lap, wary of making any move or sound he deemed slash-worthy. He came around the chair, holding the knife low and to his side. A sudden crash came from the front hall, the tinkling of glass and the splintering of wood. Before I knew what had even hit the house, he had grabbed me by the elbow, pulling me up and out of the chair, and began dragging me down the hallway. I craned my neck behind us, trying to see who or what we were running from but he'd already made it to the master bedroom with me in tow, and hastily shoved me into the closet. He looked around, panting, closed the door and slid to the floor, bracing the door with his back.

I flicked on the light. He pulled a piece of chalk from his pocket and hastily began sketching on the doorframe and across the floor, muttering the whole while. I could hear strange sounds coming from the direction of the kitchen. I moved towards the interior wall of the closet and pressed my ear against it. Beyond the echoing of the blood rushing through my ear, I could hear a strange howling, what could only be a tempest brewing over my kitchen table. I could hear cabinet doors rattling and what sounded like the entire contents of my cutlery drawer being overturned onto the floor. I was startled by the obvious aggression of the chaos beyond.

The stranger hadn't moved since laying down his chalk and sat with his back against the door. Aside from the heaving of his chest as he seemed to struggle to calm down, he was completely motionless. I joined him on the floor, sliding down the wall. I was feeling remarkably underdressed in my pyjamas, as he sat there quietly in his suit. I drummed my knees with my fingertips, debating whether to demand answers to the questions that were on the tip of my tongue. He raised his head and looked directly at me, his glare speaking louder than words.

"What -,"

He raised his finger to his lips, effectively shushing me, I pursed mine and narrowed my eyes. But the howling sound now seemed to be billowing down the corridor, a combination of a whirring, whistling, and the sultry sound of satin, sliding between exotic sheets. I could hear the hall pictures rattling against the walls, and a new, more ominous buzz added to the din. It brought to mind a TV set to static, long after shows were finished late at night. Intentional and grating in my ears, I yearned to shut it out, but I felt more and more with every passing second that maybe the sound was coming from my own brain. The stranger had closed his eyes, and I took the opportunity to study him as I tried to ignore the whirling dervish destroying my home beyond the door.

I still believed firmly that he was normally not this calm or serious. He had that look, he must have spent his whole life laughing without worry. I half expected him to crack a joke, despite the circumstances, smiling wide and toothy. But he seemed infinitely tired too. Soul-crushingly exhausted would be a better way to describe it. I noticed that the cuffs and the collar of his white dress shirt peeking out from his jacket were stained, dark blotches marring what would have been crisp and fresh in another life. I hoped it wasn't blood. Wished it wasn't, but somehow deep down I knew otherwise.

The sheen of grime and sweat and who knows what else darkened his skin and hair, and what could only be a week or two worth of stubble highlighted his jaw. Sudden noise exploded into the bedroom beyond the closet door. He firmed his position with his back against the door, bracing, eyes still closed, his lips moving silently over and over in what I assumed was a prayer. It was deafening, the roaring, I felt we were trapped directly in the centre of a hailstorm – wood creaked and broke, wind howling and shrieking, raging mere feet away. I cowered into the corner of the closet, partially hidden by hanging sweaters and dresses, trying to escape the rush and assault against my brain. I covered my ears and squeezed my eyes tight, praying the sound would just stop. Or whatever it was burst through the door, anything just to make it stop.

Abruptly it did; a light flashing under the crack of the door. The sudden absence of sound acted as effectively as a vacuum, and took my breath away. The house, suddenly so quiet, had me believe I had lost my sense completely. I swear I could hear the ticking of the stranger's watch, but maybe time itself had stopped.

He looked up at me, piercingly, and put his finger to his lips again. I nodded, pulling myself to standing as slowly as he did. I held my breath, adrenaline coursing through my veins that until this moment, I hadn't realized was surging, my heart racing. He still held the door closed with one hand, and bowed his head towards the crack, other hand on the knob. He listened, I could tell, with every fiber of his body. He hummed with concentration. Then he opened the door.

I almost stopped him. I almost threw myself at the door, slamming it shut. I almost screamed at him, a sudden feeling of despair washing over me. *It* must still be outside. *It* had to be. But no, the astonishing fact was, there was nothing outside the door. Everything, every single little detail of the room remained exactly as it had a mere half an hour ago, when I arose from my sleep to the smell of brewing coffee and followed it to my sister. The sheets remained rumpled, yesterday's clothes still lay on the chair in the corner, and nothing was touched, the alarm clock now flashing 12:00. I stared in utter confusion, my expectation of complete and utter devastation shattered, and replaced with incredulity. Was I still asleep? Am I dreaming?

Chapter 3

Moments ago, I would have sworn the house outside my closet had been torn to pieces and thrown to the maelstrom. The stranger moved slowly out of the room, again clutching his knife and heading slowly back to the kitchen. I followed; purely so as not to be alone should the insanity of the last five minutes strike again. He moved cautiously yet quickly, scanning every dark corner, and made his way to the front of the house. The only indication of malevolence was a single pane of broken glass next to the front door, innocently scattered amongst the carpet in glistening jewels. He gestured at it with his knife and shook his head, and retreated back towards the kitchen.

"Wait," I called after him, hesitantly reaching for his elbow but deciding against it.

He ignored me, sitting at the kitchen table; elbows propped, and began rubbing his eyes tiredly. His hand moved to his mouth, and he exhaled slowly. I sat at the table, and stared at him. Hands folded in my lap, waiting. Finally he met my eyes with his strange glittering ones.

"I'm sorry to have dragged you into this. It wasn't my intention. I was... meaning to only take refuge... your sister, she, well... but he caught up to me," he gestured with his knife vaguely and shrugged tiredly.

"I don't know if this means they will come for you too, and I don't know if they will make me go after you, so until I figure out what to do about that... I am afraid, I don't want to hurt you, but we might be stuck here for now,"

I sat back, consciously avoiding any sudden movements.

"What do you mean, stuck, in here? Together? Who *are* you? Who *are* they? What was *that?!*"

I abandoned all pretense of calm.

I gestured wildly at the kitchen, the hallway, the bedroom, and leapt to my feet. I stomped around the kitchen, opening and closing drawers, slamming kitchen cupboards, trying to see anything out of place, trying desperately to prove that *something* happened in this kitchen not minutes before. The coffee maker sat, still hot, bubbling away, so I grabbed a silly little clown mug and poured him a cup. Maybe a jolt would wake up him, and he'd give me some answers.

"Here,"

I slam the mug down in front of him and start flustering around through the fridge.

I was suddenly starving. He didn't move away from the splatter that shot from the cup, and continued to sit there watching me, hopefully debating whether or not to tell me all he knew. I slammed the carton of eggs down on the counter and pulled the frying pan down from the ceiling rack. I felt like making as much noise as possible, and no one was going to tell me otherwise. See if some-who-knows-who comes in my house and does who-knows-what? No, that just wasn't right. BANG. CRACK. SMASH. Eggs are on. I turned to face him. I was so close to skewering him with the closest utensil when he suddenly cleared his throat. He turned around in his chair and faced me,

"Will you sit? Just. Calm, please? I don't know if we have any time," he gestured to the chair nearest him, and turned back to his coffee without waiting for a response.

I shook my head and went to the broom closet; I grabbed the small dustpan and brush I kept for just this sort of situation; broken glass situations, of course, not mysterious stranger situations. I headed back towards the front door, fully intent on righting the situation as best I could for now. He began to follow me, an incredulous look upon his face. I was not about to give him the satisfaction of my obeisance at the moment. I brandished the brush at him,

"You, go, sit. Drink your coffee, wake the Hell up, think carefully, one more chance for answers, bucko and then I call the cops,"

He looked furious for a moment, and it could have changed my mind. Maybe it was the way his eyes almost seemed to catch fire with the shift in his emotions, becoming burning hot embers in no way that any normal human eyes should. I held my breath and the reaction faded.

I think I got through to him. He retreated back to the kitchen, and left me to the mess in the hallway. I stooped down to scoop up the shards of window from the floor, grumbling under my breath. I began cursing this morning, cursing my sister for failing to warn me of the stranger on my couch, and cursing the stranger now sitting in my kitchen.

I stomped back to the kitchen, discarded the glass, and flipped my eggs. I popped bread into the toaster, and flopped down into the chair across from my unwanted guest.

"Feeling better?" He queried, staring at me over his mug.

I could see a hint of the mirth I'd originally suspected, but I just rolled my eyes and waited. I didn't know how much time he thought he had, but I had all the time in the world to figure this strange man out.

"I'll feel better when you are out of my house and out of my life. When I have a shower, get dressed, and move on from this day like you were never in it. These eggs will make it marginally better for now," I began to stand up to retrieve my breakfast, but his hand shot out and gently cupped the top of mine.

The resulting electric shock shot me back to my seat. I squealed in protest and pulled my hand back, shaking it painfully.

"Sorry," he mumbled, looking at me reproachfully.

This lunatic sure could cycle through the emotions faster than a pinwheel. It'd be fascinating in any other situation. But for now, it was increasingly irritating.

My eyes flicked from his face to the eggs on the stove behind his head, and back to his face. I was definitely surer now in the light that the splotches on his collar were blood. They were that certain shade of rust you just can't get anywhere else. He seemed suddenly conscious of his wrists and pulled the sleeves of his jacket down.

"I've been on the run, for days now, maybe even weeks. I can't be entirely certain... I've lost a lot of time over the recent while. I think I've forgotten who I was. I've been trying my damnedest to get out of this mess, to stop hurting all these people along the way, but it just seems hopeless," he stared off into space, collecting his thoughts.

I can smell the eggs beginning to burn. I hesitantly rose from my seat again, and this time he does not stop me. I've lost the desire to eat, but plate up the food anyway. I return to my seat, placing the plate in front of him. He raises an eyebrow in surprise, and leaves it untouched.

"From what I've figured out, and from what I've was told, before, well... before today, is that they're called Collectors. And right now, I've got one following me, I've been out of their touch for a while, now," he must have seen the look on my face, as he rolled his eyes and shook his head.

He ran a hand hesitantly through his hair.

"I know, I know. You probably think I've watched too much TV or something but I am serious. Someone's been making me do things; bad things. I don't know how or why but this is so very serious. You heard it out there, you know it exists, even if you've never seen it, which is a heck of a lot more warning than I got the last time," he finished his coffee and held it between both hands, staring down into the depths of the mug.

"There are things you probably won't ever understand, and there are things that will take much too long to explain, that I don't have time to explain right now," he stressed the word *time* like a precious commodity, a note of plea in his wavering voice.

"We have to stay here, we have to fortify, until I can figure this out, figure out why I am here. I'm sure the second we step outside, it's going to know. We were lucky the first time; I don't quite know what stopped it, I didn't think it would work but we most certainly won't be as lucky again,"

My mouth gaped open. This man was completely insane. Fortify?

"Listen. I'm not crazy. I'm not, please. Just," he clenched his hands, open and closed, open and closed.

I could see the knuckles were bloody and torn, his fingernails dirty. I sighed. Aside from the obvious inconveniences he had caused, what with the threatening, he had (possibly) saved my life from the Collector (ok?) and I owed him at least that much.

"What do we have to do?"

I grimaced. Mother always told me it'd get stuck that way, since it was my common expression, at least when she was around, and the amount of it that had transpired over the last forty-five minutes was sure to add to her proof. The damage I was doing to the trim of my door frames was pretty much irreparable. Between the marker sketches and the etchings in the wood I was inscribing all over my house, around every door and every window, there was no doubt if I got through this alive, Mr. Mysterious was fixing this; even if I had to drag him kicking and screaming back here myself.

The stranger had given me a sheet of paper towel with strange symbols drawn on them, paired, one to be written in marker, one set painstakingly carved. Meanwhile, he was in the shower. I had insisted, obviously, the state of him had been pitiful. I rolled my eyes. I had to feel bad for the guy, who wouldn't? Even if his story was absolutely insane, it was still pitiful. He didn't know the last time he'd had even had a shower, and that struck a chord. I guess being on the run for your life, for God knows how long, is more important than being presentable.

We had done the windows and door frames in the bathroom first, working our way out through the bedroom, and then he'd left me to it. He seemed to be putting an awful lot of stock into me, that I'd complete them properly, that I wouldn't run screaming from the house while he was otherwise distracted. But there was something in his frantic and strange gaze that convinced me not to. I wasn't sure what it was about him, regardless of his mood, and his actions, but I felt an overwhelming sense of calm when he was near, and I felt I was drugged. Maybe I was drugged. Maybe he gave me something while I slept that made me agree with everything he said, made me believe every outrageous proclamation that escaped his lips. Whatever it was, it was working, and I was helping him.

I just hoped that these sketches would work. He had told me briefly what Collectors were. They opened up a whole new level of strange into my life, until now the weirdest thing was my sister's taste in boyfriends.

Now, the weirdest thing was a creature - sent from Hell, designed purely to hunt you down, sink their teeth in you, and pull you back to where they came from. The rushing, racing, tornado of sound that comes with them is the sound of Hell, a tear attached to their existence that goes wherever they go, to pull you back with them the instant they have you. The threat of being express-sent to Hell was reason enough for me to follow his direction, let alone the teeth attached to the Hell as it did.

After only *hearing* it in my hallway, I had no desire to see it.

When I had asked him how it looked, he had simply closed his eyes and inhaled slowly, and asked me not to ask him that. I rolled my eyes to myself again.

The knife slipped against a knot, and caught me square in the thumb. I swore and stuck my thumb in my mouth, muttering around the digit.

"Are you all right?"

I jumped.

The stranger was quiet, as proven earlier when he managed to give me a slip to the kitchen before the Collector had arrived, but being on edge, I'd expected to have at least heard him this time. He was wearing a soft hoodie and worn out jeans, leftover courtesy of Reggie, feet bare and hair wet. Reggie was taller, but not by much, the clothes slightly oversized on the stranger's lean frame. His suit was carefully folded over his arm, and the shower alone seemed to have lightened some of the load of exhaustion from his face.

"Let me see," he advanced towards me, laying his suit over the back of the arm chair and crouching down next to where I sat in the doorframe.

I recoiled slightly, and he must have noticed, as he sighed slightly.

"I know, earlier, yes, I came off as the bad guy," I clucked my tongue in response.

"But I am not. I swear. At least, I wish I wasn't. I don't *want* to hurt you, and I don't want you to be hurt on account of me. So let me see," he stared directly into my eyes, his pupils flashing in the half-light.

I hesitantly held my hand out to him, the gash angry and red, still pooling blood the moment I took the pressure off.

He took my hand in both of his, covering it completely. He pulled it up towards his face, closed his eyes, and muttered a few words under his breath. An electric shock ran from my thumb to my elbow and back again. He released my hand and stood up, turning back towards the kitchen. I took one look at my tingling hand, and fainted.

Chapter 4

Silver Barbs

I awoke on the couch, what must only have been minutes later. A cool dish cloth lay against my forehead, and the stranger sat in the armchair, legs and arms crossed, studying me curiously.

"That was the first time I did that to someone else, I didn't expect you to react that way. Was it the process, or the results?"

My brain rapidly tried to understand the situation, panic bubbling up hot and overwhelming in my throat. I fainted, why? My thumb, he did something to my - Is he not human?

He shook his head and mouthed "no".

He can read my thoughts? No reaction. Maybe he was playing it close to his chest. I know I would have. I moved my hand up in front of my face and studied it in the ray of light that managed to push its way between the curtains. The gash was completely gone. I could see a thin silver line running from the knuckle and up to tip, but no cut, and no bleeding. The silver flashed as I tilted my hand in the light.

"Um, how exactly did you kintsugi my hand?"

The ancient Japanese practice of repairing ceramics had sprung to mind – thank you second year of University – but I can guarantee it had never been used this way, not on a person. He grinned; evidently pleased I wasn't completely losing my head over what he'd done. His smile was broad and toothy – as I had suspected - transforming him into a far cry from the misery that had been cowering in my kitchen.

He pushed the sleeves of his borrowed hoodie up to his elbows, and came over to the window and held his arms out to the beam of golden sun. I gasped, his arms glittering in criss-crossing highways of silver, beautiful scars akin to barbed wire wrapping from wrist to elbow. Where his knuckles earlier had been torn and bloody, now flashed with smatterings of metal, delicate blooms against his skin. He studied me, as I studied these marks, and I resisted the intense urge to reach out and touch them. They couldn't be real? If I hadn't had my own in my own thumb, I wouldn't have believed them, a trick of the light maybe, or a strange tattoo?

A cloud passed over the sun, extinguishing the sparks from his skin and the moment passed also. He pulled down his sleeves and turned away. He collected the marker and knife from the floor, and began working on the final window for me. I pulled my knees up to my chest and watched him. He moved very quietly, and very carefully. I had assumed it was from having to sneak and hide to save his skin, but maybe it was something else. It seemed that the very air around him held its breath, the calm before the storm in a tight bubble surrounding his every move. The very fact that every time he touched me, I felt an electric shock pass through my skin seemed to propose that he himself was the storm. I shuddered.

I realized the temperature had dropped in the room. The cloud that had hid the sun must have been more than just that, an on-coming thunderstorm raging out of the west had finally blotted out the easterly sun.

Long, low rumbles could be felt more than heard from the distance, lightning not yet cracking over our skies. The stranger rose, slowly, and tentatively, cocking his head towards the sound. His eyes searched the ceiling of the hall – beyond it really, seeking something out in the storm above. I left him to it. I was still in my pyjamas and if this were anything more than what I thought it was – just another ordinary early summer shower, I wanted to be clean and dressed and ready for things to come.

The storm crashed on. It had been close to three hours already, of rumbling, crackling lightning and tempestuous rain. I had showered, dried, dressed, and returned to the kitchen, and the power had only dimmed once, wind whipping the trees outside and hail pelting the windows.

He had insisted we turn off any lights, and with the curtains still closed from earlier this morning, I could barely see my hand in front of my face, let alone where he prowled through the house, peeking behind curtains every time an intensely loud bolt of lightning smashed down.

Occasionally the lightning illuminated his profile and I became profoundly aware of how much I didn't know about this stranger in my house. How much I didn't know about where he came from, what he was doing, why he was here. I only knew what he ran from, and it now seemed to be his defining quality. He didn't want to go to Hell. A person could respect that.

I had taken the time to put his suit into the washer. I knew that was not how suits were to be treated, but I felt at this point in time, a visit to the dry cleaner was an utterly absurd notion.

For now, it was fine for the stranger to borrow Reggie's clothes. It wasn't like Reggie would be back any time soon – our brother had abruptly left us to live out the dream in California.

Unfortunately, that dream had left the rest of us in limbo; trying to piece together the bits of life he'd left here, including what he had abandoned from his time couch-surfing at my place.

CRACK.

I jumped from my seat at the table. I could've sworn the kitchen itself had been hit, my ears ringing as abruptly everything in the house shut off. All the sounds of regular life – the hum of the fridge, the swish of the laundry, the whir of the ceiling fan, were suddenly gone, their absence deafening. The fan slowed, lazily, and came to a stop. I stared at it briefly, a chill running down my back.

"Hey..." I called out, whispering.

It felt conspicuous to raise my voice any louder, even in my own home. Everything was beginning to feel so foreign, even in this familiar place.

The darkness became absolute in between the intermittent flashing of lightning through the cracks in the blinds. I felt suffocated, the dark so heavy, laced with the humidity of the storm.

"I'm here," he called, hoarsely from the front room.

I rose from the table to join him, navigating the house as best I could, my eyes unable to adjust between the extremes of light and dark. I stumbled against the coffee table, and his hand was at my elbow, guiding me to the couch.

"Look," he pulled the curtain behind the sofa open, moving aside so I could see the tempest outside.

The street was completely flooded, flotsam of garbage drifting rapidly downstream and into the storm drains. Lightning crackled all around, and hail pelted the ground. I was increasingly aware of how close he was, and the intimacy the darkness created. I was also more and more aware of how quickly he was no longer just a stranger, a threat, or an intruder. We had come to a strange impasse in knowing each other in a few short hours. He was still a stranger, in the broadest sense of the terms but unforeseen circumstances had thrown us into the trenches together.

It was then that I heard a low growl, coming from just outside the glass. I hesitated, wondering if I should step back behind the curtain. Lightning struck across the street, and the glowing reflection of two golden eyes flashed beyond the glass with it. I was startled backward for a moment, and then I moved my face closer to the window, trying to see through the onslaught. It had to have been a trick of the light, right? A plume of fog spread across the glass, condensation from warm breath spreading in front of my face. Assuming it was my own, I palmed the glass, swiping to clear it. The warm breath was on the outside.

I tripped back; all pretense of bravado stripped away, and fell head over heels backwards over the coffee table that had been lurking behind my knees. Moving incredibly fast, the stranger kneeled by my head as I groaned, twisting around so I could get my bearings. I looked up at him, where I could see his eyes sparking in the dark above me.

"You know. Since you've been here, I've been chased by a denizen of Hell, sliced open my thumb, stubbed my toe and,"

I shuffled my shoulder blades against the carpet, wiggling my hips, testing the length and stretch of my spine,

"-And almost broken my God damn neck. You, you are bad luck," I pointed at him.

He might have looked sad, but it was hard to tell in the pushing darkness. I could only see a flash of his bright eyes, lightning refracting in the irises. Deciding I was safer just laying here on the floor, out of sight, I continued,

"So, what was that? Wasn't the Collector right? I mean. There was something right? I think I saw it,"

He shifted his weight and sat down next to me, arms across his knees.

I could tell that though he was speaking to me, all of his attention was diverted to the storm beyond.

"I think it might be a creature that accompanies the Collector, I wouldn't be surprised. Sounded like it could be some sort of damned dirty dog, wouldn't you say?"

The house was beginning to feel smaller and smaller as I imagined a pack of hungry creatures trying to nose their way into my home, slipping through cracks and pawing open windows. I pulled myself up next to him. He offered a steadying arm, but I chose to use the nearby armchair instead.

"So who are you?" I pulled my knees to my chest and rested my chin on them, wrapping them tightly in my arms.

I tilted my head side to side, cracking my neck and stretching the kinks. The rain always seemed to make my bones pop, my sister had called me Kellogg when we were kids. That seemed such a long time ago, the last we were all together.

I sighed. I didn't really expect an answer from him, not any more. He was as mysterious as he was guarded, and I had already learned that in the few short hours I'd known him. Everything came out in blips and teases; it just seemed easier to accept it than to push.

"After all this, shouldn't you be asking *what am I?*"

He rubbed at his knuckles; tiny sparks flashing no brighter than static across them, a miniature thunderstorm to match the one outside.

He leaned over briefly and nudged me with his shoulder,

"I'll settle for giving you a name, if that makes it easier on you?"

Thunder rumbled overhead, a rapid pass, careening from one end of the street to the other, a drunk through a china shop.

I laughed to myself, the absurdity of the situation fluttering down around me once again. A keening howl rose from outside – and I shuddered. I hoped it was simply a neighborhood dog, left out in the rain. Better to hope for ignorance than learning the truth.

He stood up next to me, more told of by a rustle and whisper of jean and wool than actually seeing him do it. His fingers brushed my shoulder and took my hand, pulling me up to my feet.

"You can call me Deke, if that helps,"

"Adeline," I whispered.

The storm outside abruptly stopped.

Chapter 5

Deke's Tale

I longed for fresh air. I ached to throw all the windows open wide, and let in the crystalline damp of the after-storm air, cool breezes and all. The power was still out, so none of the fans were working, and I couldn't flip on the A/C. Couldn't open the windows either, for fear of something entering much more ominous than rain-scented drafts.

The air was stale and humid, and I felt myself perspiring without exertion, beading on my lip and along my hairline, droplets marching down my back. Deke on the other hand, looked as cool as marble, stony and tense. He flipped the knife around in his hand, point, handle, point, handle, flashing in the sunlight now beaming through the break in the curtains at the kitchen window. He had his sleeves pushed up to his elbows, leaning over his knees, the tendons rippling the silver linings on his forearm, as he flipped, flipped, flipped.

"You weren't kidding about the whole, waiting here and fortifying thing, huh? Have you figured it out yet? Do you know where you're going? What you're doing? Are we stuck here forever? How long do your little mumbo jumbo etchings all over my frames work for? You're fixing those by the way. If we live through this,"

A smile played across his lips. I wanted to be angry at him, for trapping me in this, explanations few and far between. Somehow though, I couldn't be angry. So far I'd only been afraid, and mildly inconvenienced. He'd had his entire existence turned upside down, chased, beat down, damaged in ways I couldn't even imagine and yet he could still smile about it.

"No. No. No. No. Probably? And forever," he counted off my questions on his fingers.

I rolled my eyes at him. I guess it was a step forward; he'd finally answered an uncharacteristic number of questions in a row. My cellphone buzzed on the table. It was Clara messaging me.

Are you at home?

Duh. What's up?

Power is out across the city. Say it's lightning. Your place?

Gonezo. Did you leave someone here last night?

O.M.G, no!

I waited, but no further response came. It wasn't often I was able to silence my teasing sister, but it seemed it had finally happened. Deke stared at me curiously, passing his knife back and forth between his hands.

"Your sister?"

He smiled, though it seemed to be covering over an anxiety I couldn't quite place, as he sat back and stilled the knife.

I nodded, slowly, not quite sure how to judge his reaction.

"I followed her last night, here. I watched her climb in the window. I climbed in after her. She didn't hear me or see me even when she left," he started playing with the knife again.

Flip, flip, flip. Ok, very creepy.

"Fortunately for me, she didn't. Of all the people I've crossed paths with up to now, I think she's the answer, and I won't hurt people anymore. I'm not sure how much more I could handle anyway," he bowed his head.

"Are we safe right now?"

I tilted my head towards the doors and windows. It was hard to believe it was still dangerous for us – the beautiful sunlight outside teasing a wonderful spring day. He shrugged, thought about it, and then nodded slowly, not returning my gaze.

"Then tell me about it," he slowly raised his eyes, both hands rubbing the bottom half of his face. He exhaled loudly.

And then he began.

Deke settled his glass down on the bar, drained and clinking, the ice barely even having had the chance to melt. He thumbed the condensation on the side, smiling absently to himself.

Today had been a good day. The merger had gone through smoothly, the clients were happy on all sides, and they'd managed to negotiate minimal staffing cuts. He felt good about this, and good about tonight. The hum of endless possibilities filled the air. He loosened his tie, catching a wink from the bartender, Dezi, as she refilled the garnishes behind bar. She leaned over, chin in hand, tossing her vibrantly red hair.

"You seem awfully pleased with yourself, Deke. I'd swear you were vibrating, that glow coming off you," she winked again.

Deke smiled, blushing up to his roots.

Damn straight, he thought to himself. No one could ruin this night.

He turned on his stool to face the crowd, a writhing, stomping dance floor in full swing. The air was heavy, the smoke machines leeching their slightly acrid moisture into the atmosphere, enhancing the dream-like state of the room.

The rock music that poured from the speakers, was just the right blend of new, old, little bit country, little bit soul, and the entire room swelled with the beat. Deke normally only came here on Fridays, a long endless week deserving of a long night out, but tonight was a Wednesday, and it was incredible. The sheer difference in atmosphere was breathless compared to the panicked anxiety of a Friday, when everyone desperately drank to forget. He settled his elbows back on the bar and closed his eyes, nodding to the music that rushed through him and letting the warm heat of alcohol rise over his senses.

The clock switched over to 11, and the dim overhead lights switched off, strobes and spots flashing on to take their place. The dance floor became surreal – flashes of skin, legs, tossing hair, grinding bodies melding into one large writhing beast. Deke's skin crawled suddenly.

He opened his eyes with a jolt, feeling watched. She was standing in front of him, at the edge of the crowd, brilliantly clad in a revealing club dress of rich, vibrant peacock blue. Cascades of dark exotic curls fell down past her shoulders, and Deke inhaled sharply when he noticed her presence. He had never seen anyone more stunningly awe-inspiring, and she was heading straight toward him with long, graceful strides.

He couldn't believe his luck, he could feel his lips curling into an enormous smile, and he couldn't contain himself. She sauntered slowly as she moved closer, savouring her steps and sashaying her hips. He couldn't take his eyes off of her, her glossy and plump lips drawing his gaze. He felt his temperature rising, the smell of flowers teasing his nostrils.

He sat up a bit straighter, adjusting his suit jacket more squarely on his shoulders. She moved in close, pushing against his knees, curling her hand around the back of his neck, lacing her fingers into his hair. Her fingers were cool against his skin, cold spots on the alcohol heat of his throat. She pulled his head closer, pulling his ear to her lips, and whispered. He could barely hear her over the pulsating beat but he caught

"I've been looking for -" What, he didn't know. Did it matter?

She teased his earlobe with her teeth, gently, and pulled back, dancing slowly. The beat faded in Deke's ears. He was transfixed. He stared into her golden eyes, star-struck, every cell in his body rioting against his consciousness. He was so acutely aware of himself; he could hardly remember how to breathe, how to swallow. She smiled, subtly, and then bit her lip.

He longed to move his own the few inches closer to hers, but surely that would end in his own death? He could believe he would simply drop dead of ecstasy. She tip-toed her fingers across his belt buckle, slowly up his stomach and towards his collar. She played with his tie, tugging absently until it fell loose to the floor. He felt hypnotized by those eyes, her slight sway almost predatory, just a cobra waiting to strike. Everything else faded away. She swiftly unbuttoned his top three buttons, caressing his collar bone, thumb stroking his chin. Her hand slid lightly into his shirt. Intense, ratcheting pains suddenly crushed at his heart, spasming across his chest and down into every limb, electrifying his every nerve ending.

He didn't even have time to cry out, before the darkness overwhelmingly enveloped him.

He awoke to complete dark and silence, sprawled across the floor. He wiggled his fingers in front of his eyes hoping to see any sort of movement, but the absence of light was absolute. Everything in his body ached, every possible fiber of his being screaming with just the movement of his hand. He rolled onto his side, resisting the urge to vomit from the pain, even as the bile gathered in his throat. He groaned quietly, as he raised himself up onto one hand, pulling his knees to him. He blinked, futilely hoping for any tiny bit of light to reveal itself. He patted down his jacket and pockets, everything missing. No wallet, no phone, no keys. He mustered up the nerve to call out – his voice rasping and harsh against the total silence,

"Hello, anyone? Anyone around? P-p-please?"

He stumbled over the word, realizing just how exquisitely thirsty he was, even swallowing becoming a conscious effort.

The words had echoed shallowly back to him. He rose to his feet and stumbled, his legs crying pins and needles as he took tentative steps forward. Only three steps forward and his grasping fingers hit rough metal. The wall felt flaky and porous, rusted but still strong against his touch. He shuffled sideways, hands passing along the wall until he hit a corner.

Damn. He turned, shuffling along once more. Damn. Damn again.

He presumed to be back where he had started. He took a step back, arms out from his sides, straight as he could make them. Ragged metal touched the fingertips of both hands. He performed a quarter turn, and reached out once again. In his mind eye he calculated that his prison could only be six by eight feet, at its absolute largest. He had felt no door when he had trailed along the wall, perhaps a hatch in the ceiling? He raised his hands slowly above his head, afraid of what could be above, but it was nothing but air. He tentatively jumped, but his fingertips hit nothing but more resounding silence.

Shit. He paused, holding his breath. Turning his pounding head side to side ever so slowly, he felt slightly more cool and fresh air to one side rather than the other. He moved towards that corner, hands outstretched until his fingers touched the edge of his prison.

He slowly slid across the wall to the corner, and moved his face as close to the crevice it created as he dared. Cool air was streaming between the join of the two walls. He sunk to his knees, hopelessly staring up into the darkness, willing any sort of light to show itself from the source of the air. He banged his fist against the wall,

"Hello! Hello! Can anyone hear me?!"

The severity of the situation hit him full in the face.

He was completely trapped, and didn't have the slightest idea of where or why. Tears pricked his eyes. He had never been a brave man, but really, he had never really had any reason to be. He had a warm and comfortable life, never stretching his means of survival, not even once.

He sat back on the floor, and began stomping his foot against the wall, pounding, over and over again. Hoping for something to break, fall, disrupt his captors enough that they let him go, explain themselves or otherwise. A giggle broke the silence, soft and musical, infinitely unnerving in the darkness.

"Oh Deke, Deke my boy. Who are you to scream, demand, and pound? Who, Deke, do you think you are?" A woman's voice lilted from the shadows.

He scrabbled along the floor and pressed his back to the corner, anxiously looking around and trying to find the source of the voice. It seemed to be coming from everywhere and nowhere, even so far as to say it sounded as if it was coming from inside his head. The voice giggled once more.

"We want you, Deke," her voice dropped an octave, and split into two voices, crying in unison

"You are ours, Deke,"

Three, four voices followed suit,

"This is the end of you Deke, we are here, and we will have you," the walls rumbled with the multitude of voices, as they called his name over and over.

He covered his ears, pushing away the sound, pushing away the thoughts and the voices, their implications and threats.

"STOP!" He screamed.

Utter silence reigned once more. He gasped, his breathing sounding ragged and deafening in the dead air.

He closed his eyes, not that it truly mattered, as a wall of overwhelming fatigue hit him fully. He pressed his cheek to the wall, willing the darkness and this nightmare away. Praying that he would wake up in bed, that this was all a terrible, alcohol soaked dream. Sleep overtook him, swiftly, silently, pulling him down below the surface.

He gasped awake. He lay curled against the wall, his head tilted awkwardly against the corner. A strange scratching sound was coming from the other side of where his face pressed, and he turned to look. He rose to his feet, tense and poised, aching and stiff, temples flaring with the change in blood pressure. The sound of a bolt being dragged back, slowly but surely. The wall suddenly swung open, and a flashlight shone directly into his eyes. He winced and cowered, arm thrown up across his face, the light seeming to burn right through him, when two hands roughly grabbed him by the elbows and hauled him forward, throwing him onto his toes as he staggered to keep up with their steel-clad grasp.

He realized he had been inside some sort of storage container, inside a warehouse. There were hundreds of similar containers scattered across the floor of the building, completely deprived of any other feature, the floors swept clean and the rafters bare. The two men maneuvering him towards the sliding door of the warehouse were clothed head to toe in black, utility grade pants and sweaters, flak vests, balaclavas over their faces. They each carried a gun in holsters snug against the small of their backs, one carrying a flashlight.

He stumbled, but they didn't falter or change their grip, merely continued pulling him along, intensely strong. The door trundled open at their approach, sunlight pouring in and a brilliant cornflower blue sky sparkling beyond.

The vast expanse of nothing was not welcoming, it presented as ominous, as foreboding as a gathering storm. He dug in his heels, suddenly longing for the quiet and dark of his jail cell. One of his captors kicked at the back of his knee, and he sunk to the ground with a cry of pain, before they hauled him up and continued pulling him along. Out into the brilliant sunshine they threw him, the blinding, aching sunlight stabbing pins into his retinas. He fell to his knees, covering his eyes, trembling as he waited for whatever they were to do to him.

This is how it ends, he thought. I am going to die here.

No strike ever came. The two men stood at parade rest behind him, arms lowered and hands clasped, feet spread shoulder width apart. He looked up slowly, through hooded eyes, and there she was.

The woman from the bar was standing in front of him, still undeniably exquisite, but somehow fundamentally flawed. The warmth of her gaze and the allure of her beauty were diminished by a sudden coldness. She had exchanged her club wear for a freshly pressed white blouse, crisp in the blinding light, a grey skirt, and staggeringly high heels. He realized what was different - it was the hatred. She was staring at him with a look of utter disgust, a creature not even worth squashing under her red-soled heel, but destined to squirm in the light until he died.

"What do you want? Who are you?" He rasped, squinting up at her against the sunlight.

The parched earth was reflecting and refracting, a dead, dry field, stubbly with the ends of hay, stretching endlessly in every direction. The sun was beating hot overhead, the massive Quonset hut he'd been inside radiating brilliant and overwhelming heat. She turned on her heel, pacing back and forth in front of him, swinging her arms, stretching and twisting, cracking her neck. She wheeled towards him,

"You really don't remember, do you? How convenient that must be. Cruel, I admit, but infinitely convenient, for us," she tapped her chin with deadly red nails, looking at him thoughtfully.

She stooped down in front of him, grasping his chin in her hand. She turned his head side to side, up and down, inspecting his face. She smelled overwhelming like lilies, and he gagged, hoarse and dry. She shushed him as he moved to speak, clucking quietly with her tongue.

"Poor, poor human. The change is already coming over you. I can see it in your eyes,"

Every nerve in his body tingled, in response to her words.

"You're our little investment, Deke, and we prefer to keep our investments safe, you are ours Deke, and you'll just learn to love it," she purred, releasing his chin and stepping back.

"What did you do to me? What," he growled, clutching his stomach, he began to feel weak, every limb bogging him closer and closer to the ground.

He longed to curl up and sleep, but fought against it, mentally wading through, slipping closer and closer to unconsciousness. She giggled softly. He realized she'd been one of the voices in the dark.

Now, now Deke, don't fight it. Trust me, it's better to be asleep when it finally takes effect, darling, just close your eyes," her whisper filled his ears, the breeze played across his face and the sunlight warmed his back. So calm, so peaceful... so perfect.

He scrabbled awake, throwing the blankets from the bed, gasping and shrieking. He had been dreaming of drowning, the light sparkling off the bubbles streaming from his mouth, down, down, sinking to the bottom of a clear blue lake, screaming and struggling, his arms bound to his sides. He lay there, panting, thinking, and shaking the cobwebs from his brain. The sheets were soaked with sweat, his hair slick to his head, his muscles tense and aching. The clock next to him flashed 12:00 over and over, beating a pulsating green light into the dark. It seared into his eyes and he winced, rolling over and onto his feet.

His legs gave way, but he clung to the edge of the bed until he could collect his control, and he waited until they stopped trembling. He staggered out of the room towards the bathroom, clinging to the wall as he went. He lost his footing once more as he crossed the threshold, stumbling onto the cold tile, hitting his knees hard. He sat, shakily, feeling as if he were recovering from a particularly long and strenuous bought of the flu, his limbs weak. He pulled himself up by the basin, slowly, painfully. He turned the water on, splashing his face, cupping the water to his mouth and drinking as much as he could.

He was so very, very thirsty. He heaved once, the water still cool flooding back up into his throat. He choked and held it down, and ducked to the tap for more. He sighed and turned the tap off, his face dripping. He closed his eyes and took a deep breath, then looked at himself in the mirror over the sink.

His irises, normally a soft and hazy blue, had turned silver, metallic and glinting in the light from the window. Heart leaping into his throat, he leaned in closer, pulling his lids apart and staring fearfully and deeply into his eyes. They flashed, subtly glowing, iridescent against the black of his pupils. He squeezed them tight, blinking back tears, willing himself to be only dreaming. He opened them again, tentatively. They hadn't changed, shining back at him.

He grabbed the face cloth from the counter and doused it in water, unbuttoned his collar and rubbed the cloth over the back of his neck, temperature rising, feeling overwhelmingly hot. He stopped when he noticed the three fingerprints burned into his skin, red and raw just below his collarbone. He ran his fingers over the minute ridges, angry and stinging in his flesh. He hissed at the contact.

Damn, damn, damn. He sank to the floor beneath the sink, pondering his options. Could he go to the cops? And tell them what; he was abducted from the bar? Taken to who knows where, for who knows how long, and changed? Changed how? He still didn't know what was wrong with him. He was hot, exhausted, thirsty, sensitive to the light, had burns in his skin, and his eyes. Oh God his eyes. He curled up on the floor, shaking, relishing the cool tiles against his cheek and palms.

"Deke?!" A man's voice called from the house beyond.

His eyes snapped open. Aaron.

"Yo, buddy, you home? I haven't seen you in days," he could hear his roommate shuffling and rustling, he must've been out getting groceries, the sounds of heavy bags hitting the floor.

The front door crashed shut. Deke managed to groan quietly in the ensuing silence; his lips were so dry once more, unable to form words. Heavy footfalls rang out through the house, down the hall, to where Deke lay inside the bathroom door.

"Deke, man, Hell, what'd you get up to?" Aaron crouched down next to him, putting a hand on his shoulder.

Deke inhaled sharply. Aaron's touch felt raw through his suit jacket, tingling like a bad sunburn.

"Let's get you up," he heaved at Deke under the arms, pulling him to sitting, and then straining, lifting to settle him on the edge of the bathtub.

Aaron was only a young college kid, renting out Deke's extra room, and even Deke's lean frame was almost too much for him to hoist in a dead lift.

Deke winced at the contact, every second excruciating. He slumped forward, elbows on knees, and put his head in his hands while Aaron filled a cup with water from the sink. Aaron stood staring at him momentarily. Deke could feel the judgement from his gaze. He didn't want to look at him. Deke gathered himself, and then he did. When their eyes met, Aaron dropped the glass, shattering as it hit the tiles, scattering everywhere.

"Kill him," the voice whispered in his ear, the sound caressing the nape of his neck.

Kill him. The voice shuddered through his head. A high-pitched whine started ringing through his ears, intense and unending.

Kill him. Kill him. Kill him. Aaron was backing away, crunching through broken glass, trapped behind the bathroom door.

Kill him! The voice started screaming louder, thundering from back to front, left to right, digging its claws into his brain. Other voices joined, the whine humming steadily louder and louder. Deke's face twisted in pain, and he clasped at his head, wishing it would stop.

In a moment of panicked blindness, Deke stooped to the floor, snatching up a curving and sparkling slice of glass and advanced forward, Aaron raising his arms over his face.

"Deke, what, no, Deke, buddy, what's happening what..." his voice cut out as Deke slashed at his arms, deep red and raw lines.

Deke plunged the glass into Aaron's stomach, over and over, Aaron struggling and retching, trying to push past Deke, trying to get away. Aaron stumbled to the floor, blood pouring from his arms and stomach, slipping and sliding in his own draining life. Deke straddled his crawling form, grabbed Aaron's hair and pulled his head roughly back towards him. Aaron gasped and wheezed, and their eyes met. Deke slashed across Aaron's exposed jugular and dropped him, gurgling and sputtering to the floor. He dropped the wedge of glass and stepped over him, out into the sunlit hallway.

The voices had stopped. Everything was a calm and breathless silence.

Aaron was the first. He wasn't the last. Deke didn't know how he left the house, how no one saw him and called the cops. His hands, his face, everything was splattered in Aaron's blood, his hair gummy when it dried. He wandered the alleys of the city, keeping to the shadows, lost and confused. Something was leading him, an internal compass, linked deep within his gut, steering him. The sunlight still burned his eyes; he avoided it when he could.

Sometimes, the voices would return. They would tell him who was next; pushing and prodding and pulling his subconscious until he met the next victim face to face. Somehow, he was stronger, vibrant with energy, faster than he'd ever been, and it showed in the brutal nature of the attacks, and how quickly they ended. The next target of the voice's rage was a man in a high-powered business suit, lurking next to the back office door having a well-deserved cigarette after hours. The next one was a young woman, innocently walking her dog through the park, jumping at sounds imagined, until he squeezed the life from her eyes.

Over and over and over, he slashed, strangled, stabbed, and even beat to a bloody pulp with his bare fists. Sometimes they fought back, but they never won, not until the day the voices led him to Dezi.

He tried to stop, he really did. Every ounce of his will screamed, he tried to throw himself away from her, screamed at her to get away from the delivery truck and go inside. She had gaped, unable to figure out what was wrong with him. When he advanced on her, menacingly, knife at his side, he hadn't realized that someone could actually beat him; that not everyone was entirely hopeless.

Dezi had a switchblade of her own, sinking it deep into his gut in the dark behind the closed bar. Deke gasped, and staggered. The ringing and screaming voices had suddenly ceased, and he became increasingly aware of his heartbeat in his ears. He clutched at his stomach, and stumbled away, slamming into the trash cans and knocking debris flying. Dezi stared after him, trembling, clutching the dripping knife, unsure of her next move.

Deke didn't make it far. Half a block away, he collapsed in a doorway to a darkened apartment building, shaking and breathless. He pulled his jacket away and untucked his shirt, pulling it away from his stomach. He winced, gaping down at the dark and pooling gash running across his stomach. He lay there, wheezing.

Finally, he thought. Finally I can end this. If I die, this will all stop. Slowly, his breathing calmed. He urged the dark to overtake him. Begged, pleaded.

"It's not so easy, the act of dying, is it Deke? You all do it, but no one can tell you just how hard it truly is," a voice quietly, teasingly called from the dark.

She was standing before him, the harpy, the devil, the cobra from the bar.

He had begun to think she wasn't real, a psychotic break, just a shift in his brain playing to his senses. She stared down at him, pouting, he looking up at her through narrowed eyes. She crouched by him, smiling sweetly.

"Now, now Deke. You're not ready, you're not done. We will tell you when you have done enough. You have to keep your head up, keep yourself healthy, eat right, the full nine yards, you know?"

She cocked her head to the side, smiling.

He could feel that he was fading fast, could feel his life slowly crawling from his body. She rolled her eyes.

"Come on, Deke, really? You're going to be like this?"

He licked his lips, unable to respond.

She reached out and grabbed his hand, leaning in close, the lilies wafting over him, suffocating.

She purred,

"Little human, little human, heal thyself," she placed his hand over his wound, the blood slowing.

She pushed his hand into his flesh, clamping down with an iron grasp. Deke gasped with the pain, and she muttered a few short words he didn't understand. Electricity ran up his arm and back down again, through his palm and into his torso.

He sharply gasped and shook, feebly trying to move his hand, trying to break the connection. After several seconds of excruciating pain, she released him, smoothly standing, and turning away. He looked down at his stomach, the blood gone. The ragged edges of his skin healed, the only scar a silver slash, flashing brilliantly in the streetlight. He looked back up to her, a thousand questions spinning a vortex through his brain but she had disappeared into the night. The questions died on his lips.

Unlike his words, they weren't going to let him die.

Hours had passed, and Deke awoke, curled on the steps he had collapsed on. Finally, his head felt clear. He felt no need to rise and hunt. The air was blessedly cool and his mind was thankfully free. The actions of the past while washed over him, and he wept. He openly and unabashedly cried on that stoop for what felt an eternity. Strangers passed by, curiously glancing at this man, blood-stained, shaking and crying, but no one ever really saw him. *They* made sure of it.

Days had passed, he had lost count how many.
Deke sat on a park bench, staring out over the bay, and farther, at the brisk waves of the ocean. The cool breeze fluttered his hair, and the setting sun behind him was easy on his eyes; he liked the dusk. The nights weren't his, that was when the voices returned, searing their demands on his brain and his heart.

The day was too bright, too vivid, threatening to expose him and his dirty deeds. He wished he had lost count of the number of people he had hurt, learned to squeeze out their cries and their pleading. Oh the begging. He wasn't in control of himself once the whine pierced his brain, slicing out through his eyes. But he could see it all, hear it all, could feel the crushing of his heart, the tears in his eyes, as he couldn't control what he did.

He pushed up the sleeve of his jacket, and then rolled up his shirt sleeve, past the elbow. He eyed the criss-crossing pattern of silver scars running a road-map of destruction up and down his forearm. He closed his eyes. Thinking back to the previous night; two, there had been two. He thumbed open his pocket knife, and sliced into his arm, slowly, no longer gasping at this task or wincing with the sting. When it had pooled, he slowly cut again.

Two, he thought to himself. When the blood began to stream down his arm, he closed the pocket knife, and slipped it away. He stared at the cuts briefly, and then palmed them with his hand. He closed his eyes and muttered, mouthing the words he now knew too well under his breath. The electric sting ran through his arm, twisting through his bones. He sighed, and pulled his hand away, revealing two fresh and shining tics, barbed wire in his flesh. Two lives he had no choice but to destroy.

He wished he was hungry. He wished he felt anything really. Other than pain, and excruciating thirst, he was shockingly numb to everything that had ever afflicted him when he still considered himself human.

How could he be human, with all the blood he had spilled?

The night began to grow cold. He pulled his sleeves back down, staring off over the water. He wished he could go home. No doubt someone would have found Aaron by now. No doubt, someone was looking for him. The past nudged at him, overwhelming.

Dark had fallen, the first time he met a Collector. He had remained at the park bench, calmly, quietly, as still as a statue, waiting for the voices to come. It was better than fighting it; just waiting for their call. But tonight was different; the humidity was rising as a storm barrelled towards him across the water. He could see the flashes, and felt the deep and distant rumble, reverberating through his chest. He relished the thought of rain; his burning skin sizzled whenever he was caught in a down-pour, steam often rising from his flesh. He felt no fear of the elements anymore; they were a part of him now.

The storm menaced ahead of him, threatening and large. Wind, rushing ahead of the storm front pummeled him, whirling dust and leaves into the air, dancing maniacally. He could feel it twisting around him caressing his face and tugging at his clothes. He breathed deeply, closing his eyes.

He heard a loud clinking sound, chains dropping to the concrete path in front of him. His eyes snapped open.

An incredibly tall man stood in front of him, casually holding a length of heavy chain in one hand, and a long silver-bladed dagger in the other. Aside from the weapons he held, he looked remarkably normal, a shock of dark hair fluttering around his head, dressed in a darkly sharp looking suit. That was, perfectly normal until he smiled, showing off his impossibly thin and needle sharp teeth, numbering in the hundreds, pressing against his over stretched chapped and cracked lips.

Deke recoiled, debating whether he could out-run the man's undoubtedly long strides; he stood a head taller even than Deke's lanky frame.

The wind had risen to a gale, rushing around, tossing trees where they stood, pin-wheeling litter through the air, rattling garbage cans across the ground, knocking them into the frothing water below. The wind suffocated, pushing and pulling and stealing the breath from his lungs. Deke couldn't believe his eyes, as behind the man, directly over the edge of the breakwater, a seam ripped through the sky, pulling slowly open, ragged, the wind growing harder as the seam edged further open. The vast expanse of ever darker black in an already dark sky threatened to envelope him.

The man moved forward, and threw the chains down in front of Deke's feet. He could feel a heat radiating off of him, low and burning. Deke cringed away, trying to maintain the man's piercing gaze, shying away from the mouthful of predatory teeth. The man leaned in close, and inhaled deeply. The pupils narrowed – vertically - and he inhaled once more. The tempest roared around them, and sparks rose from the crack in reality, seductively pouring from the seam, surrounding Deke.

The man laughed, deep and syrupy, honey spilling slowly from a bottle.

"You are not complete. The Collectors have no need to drag you to Hell yet," he inhaled again, a deep rattling sound.

Deke stumbled for words, shouting over the gale,

"Who are the Collectors? Why do you want me?"

The man straightened and bared his horrible teeth again, snake tongue slipping out and licking his lips.

"Your soul is still too clean, your destruction is not yet complete, soon, you will be ripe for the picking, and then we will come for you. Your Tender will find you, complete you. You cannot hide from us; you cannot hide from Hell,"

The Collector reached down and picked up the length of chain, effortlessly flipping them over his shoulder. He laughed once more, and was enveloped in a searing light. Deke covered his eyes, steeling himself from the harsh glare, averting his head. The glare subsided, and then the man was gone. The wind ceased; an absent and deafening silence.

Then the rain poured down, the sky opening, the storm raging on.

Deke gaped, words eluding him. Collectors? Tender? Where raindrops hit his bare skin, they sizzled. He breathed a sigh of relief, the coolness washing over him.

He needed help. His brain felt clear again, for the first time in too long, the fog was lifted. He wondered if the Collector had made the voices go away, beating them into a corner until it could assess his, what, condition, his *soul?* He wished there was someone he could go to, anyone he could tell what was happening. His solitude was exhausting; it pulled at him deep inside. He wiped the rain from his eyes, mixed with his tears.

He sat for hours, skin burning, and every raindrop that touched him was a tiny sting.

"Poor little Deke,"

Dezi's voice poured into his ear from behind the bench.

He turned sharply, springing from the bench and backing away from her. She was completely bedraggled, rain soaking her clothes, her light tank top and skirt that she wore when working behind the bar clinging to her body, the water running in rivulets through her fire engine hair. Her makeup was smudging and her lips and fingers were an icy blue.

She awkwardly came toward him, stilted, limbs and joints not quite working together in unison.

"W-w-what is wrong with you?" he stumbled as he backed away; pressing against the chain railing that separated the path from the steep drop into the tumultuous water below.

She continued her disjointed, stumbling motion, twisting her head awkwardly. She pressed against him, long and languid, twitching slightly when her hands found his. Her hands were so, so cold against his hot flesh, her fingers spasming from the tiny shocks his sent through her. She pushed her face against his, rocking slowly back and forth, pinning him against the barrier.

"Poor little Deke. Poor little Deke. Poor, poor, little, tiny, Deke," she breathed quietly, singing in a hushed tone, mouth awkwardly forming the words.

He tried to push her away, but she was much too strong, she felt too heavy, a dead man's weight dragging against him. He could feel the electricity in him building, crackling, and the spaces between them connecting with bright and tiny flashes. She gazed into his eyes, and smiled.

"I have something for you," she muttered, releasing his hands and digging around in her pocket, fingers numb, scrabbling at her pocket. She pulled a piece of crumpled paper out, the paper slick and almost transparent in the pounding rain.

She pushed it into his hand, falling against him once more. He grabbed her by the shoulders, trying to steady her; she swayed, twisting, and slumped against the railing, clinging to a support post. She stared down at the waves, rain pouring down her face. He reached for her cheek, pushing her hair out of her eyes, tucking it behind her ear. She smiled, dreamily down at the waves.

"Dezi, what do you know?"

His hand rested lightly on her back, the skin beneath the transparent hem of her shirt a horrible mottled blue, an unhuman shade of marble. He recoiled slightly, and she turned to look at him.

"Goodbye, Deke,"

With one last heave, she pulled herself across the chain and toppled over the side, down the wall, and into the waves below. He nearly threw himself after her, reaching desperately to grab her, but the waves and dark had already swallowed her.

He leaned against the support post, panting; the paper she had given him still gripped in his fist. He opened his hand, slowly peeling apart the two halves, careful not to tear it.

SAFETY was printed across the top in bold black marker, followed by a series of strange markings and symbols, swirling and jagged. *MARK AND CARVE* was printed across the bottom.

He stared down into the waves crashing against the wall, incredulous. How had Dezi known where to find him? He hadn't seen her since the botched attempt on her life, since she nearly took his. His hand strayed to the vivid scar under his shirt, the stain below his jacket a constant reminder of what he could have lost.

Mark and carve? He folded the paper and put it into his breast pocket to examine later. The rain was slowly letting up, he could even see stars between the clouds and the lightning had long ago stopped. He began to walk back towards the downtown, through the darkened park. The rain had rushed away any evening dog-walkers and joggers, he felt confident that he would not have to kill tonight.

The nights when he did, he did not choose where he went, he was drawn, and his feet took him where he did not want to go, resistant but unable to stop himself. It was a hand around his gut, pushing and pulling him until a target crossed his path and the voices began their screeching.

All was thankfully quiet now though. He reached the alley he was looking for. He moved a trashcan aside, revealing a dirty window at the ground level. He looked around, suspicious, holding his breath, and when the coast was clear, crouched down and swung it inward, pushing his legs through and dropping to the floor of the cellar. It was the basement of a foreclosed linen store, boxes still piled high with merchandise unsold in the bankruptcy.

It smelled damp and musty, the dust thick on the floor and the lone desk in the corner. He had been hiding in here in the nights, whenever he could. He did not need the warmth, but after his kills he was beyond exhaustion, and wanted to avoid being caught in the open, spattered with fresh blood. He pulled the paper from his pocket, still soaked and dripping from the rain. He unfolded it gingerly and stared at it again. He contemplated the strange symbols, committing them to memory. He looked around in the dim light coming from a stray, bare bulb near the middle of the room, and went to the abandoned desk. He thumbed through the drawers and files, until he found what he was looking for, a thick piece of blue chalk.

He turned it over in his hand, contemplating it. He wasn't sure where to make the marks, on the floor, across the window ledges, or maybe across the door? What if he put them in a circle, and stood in the middle?

There were too many options too choose from, and he didn't want to make the wrong choice. He didn't want any more people to die. Strange, that he should care more about their dying, than his blame. He knew, deep down, none of this was his fault. He had done nothing to deserve this, he was caught in an infernal game, one of which he knew not the rules or all of the players.

And if God were to judge him on that which he couldn't control, well he certainly had bigger problems than where he stood now. He looked at the paper once again. It was slowly drying to tissue quality, brittle in his hands. He flipped it over, and held it up to the lamp light, inspecting all sides. And there it was.

Roughly sketched around the perimeter of the paper were the symbols, over and over again, marching in sequence, and in the middle of the drawing was a hastily drawn sketch of a window.

Here goes nothing, he thought to himself.

All eight windows and two doors later, they were done. Painstakingly drawn, sometimes erased and redrawn to his satisfaction, carved with his switchblade into the unpainted frames of the basement, he stood back to inspect his work. The blue chalk marks glowed eerily in the light of the basement, and his tired eyes made them seem to dance across the wood work. He hoped he had been guided by the goodness left in Dezi, that whatever had been done to her was done to save him, rather than damn. He only hoped she wasn't damned for her help, lost in Hell or Purgatory or wherever she was pulled to when she finally drowned. He closed his eyes and muttered a prayer for her. He hoped it was enough.

He stayed in that basement for three days.

Waiting for the voices to call him, to make their blood demands, for the temptress from the bar to storm in and demand his loyalty; for the toothed monster from the water's edge to rise up, winds howling and drag him away in chains. But nothing happened. He paced the concrete, he slept, for the first time in too long, he meditated, and through it all, utter quiet, and peace in his heart. Even the burning in his skin was calmed, an ache rather than a stinging fire.

On the third night, he opened the window, leaning on the ledge, gazing out at the busy streets nearby, jeweled heels and heavy shoes striding by, young people on the way to the nearby club district. Hours had passed, he was certain, and he had spent most of it completely motionless, enjoying the air of camaraderie and revelry, soft breezes playing on his burning face.

These were people who had their whole lives of freedom ahead of them, passing by the man hiding in the cellar. He sighed. That is when he heard it, not the whine of incoming insanity, not the taunting and teasing voices, but an off-key ringing, akin to the vibration of a large bell. The sound grew steadily nearer, and he shrunk back against the frame, bracing for the voices to start. The sound became deafening, as a pair of red heels stopped in front of the window.

The woman standing in them stopped to light a cigarette, taking a few hesitant puffs, laughing with her friends. She tossed her hair at a particularly raunchy joke, and turned to face the alley. He altered his position until he could see the rest of her, huge sunglasses covering most of her face, strange in the night, long legs in fishnets. She had left her arms and shoulders bare, despite the chill of the night, flaunting the false warmth of youth. That is when he saw them, just below her collar bone.

Three irregular ovals, glowing dully in the streetlight, marched across her skin. He absently touched his own – the only marks he had been unable to heal himself that had remained staunchly red and angry, and knew that somehow, she was like him. She dropped her cigarette and quashed it out with the toe of her shoe. She hugged all of her friends, wishing them goodbye, and began to walk away. The ringing, now oddly pleasant compared to the usual freak show that rose in his mind, began to fade away as she left. He resolved to follow her, he felt this was his only chance to find out what she knew, and he may never see her again. He palmed the chalk on the frame, and sighed, before hauling himself out through the window and onto the dirty ground of the alley.

He moved quickly and quietly, keeping to the shadows, ducking behind cars whenever he suspected that she heard his shoes scuff the pavement. He kept the ringing in focus, ever so quiet in the background of his brain. If she got too far ahead, the ringing stopped completely, and fear would overcome him so quickly and quietly that perhaps he was just imagining that she was anything different at all. The doubt was so rapid and incensed; he knew it had to be a side effect of their lost connection.

Soon, downtown became suburbia, small lawns and low lying bungalows, and he began hanging back farther than he hoped. Finally, she stopped at one particular home, staring up at it as she finished the cigarette she had lit up a couple blocks before, and he paused, looking for somewhere to hide. She fished around in her purse, evidently looking for keys that weren't there.

She sighed and shook her head, and removed her shoes. Deke hid behind a tree across the street and watched her carefully. She walked through the grass and around to the side of the house, where she slid open the nearest window. Putting a foot on a planter near the corner of the house, she hauled herself up and rather ungracefully up and through the window. He waited to the count of thirty, and then his intuition would not let him pause a moment longer. He dashed across the street and up the side of the house, standing on tip toe to look inside the window.

He couldn't see her anywhere to be found, and all the lights in the house remained off. He took one last look around, and heaved himself up and through the unscreened window, gently rolling to a crouch once he had entered.

Silence filled the house, and he paused to collect his bearings and adjust his eyes. He knew they gave him away in the darkness. He knew from the screams when they flashed, they were always betraying him at the last second.

He heard low muffled singing coming from the hall. He crouched behind the wall, listening and waiting. Footsteps retreated, a light clicked on, then off, and then silence. He waited, breath bated.

The house settled, an unnerving crack echoing through the house. He sighed. The ringing was faint, barely audible, but he found it calming, shelter from the storm that had become his life. He crept down the hall and pushed the first door open, just the bathroom. He crossed the hall and gently turned the knob, holding his breath as he opened the door. The woman sleeping in the bed sighed in her sleep, slowly rolling over. It was not the girl he had followed home. He blushed, realizing the insanity of what he was doing. What if the voices came back? What if he hurt these women? Attacked them in their sleep? This felt different; it felt so much more wrong this time, being around these people.

He backed slowly from the room, quietly closing the door. He stopped, back against the frame, and exhaled slowly. He turned to the last door, it sat open, and he crept towards it. The ringing grew steadily louder and louder, beckoning him, calling him ever forward. He felt intoxicated, the sound filling his brain and clearing his senses. He stood in the doorway, staring down at where she had curled up on a pull-out couch.

The marks on her collarbone glowed, three red eyes shining in the dark. The ringing was deafening, and he didn't even care. He felt safe. He closed the door, still hearing the ringing as he moved back through the house. He felt so tired, limbs shaking, his feet dragging.

A great weight had settled on his shoulders, and he could sense the world turning beneath his feet, heading towards dawn. If only a few minutes of rest could be his. He curled up on the couch, giving himself a warning – fifteen minutes, and then he had to get out, head back to the cellar and figure out his next move. It would be hours before the women would awaken.

Chapter 6

Shallow Cuts

"And you know the rest... I've been here, with you,"

He was interrupted by a loud rumble, the house shaking, pots and pans clattering from their rack and falling to the floor. The clock fell from the wall, shattering its face across the tiles.

A book case in the living room toppled, cascading books and magazines across the rug. I ducked to the doorway, clinging to the frame, unsteady on the heaving floor, Deke followed, a supportive arm around my shoulders. I had never experienced an earthquake before, and certainly not one with any malicious intent. I half expected the floor to crack open, ragged, dust flying, swallowing us and my kitchen whole. The rumble ceased and Deke cautiously moved out from shelter.

"Quickly, check all the frames - make sure they are still solid, no cracks through any of the inscriptions, I don't know if they'll hold up," he loped off towards the back bedroom and the bathroom, while I ran to the kitchen window and skimmed my finger along all four sides, and repeated with the kitchen doorframe and out towards the living room.

A low growl issued from immediately in front of me and I froze. Warm breath curled along my neck and down my arm. I could feel **it** *smelling me.* A slight gasping whine escaped my lips. The smell of sulphur was filling the room, and I held my breath, urging myself not to gag. Fur tickled my arms, so close that it was touching me, and yet I could see nothing.

I peered over towards the front door and saw it – the crack running across the floor, up the wall, and damned if it wasn't straight through the window and up to the ceiling, severing the inscribed trim into four pieces. I could hear heavy padded footfalls; a weight behind the sound, and they passed around me, slowly, moving towards the kitchen. Unable to see the beast, I had no idea how large it was, or how fast it could move.

I needed to warn Deke, without having my throat forcibly removed from my body. I stepped back towards the front door, slowly, one foot after the other, careful not to stumble. I could hear it rutting around in the kitchen, no doubt smelling out the direction Deke had gone.

A pan flew across the room and smashed into the wall, clanging loudly and reverberating on the floor. I took my chance. I ran for the door, clawing it open, out into the blinding sunlight and onto the glistening lawn. Neighbors stood on their porches and driveways, chattering nervously to each other about the earthquake. I ignored their inquisitive stares.

I took off, around the corner of the house and wrenched open the gate, leaving wet shoe prints across the patio stones. I raced for the backyard; feet drenched from the wet grass and lunged towards the bathroom window. I banged on it, flat handed, smacking the glass as loud as I could.

Thunder still rolled in the distance, sharply ominous against the bright sunshine. Deke froze at the sound beyond the window, where he had been inspecting the inner frame.

I yelled for him,

"Quickly! It's in there, get out. Please!"

His eyes grew wide, and he slammed the door closed to the bathroom.

I realized what he'd done – the door and window were essentially barred to the creature stalking him - but he'd also locked himself in – trapped until we found a way to save him.

I watched him pace the room, running his hands through his hair, muttering to himself. I wished I knew what to do, where to go. My phone buzzed in my pocket.

EARTHQUAKE. I'm on my way.

No, no, this couldn't happen. What could I say to make her stay away? Any excuse would just make her come faster, she was always so suspicious.

I glanced back up into the bathroom. Deke had his forehead and elbows against the door, head in his hands. I was truly worried for him now. What had made him follow her home? What was so special about her, why was she different from any one else?

I became overwhelmingly anxious for my sister – I just couldn't stand it if she was mixed up with the same people as Deke. I couldn't imagine her out, wandering the night, ruthlessly killing strangers and hiding from preternatural forces. My baby sister just didn't have that in her.

I couldn't say the same for Deke though – who knew who he truly was before all of this came down on him, a landslide of unseen forces and extenuating circumstances.

I sat on the wet grass and thought hard. We had inscribed all the door frames in the house to keep the Collectors and their ilk out, and now, we were trapping Deke in. But what if I trapped it further, allowing Deke to get past and escape? It seemed so simple in theory, could it really work? But could I bring myself to go back into the house? The beast hadn't seemed interested in me, but I wasn't the one with a warrant on my head. Could it even sense me? There were too many what-ifs, and not even close to enough answers.

I wish Deke knew more.

I needed to get Deke out of there before my sister showed up.

I chewed my thumb, niggling at the spot that had been sliced open earlier. An odd, ozone-heavy taste filled my mouth, the taste of storms in the air before they break.

Mark and carve. Mark and carve. I rolled the words around in my tongue, contemplating the metallic scar. The note had said 'Mark and carve'.

Wait.

I slapped the window again, trying to draw the despondent Deke closer to the window. He shook his head, I could see the hope leaving his eyes, glinting steelier than ever. I rolled mine. I waved him over, gesturing wildly.

"MARK YOU!" I yelled. I jabbed my finger at him, the other drawing shapes in the air. He tilted his head, considering.

"MARK, CARVE, MARK, YOU!" I jabbed again, and I could see the light dawning.

He leapt up from where he was sitting, patting down his pockets, until panic contorted his features. He'd left his knife and the marker on the kitchen table when the earthquake had struck. He looked around, eyes filling with panic, until he spied the razor sitting on the ledge of the shower. I couldn't watch, didn't want to see if the razor slipped as he pried it from its plastic casing.

When I looked through the window again, his fingers were bloody, and he threw the blade down on the edge of the sink, pulling open the medicine cabinet, bottles and boxes raining down around him, bouncing off the floor as he searched. Triumphant, he pulled a lipstick out from the melee, a deep and seductive red I avoided wearing at all costs, a gift from my sister, and twisted off the cap.

He unzipped the hoodie to his waist, and began drawing the symbols from memory, marking blood red lines across one side of his lean stomach, framed by his hipbone. When they were done, he threw the lipstick into the sink with the other gathered flotsam and picked up the razor. His eyes flashed up to meet mine and I swear, and will always swear, that he grinned.

At that moment, I wish I believed this would work as much as he did. He studied his handiwork in lipstick for a moment, considering it, and then plunged the blade into his flesh as deep as he could, one bloody hand supporting himself on the edge of the sink. He worked away, never stopping; I feared if he stopped, he would be unable to start again. Tears welled in his eyes and he chewed at his tongue, mirroring the deep red marks he had made on the left with the slices on the right.

When it was done, he staggered, settling on the closed toilet lid. I prayed he didn't pass out, the way the blood was pooling in the etchings I was afraid he had gone too deep, my bathroom floor a slaughterhouse.

He turned his eyes to the heavens, and I could see his lips moving. He reached for the hand towel and pressed it to his abdomen, clutching at his knee with the other hand, knuckles flashing white and silver. He continued muttering through gritted teeth, flashes of static electricity escaping from the edges of his hand, and through his fingers, sparking and dropping, metal meeting a grinder, white hot.

He inhaled deeply, and pulled the towel away. The skin, though bloody and stained, was marked permanently with his silver hieroglyphics. He briefly ran the cloth under the tap, and dabbed at his skin, careful not to touch the lipstick stains. He zipped the sweater back up, and washed his hands. I breathed a sigh, not knowing if this would work, hoping to God that it did.

He came to the window, and with a last look over his shoulder, cracked it open. He waited, inhaling the fresh air deeply, eyes closed. I waited, bated breath, waiting for the door to crash open and the creature to come pounding through, waiting for Deke to be ripped limb from limb.

Nothing happened.

He pushed the window open the rest of the way, and smiled down at me.

"Brilliant," he awkwardly clambered up and through the window, dropping heavily to the ground on weak legs.

I steadied him, as he leaned against the wall, breathing deeply and wincing up at the afternoon sun. We waited tensely for the creature to come outside. We waited for the lunge and the snap of invisible jaws, but the only sound reaching our ears was that of birds tentatively twittering after the storm.

Now that we were out in the real world, outside of that humid and heavy-aired Hell that had been my home, it seemed almost impossible that anything that had happened today was real.

Except for his eyes; those were constant reminders of the otherworldly that was happening around us. In the bright of day, I could see that the irises were truly pools of liquid mercury, rimmed around the edges with electric blue, flashing with every movement of his head.

I realized I was staring, without really seeing, and bashfully turned away my face, blushing. He gently took my face in his hands and turned it back towards him.

"You, you are brilliant. I can't even believe it, I thought I was done," he swiftly brought my face towards his, and kissed my forehead briefly.

Electric tingles pass through his lips and into my head, a sensation akin to eating an ice cream too quickly, a quick and burning jolt through my brain.

"We should get moving. We need to find your sister," he turned away and began striding for the gate, leaving me to absently rub at my forehead.

I sat at the table in the café, near the intersection of Salem and Parmenter Street, nervously playing with my phone, crossed legs jittering. A cup of coffee was sat in front of me, untouched and still steaming. I checked the time again, swearing silently that the clock had stopped. Luckily, the power was back on here, and they had switched on the A/C in retaliation to the passing storms humidity.

I took a deep breath, trying to settle down. Crowds of people still wandered the streets, excited and shakily discussing the storm and the aftermath of the earthquake. The city was vibrant and buzzing, and the café noisy, full of chatter.

If I raised my head, I could see the sign for the tattoo parlor where I had deposited Deke. The only way we could ensure any permanence of the marks, was to get them inscribed right into his skin. We had debated this hotly – but it seemed to be the only way. We couldn't be scribbling on him in lipstick and marker for the rest of his life. Who needs to be attacked in the shower?

After I had paid for his body work, as he still remained wallet-less, and we mutually assumed the police would have put a trace out on his credit cards even if we had tried to retrieve it, I had retreated down the street to wait for my sister. I would never hear the end of it if she caught me coming out of the tattoo parlor.

The bell over the door jingled. My sister strode in, long-legged and confident; looking a far cry different from the straggly liquor-logged mess she had been this morning.

Dark washed denim, sensible knee-high boots, elegant navy sweater, her hair pulled up into a high and perky ponytail, and designer sunglasses hiding her face. Her appearance screamed Mother, and I knew she had probably been caught sneaking back in this morning and done herself up to meet with me in order to keep Mother quiet.

She leaned down and kissed my cheek, plopping down in the seat next to me.

"Good afternoon, darling" she drawled out the A, sickly syrupy.

"You look like Hell," she smiled.

I winced at her choice of words, and catching myself in the reflection of her sunglasses, I half agreed with her.

"So, where is he?" She looked around, bouncing in her seat. I was amazed at her energy – mere hours ago she was climbing in my window for a cat nap after the club, the city losing its power and an unheard of earthquake rattling the windows and here she was, bound and determined to be peppy.

I sighed.

"I have a lot to tell you. I mean, some really, unbelievable stuff. I need you to just, listen, he'll be over here soon, and this is really, really serious," she grimaced at me, pondering momentarily.

She awkwardly pulled at her pony tail, something she hadn't done since we were children. I knew if her hair was down, she would've been chewing on the ends. I couldn't see her eyes behind the glasses, didn't know what she was thinking. She bit her lip, and sighed in return.

She signaled for the waiter to come over and quickly and quietly gave him her coffee order. She glanced at my cup and I waved her off.

"I'm not sure how safe we are here, so hopefully, I can give you the abridged version and then we can get the Hell out of Dodge, and find someplace better. The events of today are the least of our worries so far," I began, but something about her sad smile stopped me.

She pulled off her sunglasses.

"I have a lot to tell you too,"

Her eyes glittered coolly, mirroring the room in the metallic gleam of her sparkling new irises, their normally iridescent green replaced with molten silver.

"Shit," I staggered in my seat, and almost fell out of my chair.

No, no, no. This couldn't be happening. What on earth was going on?

Deke chose that moment to enter the café, the tiny bell announcing his entry, ominous against the chatter of the patrons. I would have sworn that the air itself had been sucked from the room, an absent void dimming conversations around us and flickering the lights.

He rubbed gently at his torso below his sweater, as he looked around the room for me, and our eyes met. A look of concern coursed over his face and he strode rapidly toward me, my sister's back to his entrance. My sister, seeing my reaction to an unknown entity behind her shoulder, turned around in her seat, rising abruptly and knocking over her chair. The sudden clatter released the silence, a rush of noise washing over me and the severity of the situation hit me like a ton of bricks.

I rose as well, trying to maintain my cool, and gritted my teeth,

"Deke, this is Clara. Clara, Deke,"

They made no move to shake hands, in fact, strangely, they didn't move at all, awkwardly rigid and staring at each other, horrifyingly aware of all of each other's darkest secrets.

I stared back and forth between the two of them, waiting for any reaction. Quietly, barely moving her lips, Clara said,

"You heard it too,"

Deke nodded slightly, and reached out to the neckline of her sweater, gently pushing the top curve away from her throat and briefly touching the red marks that curved at her collar bone. She gulped, loudly, and turned away. Deke pulled the zippered edge of his hoodie aside, flashing his corresponding marks as well.

Recognition dawned in her face, and she plunked down into the nearest chair. She put her face in her hands. Deke looked at me sadly, and righted Clara's abandoned seat, straddling it in between us, body language rigid. I realized Clara was crying, silently, tiny sobs racking her body in minute seizures.

Deke looked at me awkwardly, not sure what to do.

I gestured him closer, waving his ear closer to my face, resisting the urge to pull him violently near with urgency, and whispered,

"We'll have to mark…mark her too, if she's going through… if what is happening to her, and you, it's the same, right?"

I stumbled over the words, horrified at the thought of having to hurt my own sister so badly. A second thought tripped into my head as I said it – had she been killing as well?

What was she really doing, those late nights out at the clubs?

Deke nodded slightly, shoulders rising and falling in a slow and resigned exhale. He turned, putting his lips close to my ear, the vibrations of his voice tickling the fine hairs of my ear lobe,

"It will have to be quickly… immediately; before anyone takes notice,"

I grimaced and leaned forward, away from his warm breath, and put my hand on her wrist. A snap of electric shock tingled through my fingers. I was startled, but continued on; I lowered my voice,

"Listen, Clara. We know how to keep you safe, make the voices stop, we think, for now. We need to work quickly, we need you safe, and then we can go, we will figure the rest out, but for now, we need them to not be able to find you. We just did that for Deke, it's working so far, you just have to trust us,"

Clara pulled away from my touch, crossing her arms and hunching her shoulders, body language all bristles and fears. She chewed her lip, and then nodded. The tears in her eyes magnified the silvery glare, refracting the light into sun on a sparkling pond. They were so horrifyingly beautiful, so wrong and yet filled with something intrinsically natural I'd never seen.

I stood, Deke matching my move in one smooth movement, and we all left the café together, fear of the unknown digging at my heart, despair building at the thought of what we were going to do.

Chapter 7

Discovering Secrets

Clara's story had driven me to tears, the first thirty miles of our trip, Deke hesitantly stroking my shoulder as I drove, the electricity flowing through his fingertips causing me to grit my teeth, but I desperately needed the distraction.

The voices in her head had a vastly different method than Dekes. She stalked her prey in the clubs, following them through the noise and the grinding, pounding music. She taunted them, seduced them, pulled them into the dark alleys with promises, and ended them swiftly and surely. Her friend's believed she had simply become a wild child, prowling the clubs every night. If they had only known what she had truly been doing, maybe they would have tried to stop her.

Now, surprisingly, for two people who were raging mayhem and murder across the city not so long ago, controlled by an unknown entity and fearing for their lives, they were definitely a pair of miserable whiners when it came to the pain of their tattoos.

Clara sat in the back seat of Mother's borrowed car, curled sideways along the bench, avoiding contact with the backrest. She had opted to get hers in parallel lines running across her shoulder blade, the artist giving us strange looks when Deke returned so soon and with fresh flesh. Deke had retreated with her and his switchblade to the alley shortly after, promising she would be fine and that he wouldn't let her suffer. I found out later he had gone painstakingly slow, one symbol at a time, healing the first before adding a second. Clara was still numbed from the tattoo and claimed she didn't feel a thing.

I doubted this highly.

Deke was stretched out awkwardly in the front seat of the car, legs straight out, trying to avoid bending at the waist as much as possible. He had insisted that the tattoos heal naturally, none of us were certain if his power would erase the tattoo entirely, and we certainly didn't want to test it.

Both were periodically whining and griping, not particularly at anyone, but their complaints sat heavily in the air around us, small nuisances compared to the enormity of our problem. We had been driving for over three hours, and dusk was beginning to settle around us, a heavy mantle on the car. I had always hated driving at this time of night, everything light oddly glaring, the dark deep and consuming. All manner of wildlife liked to choose this time to leap from their hides, springing across the road, lights flashing in their eyes. Deke and Clara both removed their sunglasses, quietly sighing in the dimming car.

We were heading to Mother's summer home, in Leicester, Vermont far, far away from people. There was too much uncertainty, and both Deke and Clara felt safer away from the populace. This meant I was directly driving myself into the lion's mouth, the only entity for miles around that they could hurt. Only so much pleading to their greater intentions could save me, if something were to go wrong, if their marks didn't end up actually working.

Clara had responded well to Deke's tale, nodding anxiously to the parts that meshed with hers. She too, had been taken to this ominously dark building in the middle of nowhere, blue sky crystalline over her head, and had awoken, tangled in sweaty sheets, dreaming of drowning, dying of thirst.

I think she was overly thankful that she wasn't alone in this, eager to be dependent on another person. So many unanswered whys hung in the air after the discussion, neither of them able to figure out the connection that caused this entire situation to occur. They had compared notes and memories on where they had been, who they had spoken to, in the weeks leading up to their bizarre abductions.

Nothing fit. Clara hadn't even been in the country for most of this year, visiting Belgium with her school friends. She had returned, and the troubles, the killings, had begun. She hadn't bothered to keep track of her victims, not like Deke had, preferring to dive deeper and deeper into the revelry preceding the hunt to block out the memories.

Deke could remember nothing except work; he had been gunning hard for the merger and could think of no other focus in his life at the time.

"What I don't seem to get, is why, if you were out there, doing what you were doing, why would you come to *my house?* Weren't you worried that you'd turn on me? Were you the least bit worried about my safety?"

I looked at her in the mirror, but she wouldn't catch my gaze. Deke swiveled to look back at her, raising an eyebrow.

"It felt - It felt safe there. Different. And it seemed like they had me going after scumbag jerks, I figured it was all right. And speaking of *all right.* Are those, are those Reggie's clothes?" Clara spoke hesitantly from the back of the car.

I could now feel her eyes boring into mine in the rear-view, but I chose to ignore her. Un-spoken accusations threaded her words.

I didn't want to pick a fight with her, not now. It had always been a state of discontent between us, in regards to our absentee brother. She promised, swore, deep down she knew, that he would be coming back. I was as resoundingly determined of the opposite.

Deke looked side-long at me; I could practically see him debating in his head whether or not to pierce the charged atmosphere that had expanded in the car. I tensed my hands tighter on the wheel and sped a little faster.

Clara should *know* better. She knew the circumstances around Deke donning Reggie's clothes were a little more important than her keeping a shrine to our brother.

Maybe it was because I'd been the last one to see him, absently wishing him goodnight as I went on my way to bed, Reggie sitting rigidly on the couch, awkwardly sprawling under a blanket despite the warm house. He'd been sleeping there for a couple of weeks, suddenly appearing at my door without warning, refusing to talk about why he was there, barely outside the grasp of catatonic. I had tried to get him some help, Clara had been over when she could, but I just didn't have the *time* to deal with my twin and his bizarre behavior.

He was prone to these episodes, weeks on end where he went from being perfectly fine, to a zombie, staring at the television and starving, unwilling to eat. He always snapped out of it, apologized for the time spent on my couch, and went back home.

During his stay, I would absently make sure his bills were paid and that he at least he changed his clothes every few days, but it just never seemed that big a deal. Maybe I assumed it was depression, and that it was better I could keep an eye on him. Rather the devil you know, right?

Until one day I woke up, and there was simply a note and his house keys. The note only and simply read **CALIFORNIA.**

Clara and I tried to talk to him on the phone, occasionally getting through, more often not, and leaving a message, but what could we do? And now Clara treated everything about our brother like holy artifacts, waiting for the day when he would come home. I had resigned myself that he never would. Whatever was wrong with him, it had finally come to a head, and he seemed fine out there on his own.

"Addy? Addy come on. You've barely said two words since we left the highway. You've got to be thinking something. Deke and I, we're resigned to what we are and what we've done, but there's no way you can be fine with all of this?"

Snapping me from my reverie, my eyes met hers in the mirror.

"How can you ask if I am alright or not? You know the answer to that, Clara, don't be stupid. I'm lost, I'm scared, and I'm panicked. I don't know how to fix this, I barely know who he is, I barely know who you are anymore, and I just have to keep going. I'm just; keeping going, Deke wearing Reggie's clothes is literally the last thing you should be giving a shit about right now," I banged the steering wheel for emphasis.

The road switched to gravel as I turned at an old weathered sign post for "Sunspot Cottaging" and I turned on the high-beams. No one was out here this far, the season was wrong for the cottagers that flooded these shores come June. The peeping and shrieking of tree frogs and the low eruptions of bull-frogs filled the air and blasted into the windows, an unholy ruckus compared to the void that highway speeds allowed. Tree branches slashed at the roof, ruts heaving the car as I greatly slowed down to avoid bending an axle.

I could feel them both avoiding looking at me. The tension was still building in the car, and unlike normal people, you could actually see the flickers of it at the tips of their fingers, tiny sparks that they both tried to awkwardly rub away with their thumbs, bright in the dark of the car. The snaps and pops were irksome, and I resisted the urge to yell at them both to put their hands away. Better not to poke sleeping giants.

We slowly approached the cottage, if you could call it that, rearing up out of the gloom in a sudden glare of artfully placed pot lights. The place was magnificently atrocious, grandiose and unnecessary in the rural cottage landscape. Mother loved to spend money, and spend she had. Reclaimed limestone rose two stories, arching walkways and ivied walls. Steps lead down to the water and the equally stunning boathouse, the dark lake cool and calm.

They both gazed at the lake, hungrily and at rapt attention. It was a curious reaction to the lake, barely visible in the faint moonlight that shone between the clouds. I thumbed the button on the door opener for the garage and waited patiently for it to open. I realized they had swiveled in their seats to maintain their visual contact with the ebbing water. I shook my head. The two of them were becoming stranger and stranger as time went on. Every time I thought I was getting a grasp on their behaviour, they tripped violently away from it, confused and yearning.

We all settled into our rooms, Clara on the second floor and Deke and I choosing neighbouring suites on the ground. They insisted neither of them really slept anymore, and I found this to be a strangely bizarre concept, particularly for my sister, who'd been known to while away entire weekends in slumber in college. Deke insisted privately that though the ringing he heard whenever he neared Clara gave him the warm and fuzzy, he wasn't sure if he could handle having it pulsing through his brain all hours of the night. I understood that without distraction, it could be mind-numbing. He claimed that this was the perfect distance, an underscoring hum to his thoughts rather than an over-riding sensation.

I think he thought I was safer with him nearby.

I appreciated the sentiment, but it was akin to being safe from the wolf by hiding behind the bear.

I was exhausted, physically and mentally, and however much sleep they didn't need, I knew that there would be little to say once my head hit the pillow.

And for once, I was right.

I awoke, dazed and confused, puzzled by the sparkling light refracting on the ceiling through the window. It took far too long for my brain to piece together where I was and what had happened. I sat up and groaned, rubbing my eyes, debating whether or not to investigate what had woken me from such deep sleep. A glance at the clock showed a flashing 12:00 and I wondered if I'd noticed that the power had gone out before I went to sleep.

I padded silently to the kitchen, figuring at the very least I'd get a drink of water before attempting a few more hours of sleep. The cottage was a tomb, the air very still. I felt every noise I made, no louder than a rustle or a clink of a glass on the marble countertops, was obnoxious and overwhelming.

I moved towards the wall of windows that lead to the patio and down to the lake, and was startled, the condensation-slick glass in my hand sliding towards the floor. I caught it with both hands and held it tight as I looked outside once more.

Someone was sitting out on the dock in the faint moonlight, feet in the water. I peered nervously through the glass, squinting, trying to make out who or what was out there. I resisted the urge to call out to the others in the house, when I realized it must be Deke. As he swung his feet slowly through and out of the water, great arcing lines of electricity sparked from his feet and back to the water, swish and snap. It was terrifyingly beautiful, watching the blue flashes illuminate the water and his face, running around his legs and out through his feet. Swish and snap, the bolts popping as they went. I now knew what had caused the light show on my bedroom ceiling in the dark.

I decided to join him. I carefully slid the sliding door open and stepped out into the cool and wet grass. The air was warm, the spring balancing precariously on the edge of tipping into summer, everything green and shining.

He raised his head at the sound, a smile breaking his face, white teeth flashing in the dark. His eyes glowed subtly, reflecting the moonlight, a predatory glint in the shadows.

This overwhelming power and corruption may have sharpened his edges, but I could tell that he was winning the struggle to maintain the man he was before. A man I never knew, perhaps, but definitely one you'd want to keep around.

I settled hesitantly next to him, crossing my feet to keep them out of the icy dark water. I wasn't going to admit to him that I was afraid of the patterns of lightning tracing the swishing of his feet. The few times we'd touched, the experience had been sharp and tingling, I could only imagine the effect these arcs of light would have on my skin. I could hear his skin sizzling in the dark water.

"Thank you," he whispered softly.

I cocked my head sideways and looked at him concernedly. He glanced at me briefly and turned back to the water.

"...For helping me and being with me. And trusting me. I wouldn't have. And for figuring this out," he gestured vaguely at his stomach. He sighed,

"For the first time in a long time, everything is so clear, and I feel so powerful. I can feel the charge in me and I feel it is mine alone. The voices in my head are gone. Not just quieted, but silenced entirely. I'm wondering if I can be not nearly as damned as I once thought I was; screaming in my head while I did those things. Like Aaron. Oh God, poor Aaron,"

He put his head in his hands, the sparks intensifying, and rising from his fingertips as well, a halo arcing around his head. I shushed him gently; afraid to touch him, afraid of what would happen to the current. Would it stop my heart?

"It wasn't your fault," I told him, lamely.

I knew it was the wrong thing to say the second the words left my lips, but I truly believed it. I knew they had no control, and I knew it couldn't be their fault. What hope could I have for my sister if that weren't true? The sparks settled from his hands, the ones writhing at his legs dimming. He took a deep breath,

"What are we going to do? We can't hide here forever. I don't want to grow old, like this, some sort of freak, waiting for the end to drag me down to Hell," he lamented to the sky, the moon silently standing by.

"Do me a favour Deke, and don't blame yourself. You can't have that resting on you; it doesn't help anyone, especially not you. Blame it on that woman, blame it on the Collector, we'll figure it out Deke, I promise we will. I'm just as much a part of it now as you are. Clara, she's strong, but she needs our help too," he smiled wistfully at me while I said this, his mouth agreeing, but I could still see the pain in his eyes.

He reached out for my hand, and I hesitated, subtly leaning away. He pulled away sharply as if I had bit him. He folded his hands in his lap and stared out at the far-off shore. The blossoms of silver on his knuckles sparkled in the moonlight, raw reminders of the damage he had caused.

I took a deep breath and reached out, covering his hands with mine. The sharp sting made me bite my tongue, but after the initial burst the pain subsided to an odd tingling rawness. I stroked his hand gently with my thumb, and that was how we sat, until the sun began to rise and the glare of the early morning light off the water was too intense for his sensitive eyes.

Upon our returning to the cottage, Clara was leaning against the counter, spooning cereal into her mouth, grinning maniacally, wearing pyjamas and sunglasses. I rolled my eyes at her and she snorted, spilling half-soaked cereal on the floor. If one day, Clara's maturity level exceeded that of a sugar-rushed eight year old, I will be shocked into submission. She plays a hard game, clubbing and partying, but deep down, she will always be the naughty little sister, pulling hair and putting frogs in my shoes; which unfortunately she has done, on more than one occasion, even after becoming an adult.

Deke, oblivious to my sister's antics, returned to his room to retrieve his second-hand sunglasses and came to stand with us at the breakfast bar.

"Did the water make it feel better?" Clara asked tentatively.

She hadn't been out in the elements like Deke had; she'd had an easier time of trying to maintain a normal life despite her nightly prowling. Deke meanwhile had been surviving out in the elements, relishing the inclement weather the spring had been beating down on the city. He nodded, while I looked on in confusion. Clara sighed and put down her cereal bowl.

"You've seen the sparks on the outside, obviously, and what it feels like when we touch you, but for us our skin burns from the inside, so much worse than a terrible sunburn, you can feel it just radiating out, this throbbing heat, everything is so sensitive, and it just makes you so, so thirsty. I haven't quite been able to figure out if it is the electricity or something else, but all I know is I haven't had a hot shower in weeks," she explained, taking another large spoonful of cereal.

Deke nodded. It was hard to tell if any looks had passed between them, their dark glasses masking everything but the grim set of their mouths.

I grimaced. I hated that word right now, 'our'. It implied so much about shared destinies at the moment that I didn't want to consider for my sister. Even now, in the kitchen, it felt so much greater of a chasm was between us than the marble tile on the floor. They were calling to me from an island, barely audible, unable to save them.

If sitting on the dock through the early hours of a rapidly dawning day had proven anything to me, it was that time was moving much faster than we were.

Deke said something I didn't catch, and it pulled me from the dark place I was turning to. He realized I hadn't been paying attention, and repeated,

"Is there a computer here? I'd like to try checking a few things out, see if I can find any history or lore, anything is better than nothing, right?"

I nodded noncommittally and showed him to the study where Mother's desktop computer sat. It was an older model and had bearable Internet, but she wasn't one for technology. He plunked himself down and went to it, rapidly keying across the board. I hesitated, wondering if I should warn him to watch his hands, the last thing we needed was him shorting out our only research tool. But he was already locked down in concentration, dark brow frowning and the tip of his tongue peeking between his lips.

I returned to my room, and quickly changed into my clothes, adjusting the clock before I left my room and headed back out to the kitchen, looking for Clara.

The back door was wide open, so I headed back out into the bright morning air; steam rising off the lake as the day grew hotter and hotter, burning off the low-lying fog.

I had forgotten why we stopped coming here regularly, the four of us. I am sure we all started having lives, started moving on from the family trips and chores and duties, edging out from under them, seeing the sun for the first time around our umbrellas. Maybe Mother finally became intolerable, holed up in her room. Maybe it was when Reggie decided to bail on everything with any meaning in his life and abandoned us all.

Maybe we all just got tired of chasing Clara, untameable and wheeling through time, stuck in a reality of her own device.

It struck me, the number of gaps I couldn't fill with memories lately. Childhood was hazy, relics dusty but definitely found in the depths of my head. But recently? Everything smeared into a warm blur. I pondered this. I tried to recall what I had done even a few weeks ago. I thumbed through my phone organizer, the calendar strangely empty since early March, just around the time when Reggie had up and spooked off to the West coast.

"You're gonna fall in the water, genius," Clara called to me from somewhere around my ankles.

I realized I'd walked straight out onto the dock, and was nearing the edge. Clara was floating below, submerged up to her chin, calmly kicking her feet as she held onto the ladder. Her clothes sat in a small pile on the dock at my feet. I almost dropped my phone on her face, gaping in complete and utter awe. Clara positively crackled, her entire body sending blue shockwaves out into the water around her.

She grinned, and took a deep breath, and kicked away, diving down deep into the depths of the lake. I could see her, my God, I could see her, all the way to the murky and cloudy bottom, a glowing shape as she travelled along and rocketed back up to the surface a short distance away.

As her head broke the surface, tiny lightning scattered, glowing white sparks fluttering from her hair and eyelashes as she shook the water from her eyes. She kicked and swam and giggled, splashing me, frolicking in the water. Sometimes she would lay back and simply float. Sighing deeply as she did so,

"You know, this is the first time I've felt normal in so long... I'd forgotten,"

I smiled, tentatively. It was always so easy for Clara to push away the bad things in life. I had always wished I could be the same way.

Heavy tread sounded on the dock behind me, Deke slowly coming up to see what we were doing. He seemed incredibly heavy-hearted, his shoulders drooping. He stared at me sadly, hesitating without spilling what he wanted to say.

"Deke, what happened? What did you find?" His lip trembled, and he took a deep breath.

"I think you should come inside... I need to show you something," Clara had stopped her cavorting and was treading water nervously.

It was then that I noticed the tiny teardrops clinging to Deke's lashes, unshed diamonds refracting off his eyes.

"Deke, were you crying? What, what is going on?"

Without thinking I moved forward and took his hands in mine, the contact sending sharp knives into my palms. I winced but held on, begging him to explain.

He simply held my hand, and pulled me back towards the cottage, leaving Clara to scramble dripping from the dock after us.

I stared, agape.

My picture stared right back.

I remembered it being taken, at a picnic several years ago, after an intensely competitive game of Frisbee with Reggie. I stood behind him, arms around his neck, we were laughing, sun-kissed, the matching freckles standing out across our noses. Reggie was wearing the horrible neon-green tank that we had begged him to throw out year over year, until it became his official uniform of summer. Mother had tried to destroy it every time it made its way to the wash.

The headline immediately below the photo read, in glaringly painful few words:

Whistler Avalanche Claims Two More Lives –

American siblings vacationing in Whistler had their trip brutally cut short as...

I stopped reading after a few more lines. There was no way. I couldn't take it.

I pushed away from the computer, staggering away from the online journal reporting my apparent demise. I tripped backwards, falling against Deke, gasping.

"What the Hell, what, what, Deke, where? What is going on?"

He held me tightly as I shook my head despairingly at the screen, refusing to accept what I was reading.

"It's a joke, it has to be a joke, Reggie, Reggie must have done this, it's fake,"

He steadied me and let go as I pushed him away, shaking his head. He approached the computer, and switched to another tab; then another, and another, each one hiding another journal or newspaper, each one with a new variation of the same story.

I was supposed to be dead. This macabre slideshow told me so.

Reggie was supposed to be dead.

We had died over two months ago, tragically, far from home, lost to the snow and cold on a mountainside.

But, I was here.

Why was I here?

"Oh Addy," Clara gasped, dripping in the doorway.

I turned and clung to her, ignoring the wet and holding her tight. Deke sat awkwardly on the corner of the desk, massaging his forehead tiredly.

"This is going to sound...odd. But, have either of you spoken to Reggie? Since, this... this, whatever this is, happened," he leaned in closer to the screen, reading a date on the page,

"....Since around March First; either of you?"

We turned and looked at him strangely, and then at each other.

I nodded my head slowly,

"He was staying at my place through the first part of March... and well, he left, not long after, there have been some phone calls, nothing concrete, the connection has been bad... I guess..." Clara nodded in agreement.

A sudden panicked feeling rose in my throat, threatening to crush at my heart.

I fumbled for my cell phone in my pocket, the jeans fighting against my fingers. The phone slipped from my grasp, plummeting towards the hardwood floors, but I quickly managed to scoop it to safety, diving to my knees.

I sat on the floor and scrolled through my contacts, finally finding Reggie's number and pressing the dial button. Overwhelming emotions were crowding in. What if he was one of *them*? It rang.

Rang.

Rang.

Disconnected.

I pushed the dial button again. This time, it went straight to voicemail;

"Reggie's phone, you know what to do,"

My eyes welled up at the sound of Reggie's voice. Had it really been so long since we actually spoke? I knew that time was moving ever forward, we were busy, adults, going about our lives, and he was time zones away, having his little brain vacation, but had we really not spoken? I realized I had been crying into the dead air of the recording.

"Shit. Reggie, hi, it's Addy... can you, can you call me and Clara? Just, just as soon as you can?" I wiped the tears from my cheek.

"It's really important. Like, really, really Reggie. Please, when you can," I disconnected the phone and hung my head.

Clara hovered nervously and Deke had returned to his web search.

I felt numb. Everything was upside down, and I was sinking fast. Was I still me? Was I going to turn into one of them? I shuddered at the word. I didn't want 'them' to know I thought of them as something else, I didn't *want* to be one of them. Had Deke died too? Clara?

Deke was clucking his tongue at the screen. He was flipping through various pictures and head shots of himself, but from where I sat on the floor, it didn't look like obituaries. He sat back, puzzled, hands behind his head, swiveling gently in his chair.

"So I'm not dead. I don't think; missing, after a career changing corporate deal, and wanted for questioning in the death of one Aaron Devon by Boston PD, but definitely not dead," he turned to face me.

My heart sank. That couldn't be what this was, then. We were right back where we started.

Clara had gone to retrieve a towel, and had returned, bundled in Mother's expensive cotton.

"So Clara, you were in Belgium, returned, what, last week of February? When did the changes start happening?"

"Just after that?" She muttered hesitantly.

"And I've been missing from work for…" he turned back to the computer and scrolled,

"I've been *missing* for a month and a half myself; but Aaron was found five weeks ago and the merger was a week before I was reported gone, so I'd say I've been changed for those full six weeks...shit. I would've said two, at the very most. Adeline, are you missing any time?"

He whistled. I had zoned out thinking back to my planner.

I handed him my phone.

He scrolled through carefully.

"There is nothing in here since February... No texts, no emails, no calendar notes...no browser history even, how did you not notice this? Where the Hell were you?" He handed me back the phone.

They both looked at me expectantly. I was with Reggie. Reggie was at my house. He'd been sleeping on my couch. I'd been working, busy, and too busy for Reggie. Was I making it up? Had I imagined it all? I had no answer, if I had died, why was I here? If I hadn't died, why did the world think I had? Was Reggie still dead? Had I even made up his leaving?

Deke moved closer. He sat down next to me on the floor, cautiously keeping his distance.

"Do you even remember going skiing?"

The colour drained from my face. I could feel it rushing away, steaming ribbons settling in the pit of my stomach. Everything was in knots and everything felt fibrous. Nothing could be trusted, even sitting here now, was any of this real? Maybe it wasn't, maybe this was all my personal version of Heaven or Hell, a convoluted reality that I was trying to break free from.

Deke snapped his fingers, trying to pull me back from the edge of where I had been. Maybe Reggie and I were more alike than I realized.

"Adeline, you're real. I'm real, Clara is real, and we are all here. We'll find out what happened. I know you don't want to hear it, but this could be a real lead. Clara and I weren't aware of time passing, but we were definitely in it. You were here, and didn't know, so if we can figure out what happened in the meantime, and why Clara didn't know either, we might be making great strides in this, maybe even find out why we are now the way we are, and you aren't,"

"I almost wish I was, like you. It'd be an easier problem to wrap my head around," I spat vehemently.

Deke shook his head and wrapped an arm around my shoulders, pulling me closer. I rested my cheek on his shoulder, squeezing out the tears, just wanting them to stop.

"You're not dead, Adeline, you're here with me, I promise, it feels like a nightmare, but you're here,"

I nodded shakily, eyes still closed.

When I finally opened my eyes, Clara had left the room. Deke stirred when I straightened my position; he must've been staring off into space, eyes unfocused. The strangeness of them was so much a part of him now, a defining characteristic that gave him away to everyone else, that something was wrong, with him, and with Clara.

But I'd never known them any other way. He'd pushed his sleeves up when he had been working at the computer, and I took this opportunity to study the markings marching down the arm draped around my neck.

The lines glowed in the early morning sunlight, a tapestry of misdeeds threaded with silver. He tensed as I reached out to touch one, a short dash etching the knob of his wrist, the now-familiar tingle shooting up through my finger and spreading across my arm. He turned his hand over, so his palm pointed to the ceiling, where there were no regular barbed lines here, no counting tickers of lives he had kept track of. There was only one line, deep and wide and dark silver, running from his wrist to elbow. I exhaled lightly, a tiny 'oh' that should've stayed deep down inside. This was worse than I ever could have imagined. He turned his other arm over, the one that rested across his lap, revealing an identical match.

"It was not too long after Dezi's attack... I wanted to see, if I could make it stop. But now you see, you're more like me already, they won't let either of us stay dead," he uttered quietly, twitching as my fingers traced the highway running up his arm.

It was so sad, really, when I thought about it, this man had done everything he could to stop, going to unimaginable lengths, and he simply had the opportunity pulled away from him, no matter the cost. A sudden thought occurred to me,

"Dezi, did she? Did she stay dead? You said something happened to her, before she fell into the lake, that something was wrong with her, did you look her up?" Deke's eyes widened.

He snapped his fingers, scrambling up from the floor and diving at the computer, fingers clicking wildly across the keys. I could see him shaking his head, still furiously typing. He sat back, stunned. I looked over his shoulder, reading the headlines,

Local bartender murdered, left behind bar –

He turned to look at me, rising from his chair, trying to block the words from my view, ashamed. He moved towards me, pleading, not knowing what to do with his hands,

"I didn't do this, you know I didn't. You know I left, right? She had attacked me, she got away, in that alley, I didn't...I saw her alive, later, down at the lake," he gaped at the screen.

I shushed him gently, gesturing for him to settle down.

I placed a hand directly over the healing tattoo I knew was under his sweater. I could feel the soft bulk of the bandaging.

"This is why I believe you Deke; she brought you the message that saved you from the Collector and its Hell-Beast, the same one that is protecting my sister now. She couldn't have done that if you'd stabbed her in the alley. It couldn't have happened. According to these articles, I'm dead too. Something is going on here,"

He was shaking and crackling, whether from fear or anger I couldn't quite tell. Every time these extreme emotions took over him, his skin visibly electrified. It was always there, the briefest of touches of skin to skin conducting the energy between us, but when he was truly upset, it was watching an invasion of lightning crawling from pore to pore. It was utterly terrifying.

He must have seen the reaction on my face, whether it was judgement or fear, I didn't even know but he immediately calmed in response.

He looked at me reproachfully and sat heavily back down in the computer chair. Clara returned to the room, dressed in dry spare clothes that we left here for short weekend trips. She'd found time to dry her hair and apply her makeup, dark eyeliner highlighting her intense eyes rather than masking them.

She sat in the chair next to Deke and swiveled hesitantly.

"I was thinking, we should go find Reggie,"

A million possible scenarios went through my head, none of them pretty. We'd come out here into this lonely wilderness to keep the world safe from them, and we'd have to throw ourselves right through Middle America to travel to where we *might* find Reggie. It was only a might, however, as we didn't truly know if he was even still alive. What if they lost control in the car, I the only possible victim? Could we fly? Being trapped on a plane with the pair of them, any second they could break their chains and be unable to stop? We honestly had no idea how long they, and I, would be safe for.

The tattoos made them invisible to the Collector and whoever was giving the orders around here, but could the magic wear off?

But this might be the only lead we had, and it was a slim one at that. Reggie was definitively a piece of this puzzle, and we had no corners yet to define the borders of the problem.

They were both staring at me. It was unnerving, being thrown into this caretaker and keeper position of my sister and a stranger. If they were going to look to me for direction, I'd have to start making the right decisions.

Clara looked at Deke, and tugged at her earlobe nervously. Something swept across his face, a recognition; darkening his features and he nodded slightly.

"We found each other, through the ringing, a deep vibration, just about right here," Clara gestured to the soft spot behind her ear, rubbing it gently.

"It's different, than from when we feel, compelled to, you know. That's more aggressive, bees in my head, behind my eyes, shooting through my body, just a mindless, dark sensation,"

She ticked her glance towards Deke, he nodded again. I looked slowly back and forth between them, waiting for the other shoe to drop. Why was she telling me this?

"But when we are with you, close to you, the same room, the ringing just stops; it's just dead air humming. It's quite a relief. Relief to have the silence back,"

Deke was avoiding my eyes.

"So, what do you think it means? I'm blocking the signal?" I knew I was being incredulous. It was hard not to be lately.

"I think that whatever happened when you and Reggie went on vacation is related to this, well, me at least, I won't speak for Deke since we didn't know him then, and I think we can use this sensory absence to help find him when we get there. Maybe he's one of us, and we'll hear the ringing, or maybe he's like you, and we'll hear nothing when we are together, but either way, we will know as soon as we get near to him,"

I took a deep breath, settled.

This roller coaster of emotions wasn't going to help anyone. Clara was completely right, I knew this now. Something niggled at the back of my brain, something about Reggie and why he had left. I couldn't quite grasp it and tease it to the forefront, but I knew deep down that he had to have some of the answers. Twins were always closest, right? Maybe we had a greater bond than I even knew.

I took another deep breath, letting another grasp of panic lose its hold.

"How do you want to get there?"

Deke and Clara exchanged glances, relief passing as visible as a lightning bolt between them. I guess deep down, I hadn't really been the one making the choice.

"Road trip," Deke announced huskily.

Chapter 8

Preparations

As I still had access to Reggie's phone account from keeping track of his bills every time he took his little brain breaks, I logged in and checked his call history. I was no super sleuth, but we needed something greater to go on than the entire state of California being a possible location for our wayward brother.

I hissed with excitement, a brief exultation escaping between my teeth. He had been calling a number of places with a 650 area code – somewhere around San Francisco. I tapped my fingers on the mouse. Deke and Clara were absent. I had sent them off to gather supplies in town, and to get Deke some more clothes. I had hesitated for quite a while before letting them go, as we debated whether they should even be allowed out on their own. I figured if they hadn't gone batty yet and sliced my throat out, maybe we were doing ok. Somehow, these decisions were what my life had boiled down to.

I pulled out my phone, checking it for any word from Clara. Nothing flashed across the screen. Should I call her? Are they ok? I hated the feeling of worrying sick. Worse, I hated the feeling that I was worrying sick for *other* people's well-being – not theirs. I glanced back up at the list of numbers on the computer, selected the one he seemed to call the most, and dialled through. Here goes nothing. It rang once, tinny and full of vibrato, the long distance smearing the sounds.

"Dizzy Moon Pizza, how can I take your order?" I smiled. Reggie and his pizza, it always ended up being pizza.

"Hello, I think I may have misdialled, could you please tell me where this location is?"

There was a moment of silence, I heard the speaker talking to someone quietly on the other end, and I frowned. Was it that confusing a question? The voice responded hesitantly,

"Half Moon Bay, ma'am, can I take your order?" I thanked the operator and hung up.

That narrowed it down greatly. I pulled up a search and keyed it into the computer. Half Moon Bay was a relatively small town, right on the coast. Small neighbourhoods, two highways, it should be a piece of cake with the disruption that Deke and Clara feel in order to track him down. I hoped, deep down, that this would be the first of many answers.

I shut down the computer, rising from the chair and stretching the kinks from my back. It was becoming late afternoon, and we had an excruciating amount of driving ahead of us. Even though it would be shared, we had roughly three thousand miles of ground to cover. Luckily, with the three of us, we wouldn't have to stop to sleep, and if we kept all the breaks to a minimum, it wouldn't be too long before we could hunt down Reggie. It felt good to finally have a plan.

I wandered to Mother's room, the drapes drawn, and the room dark and cool, chilly compared to the rest of the cottage. Everything within was heavily perfumed, exposed to the rich floral scent she always wore over many years of vacationing. I could never stand it for more than a few minutes at a time as a child; we had always kept the door closed, even when she was staying over.

I tried to piece together the last time I had even seen her here. Everything was so faded and hard to grasp, I couldn't get a hold on anything inside my own head. I settled on the bed, relishing the cool, and put an arm over my eyes. It would be a long time before I was this comfortable again. I quickly fell asleep.

"Deke, what the heck are you doing?" Clara was regarding Deke suspiciously through her dark lenses. She had approached him silently in the grocery store, arms full with produce. He held up two different bags of salty and sugar coated snacks.

"All the memories of food have completely escaped me...I don't eat anymore... not really, what do you think Addy will want?"

A sly smile played across Clara's lips, she snatched one of the bags with a raised eyebrow and tossed it into the basket over her arm.

"You maybe not, but I'm ravenous. I've been stuffing my face since this happened. You think I was born with this ass?" She briefly hip-checked him as she pushed past, scanning the shelves for treats.

He stared after her for a moment, processing what she said. He blinked behind the glasses. Maybe they weren't as alike as he thought. Did that make him better, or worse? She had also been able to control herself better than him, or maybe whoever was controlling them didn't have as many missions for her. Maybe he was more deadly or harder to control once he started.

He massaged his temples; the fluorescents in the grocery store were beginning to burn pinpricks into his sensitive eyes. He was hoping that Adeline could do most of the day driving. Obviously it was the longer pull across country, but there was no way he would be able to concentrate on driving, especially across the long flat Mid-West if the sun was going to be such a painful enemy.

Clara was speaking, but he wasn't listening. They had stopped moving too close together; the ringing was beginning to drown her out. He watched her lips move, then falter, then stop altogether. The delicate lips pursed together, the only way of determining her emotion. He knew damn well she couldn't hear him either, why was she even bothering? If only Addy were here, and then the blessed silence would return.

Clara was snapping her fingers in front of his face. He made a gesture across his throat, a "cut it out" and then pointed at his ears. She shrugged and turned away. How were they supposed to accomplish anything if they couldn't even hear each other, let alone think without the pealing of every bell in Notre Dame ringing inside their heads? When she had strode away several feet and then turned, shrugging her arms half-heartedly again, she called,

"Better?"

He nodded, not relishing the fact that they still had to go buy him his own clothes. Clara seemed desperate to get him out of Reggie's clothes, and not in the exciting way he would have hoped for from a girl of her beauty only a few short weeks ago.

If only Adeline were here.

I awoke with a start. I was disoriented by the dark and the scent of the room, it had settled deep into the back of my throat, and I had been dreaming of drowning. The clock ticked away, much more loudly than I remembered; Mother's old wind-up she had inherited from her grandfather. The hands showed seven, and I hoped in my confusion that it was only seven at night.

My skin was prickly feeling, the strange sensation arising from rapidly ascending out of deep sleep. I felt oddly hot; my clothes clinging sweaty against my skin. Oh God, was I turning into one of them? I stumbled off the bed and towards the door of the ensuite bathroom, yanking it open. I practically crashed into the sink basin, flicking on the lights and staring deep into my own eyes.

Thankfully, they remained their rich shade of green, gold flecked and truly my own. I studied my reflection, giving myself the side-eye treatment, hoping not a single flash of silver would spark back at me. It was me, it was fine; I'd been napping and had just woken up. It was only a nightmare. I turned on the tap, patting my neck and face with cool water. I felt I had run a marathon, my dark mahogany hair standing up in every direction, while somehow also mashed to the side of my head. My face had gone pale, the freckles across my nose and cheeks prominent against the ashen skin.

"Fine, fine, everything is fine," I breathed, calming.

Slowly the colour came back to my cheeks, the terror in my eyes slowly trickling away. Things weren't fine. Not really, not at all. But at least I still wasn't one of them. I flushed at the thought. They weren't monsters; I needed to stop thinking of them that way. One of them was my baby sister for Pete's sake, and no matter what she needed me. And Deke well, he needed me too. I heard the front door slam, groceries dropping heavily to the floor.

I wandered out through the bedroom, tightly closing the door behind me, and moved to the top of the stairs, looking over the banister to the open kitchen space below. Deke was looking up, clad in new dark jeans and a navy sweater over a white dress shirt. He looked positively preppy. He held his arms out and did a slow spin, no doubt mischief in his eyes behind the dark glasses.

"You let my sister dress you, huh," he hung his head in mock disappointment.

"You loved it," she tweaked his nose as she went by, carrying bags in from the car and leaving them heaped on the breakfast bar.

He shrugged, I giggled, and I came down the stairs. They both seemed to have dropped a weight from their shoulders, coming back into the house had reaffirmed something to them. I hadn't been through the cottage since the sun had started to set, the shadows creeping into the corners and only the sparkles on the lake outside the windows lit the grounds.

They both removed their glasses, light flashing in their eyes as they set to sorting out the groceries so they could repack them into the car properly. Deke stopped to look at me for a moment, studying my no doubt puffy eyes and sleep lined cheeks. His gaze scanned my hairline and his intense look broke into a little boy's toothy grin. The laugh lines I swore I saw when I first met him crinkled prominently around his eyes.

"Your hair is just. It's fantastic,"

I groaned and started patting at it, hoping to resolve it to some semblance of order. Clara snorted and continued sorting, pulling a cooler from the cabinet under the sink.

"She's always been like that, you know, Queen of the Bedhead, just spectacular,"

I huffed at her, Deke smiling and looking back and forth between us. I grabbed an apple from the bag, and took a huge bite. I hadn't really eaten all day, emotional rollercoasters taking any desire for food right out of me until now.

"Do you have any family, Deke, any brothers, sisters, kids?" His face clouded briefly, a small frown flitting across his face. He shook his head,

"No, not anyone really, only child, parents have been gone for years, been on my own for quite some time," he took an unsteady deep breath, and then plastered a smile on his face.

All I could think, after all this, was why did he feel the need to lie? Something about the way that smile had stretched across his face seemed disingenuous. He must be terrible at poker. Clara didn't seem to notice, and began prattling on about the clothes they had hunted down for Deke. An absent sort of atmosphere had filled the room, and I wondered what line I had crossed by asking.

"Luckily, this guy, completely average, very easy to shop for in this little cow-poke town," she waggled a package of jerky in his direction. The tension broke, if it had ever really been there. I realized that it had just become completely dark in the house, and I wondered how they could even see what they were doing. My eyes had been adjusting, but they were still only just vague shapes in the dark, the brightly coloured groceries slowly fading in the ink. Their eyes glinted, predatorily, and I got a chill. Deke had stopped what he was doing. He was watching me carefully. Clara stopped what she was doing and rested her hands on the cooler, waiting.

"You guys can see in the dark, can't you? Like cats. The two of you are like God damn freaking animals," I threw my hands up in the air.

Deke and Clara glanced at each other. At least, that's what I think they did. All I could see was the quick flick of their eyes in the dark. I made an exasperated sound.

"Well, I'm turning on a light. Deal with it. Sorry the only non-super human in the room can't see," I turned and stumbled on the edge of the rug, banged into the corner of the end table, almost knocking the lamp down.

I fumbled for the light and switched it on, triumphant. I turned back to see they had donned their glasses once more, smirking in the half-light filtering from the adjoining room.

I stomped off to pack my bags, the sooner we got out of here, the better.

I had only been in my room for a few moments when I heard a rustle at the door. I turned to see Deke leaning against the frame, his lips set in a grim line. I wished I could see his eyes; it was so hard to get a sense of what either of them was feeling when that part of their souls was hidden from view.

"Are you alright?" I asked him, distracting myself with rolling socks into their pairs and tossing them in a backpack.

I couldn't get his strange response to my earlier question out of my head, and I knew he could tell what I was thinking.

He moved into the room, hands jammed into his pockets, and settled awkwardly on the edge of the bed. The clock next to him on its stand made an odd sizzling noise, followed by a *pop* and flicked back to 12:00, flashing weakly. I raised an eyebrow and he shrugged.

"I think the current is getting stronger, I've noticed a lot of things going on the fritz lately when I'm in the area," he fumbled with the buttons across the top, adjusting the time back to something closer to correct.

The poor clock lasted a mere few seconds, before it shuddered and switched back to flashing.

I stopped packing and climbed onto the end of the bed, sitting cross-legged and waiting patiently for Deke to spill whatever was bothering him out into the space between us.

"I'm worried about you," he finally mumbled.

I was taken aback, it wasn't what I was expecting in the least, and I had no idea how to react. He must have seen the confusion on my face, as he began awkwardly picking at the bedspread, avoiding looking at me directly.

"Deke, you barely know me, you aren't responsible for me, or my safety. I got this, Deke, no need to worry. I'm in a much better place now, about all this, than I was before. We even have a game plan now, I found out where Reggie might be, we can find him, sort this out, and to be honest I am glad, that I'm not dealing with this with Clara all alone," his smile lit up at the news about Reggie, and I could only assume his eyes did too.

I filled him in on what I had found out, emphasizing that the town was very small, that between the two of them they should have no trouble hunting Reggie down. His face clouded once more,

"But are you sure you are ok with, being with us? You know, tight quarters? I'm so afraid of hurting you, or Clara hurting you and... well, to be honest, I think I'd have to hurt Clara if she hurt you,"

He must have struck me dumbfounded, as I could feel my jaw drop.

110

I hadn't thought of it that way. He pulled off his glasses, wincing slightly. A muscle in his jaw twitched. He searched my face, and I could see in his eyes how distraught this made him, a total stranger willing to go to bat for me, in these life altering circumstances.

"Well, hopefully, we've done what we can, and we won't have to worry about it coming to that," I tried smiling reassuringly, I really did.

"Still, I worry. But I promise, I promise, it'll never be me, I'll manage...I'll, I'll throw myself out of the car if I have to,"

His hand moved subconsciously and rested on the bandage below his sweater. I smiled at him, and I assumed that all in all, my response was enough for Deke, even after his proclamation, as he then stood up to leave. He came close, reached across the distance and gently pulled my face towards his lips, and kissed the top of my head. He stopped, dead.

Did he just smell my hair?

He stepped back awkwardly, whole body held rigidly. Something passed across his face, unbidden.

"What? Deke, what's the matter?"

The moment passed and he relaxed, shaking his head.

"I just thought, something was familiar, for a second there, I'm not sure," he finished lamely.

What the Hell was he talking about? He smiled a much better poker face than his previous attempt in the kitchen and shook his head.

"How's about; twenty minutes and we're out of here? Want to get as much rubber on the road between now and dawn as we can," he patted the doorframe as he left, awkwardly escaping the room.

I didn't know what to think. Something had rattled Deke, on a deep level, and I didn't know what had set it off. I realized my heart was racing.

I also realized at that moment, that I had seen the Deke that all those other poor people had seen, coming at them out of the dark, as the light left their eyes. It was the predator we had locked away, and now I knew how shallowly it lurked below the surface.

Chapter 9

False Steps

"I *have* to stop," Clara announced from the back seat.
She startled me awake from the doze I had fallen into while
Deke drove. We'd been on the road for several hours,
Leicester and the cottage far behind us, the wide dark skies
wheeling the heavens and stars overhead, and the edge of
the horizon behind us was just beginning to glow. It would
still be quite a while before the sun rose, but we had been
making fantastic time.

I knew I'd be getting the shift from noon to sunset;
driving West into the sun would be much too excruciating
for either of them. It helped having Deke do the middle of
the night run, as he did not have a wallet or identification
on him, and we hoped to get by without him being pulled
over; leading to an awful lot of questions we couldn't
answer.

Deke looked over at me and playfully shook my knee. I
jumped at the mild voltage tingling into my patella and
deep into the cartilage.

"What about you, sleepy head? Need a break?"

I simply groaned in response and tried to twist into a
more comfortable position. I turned toward the dashboard

113

clock and realized that instead of the time, the letters were flashing ZZ:ZZ, the lights within the timepiece themselves having fried.

"When did that finally give in?" I yawned sleepily, my voice cracking.

"About an hour or so back, I think the car's juice was keeping it stable for a while but it finally just gave up the ghost,"

I looked at him suspiciously, and then turned to look at Clara. She shrugged, and I shook my head. I could hear Clara's whine strumming through her body, ready to break free and start causing Hell.

"Alright, alright, let's find someplace to stop," I conceded, knowing I might as well stretch my legs while I could.

The days weren't getting long yet, but I'd still have a long time to go once the sun reached its peak.

We found a Kwik-Fill in Dunkirk a short while later, lights blazing a brilliant white through the darkened landscape. I swore I went blind, let alone how Deke and Clara must have felt with their heightened sensitivity to the light. Deke pulled the car into the farthest bay for pumping gas, and Clara practically launched herself out of the car, running for the ladies.

She had always gotten car sick when we were kids, the number of road trips cut short because dear little Clara just couldn't handle the drive I couldn't even count. I had hoped she had grown out of it, but no such luck. I remembered a spectacular display one year on the way to Yellowstone that led to Mother switching to an entirely new rental car. I will never forget the look on the attendant's face, as she, fully smiling, paid the cleaning fee.

"I'll go pay, want anything?" I was halfway out of my seat.

Deke shrugged, and unfolded out of his side, going through the ritual to start pumping the gas. He'd been pensive for most of the ride, and only just now had he snapped out of his reverie.

Inside the gas station was oddly cold, I thought maybe the air conditioning was on but really, it was much too early in the year. I rubbed my arms briskly and traveled up the aisles, looking for anything to perk my interest. I stopped at the cooler displaying chocolate milk, and glanced up in the security mirror above my head.

The attendant was ignoring me entirely, engrossed in a news bulletin on the small television on the counter. I retrieved a carton, and headed toward the register. I set the milk down, awkwardly waiting for the attendant to turn around. I coughed lightly, hoping to catch his attention. He swung towards me, half-dazed.

"Just this, and whatever number 8 charged to the pump," I smiled.

His eyes flicked from my face, to the chocolate milk, to the television, down to the security screen for the pumps, and back at me. He rung it up and put out his hand, eyes flashing back to the television. As I pulled out the cash and he was distracted with the till, I checked out what he had been so avidly watching on the screen.

A chill ran down my back.

Deke's face was plastered across the screen, the ticker practically screaming for his capture, rolling across the details of his disappearance and the authorities desire to question him in the brutal slaying of one Aaron Devon.

Deke had been missing for weeks, why were the authorities suddenly looking for the public's help *now*? No one knew we had left – no one knew where we were going, why the manhunt? I snapped back to attention, and realized the attendant was scrutinizing my face.

I smiled again, and turned tail, almost forgetting my milk. I had to remind myself to play it cool, walk, slowly, don't run. There was no way he could have seen Deke from there. He was too small, too vague; the cops wouldn't believe him, would they?

I could see Clara was in the car, at the wheel, ready to take her turn, Deke in the front seat. I could see their eyes glowing dimly in the fluorescents, knew they were resisting the urge to put on their glasses, a strange thing to do at four a.m. on a country highway and any witnesses sure to call them out on their strangeness.

When I threw myself into the back seat, I could barely contain myself,

"Go, go, drive, drive, just, outta here, now!"

Clara hesitated momentarily before cranking over the engine, spurred on by my slapping the back of her head rest. Deke twisted in the seat, wincing from the pain in his gut, trying to get a read on my face.

"What the Hell, Addy?"

My heart was racing and I shook my head. Clara had pulled out of the rest stop, and the bright lights were fading behind us.

I could see them reflected in the metallic blur of his eyes.

"You, you were on the news, you're wanted Deke. The Boston cops have extended the search out to the FBI, a country-wide manhunt, a big ol' ticker with all your details all over the screen, Deke! The guy at the counter was incredibly suspicious that it was you at the pumps. They want you for Aaron. Why now Deke? Why?"

His skin flared, briefly lighting up the car with his brilliantly blue sparks, until he took a deep breath and calmed. Clara had a steady crackling in her hair, a tiny lightning storm winding across her scalp. Deke touched her on the shoulder and they dimmed, finally settling back to the darkness of the highway weaving through the car.

Deke turned back to me, studying my face for a moment, his face deep in shadow, before maneuvering his leg between the seats, sliding carefully from the front to the back, teeth clenched as he avoided hitting his tattoo against the shoulder rest. I squeezed against the window until he slid past me to sit behind Clara. He lounged back against the window, his whole body turned to face me. I pulled my knees up to my chest, avoiding turning towards him. I could feel Clara looking up in the rear view at me, eyes flicking between me and the road.

"Do you think he knew enough, to call it in? Is he going to be a problem?"

His tone of voice had reverted back to when I first stumbled across him in my kitchen, steely, rough, but underneath it all, completely terrified.

I didn't want to look at him. I was afraid that I would see the Deke I had seen in my bedroom at the cottage. He reached forward and touched my hand, and this time, I did pull my hand violently back. A surge leapt between his hand and my arm, white-hot, a hot ember landing on my wrist. He jumped back just as quickly, apology scrawled across his face.

"Deke, it's fine. If he called it in, he called it in, we can't stop him now. Damage is done. The best we can do is just keep going and hopefully get past any barricades before they can even go up," I rubbed absently at my wrist, trying not to call too much attention to the hot sun-burn sensation he had left behind.

He turned away from me, silently pondering what I had said. I desperately hoped we wouldn't cross paths with any more innocent people, who were only trying to play hero, if only for their sakes. He rubbed his hands through his hair, scattering sparks, tiny fireworks in the gloom. The glow along the horizon was getting brighter in the rear-view, and I dully wished that the sun would stay down. It was easier to be honest in the dark.

The sun was just beginning to fully rise as we crossed the Maumee River near Toledo, Ohio. The sun glinted off the girders, reflecting softly in the water. It reminded me of how far we still had to go, the Wild West of America still looming in our headlights; Nebraska, Wyoming, Utah and Nevada, not to mention the mountains, the desert, until finally, hopefully, Reggie and answers. This lonely stretch of bridge we now drove over, crossing an inconsequential strip of river, feeding into the lakes, until it went onward and outward back home to the Atlantic, made me feel so small in this vastly expanding universe, my eyes open to the unknown and the terrifying in such a short amount of time.

I had never felt so tired. I felt drained, every movement a supreme effort. If only I could blame it on a flu, or a virus, dragging down my defenses. I didn't, wouldn't tell Clara and Deke. There was something else at work here; I could feel it humming deep in my bones. I thought it had something to do with them, some sort of fatigue from exposure to their unnaturalness.

Sometimes, as crazy as it sounds, I thought the car could feel it too. Regardless of the fact that it was a mostly new car, sometimes the engine would stutter, hiccup, the headlights flaring brightly, even turning off occasionally, and leading to more than one near heart-attack on the dark and winding roads. The radio no longer worked, only issuing a defiant screeching when it was clicked on. I had confiscated Clara's cell phone to keep it safe, back in the trunk with my own. Whatever these two were, it wasn't just human life they affected.

Maybe they were radioactive, I mused. In a moment of over-tired delirium, the old Spiderman theme chose that moment to play in my head, and a smirk came to my lips.

Deke chose that moment to awake where he was dozing, settled into the curve of the door. It was easier for him to stretch out that way, his feet resting across my knees. Lucky for me, his charge didn't seem to extend through his runners.

"What are you smiling about," he rubbed his face tiredly, flashing me a quick smile.

I just shook my head, blushing slightly. I didn't think I knew him well enough to try to explain myself.

He turned in his seat, pulling his feet back to himself, grimacing with the ensuing stiffness in his legs and back. He pulled himself forward by the driver seat, looking out at the road ahead.

"Toledo, Ohio" Clara stated, flatly, to the question not asked.

Deke glanced back at me, and we shared a look. I noticed that Clara was awkwardly gripping at the steering wheel, knuckles white.

"Do you need to pull over?" Deke asked lightly.

Clara responded with slamming hard on the brakes, twisting the steering wheel violently to the right, swerving past the breakdown lane and onto the shoulder, dragging the car across the gravel. She stopped just short of throwing the car into the deep and marshy ditch. Deke and I were thrown forward against the seats, clouds of dust rising up around the car, obscuring the early morning traffic from view.

She threw the car into park, and unbuckled her seat belt, leaping out of the car and slamming the door. Deke and I watched, gripping the headrests in stunned silence, as she stalked around the car, down through the boggy ditch and into the line of trees on the far side. My heart beat slowly returned to normal, and I untangled my fingers from their grip on the passenger seat, and sat back.

"Should we go after her?" Deke asked hesitantly.

I struggled with an answer. If she was being more than just Clara, her new self - I would be in danger. If she was *just* being Clara, Deke wouldn't be able to handle her. My sister had taken a bite out of more than one guy who tried to sort her out – both literally and figuratively, and I wasn't sure if I should throw Deke to the hounds just yet.

I swallowed roughly. My mouth seemed to have gone sand-dry in the mere moments since Clara left the car.

"I'll go," I finally volunteered.

Deke nodded, eyes wide, his strange irises shining dull pewter in the early rising sun that hadn't quite broken through the treeline. I took a deep breath, nodding to myself, and opened the door, sliding out of the car. Rather than tromping through the ditch, I took a light leap across, stumbling slightly on a loose stone on the far side. I scrambled up and through the tall grass, pushing through the low growth between the trees, following Clara's trampled path.

It was cold, briskly so, and absolutely quiet. The hum of the few cars that had been on the road was absent here, blocked by the trees. I could feel my heart in my throat, a strange sensation running down my back. I was terrified of my own sister, for the first time in my life. And a dull certainty hit me – this wouldn't be the last time. I called out her name, hesitantly, shakily, cutting through the quiet.

I paused. Waited for any sign of where she had gone. I could see my breath rising in the air. Apparently no one had

121

told this copse of trees in Ohio that it was late spring, nearing summer time. I rubbed my arms and continued moving forward, stepping high in the tall weeds that strangled the ground. I could see a clearing up ahead, and hoped that I could find her there. I couldn't lose her now, not after all that we had gone through already.

The clearing was dark, surrounded on all sides by tall trees that didn't allow the early morning sun to pierce through. It was eerily quiet – no bird song, no squirrels chattering from the branches at their intruder.

I took a step forward and the hair on the back of my neck stood on end, a chill running down my spine. Goosebumps marched up my arms and legs, a branch cracking behind me, but I turned too late. The full force of Clara tackling me knocked me to the ground, pressing the air from my lungs with the impact. I wheezed, and tried to push her off and away, grappling with her shoulders. Her hands reached for my throat, pushing down against the soft spot above my collar bone, crushing at my windpipe.

Every time I tried to claw at her hands or arms, or even shove at her face, I received a shooting flare of heat and electricity through my hands, fingers, burning the flesh even on my forearms as I tried elbowing her away. My feet scraped at the ground helplessly as she knelt on my chest, pinpricks of lights flashing before my eyes. Clara's face was inches from mine, teeth bared, and pupils fully dilated, showing no trace of the steely flash of her irises. I wheezed, gasping for air, no longer caring about the burning in my hands, pulling weakly at her wrists.

She was muttering something; I couldn't understand it, a strange clicking in her throat. I swung at her face, an awkward punch to her jawline, and her head cracked back, only serving to make her push harder against my already crushing wind pipe.

Deke was there, suddenly, unexpectedly, grappling with Clara around the shoulders, dragging her backwards. Her nails raking tracks across my throat as he pulled her away. A sudden expansion of bright blue light rippled between them, a loud crack echoing through the forest, throwing both of them back several feet apart. They both landed hard into a crouch, lightning crackling across their bodies in a violent maelstrom. I panted and gasped for air, half pulling myself across the forest floor, cowering against an outlying boulder, sheltering my face from the brightness.

Their faces were lit eerily by the light, emphasizing hollowness in their faces I hadn't noticed before, their eyes both flashing the reflection of the sparks. Clara made the first move, lunging forward, swinging wildly.

Deke caught her wrist, ducking the second punch from her other hand, and deftly twisting her arm behind her. His leg kicked out, knocking against the inside of her knee, dropping her awkwardly to the ground. Sparks flew everywhere they touched, metal from a grinder, the smell of ozone rising heavily in the air – and an underlying odor of my own burnt hands. Deke knelt on her back, gently but firmly, pinning her to the ground as she struggled. The lights went out from the air, sparks gone.

Holding her shoulders, he leaned forward and muttered in her ear, too quietly for me to hear. She slowly began to settle, starting from her toes, which stopped kicking in the dirt, up to her hands, which quit scrabbling in the leaves. Finally I saw her eyes close, and she muttered something in response to Deke. He nodded, and slowly released her shoulders, shifting his weight onto the other knee, but still cautiously holding her down. He brushed her hair gently away from her face, and stroked her head. She opened her eyes again, and I could see the wild look had drained away, to be replaced with apologetic tears. She mouthed my name, and her face screwed up as she silently sobbed.

Deke slowly moved backwards, sliding back into a crouch, hunkering back on his heels. He studied her for a moment, and then stood up, never taking his eyes from her. He slowly moved cautiously back towards me, treating Clara like a wounded animal he was afraid would lash out and bite. In all honesty, that was truly what she was.

His eyes roamed over the burns across my throat, the slow rise of the deep bruising that mottled the skin underneath, the blood pooling in the scratches, and my singed and stinging hands. He extended a hand to help me up, but I ignored it, struggling to stand, pulling myself up the boulder awkwardly, and hissing every time I put pressure on my palms. He tried to help, hoisting under my arm, but I twisted away from him, and slowly made my way back to the car, biting back at my own tears, the hiccupping sobs stabbing my throat with needles every time they tried to make their way out.

Back at the car, I allowed Deke to touch me. He had to, after guiding a shaking Clara back to the car, gently settling her into the back seat and closing the door. She remained sitting there, stiffly, mud splattered down her front where she had been pinned to the forest floor.

After all my defensive posturing, I had to let him, have you ever tried bandaging your own hands? I sat on the rear bumper, wincing as he wrapped them with supplies from the kit in the trunk, then tenderly applying ointment to my throat. He smelled strongly of ozone, and a fire seemed to burn in his eyes, a flickering behind the pupils. He twisted the lid back onto the tube and sighed. I continued staring dully off into the distance, a hundred different scenarios playing in my head of what could have happened in the forest, so close to so many other people.

He took me gently by the shoulders, shaking me slightly, ducking his face to look into my eyes.

"It isn't your fault," he spoke low and softly, making sure Clara couldn't hear.

Tears were welling up, uncontrollable, and I struggled with the burning behind my eyes, trying so very hard not to cry. He swallowed nervously, staring into my face. I didn't want to make eye contact. I just couldn't. He responded by pulling me close, wrapping his arms tightly around my shoulders, pressing his cheek to the top of my head, reassuringly and gently rocking. I resisted at first, but slowly melted into his grip, it wasn't his fault either. All Deke could do was try, and he was, even though he was a perfect stranger, and he was trying so damn hard to fix what my sister had done. He was as lost as I was, and I clung to him, drowning in my own tears. He patted my back quietly, waiting for me to collect myself.

"I thought we could do this Deke, I thought this could work," I mumbled into his collar bone, awkwardly aware of the damp patch I was leaving on the collar of his sweater, the heat from the three little scars warming my cheek.

"Baby steps, Addy, baby steps, it's all we can do, we're all new at this," he responded, gently pushing me back so that he could look at my face.

I hiccupped, eyes and throat stinging. I wiped gently at my eyes with the back of my hand, dampening the bandages.

"What happened back there? How did it happen? I thought we were safe now, with the tattoos and, and the-the scars," I stuttered.

He ran a hand through his hair, a small smattering of static following his fingers, dim in the bright morning light that had broken finally past the treeline.

"From what I can tell, from what I could barely get out of Clara - she didn't hear the voices. Not even once. But, she did feel a buildup. It was a frenzy of energy inside, building up since we left Dunkirk, breaking her to get out, completely undirected. She left the car in a panic, was hoping to take it out on the trees or something, I'm not sure, but you crossed her path first, and she just went manic. She had no idea what she was doing Addy, she was overwhelmed. When I grabbed her, it's like our fuses blew - lightning to a transformer. She had a moment of confusion and panic after that, when she came after me, and then she was done. I'm starting to think we're close to thunderstorms, you know when you can feel it in the air and it tingles under your skin until the storm finally breaks. Unless we can release that energy somehow, this is going to be happening. I think maybe... before, when we were... well, taking it out on other people, whoever the voices chose - it kept it low and in control," he stopped, looking pained and stepped back. I took a deep breath,

"And how are you feeling now?" I asked quietly. My face felt tight and hot from crying, a warm ache deep in my stomach.

"I think whatever happened back in there, whatever it did for Clara, it did for me too, I feel very, um, I don't know, kind of feel like jelly to be honest. Like every muscle in my body has stopped being tense, but I didn't realize everything was clenched until I stopped,"

I nodded. I think I understood. He smiled lightly, not quite extending it to his eyes, cupped the side of my face in his hand, and clapped me on the shoulder.

"Come on, come sit with me up front, we should get this freak show back on the road,"

He turned back to the car, and I gently touched my face where his hand had been, the skin crawling from the light buzz that had tingled through and through. I knew in that moment it was all true – his touch in the car outside the gas station late in the night had been white-hot on my wrist, but now, after that expulsion of brilliant energy in the forest, he felt almost normal.

Almost.

Chapter 10

Just Scraping By

Clara sat rigidly in the back seat, avoiding looking in our direction. Her face was puffy from crying, but her cheeks were now dry. She occasionally sniffled since Deke had put the car into drive and pulled back onto the long road ahead of us. Other than that, Clara had no follow up to her behavior, and the side long glances I threw her way.

It was a beautiful spring day, and I now had a greater appreciation for it. I rolled down the window and tilted my head out, eyes closed, feeling the wind rush over my burns and through my hair. I wished the radio worked. I wished this was just a regular road trip like I had as a teenager, care free and sun kissed.

Reggie and I had taken one the summer after university, reveling in our new found freedom from responsibility and the heavy hand of Mother's rules. We had traveled from Boston to South Carolina, spent our days roaming the beaches, and our nights camping in the woods.

Sometimes I wished we had brought Clara along, letting her share this experience, letting her in on the intricacies of our twin relationship, the inside jokes and the shared mindset. And sometimes, I was glad we didn't. I think the bond that Reggie and I had shared bothered her at times;

she idolized her big brother and this often meant that there was none of her left for me. If we ever found Reggie, and if it turned out that he was like her, and not the same old Reggie we had grown up with, this chasm would only grow deeper between us.

I opened my eyes and turned back to the road. I must have fallen asleep. The darkened clock didn't give me any indication of the time that had passed. Any sign of trees had long since retreated into the distance, the hints of the wide open fields creeping in, gently expanding. Deke had donned his glasses against the glare of the road, I realized that the sun was fairly high in the sky now, must have been noon or later.

We had switched to more obscure country roads, our route originally was taking us past Chicago and in the light of recent events, it was probably better that we avoid any major cities where we could.

There was too much of a chance that Deke would be recognized, too much of a chance that someone could get hurt. I glanced back at Clara; she had curled up, lying down across the back seat, arms hiding her face. I could see the bruises on her forearms where Deke had grappled with her. Their powers couldn't heal burns or bruising I realized, the effect of the silver couldn't replace what only time would heal.

I caught Deke watching me as I studied the prone form of my sister.

"It's been pretty quiet in here," he muttered softly, clearing his throat quietly.

I squinted up at him. His face look tired and he definitely needed a shave. I realized with a start that we'd been on the road already for an entire day, stopping only for quick bathroom breaks and gas when we could find an out of the way station. Deke absently scratched at his stomach, wincing as he did so, keeping his focus on the road.

"When was the last time you changed those bandages, Deke? You've got to take care of it, or it won't heal right," he flushed under his day-old stubble, and stopped scratching.

"Deke! Come on, what do you think will happen if it doesn't heal right? That's going to be really, really bad! I don't need to be worrying about you going Jekyll and Hyde in this car on me, alright?"

He nervously scratched at his face instead.

"Pull over. Now," I said firmly.

He looked at me incredulously, but obeyed, slowing the car and indicating that he was pulling into the rest stop we were approaching. He pulled the car around to the back of the washroom building, partially obscuring the car from the road. He moved to get out of the car, but I grabbed his shirt tail, pulling him back into his seat. He clunked his head against the edge of the door frame, and yelped, holding a hand to his temple.

"Let me see," I grabbed at the bottom of his sweater, yanking it up past his belt, holding it up near his arm pit, and pulled at the edges of the tape holding down his bandage. He yelped again,

"Jesus Christ, Addy, what the Hell,"

I fixed him with a look that shut him down quickly. The tattoo looked raw and itchy; it hadn't scabbed yet, as it hadn't been long enough. I poked around it, and he whistled through his teeth, glaring at me behind the glasses.

"Look at it Deke, tell me, is it still fine? Is it still going to work?"

He twisted awkwardly, looking at it from different angles. He had since taken his sweater hem from me, and pulled up the other side to compare it to the silver scars he had left in his abdomen.

"What the Hell are you two doing?" Clara rubbed at her face sleepily, pulling herself up to the space between the seats to get a better look.

"How about you, how are your tattoos looking?"

She shrugged and pulled her sweater over her head, clad underneath in a light weight tank.

She leaned her head down between the seats, and I pulled at the gauze on her shoulder blade until I could see her marks. Deke turned in his seat to check them out, our faces close. They didn't look as red as Deke's did, the healing process going well. The silver scars glittered, the appearance of silver ink next to black masking what they truly were.

"Stay there,"

I rummaged through my purse, skimming through the flotsam of a life that I felt had ended years ago.

Triumphant, I pulled out a tiny bottle of lotion. I applied it to Clara, using only my fingertips, the rest of my hands being covered in bandages, tiny sparks leaping where the lotion first contacted. When I was finished I let her come back up to the surface, her face flushed from the awkward position. I waggled the bottle at Deke and he twisted to a better position for me to see, hissing as the cold cream touched his skin. He was blushing again, awkwardly staring out at the parking lot until I finished. I realized I could see the scar from his near fatal stabbing from Dezi, an ugly metallic gash just under his rib cage, wide and sharp.

Their powers gave their scars such strange beauty, keeping the wound looking fresh with a terrifying permanence, when normal scars could eventually fade. He pushed his clothing down, flushing up past his collar to his hairline, and cleared his throat.

"Anyone want to use the facilities before we head out again?" I looked at Clara, who smiled faintly, a haunted look in her eyes.

I smiled reassuringly, wanting nothing more than to forget what had happened this morning, needing us to move past it. She climbed out of the car and headed off towards the bathroom.

"Are you two going to be alright?" Deke looked at me seriously, studying my face. I took a deep breath,

"No, not really," I smiled sadly and looked away, climbing out of the car and following Clara once more, hoping against Hell that this time, the end results of following her anywhere would be much, much different.

Deke studied his face in the bathroom mirror. The bathroom smelled vile, a mixture of cheap cleaning products and an undercurrent of vomit.

He looked old, his stubble standing out against his pale face, exhausted circles under his eyes. And his eyes, he didn't think he'd ever get used to them. They were so wrong, so unnatural; he couldn't keep eye contact with himself. They reflected his brief flirtation with destruction – the weeks of insanity that were now feeling like a horrible dream. He'd been weeks without a haircut, and he was still getting used to the idea of not wearing a suit.

He breathed deep. He began shaving, only using the tap water, tapping the razor against his fingers, avoiding the grimy basin. The water sizzled when it came into contact with his skin, steam rising from his face, fogging up the glass. He hoped no one came in; the water only came out cold. When he was done, he put his glasses back on, splashed water around his neck and scrubbed his hands.

The door to the bathroom opened. The heavy footfall of booted feet entered, clunking against the concrete, a jangle of keys at the hip. A state trooper entered, pulling off his aviator sunglasses, tucking them into his breast pocket. The wind was knocked out of Deke, as he held his breath, plastering a small smile on his face, nodding slightly in the mirror in the officer's direction.

He hoped that his sunglasses covered enough of his face, that his disheveled appearance looked different – enough – from his circulated photo to escape without notice. He reached for the towels, scrubbing around his neck, trying to hide his face while pretending to dry the water. The officer nodded slightly to return his smile, and turned towards the stalls.

Deke threw out the wad of paper towels, and did everything possible to avoid scurrying for the door. He measured his steps, heart quickening. He had not quite touched the handle when he heard a deep voice behind him,

"Son," he avoided flinching – he was damn certain of that, and turned around. He turned slowly, debating his options.

"You forgot this," the officer smiled, handing him back the little plastic razor he'd carelessly left on the basin, something he would have left, a million times over, to avoid any more contact with this man.

He nodded, shakily, smiled, and turned back to the door, pulling it open and walking out into the piercingly bright sun. When the door shut behind him with a dull clang, he bent over his knees, gripping them tight, deeply inhaling the freshly mown smell of the field surrounding the turnpike. When his heart beat returned to normal, he hurried towards the car, ready to get out of this place.

Adeline was behind the wheel, waiting patiently, car running. He slid into the front seat, buckled up, and sat stiffly waiting for her to go. She looked at him curiously.

"Cops," he coughed out, suddenly realizing to breathe once again.

He removed his glasses and rubbed at his face. Adeline pushed the car into drive and swung around the rest stop structure, passing the door to the men's just as the officer stepped out, adjusting his belt. He looked up and into the car as they pulled by, and Deke swore he saw a spark of recognition in his eyes at the very last second. He couldn't be certain – never would be, but by then they'd reached the highway, carefully pulling out into traffic and blending in with the steady stream of people travelling through Watseka, Illinois.

"Onward and outward," he muttered.

Both Clara and Adeline fixed him with identical skin shriveling glares. No denying they were sisters, that was for damn sure.

Chapter 11

Do Not Disturb

We ate up the miles, our three person rotation helping us to keep maximum time on the road. We avoided people, avoided stopping during rush hours, avoided discussing the near-death experiences near Toledo.

Every few hours, in a patch of isolated forest, or once in the middle of the night of the fourth day, in a cornfield outside of Lincoln, Nebraska, Deke and Clara would leave me in the car, and spar. I comment on the Lincoln incident, because it struck me as truly awful, and truly beautiful. It was a clear night, the stars wheeling overhead, but a dark thunderstorm rolled off in the distance. It would be many hours before it caught up to us, but the two of them had been practically vibrating with the charge in the air.

Deke always allowed Clara to strike first, crackling, electricity arcing between her hands, a vibrant and deadly chain. He would block, inevitably resulting in a loud *crack*, and a flash of light, pushing them back in opposite directions, a formidable force.

Deke's silver scars tended to spark, his forearms throwing embers, as he fought in his shirtsleeves. Together, they were a beautiful and horribly frightening firework show, a deadly Tesla coil. Back and forth they would throw punches, sometimes landing one carelessly blocked, neither of them actually fighters, operating purely on instinct, until slowly the lights would fade. They'd run their hands through their hair, brush off their arms, until they let off no more than static, and come back to me, panting and sweaty and bruised.

Thunder rumbled in the distance, and I was beginning to think that the two of them together somehow attracted the storms, moths to a flame.

Maybe together they even created them.

I was always afraid that one of these times, it would all be for show. That something would escape from one of them, or both, and they would come back not as themselves, but as whatever we had locked up inside them, finally free.

I was taking my turn driving now, as we made our way through Loveland, Colorado, staying north, wanting to avoid Denver and Boulder, entirely. Boulder was a mysterious place, so often regaled in the worn paperbacks I had read as a child.

There seemed to be a magnetic force among the mountains, it was often said that it attracted psychic energy, often malevolent. A chill ran up my back every time I thought about it, and I resisted at every turn-off from the main road to head towards it. The last thing we needed was a bulls-eye on our backs, larger than the one we carried even now, and tempt the forces of nature – or darkness.

The sun was setting, already deep behind the mountains, every shadow the colour of a bruise. Clouds were scuttling rapidly across the sky, blending with the fog rolling down from the hills. This country never ceased to amaze me in its brilliance, when I took a moment to breathe and truly consider it.

I realized we were going to have to stop for supplies, and soon, as we were running out of towns nestled in the foothills. As much as we didn't go near the large cities, we also wanted to avoid stopping where a strange face would stand out too greatly. If I was honest with myself, I needed out of the car. I needed to stretch. I needed to not be in a moving vehicle, if only for a few hours. My brain was running on fumes, regardless of the state of our gas tank. I also had started loathing driving in the dark, the headlights spastic behaviour was become more frequent, and I didn't want to hit a hairpin curve on a cliff the wrong way in complete darkness. I cleared my throat,

"Hey, guys, we're making good time, what do you think we take a break, huh? We'll camp out somewhere, get our legs out of the car, campfire?"

They both stirred in their seats, snapping out of the daydreams they had been lost in. They took off their glasses as the sun dipped finally below the crest, irises subtly glowing in the half light. Another chill tickled at my spine as the feeling of being in the car with a pair of predatory cats washed over me.

Clara smiled.

"That sounds brilliant, is there somewhere we can just pull over?" she asked, leaning forward to see through the windshield.

I pointed, directing her view towards the signpost we were passing. A rest stop was up ahead, and the area was slowly becoming heavily forested.

"We can park in there, and head out into the trees a bit, find a clearing. Might even already be a fire pit or two out there. It's too early in the season for anyone else to be camping," I told them.

I felt I was only convincing myself. Deke was oddly quiet, absently rubbing at the fingerprint scars on his collar bone.

"Any response from the peanut gallery?" I looked at him directly in the rearview, waiting for eye contact before turning back to the road.

He blinked, once, twice, eyes flashing, snapping out wherever he had been, and then finally smiled, nodding. I let out a long slow exhale. I didn't know how much I needed this rest.

I pulled the car into the rest stop, nothing more than parking spaces, a water tap, and an outhouse, and found a spot in the far corner, tucked under a low-branched pine. The needles brushed off where the car rubbed against them, the branches still dry from the winter. I wanted to avoid being seen from the road, the brush up with the state police, miles and miles away was still fresh in my mind and I didn't want to repeat the experience. Clara and Deke were out of the car before I could even turn the engine off, hauling out sleeping bags we had pinched from the cottage garage and food out of the trunk. We hadn't even had an opportunity to use them yet, our rolling rotation of drivers sleeping in fits and starts had managed to sustain us so far.

When I got out of the car, I realized something was wrong with it. I couldn't quite place it however, and the thought tickled at the back of my brain. I grabbed my stuff from the trunk, shutting the lid, and pressed the lock button on the fob; a strangled and stuttering squeal coming from the car instead of the regular short beep. The lights didn't even flash in recognition of locking.

I realized what had been different. The interior lights hadn't come on when they got out, we had remained surrounded in darkness as they had grabbed their stuff.

I think they were slowly killing the car, absorbing the electrical functionality right out of the parts, aging it prematurely. I sighed, and followed them on the narrow deer path through the trees, an owl calling, lonesome through the quickening dark.

I couldn't see, and I couldn't find my flashlight. It should have been in the side pocket of my knapsack and it wasn't. I wondered if it had fallen out in the trunk somewhere. Flashes back to Toledo were replaying in my brain, and I paused, listening. The owl hooted again, making me jump. I cautiously moved forward a few steps, the curve of the path blocking what lay ahead. No doubt, I was going to give myself a heart attack.

The wind had died down when I entered the trees, the night breathless and still around me. I could feel the darkness pressing in on all sides, a closeness tangible in the cool but humid air rolling through on the fog. A sudden movement and a realization that something was standing in front of me caused me to jump back, clutching at my chest.

Deke was standing in the middle of the path, one hand holding the strap of his bag on his back, the other cradling his rolled up sleeping bag. I could only define him by the white of his skin in the darkness, his clothes blending seamlessly, his eyes glinting, forgotten diamonds in the dark.

"Jesus, Deke, you scared the Hell out of me,"

He smiled in response, crookedly.

"I guess it's better than scaring the Hell *into* you," he cracked wryly.

I punched him in the arm, and he turned to walk with me. The path widened, and we came into a clearing, ringing with heavy pines and cedars, effectively blocking light from the sparse cars on the highway from penetrating through. It was eerily calm in there, and I was again reminded of Toledo.

Clara was knelt in the center, sparking flames from a lighter amongst some dried kindling and leaves she had pushed together.

"I'd better go grab us some proper firewood, since unlike some people, I'm not completely blind," Deke winked, and proceeded to wander off.

I dropped my stuff near Clara and looked up. I gaped. The stars were slowly coming out, the clouds from the sunset had passed by, leaving the view above the clearing bright and sparkling, the air crisp. I'd never seen so many stars in my life. Even up at the cottage, growing up, I'd never stopped to appreciate what was right above my head.

Soon enough, smoke began to obscure the scattering of celestial embers, as between Clara and Deke the fire was built up enough to warm us – well, me - and fend off any would-be scavengers. I sat down on my sleeping bag, and pulled out my phone. I thumbed through my contacts until I reached Reggie. I chewed at the inside of my cheek, debating hitting the call button. Why not?

It rang. Once, then twice. I closed my eyes, calming my breathing.

"Hello?"

The voice was cracking, sleep-filled. Did I wake him? Was he really on the other end?

"Reggie! It's Addy! Oh my God, I can't believe I finally –"

I was cut off by a loud screech of feedback, practically shaking the phone and blasting my ear drum. I looked at it incredulously, and then put it back to my ear.

"Reggie? Reggie?"

There was silence on the other end of the line, but not of dead-air. I looked at the phone again, and then listened carefully. I could hear distant muttering, someone had put their hand over the receiver to cover up a whispered argument. Clara moved closer and crouched next to me, and I thumbed the speaker button so we could both hear what happened next.

Reggie returned to the line,

"Addy. Listen, hon, don't come here. Don't find me. Don't, just don't call ok? Delete the number, burn the phone. Stay away Addy, stay away from me, and for God's sakes, *stay away* from Clara, stay away from us all. Goodbye,"

I tried to interject. I really did, my stuttering *whats* and *buts* not piercing through his dialogue. The line went dead in my hand. I stared at it, feelings of confusion and broken heartedness competing as I sat dumbfounded.

Clara sat down hard, dejectedly, concern troubling her glowing eyes, reflecting the firelight. She looked like a child, the baby sister I had always tried to take care of, always tried my damnedest, rising to the surface. Her bottom lip trembled.

"Did you hear all of that?" I spoke, hoarsely, choking out the words, my lips tripping over their formation. My throat felt raw, and the warmth from the fire was making the burns on my neck and hands tingle. Clara nodded, and choked back a sniffle, wiping at her face. I dropped the phone like it had bit me, a venomous snake in my hands.

I pulled Clara to me, awkwardly hugging her as she buried her face in my shoulder. I took a deep breath. I wasn't going to cry. All of this was too far beyond tears, I knew tears were worthless now, they didn't change anything. I didn't care what Reggie had said. I was finding my brother, and he was going to give me answers. He knew something.

I didn't care any more, how much danger we were in, or what he might have gotten into. I knew now, that behind all of the bravado and determination, and the bald-faced lie that was his warning – I knew that Reggie was terribly, terribly afraid, and that he knew exactly why he should be. If he knew why, I needed to find him.

Clara pulled away, and flopped back onto her sleeping bag she had straightened out next to mine, hands covering her face. I stared blankly at her for a moment, and then looked to Deke.

He sat halfway around the camp fire, far outside the warmth, knees pulled up, arms dangling loosely where he leaned his elbows on them. His face was half in shadow, the firelight licking at his shadowed cheekbones, embers flashing in his eyes. I couldn't tell what emotion was on his face, the hood of his sweater pulled up, not for warmth, as he didn't actually need that anymore, but to hide.

I ran my hand tiredly across my face, willing the motion to clear the exhaustion. It didn't work. There were too many words left unsaid right now, the very existence of them stopping up my mouth as effectively as a cork. I flopped backwards, wriggling around until I had managed to stuff myself into the sleeping bag, and turned myself away from Clara.

I could still feel her preternatural heat radiating through my back. I sighed, and resigned myself to sleep.

That was the night the dreams started.

I was running hard, legs pumping, pushing through tall grass scattered with wildflowers, daisy heads being lopped as I kicked out with my feet. I was winded, exhausted, the sweat dripping from my forehead, stinging at my eyes. The sun burned brightly overhead, too hot, too close, my skin feeling singed. Ahead was a Quonset hut, dark and looming, a shadow of an enormous beast crouching in the distance. No matter how long I ran, no matter how hard I was breathing, it was getting no closer. My muscles were screaming, I could hear them, their voices getting louder and louder, ringing in my ears. I crested a steep hill, and an unseen force hit me hard in the chest, knocking all of the limited air from my lungs. I stumbled, falling down the hill, the ground rumbling around me, the sky cracking open with a deep pulsating wound, black air shimmering in the heat. Flames licked the edges of the portal, spitting out long fingers of flame and showering me with sparks. I continued to fall, rolling and bumping, until I landed, screaming, into a lake. The lake burned my skin, bubbles rising as I continued down, silently shrieking to the bottom, pulled by a skeleton hand around my ankle. Down into the dark, until it was too dark, too cold, my skin burning in the ice. I should be dead, drowned, long gone from consciousness, and yet my lungs continued to strain, water long ago filling my mouth, throat, I clawed at my own chest, the pressure and the breathlessness pushing at my organs, stars flashing before my eyes. Only the red sensation of terror, the overwhelming and exhausting need to breathe were left of me.

Suddenly, gasping, I was through to the otherside, weakly crawling onto a dark shoreline, the rocks sharp, cutting at my palms and knees, leaving a trail of red mingling with the water as it ebbed and flowed along the stones. I breathed, deeply, eternally, cherishing every moment that air entered my screaming lungs. Stones crunched above my head, and I squeezed my eyes shut, willing whoever it was to go away. A low laugh brought me to attention, raising my head from between my knees. I shrieked. The grinning man of Deke's tale stood before me, flaming chain in hand, knife held loosely at his side. His teeth flashed, hundreds of them, sparkling tiny needles in an over-stretched mouth, lips raw and chewed. He smiled wider, shivers running across my skin, goosebumps rising as I was paralyzed at his feet. He dropped the chain on the ground in front of me, and slowly reached out for me, the nails of his fingers broken and dirty, the knuckles bloody. I couldn't move. I couldn't scream, I couldn't –

"ADELINE!"

Deke screamed, so close I could feel the heat from his face, shaking at my shoulders, pinning them to the ground.

I gasped awake, panting, realizing that Deke held my shoulders, and Clara my ankles, electric shocks passing through their hands. I relaxed in their grip and stopped thrashing. They both removed their hands at the same time, held up in surrender. I felt limp, tired, I had been running for my life, that I had climbed the mountain in my sleep.

Both their eyes were filled with concern, their breath in clouds of white plumes around their faces in the pre-dawn cold. Deke reached forward and stroked my cheek, brushing the hair from my eyes. My skin tingled, static shocks crackled quietly in the dead-quiet forest. I knew he could see the terror in my eyes, I could feel it still filling my head and coursing through my veins.

I rolled over and vomited, Deke crouching close, gently stroking my shoulder blades. Clara passed him a water bottle, and he presented it to me, just at the edge of my field of vision, and waited for me to calm myself. I sat back on the sleeping bag, wiping at my face and taking deep stuttering breaths.

Clara hovered at the edge of the slowly dying fire, anxiously rubbing at her arms, quiet blue lightning flickering up and down with each pass of her hands. Deke stood, surveying the situation, looking down at me. I couldn't see his emotions, but I could feel that strange absence, the approach of a gathering storm I had felt back at my house, close to a million years ago in my mind.

"Were you dreaming of drowning?" he asked quietly. I nodded, hestitantly. I took a deep breath, "and running… and, I saw the Collector, he was, he was so horrible Deke, how could you stand it? " my voice cracked at the memory.

I could hear his sharp exhale, and he knelt down to one knee, and quickly in one swift move, scooped me into his arms, and pulled me up to standing, hugging me tightly against him, my arms around his neck. I could feel the electricity coursing through the direct touch, a ringing in my ears, *I thought,* until I realized it was a ringing I could *feel* all over my body. Where I had felt unnaturally cold and clammy after awaking so terribly, from being sick all over the campsite ground, my clothes clinging to my body in a film of sweat, I now felt warm, vibrant, and calm, the sensation spreading through every nerve ending in my body.

I pushed him back, and he stumbled slightly, a strange look on his face.

I felt so much better.

I felt, *infinite.*

Clara looked between us, confusedly.

My skin glowed, and then faded, a trick of the eye in the early, early dawn light barely highlighting the edge of the sky.

I fainted.

When I awoke, the sky was still a deep indigo bowl above us, the sun still trying to wade its way through to the shallows of dawn. Clara was next to me, her back facing me, her blond hair the only bright spot in the dark, the warmth of her radiating towards me. One side of my face was resting against something very warm, very soft, and I could feel a warm weight against my back. My eyes followed where my head was resting, and I realized there was a hand at the end, the fingers curling in response to my shifting. My head was nestled into the crook of Deke's shoulder. I rolled over towards him, and realized he was looking at me, sheepishly.

"You were really, really cold when you passed out. We didn't know what else to do," he whispered.

I blushed. I hoped he couldn't see that in the dark with his superhuman vision. They had used their unnatural body heat to warm me up after my ordeal, and as embarassing as it was, I was grateful. I closed my eyes and smiled. When I opened my eyes, he was studiously looking up at the stars that were silently winking out so many millions of miles away.

I studied his face.

"Do you ever miss it?" I asked quietly. Without taking his eyes from the skies, he replied,

"Miss what?"

I pursed my lips, settling more closely against his side, feeling only warmth without lightning, no electrical currents shivering through the sleeping bag draped across me.

"Life. Being normal. Everything before all this," I whispered.

He smiled, bit his lip. He seemed to be considering his answer very carefully. He tilted his head and looked down at me.

"I don't think I was a very good person before. Don't get me wrong, I wasn't a *bad* person. Not the nightmare that I became, later, when this all started, but I wasn't *nice.* I wasn't going to get very far, not in life, not with people. I made deals, that was my job, no matter what, no matter who got hurt in the process. I was cut throat before I was ever, literally, cut throat," he winced at his joke.

"But, it was my life. I can't help but think I was just dragging myself through it. But now, I don't know, it's all so different, it's like there never was that me anymore," he looked back up at the sky.

He must have realized what he said,

"I'm sorry Addy, I didn't mean it like that, you know I didn't,"

I sighed. Sure, it was all fine and good that he felt the old him didn't exist anymore. For me, that fact could be entirely true. I had died, and I didn't know why I was here, or if I was even really me anymore, and here he was, thinking it could be a wonderful thing.

He curled his arm around my shoulder, gave me a reassuring squeeze. When he stayed silent, I continued,

"For the record, as scary as this all was to me in the beginning, I'm kind of getting used to having the two of you around all the time, you guys have your benefits, terrifying as they are," I grinned, elbowing him in the side. I heard his sharp exhale in the dark,

"I take it, you're nice and warm now?"

"Snug as a bug," I felt him nod above my head.

"You should try to sleep, we've got an hour or two before proper daylight, and we still have a long drive ahead of us,"

I murmured in agreement and settled back, comforted by their shared heat. There was too much to think about. The strange call with Reggie, the horrible nightmare, the strangely burning certainty that somehow, the Collector could see me. Was he closing in on us? It was too horrible for words. I closed my eyes, but I didn't sleep, listening to the sound of Deke and Clara's breathing around me, the forest slowly waking up to the steadily rising sun.

A new day for the freak show, ready to go.

Chapter 12

French Mistake

We packed up the campsite, scuffing out the ashes with our shoes, slinging our bags across our backs. It was setting up to be a brilliant day, the sky a sparkling blue, not a cloud to be seen in any direction. The great big round bowl of azure over our heads stretched in every direction. The air was crisp and cool, dew still scattering the grass. We followed the way through the tall weeds and along the deer trail that hadn't quite rebounded from our trek the night before, the forest green and lush now in the light, instead of cold and dark. It had felt like miles to the campsite the night before, but we realized now we had only just barely crested over a hill and a short span of trees.

I could see the car, and I loathed the thought of climbing back in, cramped quarters for many more hours. Clara hadn't said much this morning, but she hadn't needed to. Her eyes said everything. I have never seen her look so scared and hollow-eyed before, looking like she hadn't actually slept last night, but lay awake, waiting for the worst to happen. There was a good chance that was exactly what she had done.

Deke was bright eyed and bushy tailed however, and I didn't know how long I was going to last without giving him a cuff over the head. Morning people, am I right?

They had both since donned their sunglasses against the glare, and being unable to see their eyes made me feel a little less terrible about shattering the night with my screams. My voice was hoarse this morning, and Deke had filled me in on their end of my hysterics.

From their point of view, I had been thrashing around, sound asleep, becoming increasingly violent, until I was almost ending up in the embers of the fire, muttering in a strange language. I had alerted Deke first, as he was only dozing, but he soon woke Clara for help with holding me down. When I appeared to be suffocating however, they were truly at a loss, as I was clawing and kicking too hard for them to check if I was choking, or even perform any form of CPR. Deke figured, if I still had the energy to fight them, I must be doing just fine where air was concerned.

They sure thought I was fine, once I had gone limp in their arms.

Until I started screaming.

Clara thought for certain that every state trooper would be swooping down on our heads, as I hollered bloody murder. Lucky for us, no one was around to hear me scream. She had frowned at the memory.

Deke had figured that I vomited after purely because my body didn't know what to do with the adrenaline. He seemed especially concerned about the drowning part of my nightmare, as both Deke and Clara had mentioned rising from dreams of being pulled under in a lake when they had made their change. I could see them both looking at me sidelong when they thought I wouldn't notice.

Trust me, I noticed.

I was doing the same to myself, every time I caught my reflection. I was secretly glad I hadn't dreamt of being smothered under a million tons of snow and ice, as I now realized it was more than likely that this memory lurked somewhere in my subconscious, and I didn't want to know what would finally be the trigger to remember it in horrible soul crushing detail. Maybe I didn't want to ever remember.

We had finally made it to the car, and I keyed the fob to unlock the car.

Nothing happened. I frowned, pushed it again.

Nothing happened.

I put the key in the lock, and manually unlocked the door. I put the key in the ignition, muttered a short prayer, and tried to turn the car on. The engine made a plaintive sound, but wouldn't catch. I had heard this sound before. I didn't ever want to hear it again, and certainly not now.

The battery was dead. I sat back, defeated, and stared at the ceiling. What on earth were we supposed to do now?

We were at least eight miles from the next nearest town, Estes Park, as I remembered seeing a sign not far back when I first decided we should camp down for the night. We couldn't call for help, we couldn't draw attention from the police or AAA, anyone could recognize Deke. Clara settled dejectedly against the hood, Deke rested with his arms on the roof, looking in at me through the passenger window.

"Well?" he mouthed.

I could feel his eyes boring into me, even behind the dark shades. I banged my head gently against the headrest. I climbed out of the car and slammed the door, locking it behind me. Maybe, I'd be back for it. Likely as not, it would eventually get put down as abandoned and towed. It was licensed under Mother anyway.

"Well, I guess we walk, cowboy," I smiled, glumly.

He flashed me a can-do grin, all white-teeth and dark scruff, and hitched his bag up higher on his back, sleeping bag tied down firmly.

Clara was already up at the road, climbing up through the ditch, long-legged strides pushing through the rushes. I sighed. Would anything between us be right, ever again? Was she honestly blaming me for what Reggie had said last night?

I felt apologies were no longer a worthy currency for our relationship, and the shots fired on both sides were just building up to some terrible collapse. I didn't even know what I was doing wrong anymore. No matter what Reggie tried to make me do, I was still with her, wasn't I? Shouldn't that be a damn good indication of whose side I was on?

Deke was studiously ignoring the tension. I realized I was impressed with him, half the time Reggie could barely handle the both of us at the same time, and Deke had been cautiously navigating our tenative sisterly bond for days now. Good thing Mother wasn't here, she'd eat him alive.

My thoughts turned to Mother as we strode along, and where she probably was, and what she'd been doing. Had she heard about what had happened in Whistler? Did she know Reggie was hiding out in California? She, like Reggie, had a habit of disappearing into herself for weeks at a time. Unlike Reggie, she liked to do it elsewhere, away from us. For a time being, it had been the cottage, but the older we got, the farther she went. I remember trying to study for a final exam, second year of University, and Clara calling me in hysterics, home alone and terrified, because Mother had left her for San Cristobal, with nothing more than a note and a wad cash for food.

It wouldn't have been so bad, if she ever warned us she was leaving. But Clara had just come home from school to an empty house. I had gotten the phone call, but Reggie made the drive. He was done exams, he had time on his side. I'm sure that ended up as another tick against me in her book.

She had wanted her sister, for once, and it wasn't a luxury I had afforded her. Sometimes, it came up in conversation, always starting as a joke, but always ending in a numbed silence. Reggie the hero, the half of me that I couldn't ever seem to be. Mother always said we were two parts of one personality, and Reggie got the better half.

Eventually, we stopped expecting her around, stopped looking for her notes. She'd be back, she always was, and there was no point in worrying about her - she certainly wasn't worrying about us. Reggie ended up heading down the same path, but until recently, had never disappeared entirely. I think maybe he was afraid to. Sometimes our conversations led in circles until he admitted he was afraid he'd get lost, and couldn't find his way back to us.

Clara still lived with her, though I use the term loosely. They were two ships passing in the night, for weeks at a time. When they did cross paths, it often ended explosively,

Mother, despite her abandonment and her less than favourable consideration for our feelings on the matter, became a tyrant when she was at home, expecting Clara to adjust to her rules the moment she returned.

I studied Clara's back as we walked, her sure stride, the ease she carried her heavy backpack. She had recently become a jetsetter herself, backpacking far and wide. Though she always left me a note, or a well thought out email, full of flight plans and schedules and directions and phone numbers. You know, all the things that someone would give you when they *care*.

The latest in a long string of getaways was her tour of Belgium. This was normal for her now, getting along with only what she could carry on her back. I guess I was the only one that hadn't turned into a wanderer. Life had just seemed to always get in the way, and despite our fear, and our hardships, and the fact that we were now navigating the mountains on foot, I felt so much more free.

If I only knew what Reggie was hiding from us now. I resisted the urge to try calling him again. Thinking about it now, the strange shriek of feedback had given me severe heebie jeebies, something was purposely trying to interrupt us, not from a technical problem with the phones, but something else entirely.

"Car," Deke called.

Clara and I both turned to look, and headed rapidly for the ditch. We scrambled down in the brush, and even I avoided rolling my ankle on loose gravel. Deke followed us, sliding deftly along the rocks. We didn't want anyone stopping to pick us up, we had no idea how far the police bulletins had spread, couldn't chance a friendly face up here in the mountains who'd ask too many questions.

Better to look like we were hiking on purpose, with no need for assistance, than to look like the car-less saps that we were. I took this break to adjust the straps on my bag, and try to hitch the load a little higher. I wasn't used to this, not in the slightest, and I could feel every joint beginning to groan just a little, and in light of the night I had had, I was already growing tired. I couldn't let them see that though. They knew they were stronger, as did I, but there was no point in bringing it up, or pointing it out. We were all in this together, and if they could continue on, so would I. Deke passed me a water bottle, and I smiled gratefully.

"What's the matter with sprout?"

He gestured with his bottle at Clara as she continued on ahead of us, always maintaining the same speed no matter what we did or how far behind we got.

"If I had to guess, everything. Between whatever the Hell Reggie said last night, Toledo, me, the sun, the moon, who knows. Everything becomes personal to her, everything turns into a vendetta or a grudge," I shrugged as we continued after her, walking just out of ear shot.

Pushing Clara out of my mind, I was focusing my attention on admiring the scenary, and the warm sun on my face. The hills around us were definitely majestic, I understood now why everyone used that term to describe this side of the country.

Deke, delayed, nodded in agreeance to my words about Clara,

"It broke her heart, you know, all that, back in Toledo. She's so afraid of it happening again, and just from the experience, she's terrified about what she'd have to do if it were me, if I was the one that cracked, she just wouldn't have a chance,"

He sipped at his water.

He was being nonchalant, but completely honest, and it hurt a little. Maybe I just should've let them go at it alone, and just stayed out of it all. Everyone would be safer.

"So what are we going to do, when we reach Estes?" I asked, looking for a change of subject.

Deke kicked at a stone in his way, sending it skittering into the underbrush. I wasn't planning on walking all the way to California, especially not through the mountains and Nevada. Deke remained silent for a few paces before kicking at another stone.

"Just going to go out on a limb here, and say, we will probably have to steal a car, we can't be putting pen to paper, and to be honest I'm not certain there would even be a car rental place in Estes," he chewed his cheek and continued on in silence.

I thought for a few beats, watching a hawk circle overhead, and then smiled,

"Do you even know how to steal a car? Weren't you a lawyer before all this?"

He hung his head for a moment, and then elbowed me,

"Smartass. I thought I'd use *the* Google. Heard it's pretty helpful,"

I smacked him in the arm, and we continued on again in comfortable silence.

I noticed Clara had stopped walking up ahead, and tried to see what was catching her notice. We broke even with her shortly, she was craning her head sideways, looking at the ground, disgusted. I grimaced. Deke sniffed his nose in derision, and stepped around the bloody mess on the ground.

"That is some grade-A roadkill ladies, what are you standing around for? He ain't going to get any less dead for your looking," he mockingly drawled.

Clara sighed, toed the poor carcass with her boot and stepped over it. With Deke up ahead, I settled into pace with her, hoping we could talk.

"It brought back memories," she finally said, quietly, squinting up at the sun.

I looked at her directly, thumbing back at the ex-groundhog we'd just passed by. She nodded, and bit her lip.

"Well that's, disturbing," I replied, shortly.

This wasn't really the conversation I'd had in mind. Clara nodded in reply, staring blankly ahead at the back of Deke.

"I just don't know how I never got caught," Clara ran a hand through her hair, frowning down at the ground.

I cleared my throat, side-stepping her statement,

"You know, Clara, in case you were worried, I don't plan on banishing you, just because Reggie said so. Even after everything that has happened. I know it hurt you, to hear him say that, I know Reggie has always been your hero, but I don't plan on ever not being here for you,"

Clara nodded, swallowed hard,

"I always figured one day, the two of you wouldn't have to look out for me anymore, that I'd be able to figure it all out. I thought I'd gotten pretty damn close, Addy, and then this curve ball comes my way and of course, once again, I've coming running back to you guys,"

"Well, at least you've got Deke in your boat now too, huh? It'll just be more the merrier until we can get this figured out, alright?"

I nudged her, and I could have sworn she blushed, but it could have been a trick of the light, or the heat of the sun beaming down at us from this elevation. Whatever it was, she tentatively reached for my hand, and we walked that way, comfortably, the three of us eating up the next few miles.

I only caught Deke looking back at us, grinning, once.

Ok, maybe twice.

Estes Park was indeed, a very small town. I was sure it was bustling come summer time, filled to the brim with adventure seekers, RVs trolling through chocked to the teeth with sweaty kids and tired parents, bikers running in packs, and the smell of *tourism* heavy in the air.

Unfortunately for us, this time of year, meant that the pickings for spare vehicles were reserved to the few locals who stuck it out year round, and a random assortment of over-zealous weekend warriors. Not far after crossing the townline, we straggled across to a diner, legs tired and cheeks burnt, and plopped ourselves heavily down into a booth in a darkened corner. Clara and Deke kept their sunglasses on, and Deke added the totally non-threatening touch of raising his hood over his head.

Despite my insisting that he looked like a bomber, or possibly a wayward rapist, and likely to attract more attention than simply being one of America's most wanted, he merely smiled behind the dark lenses and waited patiently for me to drop the subject.

The waitress, chewing gum, and wearing an obscenely pink uniform came over shortly, and gave us the once over. Her eyes lingered on the bandages at my neck and hands, and her eyes flicked to Deke momentarily. She put down menus and asked us if we wanted coffee. Clara and I nodded profusely, and she raised an eyebrow at Deke, who smiled brilliantly in return. The waitress blushed slightly, and turned off to get the coffee. Clara and I stared at him.

"Still got it," Deke smiled at us, drummed the tabletop and stared out the window.

Clara laughed under her breath and picked up a menu, casually looking it over, the pages and pages of assorted breakfast specials alone enough to choke a horse. She scrunched up her nose,

"Bread dipped in egg, wrapped around sausage, wrapped in bacon, and deep-fried in beer batter, what, what the Hell?"

She looked up at me questioningly, or as far as I could tell behind the glasses. I picked up the menu and looked where she was pointing.

"The French Mistake? You got that right," I grimaced. I elbowed Deke,

"Hungry yet?"

He didn't respond, but instead seemed to be carefully watching a man get out of his truck, sliding down to the ground from the high cab, all denim and cowboy boots, baseball cap pushed firmly down on his head. He strode into the restaurant, greeting the waitresses familiarly and taking a seat at the counter, the barstool creaking underneath him. I could feel Deke concentrating next to me, every line of his body tense. Clara leaned forward and whispered carefully,

"What, do you think that's our chance?"

Deke bit his lip and rubbed the back of his neck, then exhaled sharply,

"Just might be. He's parked far enough out of his eye line that he might not miss it until long after it's gone. And he left his keys in it," Clara swiveled to look at the blue jean man, pretending to scope out the specials menu above the service window where a number of orders waited to be filled.

"How the heck do you know that?" she leaned in, whispering loudly.

Their stage whispers were getting annoying, only a slight notch below everyone was definitely going to hear us conspiring to steal this man's truck.

The waitress returned, pouring the coffee expertly and stepped back, patiently waiting for our orders. We glanced at each other awkwardly, having not really been prepared for this moment, when Deke spoke up, gathering our menus and passing them into the waitress's hands.

"Three French Mistakes, extra whip cream, please,"

Clara and I looked at him, horrified, but the waitress had already nodded enthusiastically and promised it would be right on out. Clara whipped around and looked at the specials menu again, then turned back to him angrily,

"Whipped cream? Really? You needed to make that abomination worse?" Deke shrugged and stared her down, and then nodded his head towards the man at the counter.

"Look, see the breakfast he got? He's settling in for the long haul,"

Indeed, he seemed to have gotten the works from the short-order cook, the pile of food dwarfing his plate. The waitresses must know his routine, because I'd never even seen the man order. I turned to Deke again,

"You didn't explain how you knew he left the keys in the truck, what, are you psychic now?"

Deke paused for a moment, then pulled his glasses down and gave me a wink with his strange silver eyes over the rims. He waited for my gape-jawed reaction and then shook his head,

"Nope, not psychic, just saw him take them out of the ignition and tuck them into the visor while you two were too busy being disgusted by the menu options. Small towns, huh" he sipped at his coffee, a self-satisfied smile on his face.

Clara was glowering on her side of the table, coffee left untouched.

The waitress returned with what only could be described as a trio of deep-fried baseballs smothered in dripping dollops of whipped cream and unceremoniously clanked them down infront of us, cutlery rattling. Clara's eyes were going to bulge right out of her head, and if I wasn't mistaken in the bright noon light, she looked quite green.

Deke lounged back in his seat against the window, arm across the back of the booth, and waited patiently. I could feel the hairs on the back of my neck rise in the static closeness of his skin, bare from his pushed up sleeves.

Clara and I dug in, at first merely poking and prodding at the doughy and crunchy layers, trying to find the best point of attack. Deke's attention was fixed on the man with the truck, who was half distracted, chatting up the waitress as she refilled his coffee, meal forgotten. Deke drained his coffee, and gestured for me to get up. He thought differently for a moment and grabbed my hand, preventing me from standing. He leaned in close, and whispered in my ear, his five o'clock shadow rough against my cheek,

"I'll meet you on the far side of town in two hours. You're gonna have to act with me a bit here. Give me a good smack, right across the face, you'll know when,"

Suddenly he was on his feet, yelling, pushing me bodily from the booth, pulling me up by the elbow,

"You know what, I've had enough of this, you and your slut sister can just go by yourself, I'm done with you two,"

164

he dug in his pocket for some cash, flinging bills down on the table, coins scattered into our dishes.

I was disoriented by his outburst, and I hoped it lent some credibility to his performance. The entire diner was staring at us, more than one waitress standing motionless, the coffee they poured over-flowing their respective patrons' cups. I caught a glimpse of Clara, red faced behind her glasses, before I wheeled back on Deke, smacking him hard across the face,

"Don't you dare call my sister a *SLUT*, she's an angel!"

He laughed, scoffing, then Deke clutched at his face, attempting to re-square his jaw,

"Then you get her to tell you what *WE* did last night! I'm outta here!"

He angrily pulled down the sleeves of his sweater and hauled up his pack from the pile next to our booth. He stomped bodily through the diner and out the door, slamming it hard, the tiny silver bell jangling so hard it fell from its casing and rolled across the floor. He continued along the street, heading across to a park in the distance away from the diner, visibly raving as he went.

I primly sat down, and went back to what I was eating. Clara was shaking, and I looked up at her carefully. The diner went back to an uneasy motion, spills being mopped up, and our waitress retrieved the bell from where it had rolled under a bench. I realized Clara was stifling laughter.

The jeaned man continued to stare at us a heart beat longer, and I caught his gaze. He raised his mug in a mock-cheer and smiled,

"Good riddance to bad rubbish, am I right?" He then turned back to his food.

"An angel?" Clara blurted out in a half-whisper, half-giggle. I rolled my eyes and kept eating.

Deke circled the park, keeping one eye on the diner, taking stock of who was around that might have seen him exit. An older woman sat on a park bench, feeding the pigeons, but other than that, the street was eerily silent. He rubbed his jaw, and reminded himself never to get into an actual fist fight with Addy, she had one Hell of an arm on her. Clara was one thing, but Addy seemed to have a lot of angry behind that swing.

He ducked across the street, making his way between two cars and into an alley between an outdoor gear shop and a butcher, both advertising half-off carving services for fresh hunts. He grimaced and moved quickly, avoiding the block the diner sat on and passing through alleys and behind stores until he had circled back around, a strategic view of the blind side of the pickup truck he had targeted ahead of him. He crouched by some bins, and scoped the area again.

The old lady from the park had moved on, and the street was once again empty. He knew he had to move quickly, the man in jeans could be finishing up even now as he sat here, and if he got caught, the chances of them getting out of here intact slid straight down to nadda.

It was a fairly old truck, too old for power locks or power windows, maybe so far gone as to not even having power steering. He thought this might be for the best, less for him and Clara to screw up. He pulled his hood down from his face and strolled forward, crossing the street to the corner of the diner, carefully looking around him while trying to act completely unsuspicious. He moved forward carefully, trying to keep an eye on the door, and up the street to see if anyone was coming towards him.

A small town like this, someone was bound to know Jeans and bound to recognize his truck, but once they were out of town, they'd blend in as just another country bumpkin. Deke ducked when he got to the bumper of the truck, on the passenger side, and scuttled along the door to the rear of the cab. He stood up, back pressed to the truck, and cautiously looked around. He angled his head until he could see through the passenger window, through the windshield and on into the diner. Addy and Clara still sat by the window, engaged in conversation.

He smiled, thinking of what it would be like to be a fly on the wall inside right now. The owner of the truck appeared to be finished his meal, but at that moment a waitress offered him another cup of coffee, which he accepted excitedly. Deke tried the handle of the door, and found it unlocked, and exhaled roughly. Looking around one last time, he cracked the door, wincing as it screeched, and folded himself into the seat, keeping his head low, barely peeking over the dashboard. The door screeched shut. He pulled his knee to his chest and moved it over to the driver's side, sliding his hips across the center console and then paused, awkwardly half in one seat, half in the other, and waited. Jeans had risen from his seat. Deke's heart pounded. If he came outside now, they'd definitely have something to fight about.

He let out a long gasp of air as he realized the man was heading towards the bathroom, on the opposite side of the diner. He quickly folded his other leg into the driver's seat and pulled down the visor, dropping the keys into his lap. He glanced up and saw Clara and Adeline staring at him, gape mouthed where he had suddenly popped up over the dash.

He waved the keys at them, then pointed off towards the west end of town. He flashed two fingers at them and then smiled. Addy nodded, but Clara just continued to stare. He put the keys in the ignition, and cranked over the engine.

The truck had a low rumble, but was tuned well enough not to draw attention. He reversed quickly and smoothly, and headed out for the hills to the west, hoping to find somewhere to stash the truck, and meet up with the girls. He focused on calming himself – sparks were wreathing his wrists and he could feel them coursing down his face. What was one more crime on his hands?

Clara moved to get up to leave, but I put a hand on her wrist, rewarding myself with a shock in return. She cocked her head questioningly, but I tilted my head towards the bathroom.

"If he comes back, and we're gone, who do you think he's going to tell the cops to be on the lookout for? It's better to stay here for now, slip out when we can later. Have some more coffee,"

"But what are we going to do if the cops question us? Ask us how we got into town? Why we are here? What if I get a little stressed?" Clara whispered angrily.

She reached for her fork, electricity zipping between her finger tips and the tines, and then waved her hand at me.

"And I don't think they'd take too kindly to interviewing me with my sunglasses on either," she crossed her arms, and sat back hard against the bench.

She was right. I knew she was right, but I knew I wasn't wrong either.

"Okay, so we wait for him to come out, thank him for his kind words of support, and head out, make sure everybody watches us leave, by the time he settles his bill and heads outside, he'll know for sure it wasn't us, but we will make ourselves scarce in the meantime, deal?"

Clara considered this, then nodded.

The sound of a hand dryer filled the diner momentarily as the man of the hour stepped out, swiping his hands on the legs of his pants.

I scarfed down my last bite of French Mistake, savoring it in all its salty, meaty, artery clogging terribleness, the first real meal I'd had in too long that didn't come from a rack in a gas station. I threw down a couple of bills to go with the odd assortment of loose change Deke had scattered.

We both stood, plastered matching sad yet hopeful smiles on our faces, and headed for the door, pausing momentarily at the register,

"So sorry, ma'am, about that scene earlier, we just wanted to apologize, and hope none of your regulars think none too badly about eating here again,"

I glowered at Clara. Where was this awful Texan accent coming from? The waitress smiled warmly and patted Clara's hand.

Jeans reclaimed his seat and gave Clara a brief once over, smiling and touching the brim of his worn and ratty hat. We hitched our packs up higher and headed out the now-silent door, careful to swing right, away from the parking space that now only featured a crumpled and faded soda can. The moment we were out of eyesight of the plate glass windows and their accompanying flyers, we hurried onward, just short of breaking into a run.

We were several blocks away, going in the wrong direction, surrounded by small cottages and motels lining the street, the only people around for miles, when we heard the sirens.

They were coming directly at us, barreling down the street, dust clouds billowing behind them. Two cruisers flew by, hardly even slowing to notice us, and we coughed on the grit they had kicked up. I figured if we headed east enough, back the way we came, and then circled around through the suburban areas, we'd miss any attention focused on the downtown core where the diner resided. I hoped that Deke was alright, that he'd managed to slip away without any locals noticing he wasn't the right driver for that truck.

"This town makes me dizzy," Clara confessed, breaking the silence.

"What do you mean?" I tilted my head at her, wondering what she was getting at.

170

"There's something wrong about it, there's nobody around, no kids playing on the streets. I feel like even though we saw people half an hour ago, that those were the only people for miles,"

I knew what she meant.

The skin on the back of my neck had been crawling since we left the diner, and the wind had picked up its hollow whining a little bit louder since we got here.

"I'm sure it's just because it's early season, no one is really visiting yet, so no one is out doing anything to keep the town running right now," I explained.

She nodded, and we plodded along in silence. I felt my pack was getting ever heavier and despite the close quarters, I couldn't wait to be back in a vehicle and on our way. Clara broke the awkward pause,

"Do you think, your dream, that it was two-way? Do you think maybe the Collector could actually see you?"

Clara's voice was shaky, she sounded nervous. I wasn't sure if there was anything I could say that would alleviate her feelings – I had been thinking the same thing. I didn't respond, waiting to hear her out.

"I'm afraid that might be true, that he can find us, by using you, using your dreams to track us down," Clara blurted out, blushing ashamedly.

I considered this. Could the Collectors only track down people that were on its list, or was everyone up for grabs, if the opportunity presented itself?

"I think you should get marked up too,"

She looked at me hard, screwing up her face, hair blowing in her eyes.

Maybe she was right. I cringed at the thought of scarring myself, of the unnatural symbols scrawled across my body. But if it meant that the Collector couldn't see me, if that's what he was doing, maybe it would be safest for everyone.

I non-committedly shook and nodded my head, and she pursed her lips in response.

"We'll see what Deke thinks, ok? We'll figure something out," I adjusted the straps on my pack again.

I felt it was weighing me into the ground. She looked at me concernedly.

"Do you need me to take that for a while?" Clara asked quietly.

I sighed and shook my head. She rolled her eyes.

"I know you feel bad, about what you did, but it's ok, really. I'm fine," I was lying through my teeth, I wasn't fine. I was exhausted and sore and aching and scared and nervous.

I felt like that was enough – but I wished there was a word big enough to encompass all those feelings. Clara nodded, but I could tell it was half-heartedly.

"I just don't want you to hate me," Clara muttered.

I shrugged and stopped walking. I stopped her by placing a hand on her shoulder and turned her to face me,

"I'm not going to hate you Clara. You haven't seemed to figure that out yet. You're one of the most important things in my life, and with Reggie pulling his stunt right now, you're all I have left, there's nothing you have done or could ever do that is going to make me hate you, ok? Absolutely nothing,"

Clara avoided looking at me, eyes downcast.

"How can you say that, after all I've done already; the people that I've killed, the pain that I've caused you?"

She shrugged my hands away and turned to keep walking. I sighed in frustration. I wished that for once, Clara could see the bigger picture, the consequences that were larger than her.

"Maybe it's because I'm not our Mother? You know I've always tried to be here for you? And I've always forgiven you?" I called after her.

She stopped, feet scuffing the stones. She turned back to look at me, but I couldn't see the expression she made. The sun was high in the sky, and everything was too sharp, too harsh, her sunglasses hiding half her face. After two long moments where I felt my heart had stopped in my chest, she turned away, continuing on down the road.

We had crossed back onto a narrow road masquerading as a two-lane highway, the sun beating down on the blacktop, and the only thing for miles ahead were hills and mountains and scrub brush. A lonely billboard sat out ahead, proclaiming the wonders of a scenic viewpoint three miles down the road. We hadn't seen a car in hours, the town of Estes Park could have only been a dream we had shared. Occasionally, I would walk backwards, shielding my eyes, looking for Deke.

It worried me, his absence, it had been over two hours now, the longest any of us had been apart in days, and he was nowhere to be seen. Clara didn't share my worry; she fully believed that Deke was more than capable of taking care of himself. But she hadn't seen him at my house, seen him running scared, she hadn't seen him cycle through the emotions of anger and desperation and surrender faster than a pinwheel. I was afraid of him being cornered again.

She had been a calming force to his frenetic energy, despite her anger, and didn't understand my worry. Behind it all, Deke seemed to have very little faith in himself, and despite his often gratuitous bravado, the jokes and the laughter, I knew he was only keeping face for us.

Like stealing a car, so we could continue on this crazy mission to God knows where.

A low thrum of an engine caught our attention on the horizon from where we came. Dust clouds billowed out behind, the vehicle traveling much more rapidly than the posted limit, sunlight glinting off the windshield. We shaded our eyes, straining to see what the vehicle was, and who could possibly be driving it. I could hear the gears shifting smoothly as the hum of the engine changed and the driver navigated the hills that rose up to meet us.

"Is that Deke?" Clara shrieked.

This was no heavily used pickup truck that had dedicated its life to trundling along the mountain roads and visiting local diners. Now this, this was a car, cherry red and growling. As he slowed on the approach, he put his arm out of the window and waved, neatly pulling it to the shoulder in a cloud of dust and grit.

"Deke, what the Hell is that! What happened to the pickup?"

He grinned toothily through the driver's side window, a smile that could light up a whole town, and waved us in,

"I'll explain on the ride, we got places to be!"

I began to shoot a look at Clara, but realized she was already eagerly stuffing her bag in the backseat, scrambling in behind the pushed up passenger seat.

Of course, he got a two door. What was he thinking? I sighed, Deke still grinning like a fool, and slammed the seat back into position, clambering in and slamming the door behind me. I'd barely time to grab my seat belt when he took off, rear end fishtailing in the gravel, Clara whooping in the back seat.

"Deke, seriously. What is this? Where the Hell did you get this from?" I looked around the white leather interior, the rabbit foot hanging from the rear view mirror. Clara leaned forward over the front seat, grinning ear to ear.

"Do we care? I was *not* looking forward to sitting in that stanky-ass truck from here to California,"

"Clara, shut it. This car is going to attract so much attention, how did you even get out of town with this?"

He turned to look at me, sun glinting off his glasses, wind ruffling his hair, grin still plastered across his face,

"Turns out, our Mr. Blue Jeans, he's been playing some backroom poker for a couple months now, and by the sounds of it, doing pretty poorly,"

He shifted into another gear, combating the sudden steep incline as we banked towards the famous scenic point ahead. The car hummed in response, engine purring.

"A couple of gentlemen caught me sneaking down an alley, looking for somewhere to stash the truck for later. They thought I was him at first, but we worked out an agreement, a trade you could say. There was quite a bit of persuasion involved. But he's a quarter of a million in debt, and they were eager to get some bait to lure him back to them. A 60's Mustang seemed like a good trade to me,"

I looked at Deke incredulously.

"Persuasion, Deke? What kind of persuasion?"

He turned back to me again, tipping down his sunglasses. I realized his cheek was swollen behind the frames; bruising rising to the surface, and the collar of his shirt was torn.

"They uh, started throwing punches, but they quickly regretted it," he went back to facing the road. Clara settled back in her seat nervously.

"Deke, what did you do? You didn't... you didn't, kill them did you?" I asked him anxiously.

"Nah," he shook his head, giving me another reassuring smile.

"Gave 'em the shock of their lives though," he threw his head back and laughed, Clara issuing a high-pitched shriek of laughter from the back seat.

I couldn't believe they were joking about this.

"Deke!" I shouted indignantly,

"You can't just be shocking people, willy-nilly, someone is gonna report you somewhere, and then what, get you all over the news again, or more, or whatever," I smacked his shoulder.

It did nothing to quell his laughter.

"Addy, seriously, these guys, the things they do, you think they're going to get the police involved?"

He looked at me over his glasses, a flashing of his eyes in the brilliant sun.

I thought about it for a moment. He was right. If a bunch of card sharks wanted to trade punches and a beat down pickup truck for this beautiful piece of muscle car that was their business. Might as well enjoy it while I could; we were eating up the miles, and we were doing it in style.

And we were doing it in a car that was old enough to hopefully survive Deke and Clara and the next twelve hundred miles.

Chapter 13

The Space Between Us

It took a lot to get Deke to relinquish the steering wheel to anyone else, the smoothly curving road through the mountains addictive and unrelenting.

But after the fourth time the wheels gently nudged the ridged warning strip over the yellow, and my heart leapt in my throat as I realized how precariously close we were to the scrub clinging to the cliffs, Clara and I insisted he'd had enough. Though they were both tired, I could see their skin crawling, light highlighting their cheeks in the rippling moonlight and I considered the currents of energy pouring from their pores. Even bone tired, no real sleep in a couple days, and yet still the power controlled them, overruling their basic nature.

They were dictated by what wanted to consume them, by the desire to keep themselves buried underneath the enormity of the situation.

We were stopped at another lookout, the view stretching out over a canyon, sparklingly lit by the full moon, leaning against the Mustang, stretching our legs. The wind was still cool from the passing winter, up high, up here; I could imagine that there were still spun sugar pools of snow lurking in the shadows. Deke had his hands shoved into the pockets of his hoodie, head tilted back, eyes closed, inhaling deeply. Clara was looking at her shoes, scuffing in the dirt. Her eyes glinted as she looked up at me, the glow reflecting from her skin in her pupils.

"Smells like snow," Deke commented, bringing himself back to us, from wherever he had been, deep in his own head.

I wondered if Clara noticed that he was leaving us more and more often, distracted, locked away behind those strange eyes. I didn't know if I should be worried or not. If it was a symptom, or if it was a side effect, either could spell out horrible things for all of us. Clara nodded in agreement to Deke's comment, taking a deep inhale of her own.

"You ready?" She asked him, wry smile on her face.

I rolled my eyes and walked around the car, hand drifting across the smooth cherry red hood, still warm from our long haul out of Estes. Deke did good, real good.

I glanced back as they readied themselves, stripping off their sweaters and then I started the engine, pulling the car forward as far as I could on the narrow shoulder, giving them the space they needed to spar, without putting myself or the car in danger.

I considered letting the car idle, so we could pull away quickly when they finished, get back on the road, get on toward finding Reggie and whatever secrets he hid. Bright flashes reflected in the rear view mirror and off the chrome highlights on the dash. I tried following what was happening, but the difference in lights and darks were flashbulbs in the dark, blinding if I stared too long. I closed my eyes and settled back, the leather still warm in the backrest from Deke's overheated frame.

I was running hard, legs pumping, pushing through tall grass scattered with wildflowers, daisy heads being lopped as I kicked out with my feet. I was winded, exhausted, the sweat dripping from my forehead, stinging at my eyes. The sun burned brightly overhead, too hot, too close, my skin feeling singed. Ahead was a Quonset hut, dark and looming, a shadow of an enormous beast crouching in the distance. No matter how long I ran, no matter how hard I was breathing, it was getting no closer. I could hear heavy foot falls around me, following me, chasing me, flocking me, herding me. They sounded four legged, from the beats that matched mine. I couldn't tell how many there were, I couldn't see them at all. I ran harder, hurting, stitches pinching in at my ribcages, but I couldn't stop. The intrinsic and delicate fear of pursuit iced my veins. I ran with the pack, I could hear their breathing now, hoarse rasps in the sunlight. I crested a steep hill, and an unseen force hit me hard in the chest, but this time, instead of rolling down, violently knocking every bone in my body, another invisible push shoved me aside, tripping me, pressing me hard to the ground. Heavy steps gathered around me, tufts of grass flattening, puffs of pollen and sprays of tiny insects floating off in their wake. I whimpered, feeling their heat, two firm pressure points pressing down on my shoulders, hot breath on my face. I squirmed, feeling claws lightly pricking at my skin, a low guttural growl coming from inches from my chest.

"We can smell you, Adeline," a deep rumble pervaded the air, and I gasped, looking around for the source of the voice.

"We know where you are," the air reverberated again. I twisted, hard, trying to roll off the force holding me down,

struggling against the weight. I managed to free an arm, scraping against the earth, tugging at the grass, trying to break free. For a split moment, I understood, as you do in dreams, that it couldn't hurt me, it wasn't real, I just had to awaken, release myself from the fear. My wrists were unmarked, my throat had lost it's ache. How could I be healed unless this wasn't real? I urged myself to wake up, squeezing my eyes shut. I went limp in the puncturing grasp on my shoulder, willing it to disappear. A low malicious laugh filled the air, deep in my bones, making my soul ache. My eyes shot open. Deke's Collector stood before me, grinning.

"No," I whispered. He cracked his neck, slowly, the joints popping, sounding as gravel under shoe. He moved forward slowly, hiking up the legs of his suit, and crouching down next to me, head tilted, studying me with his odd vertical pupils. I tried to ignore his teeth, the flayed and chapped lips, cringing back into the grass and daisies, ignorant of the monstrousity above their swaying heads.

"The Hell Beasts will find you, they're waiting their turn, and when they do, we'll have him too. And her. And all those who try to hide from us," he winked at me. He actually winked at me. And then he reached for my face.

Screaming. I shot awake, kicking at the accelerator and causing the car to rev furiously, growling low like the beast in my dream. Deke appeared at the window, gripping the sill, sweaty and panting,

"Woah, woah, woah, hey," he calmed, and I relaxed off the pedal, furious with myself, the car slowly grinding to quiet, wrenching the keys into the off position and chucking them out the window past Deke, pushing my head into my hands. Thank God the car had been in park.

He glanced at the wayward keys, and then back to me, pulling open the door to the car, and crouching at my feet. He rested his hands on my knee, a dull glow of heat compared to the usual sparks, a normal sensation, comforting in the dark.

"Did you see him again?"

I took a deep breath and nodded, resting back against the headrest, squeezing the steering wheel in white knuckled hands.

He smiled at me gently,

"I guess you should be getting used to it now, you've seen him more than I have," I looked at him directly, not wanting to hear the humor in his voice.

"He told me something Deke, and it's bad, it's really bad," his smile quickly reversed directions, and he ran his hand through his sweaty hair.

"What do you mean, he told you something? It was just a dream, wasn't it?"

The hand on my knee clenched, and I softly laid my hand on top of his.

Clara had appeared behind him, similarly drenched in sweat, barely visible in the darkness of the mountaintop. Fog cluttered my brain, creeping tendrils slowly erasing the dream, the fear, the embers of the nightmare.

"The Hell Beasts were there, this time, like they were at the house, I could hear them breathing, all around me, and he said they were hunting me. That they can find me, and that they will find you, he knows we are all running together,"

Deke's grip was too tight, prying at my kneecap, knuckles turning white. I gently pulled his fingers away, loosely holding his hand.

"I told you," Clara spat, voice all poison and indignant.

Deke squeezed my hand, rose and turned to her, waiting for her to continue. She pointed a finger at me, voice shaking,

"You need to get a tattoo, you aren't safe either, and you're on his radar. He's using you, to get to us, all because you don't want to get a tattoo. Well tough nuts, Addy, you might not be one of us, but you're with us, whether you want to be or not,"

Deke's head swiveled back towards me, eyes wide, studying my face,

"You guys have talked about this?"

I groaned and nodded. It was obvious what I had to do. I just thought I could have passed it off just a little bit longer. I winced at the thought. Clara stooped to pick up the keys, and dangled them, twinkling from a finger.

"We aren't going anywhere, unless you mark her up Deke. At least get half on her, see how that works, maybe it'll dull the signal until we get to Salt Lake City, we find ourselves some parlor that'll take her in, do her up quick," she raised her chin, firm set to her jaw.

They were both exhausted, and I could tell Deke didn't have it in him to argue. He looked back at me and shrugged.

I rolled my eyes and got out of the car, pushing past Deke and plunking myself down on the nearest boulder I could find. I unzipped my sweater, glaring daggers at Clara, flapping my arm out of one of the sleeves and rolled up the left side hem of my t-shirt, exposing hip bone and a long slim expanse of white torso.

"Come on Deke, before I change my mind," he glanced at Clara and she gestured at me, rolling her eyes.

"Addy, come on, this can wait, wait until daylight even? We don't have to do this now, get in the car,"

Deke pleaded, eyes glinting in the half light from the car's interior bulb. Clara crossed her arms, tapped her foot. She wasn't letting him go anywhere. He was torn between the two of us, our identical stubborn natures forcing him to make a decision.

Deke closed the car door and pulled his switchblade out from his jeans pocket, shrugging half-heartedly, and approached me. I smiled at him nervously, wishing there was another way to go about this.

He knelt down beside the boulder, and I leaned back on my elbow, staring up at the stars cycling overhead, frosty scattered diamonds, the full moon shining down. I swore I could see my breath now; my exposed skin was goose-pimpling, sure to make Deke's job that little more difficult. He steadied a hand on my hipbone, his touch warm and electric, and looked up at me.

"Really, Addy, we can do this later, you don't have to do this, you don't have to let her bully you,"

He gestured over his shoulder, the point of the knife glinting. I wouldn't look at him.

"Deke, just, go ahead. Anything you could do, wouldn't be anywhere near as bad as what he could do to you, or to us, or to Clara, she's right. This isn't about me, so just do it, ok?"

He nodded and sighed again, offering a quick squeeze of my hip, and began.

I bit back the pain, tiny burning slices, over and over, and stared directly at Clara, staring her down, and waiting for the defiance to soften in her eyes. Rather than allowing me the pleasure, she turned away, sitting down on the hood of the car and staring out over the valley once more. I felt Deke's warm breath on my side as he looked closely, inspecting his work.

"Can you tilt, just a bit? Trying to catch the moon," I settled down farther onto my right, resting my cheek against the cool boulder.

A couple more strokes of fire, a quick intake of breath; whether from myself or from Deke I couldn't tell, and I think he was finally done.

"Ready?"

Somehow I knew this part would hurt more than the knife strokes, but I wasn't ready for the flaming sensation, the electric fire spreading through my side, tingling deep into my spine, and across my hipbones. I cringed, gasping. The flare ceased and the electricity stopped.

"Hey, hey, it's done ok, it's good, look," he smiled reassuringly, and I looked down at the glittering symbols that now ran down my side.

185

And there they were. We had no idea if they were enough, but it was a start, for now. He pulled down my hem, and helped me sit up, sitting back as I pulled my arm back into the sleeve of my sweater. I winced, pressing a hand to my side and rose from the boulder. Clara had moved to the rear of the car, leaning on the trunk, facing us, arms still crossed. I pushed past her, shouldering her as I went.

"I hope you're happy," I muttered, popping open the door, and folding into the driver's seat, trying to ignore the dull ache in my side.

Their powers took away the wound, but it didn't get rid of the pain; interesting to know. When Deke had left himself to die after being stabbed by Dezi, he must have been in agony for days, even if he was no longer in danger of dying.

I watched in the mirror as Deke approached Clara, appearing to mutter a few words to her. Her posture stiffened, and her hands dropped to her sides. He touched her briefly on the shoulder, and gestured for her to go ahead of him.

I grabbed the keys off the seat where Clara must have thrown them while Deke had carved the safety symbols into my flesh and cranked over the engine, the throaty rumble drowning out any chance they had at continuing conversation.

Clara opened the door and adjusted the passenger seat, sliding into the back. Deke pushed the seat back into position, a little more aggressively than necessary, and slipped into the front seat, slamming the door. He rubbed his eyes with one hand and gestured with the other in a circular motion.

Here we were, rolling on out once more. I shifted into gear, and we were off onto the winding roads once more, Salt Lake City a distant jewel on the horizon.

We locked up the car on a lot just short of downtown, the sun only just rising, the lake sparkling in the distance in the early morning light. The pair of them had donned their sunglasses, and we strolled the streets, taking note of where the nearest tattoo parlor was. I had made both of them change their bandages before we left the car, and as it was still too early for any self-respecting parlor to be open, we looked for a place to eat.

Very few people were on the streets, and that's the way I liked it. Less people now always meant fewer complications. The walk was pleasant; the trees lining the street were well on their way to being full and leafy, and the air, though crisp, was being warmed by the bright sunshine.

Clara had thawed during the rest of the drive, but still wasn't speaking much. I hope she realized I knew her reaction had come from a place of fear. The dream had scared me too, and every moment I waited for the warm breath on my neck, the brush of hair against my face, waiting for the inevitable presence of the Hell Beasts. It was much easier to be afraid in the wilds of the mountains, and not in the sunny and shiny city during broad daylight.

We found a place for breakfast, a hole in the wall, once more named after a woman who may or may not work there, or maybe was someone's mother at one time, and ordered up coffee and all-American breakfast. Deke sniffed at his food, and made a half-hearted attempt at eating it, while Clara ate all of hers down swiftly, and half of mine. She ignored my indignation, and we all sat in silence, peering over our steaming mugs.

"You two gonna kiss and make up?"

Deke swallowed and settled his empty mug down on the condensation-ringed wood. Clara rolled her eyes at him and looked at me,

"You know, I was just concerned, right? We don't need you to be a liability right now," she explained, clearing her throat.

I scoffed in response. If anyone had been a liability this entire time, it had been her, and I resented her implications.

Deke tipped his head at her, a clear look of disdain on his face.

"You know, Clara, you can be a piece of work sometimes, your sister was scared awake, afraid for her life, and yours, I might add, and then you make me take a knife to her? It's cold, Clara, no matter what your reasons,"

Clara's face hardened, and her eyes smoldered, but she soon looked away, pouting down at the table.

Deke fixed me a small smile, the corners of his mouth barely twitching, but it was enough. He'd cut right to the heart of the matter, and wrangled Clara into silence in one fell swoop.

Maybe he did have a chance against the Byrne sisters. Maybe he would be able to handle Reggie once we found him.

Reggie, that hot-headed, red-headed, tried and true Boston boy, always something to prove, always reaching for something more out of life.

God forbid, you called him Reginald, as Mother did. All of us, always our full names; they were as important to her as what you wore, what your hairstyle was, it was essential that you be who your name promised you'd be. It lead to us all adopting short forms outside her ear shot, at school, work, it was important to distance ourselves from the persona she made us reflect. The strange and twisted personas she wanted from Reginald, Adeline, and Ellaclara; really, no joke, were so beyond who we all yearned to be.

Only the Byrnes could be the best, she made sure of it. If only she could see us all now.

Deke regained my eye contact and tapped his wrist. I checked the time, the last one out of all of us who could hold onto a cell phone, or wear a watch. It was ten, meaning the shop would be opening its doors, and I could get in there for an early appointment, and we could get back on the road as soon as possible.

"I'll go with you, if you want?" Deke smiled, hesitantly.

Clara rolled her eyes, and pushed her last bit of waffle around the plate. The waitress buzzed by, the offer of more coffee in her hand and in the air. We waved her off.

"Do you guys think we could take a break here? Have a breather, stay out of the car, have a shower maybe?" Clara looked around at us.

I suddenly became very aware of how long we'd been on the road, how long it had been since the cottage and the last hot shower we'd all had. I grimaced. Fresh clothes and deodorant only got you so far. I agreed with Clara, hoping it was enough of an olive branch for now. Reggie would keep for one more night. If all went well, we'd be in Half Moon Bay the following evening. I'd love to actually sleep in a bed again.

Hell, I'd love to sleep without having the nightmares. Deke slid the car keys across the table to Clara.

"Go find us a place to stay then, take the car, we will meet up with you after, give Addy a ring when you've found a place," he smiled, the motion not quite reaching his eyes.

Evidently, he was bothered more by what happened up on that mountain top than either of us was. But it was par for the course for us right? Clara huffed and scooped up the keys, sliding out from behind the table and sauntering out through the door, not a word of goodbye, the bell tinkling merrily behind her.

"You don't have to protect me from her, Deke, I don't know how it was in your family, but it happens, we needle each other. It comes from love, deep down, though,"

Deke's face darkened at the mention of his family, brow knitting into a frown.

"Yeah well, sometimes family doesn't know what it has, until it's too bloody late, too, Addy," he stood up from the booth, dusting the crumbs from his barely eaten meal off his sweater and waited for me to join him.

I waited, torn between the urge to ask him what he meant, and to leave well enough alone. This was the second time that Deke had reacted unfavorably to the mention of family, and I was beginning to seriously wonder what had made him so vindictive.

The look on his face, even behind the sunglasses was enough to stop the words in my throat. I pulled out my wallet and laid the money down on the table, and followed the sound of the ringing bell that marked where Deke had already left without me.

I was about to push the door open, when a hesitant touch was applied to my elbow. I turned, looking down at our diminutive waitress, grey hair carefully coifed and pinned, and her apple cheeks a healthy shade of red.

"Honey," she smiled and drew me aside.

I wondered if there was something wrong with the payment, if it was too little or too much. I could see Deke standing on the sidewalk, hands shoved in his pockets, carefully watching what was happening inside.

"I don't want to alarm you, but have you been travelling with that boy long? Do you know him?" I could see the calm concern in her cool grey eyes.

"Uh, yes, yes ma'am, known him forever, why?"

She pursed her lips and pulled a folded half page of newspaper from her apron pocket.

"I was worried it might be this boy, the one the FBI has been looking for, news is he was headed west, so we all thought to keep an eye out," she jabbed a finger at a photo, blurry, of a gas station, surveillance footage, grainy and dark, a person that quite possibly could have been Deke squinting up at the camera.

Next to it was the circulated photo from the news bulletin I had seen back on the television in Dunkirk. Up close I could see how blue his eyes used to be, long before any of this ever happened. She was watching me carefully, so I smiled,

"No, ma'am, that says it was taken back in New York state, we've never been there, certainly not in the past week," I flashed a wider toothy grin, hoping it was reassuring.

The car with the Massachusetts plates was hopefully still sitting in a dusty parking lot back in Colorado so how was she to know any better?

She nodded, grimly. I could tell she didn't quite believe me. Deke was moving to come back into the diner, and I willed at him that he'd stay where he was. He abruptly stopped moving. I wondered for half a second, before the waitress continued,

"Alright, just wanted to make sure, I hoped you weren't being taken against your will or nothin',"

I nodded, maybe a little too aggressively, and smiled,

"Not at all, I am just traveling with my man and my sister, taking her up to Seattle for a trip for the weekend. Thank you, ma'am, for the concern, and we'll keep our eyes out for him too," she nodded sagely, as if we'd entered into a great binding conspiracy.

I turned away, feeling the sweat on my palms, wanting to vomit. Great, I thought, another town where people were actually diligent as to their civic duty.

I exited the diner, where Deke was about to ask what had happened, when I linked my arm through his, and rose up on my toes, kissing him lightly on the lips, greeting my man for the eyes of those watching in the restaurant behind me. I turned him away, steering him to go down the street,

"Don't act surprised, act normal, keep walking," I muttered, and he smiled down at me,

"Why, Adeline, I never,"

"Shut it, keep going,"

He patted my hand that linked through his arm, and laughed, loud in the quiet morning.

"So, are you going to tell me what that was about?"

"She had you made, Deke, she recognized you. You're in the papers now, even here. I had to convince her that you weren't who she thought you were," he craned his neck to look back, and I elbowed him in the side.

"Should've kept a copy," he grinned.

"Deke!"

He pushed his sunglasses up his nose, as we reached the end of the block, and turned down a side street off the main drag towards the tattoo place we had noticed earlier. I pulled my arm out from his and crossed my arms, continuing that way down the street.

"I don't know why you make it such a joke, running from the law, while all else is going on in your life, you'd think you'd take it a little more seriously,"

I'd ended up several strides ahead of him, as he'd stopped dead in the middle of the sidewalk.

"You know, you made me realize something, back at the cottage, about a billion miles ago, but I didn't understand it until Estes," he approached slowly and took me by the elbows. I craned my head up to look at him.

"That if I'm screwed, royally, forever, eternally, until Death I do part, and especially if I'm going to Hell for it, I'm going to have fun. I'm going to joke, I'm going to laugh, I'm going to drive that damn Mustang right into the ground, I'm going to pretend to be other people, I'm going to take on card sharks singlehandedly, I'm going to watch as many sun rises, sun sets, moon rises and moon sets as I can. And I'm going to dance in the streets, because..." he took my hands and spun me around,

"None of it, not even a little tiny bit, is ever going to matter anyway," he smiled wistfully, and continued holding my hand.

I didn't know what to say. What was this, to be so joyful – while being so fatalistic? It was a bizarre concept to me, and it made me wonder even more if we were somehow losing him deep down inside.

"And how did I inspire this, exactly?" I frowned at him.

He merely chuckled, and shook his head.

"Come on, let's get you inked up," he pulled at my hand, and we continued down the street.

He'd given me a lot to think about. What were we going to do, if nothing could be done? Where could they go?

I was overwhelmed with the sudden feeling that we'd done this all wrong, were we insane, driving across the country with a pair of trussed up maniacs? What was I thinking? We'd been through so much already, and we hadn't even gotten to where we were going yet. What more could we possibly take?

Deke pushed the door of the parlor open for me, holding it to allow me to pass through in front of him. He had pulled off his glasses, and gave me a reassuring wink. I took a deep breath and walked up to the desk. A slim redhead with double sleeves of roses and a labret piercing smiled at me, asking kindly what she could do for me. She gave Deke a once over, taking in his strange eyes for a moment longer, and then turned back to me.

"Go on, show her," he smiled.

I unzipped my sweater and pulled up my shirt, twisting towards her to show her the silver marks. They flashed in the bright morning sun streaming through the windows, sparkling on and under my skin.

"Dude," the girl smiled, coming around to take a better look.

"How the Hell did you get that?"

She gently traced the symbols with a finger, and I tried not to wince. Deke looked at me and I shrugged, helpless, so he answered for me,

"New technique. Surgical grade wire and light bulb filaments. Really, really uh, tricky. All the rage out in Boston right now. But she wants a matched set, so she needs another one tattooed, right there next to it. If I draw them out, do you think you can match them up?"

He ran a finger alongside the carvings he had given me this morning, my skin tingling in the after-burn of his

195

electric touch. She cocked her head, made a face, and nodded.

"Yeah, no problem, you got a couple hours?"

Turns out, we did.

Chapter 14

The Last Straw

Deke held my hand. Of course he did. As promised, he was there for me being quite possibly the biggest baby to ever grace a tattoo parlor. The artist got a kick out of it, alternatively gently mocking me, and flirting with Deke. I just wanted it all to be over with.

She sat back, inspecting her work, Deke hovering over her shoulder checking that every line was perfect, when my phone rang on the table next to my head. The display said blocked, and I assumed it was Clara. I thumbed the phone to answer the call, putting my phone to my ear,

"Hey, did you find a –"

"Addy?"

"Reggie?!" I sat up, knocking a tray of instruments flying.

The artist cursed and ducked down to pick up the scattered tools. Deke stooped to help, while carefully trying to listen in on the conversation.

"Adeline, where are you?"

I heard some strange noises in the background, muffled yelling, and a roar of outrage in the distance.

"Um, Salt Lake City, Reg, why? I thought you wanted me to burn this phone? Why do you care now?"

"Well, it's obvious you haven't,"

He paused, and I could hear him yell to someone in the background of where he was, even though it sounded like the phone was pressed against his chest,

"Will you just put him down? You've got enough juice to lay out a rhino, what are you two doing?!"

The phone was abruptly put back to his ear, his voice back to full volume, and I winced,

"And I'm guessing you're still on the way to find me, but something's changed, Addy. Something important. I'll have to explain later. We'll have to meet up, I guess, I'll call again,"

"Reggie, I-"

Click. The line went dead. I growled in frustration, and threw the phone at Deke, flopping back in the chair. He caught it awkwardly, fumbling it against his shirt.

"Seriously. Seriously, I am sick and God DAMN tired of that man,"

Deke and the artist exchanged glances.

The artist pulled off her gloves, snapping them into the nearby garbage can. The phone rang again, and this time, Deke answered, leaning out of my reach as I tried to take it from him,

"Yeah, cool, yeah Clara, we will see you there,"

He thumbed the phone, ending the call. He held his hands up in surrender, and tossed me back the phone,

"Just Clara, she's down at the Western 89,"

The artist raised her eyebrows at us and I shot her a dirty look.

"I guess she found us a place that would take cash,"

I straightened out my clothes and zipped up my sweater against the cool air that would be greeting us outside.

The artist snorted and headed for the register. Deke winked at me and gestured for me to go ahead of him. We paid up and left the parlor, the whole day stretching before us, long and languid compared to the tense drives and furtive glances we'd been operating under for too long. I beamed, thinking about a hot shower and a soft bed. I was starting to feel my age, and sleeping in a cramped car for mere hours at a time was starting to make me go stir crazy. Deke caught the look on my face, and his lit up, and I wondered how long it had been since I'd really smiled, honestly and naturally.

"So what did you think Reggie has to say for himself?" Deke asked.

"I don't know, but he knows something, I am not sure what, but I think it might have something to do with the marks. There's something going on here, and he's been way too careful about using the phone. It was blocked every time he's called,"

I took a deep inhale, the crisp air refreshing in my lungs.

"And I heard him yelling to someone about rhino tranquilizers?"

I laughed hesitantly at the look that Deke shot me, and shrugged in response. I looped my arm through his, both of his hands deep in his pockets as we walked.

"So do you still want to see him? Do you think it'll be safe?"

He avoided looking at me, seemed afraid to ask the question. I thought about it, hard. Reggie was making it an awfully intriguing concept, finding him, but at the same time, it felt dangerous. Something else was at work, and he was trying to hide it from us. I eagerly awaited his next call, even as frustrating as they had become. I shrugged, not really feeling like answering the question just yet.

We walked along, lost in our own thoughts. For once in a lifetime, I didn't feel like I needed to keep everything together. Deke was right. Who's to say we weren't all going to end up in Hell for this whole thing anyway? The sun warmed my face, and the breeze ruffled my hair.

The city was finally properly waking up, though it was mid-afternoon. I'd lost track of days, we traveled so much at night, sleeping strange hours or barely sleeping at all, so it bewildered me seeing civilization continuing on like nothing had ever happened to them. Children were being bundled into cars, the Saturday shopping desperately needing to be done. Dogs were being walked; yards were being raked of the winter's soggy leftovers, browned leaves and dead vegetation. No one knew who walked past them, the secrets they were hiding, the things they had done.

I blushed, thinking back to the evening in the mountains, how these people would gasp, knowing someone I now considered a friend had taken a knife to me. And that I'd let him. And that it was honestly in my best interests. If you'd told me a week ago that any of this would have happened, that I would have dropped everything, and taken off across country, I would have called you a liar. But here I was.

"How does it feel?" Deke squeezed my arm, pulling me back to myself. I cocked my head at him,

"How does what feel?"

He wrapped an arm around my waist, gently resting a hand on the bandage that now covered my left side. I winced and he let go abruptly.

"Well that answers that," he chuckled lightly, turning away and continuing down the street.

I shook my head and followed him. He was a strange, strange man, and the layers I knew I didn't know well at all. Anything that I thought I knew was all new to him too, and that didn't really help anybody.

"Hey, Deke?" I called ahead to him, his body swinging around in response to my call, stopping and waiting for me to catch up.

"Don't get me wrong, I appreciate what you did for me back at the diner, I like having you on my side. But just while Clara isn't here, since…since you seem weird about it, like every time it comes up. Can I ask, what's the deal with you and your family?"

I swear I could see the hair rise on the back of his neck, every limb tightening, and his mouth set in a steely line. The sunny day darkened ever so slightly. I regretted it the moment the words came out of my mouth.

He pulled me aside, stepping out of the way of a young woman pushing a stroller, her child waving happily at us as he passed.

"It's a long story, Addy, one I would love to tell you. Eventually, but right now, I don't think this is the time, or the place. We've got too much on our plate right now to be trying to figure out where my past went wrong. The how and why I'm here now, how I got myself into this mess. It's on me. My brother was a cause of a lot of things, but he has nothing to do with this,"

"Your brother? You said you were an only child?"

"I know, Addy, I lied. I lied to you about my brother. But I didn't lie about my parents. They are dead, for sure, and I sure as Hell haven't been keeping tabs on my brother since,"

"But Deke,"

"No. Let's not, ok? Things happen. Things you try to forget, and I am not going to try to remember them for you right this minute,"

I grabbed his hand, willing him to calm down, feeling the sharp shock in my palm, the jolt running up my arm. He winced when I winced; leaning defeated against the white picket fence wrapping the well-manicured lawn of the house we stood in front of.

"You owe me, Deke, after all of this, you owe me, one of these days, and I want to hear your whole story,"

He nodded, scuffing his sneakers on the sidewalk, avoiding my eyes.

"We've all got our family crap to deal with, hey, I got a brother that is stirring up the muck on both sides of the country right now, but it happens. You have to deal with it eventually,"

I smiled reassuringly. It hurt me to think that he felt he had to bottle it all in, whatever his past was. It made me so curious though, to know, who his brother was, and what his brother had done. It had to have been terrible, and did it have anything to do with his parents being dead? I couldn't imagine any family member having anything to do with the deaths of another, but horrible things happened every day.

Deke squeezed my hand, and pushed off the fence, continuing together down the street.

Eventually, pleasant downtown streets turned to grey hazy industry, cement lots and high fences, the edges of a city where the exhaust pipes and steam pipes and smoke laced air filled the sky. We'd already been walking for a couple of hours, and I was tired, dusty, and ready to collapse where ever the fall took me. We finally happened upon Western 89 on the outskirts of the city, and it was everything the tattoo artist would have smirked about.

My overall perception was of grey. Grey walls, grey windows, grey curtains in the windows. Only two cars sat in the parking lot, a rusted out Chevette, older than I was, and the beauty we had brought with us from Estes, looking gaudy and flashy next to the drabness of the motel. The sign indicating vacancies stuttered dully, half of the neon bars flickering and the other half dead. Deke must have seen the look on my face, and if I had any indication of what I was feeling - it was mirrored in his.

Where the Hell had Clara gotten us into?

The mountains were hazy in the distance all around us, dust kicking up across the empty parking lot, a can rattled across the ground, stirred up by the emptiness.

A shiver ran down my spine. I checked my phone, a text from Clara gave me the room number – number 8. It was the last room on the end of the row, the number faded against the cracked paint of the door.

"You can check out any time you like, but you-u can never le-eave," Deke sang softly under his breath. I wished he hadn't.

"Such a lovely place," he smiled and winked at me, heading toward the door.

Before he had a chance to knock and dislodge more paint chips off its frame, the door swung open, Clara beckoning us in from the darkened room beyond.

"You know, it came out the month I was born," he smirked at me as we followed her inside.

"God, you're ancient," I mocked him.

A note of derision came from him, and then the door closed, leaving us in a half-grey darkness, the bright sun outside barely filtering through the curtains.

Clara had settled into the chair in front of the television, watching us looking around at the shabby surroundings, the carpet that was an odd crispy texture and an indescribable shade of who knows last time it was cleaned, the water stain running from the floor above, and the dust-coated wet bar.

"So did you purposely look under "horrifying" in the phone book when you made these reservations?" I asked Clara flatly.

She shrugged and grinned. Deke had wandered into the adjoining bathroom to take a look at the situation inside.

"They took cash and my word on what my name was; I thought we were avoiding any paperwork since Deke's such a hot commodity around here,"

'What's this I hear about hot?"

Deke had reappeared in the doorway. Clara scoffed.

"Not the water in there, if you're looking to take a shower,"

I groaned and rolled my eyes. They were giving me a headache.

"Alright, fine, yes. Smart thinking on a cash only motel, on the murder-y side of town,"

I glanced around the room again, afraid of looking too hard at any of the finer details.

"Sleeping bags are still in the car, if that was what you were thinking," she waved a hand back towards the parking lot.

I nodded and sighed, pulling off my sweater and settling tentatively onto the edge of one of the beds.

"I'll grab everything,"

Deke headed outside, the door clicking softly behind him, dust motes floating in the brief flash of light from the warm sun outside.

"So, how'd it go? Did they say anything about your marks?"

Clara gestured with the clinking glass she had picked up from the top of the television.

"Went alright, had to convince her that the silver was some sort of new trend in tattooing. What are you drinking?"

Clara looked in her glass, shook it, dislodging ice cubes and making them ring for a moment. She shrugged.

"Whatever was in the mini bar?"

I stared at her for a moment. I was not in the mood to deal with this. I headed for the bathroom, dreaming of a shower, whether hot or cold, I realized I just needed to get away from it all, just for a moment.

I winced as I pulled off my clothes; bending and twisting were no longer options, not until all that was going on had finally healed. I pulled away the bandage covering my new tattoo and took a look in the mirror, my side red and aching. The hieroglyphics glinted in the weak light coming from the florescent over the mirror. I wondered at their meaning, their origin, whether good or evil. I wondered at how Dezi knew what they were. I wondered why these marks were even a part of me now. What had happened? Why Clara? Why Deke?

I sat down roughly on the edge of the tub, feeling the warm rush of tears spreading across my face. I pulled the bandages from my neck, carefully unwrapped my hands. I thought of a boxer, winding down after a fight, the wrapping sticking in spots. The skin was off-color from being bound, the blisters healing but still raw looking.

I was tired of being strong. I was tired of pretending like I knew what was right, what to do, where to go. Years of this, Clara the rebel and Reggie, well, Reggie was Reggie, and there was nothing to be done about that. How had we gotten through life, as we did? I felt like there was a hole in my life, a chunk missing that I didn't understand. Did I forget something, or someone, that was terribly important to me? Did I forget them when I died? Did I come back wrong?

I took a shuddering breath and attempted to play with the knobs in the shower, tried to make anything come out warmer than cold. After six or seven minutes of cursing Clara, the motel, the health department of Salt Lake City, and water in general, I managed to convince the tap to produce a mediocre amount of hot water.

Once the days of traveling in the car, gas station bathrooms, terror dreams, and terrible diner food had been washed from my skin, I felt a little better. Wiping the mirror clear of a thin layer of condensation, I checked my face. The redness from crying could be mistaken for the rosy glow of hot water. As if Clara would believe that, but maybe it would be enough to fool Deke.

I exited the bathroom, wrapped in a threadbare towel, to an empty motel room, my bag sitting on the bed, the air still and quiet. Clara's now empty glass sat, half-melted, on the top of the television. I stepped carefully across the oddly textured carpet, and glanced out between the curtains. Clara sat on the curb outside, cigarette in her hand, exhaling at the sky. Deke sat next to her, legs stretched out in the dusty gravel. They looked to be in depth in conversation. Clara only smoked when she drank, or was incredibly angry. I hoped for the first, and rolled my eyes at the thought of the latter.

Clara drew slowly on the cigarette. She was down to her last three. She figured she'd stop when she was done. Life was hard enough as it was right now, without supporting an addiction that now seemed like a waste of time and energy. But there was no reason not to savor it

Deke sat quietly nearby. He was good at that, just sitting, patiently, listening to nothing, but understanding everything. It probably had something to do with the fact that they couldn't actually hear each other, not over the incessant ringing, but it was comforting nonetheless.

She studied his profile, straight nose, strong jaw. There could be worse travel companions. And the longer they traveled together, the more she appreciated his strange brand of humor that kept the edge off when it was important.

"Sorry about earlier," Deke caught her eye, smiling slightly, mouthing it more than anything.

Clara shrugged and waved it off with the hand holding the cigarette. He was drawn to it for a moment, and then spoke up,

"You know, the first time I saw you, you were having a cigarette, and sometimes I can't help but think, where we'd both be right now, if you hadn't stopped outside of where I was hiding, if I hadn't heard the ringing,"

Clara smiled to herself. That had been a good night. The voices hadn't made her kill, she'd managed to just be – had gone out, enjoyed her friends, enjoyed a few drinks, and unbeknownst to her, dragged back a momentous force in the shape of Deke into their lives.

Deke scuffed in the gravel with his shoe, looked like he had more to say, but then thought better of it. He slapped his hands on his jeans, brushing off the dust from the walk earlier, and headed inside, patting her softly on the shoulder as he went.

She shuddered at the electric jolt that flowed through her shoulder, wondering if he felt hers coursing up to his elbow, and took a deep final drag on the cigarette, before dropping it down between her knees, and crushing it under her shoe.

"Decent?" Deke called, the door cracked, letting in the warm breeze from outside.

I was just finishing toweling my hair, combing my fingers through the long mahogany tendrils, attempting to make it behave as it air dried.

"As much as I'll ever be," I straightened up, pushing my hair behind my ears.

He chuckled and closed the door. His eyes flashed in the half light, catching the dim light coming from the bathroom door.

I tossed him the towel, which he caught with a grimace.

"How's she doing? Did you tell her Reggie had called?" I asked him, judging the look on his face before he answered. Deke just shook his head.

"She's got enough going on, without worrying her about Reggie. Until he calls again, gives us some better information, I wouldn't bother, it would probably just upset her," he headed towards the bathroom, paused and looked back at me.

"Just, let it all go for a night, ok? We can all just pick right back up in the morning, all our baggage will still be there, don't you think?"

He closed the door behind him; the only light in the room now was the light coming from under the door. I heard the shower crank on, and I inhaled deeply. Deke was right. There was more than enough baggage going around right now, and not all of it was sitting on the beds, waiting for us to unpack.

We all needed this.

I dozed on one of the beds, using my backpack as a pillow.

It was thankfully dreamless, wonderful and quiet.

Eventually the shower turned off, the small change in white noise enough to draw me up from sleep, but I kept my eyes closed, willing myself back under. Eventually Clara came back into the room. I sat up sleepily when Clara announced her purchases. The plastic bag she carried held a vast assortment of junk food and underneath it all, a deck of cards. Tucked under her other arm was a case of beer.

"Figured we'd order a pizza? Play some poker? What do you say?" Clara smiled, shaking the six-pack at me.

"Is that all the beer you got? Really?"

Deke commented as he came out of the bathroom, padding along softly in only his jeans, running a towel across his head. Sparks flew in every direction, lighting up the dark corner by the bathroom door where the dim bulbs by the beds didn't quite reach, his scars flashing on his arms and torso, catching the light from his static.

"There's another one in the car, smart ass," Clara pulled her eyes away from him momentarily as she pushed the beer into his arms, and slung the junk food onto the table.

She stared hard at me for a moment and mouthed something, rolling her eyes, and went back out from where she came. It had grown dark outside, I realized, the sun dipping behind the mountain ranges that surrounded the city.

I pulled my sweater tighter around me, feeling chill after my nap. Deke lounged back on one of the dinette chairs, bare feet up on another, pulling the food out of the plastic bag and inspecting each of Clara's purchases.

"Uh, aren't you cold?" I asked tentatively, throwing him a raised eyebrow.

"For once, in a really long time, I'm pretty comfortable. Clean, cool, not murdering, feels pretty fantastic," he scratched at his scruff and studiously went back to reading the labels.

I rubbed at my face,

"Are you honestly telling me you had a *cold* shower?" I shivered at the prospect.

Steam still rolled out of the door where it met with the cool air of the room. If he'd had a cold shower – then that steam I could see was purely created from contact with his skin. I could see it in the half light, curling wisps. Clara entered the room again, sliding the chain lock in place, and set the other case of beer down with a jangling of bottles.

Deke shrugged,

"What, I can't help it if I'm hot," he passed me a wink, and Clara rolled her eyes. He threw down a packet of cookies.

"Yeah, yeah, before you all suffer from aneurysms from rolling your eyes too much, you both know it feels better on the skin, especially you, Clara," he tossed her a bag of gummy bears and she scoffed in return.

She stared at the bears for a moment, and then tore open the bag. She settled into a chair at the table with him, and ripped open the pack of cards.

"Are you in?" Clara turned around in her chair and looked at me.

Deke threw a gummy bear at me, badly, so much so, it smacked into the wall above the headboard and down behind the bed, where I am sure it would stay until the end of eternity; or maybe until one of the cockroaches found it.

"Deal me in,"

We were each three beers in, and I absolutely did not drink beer. Wine, sure, I had been known to indulge in a good sweet Riesling from time to time. I'd even made my way through college with a healthy love for rye and cola, the same as Reggie. But beer was not my friend, it rushed for my head, pulled down my defensive line. It was the Byrne family curse, and always Reggie's warning – don't drink the beer, unless you want everyone to know your darkest secrets.

I was eighteen gummy bears down, constantly begging Deke for another loan to keep playing the game. Clara had four left to her name, Deke, the apparent card shark in our midst, was up thirty-five.

Clara slammed her cards down and sat back heavily in her chair. High card eight.

"Nothing. Again, how are you doing this?" She glared at him ominously. He shrugged and smiled, laying down his cards.

Two pairs, queens and threes.

They both turned to stare at me, waiting for my hand which inevitably had been terrible this entire time.

I laughed, incredulous.

I threw down my hand, three nines, a six and a two. Deke stared.

"She *can* learn, amazing," he smirked and dodged popcorn I threw at his head.

"Listen, you," I brandished my beer at him, taking another swig.

I pointed at him, and Clara leaned in to hear. The room took on a golden glow, effervescent in the beer cloaking my thoughts.

"I'm upping the ante,"

He cocked his head, listening closely, eyes lit up with laughter.

"I beat you on this next hand, the *last* hand, mind you," I settled the empty beer down, and Clara absently passed me another.

"I get to drive the rest of the way to Half Moon, your precious little car is *mine*," I pushed six red gummy bears at him.

Deke tapped his beer on the table thoughtfully, and then took another deep pull, draining it.

"And if I win?"

He stared directly at me, challenging with his eyes, waiting to see where I was going with this.

"I never ask you about your brother again," I cracked open my final beer, saluted him, and took a sip.

Instead of frowning, as I had suspected he would, he considered my offer thoughtfully. Clara shot me a look, raising an eyebrow. I shook my head at her and turned my attention back to Deke.

"Deal," he gestured at Clara, who currently sat in the dealer position.

He sat back, arms crossed, and waited for the cards to lay out. Clara looked at him worriedly as she dealt, suddenly worried about doing the wrong thing, not wanting to see the outcome of the cards.

We all picked up our cards, silently reviewing our options.

Deke looked at the cards, and then looked at me up through his lashes.

I suddenly doubted my brashness, wondered if I shouldn't have brought it up again. Why did I insist on finding out his past? Why did it matter so much?

Deke chewed his lip thoughtfully. I pushed five more gummy bears into the pile in the center, holding my cards tight to my chest.

Deke sighed. He folded his cards down on the table, face down, and stood up, pushing off and striding towards the beds.

"You win, I fold," he slapped at the pizza crumbs on his jeans, washing his hands clean of the game.

He grabbed his sweater off the end of the bed where he had thrown it after his shower, zipped it up, unlocked the door, and headed outside.

The door slammed home with a note of finality.

I may have won, by his surrender, but I felt at a loss. I shouldn't have pushed.

Clara sat back, and stared at me, arms crossed.

I pulled his cards across the table and looked at them. I flipped mine over, and stared at them side by side.

What I saw confused me.

He had a royal flush, there was no chance I could have beaten him, and yet, he had surrendered the game. Had he changed his mind? Did he want to confess? Was he looking for an opening? Had I changed his mind?

I could feel a headache coming on, and left the table, crawling into my sleeping bag on top of the covers, lying with my back to the door. A million thoughts crawled through my brain, each one more outrageous than the next. I don't know when Clara crawled into her bag next to me, or when all the lights were switched off, but I do know, we slept like the dead that night, falling hard, barely breathing; the soft weight of consciousness lifted from our shoulders.

Dawn glittered dully through the gaps in the curtains, reflecting off the ceiling, bird song filtering through the paper thin walls. I stretched, working out the kinks in my back, somehow now unused to sleeping in a bed. I rolled over toward the door, and saw Deke lying on the bed closest to the exit, curled in the fetal position, head resting on his arm, and he was looking at me, his eyes looking more molten grey than liquid silver in the strange light.

He wiggled his fingers at me, and mouthed 'hello', trying not to wake Clara, who was snoring gently next to me, her long honey hair the only part of her sticking out of the sleeping bag.

He tilted his head toward the door, and slowly sat up. I nodded, looking at Clara over my shoulder as I tried not to rustle the sleeping bag or jostle her too much on the cheap mattress. Sometimes I swear sleeping bags are made of tin foil, the amount of noise they make. But Clara continued snoring on, and I padded barefoot across the carpet to the door, following where Deke had already unlocked it and snuck out, quieter than I would have guessed.

We walked along the concrete pad that acted as a porch across the front of the motel, both barefoot, Deke wearing his borrowed sunglasses against the bright morning light. The day was already dry and getting warmer. It must have been late in the morning; the sun was fairly high in the sky.

A vulture circled above, a broad kite floating on the thermals far, far away. I hadn't even thought to check the time. It was quickly becoming irrelevant; especially when your clocks kept getting blown by the company you keep.

I noticed Deke's clothes were hanging much looser than when he and Clara had gone shopping, an eternity ago, his frame slowly transitioning to bony from lean. The man nearly never ate, and hardly ever slept, I wasn't surprised.

I wished there was something I could do.

He was watching his feet as he walked, occasionally tapping my arm when he noticed a piece of glass or sharp pebble in my way, and I realized walking barefoot in this part of town probably wasn't the smartest idea we'd had. We found a bench near the ice machine, and sat down. I basked in the sun, enjoying the fresh air, ignoring my growling stomach.

I waited for Deke to speak. This was all on him; I was done trying to convince him otherwise.

After several minutes, and my feet were finally frozen from the still cool cement, he finally cleared his throat.

"Seven years ago, I was in school, finishing up, actually, my final year. We'd been out, the bunch of us, at a party, celebrating that we'd all passed, ready to go, and ready to be adults," he chuckled, hoarsely, staring off into the hills that seemed to have fallen silent once his story began.

"The world was before our feet. I remember, how triumphant, how just, spectacular and shiny everything had become. I came home later that night, morning even. It was so, so early. Four forty-five. I remember it, because I had to check my watch. All the clocks in the house were flashing, the time was all wrong. I was drunk, I knew that, but I wasn't that drunk, I knew something was off," he nervously swiped at his hair, which was tousled oddly from laying on the bed.

"I figured the power must have gone out, during the night. No one would have noticed yet, everyone should have been asleep. I was going up the stairs, quietly. I skipped the eighth step, like I always did, it always creaked. I was three stairs from the top when I slipped. Something sticky on the hardwood, I couldn't really see in the half light. I reached out, felt out how thick it was, and then the copper smell hit me. I almost puked. I've never...I hadn't ever..." Deke trailed off, his Adam's apple bobbing in his throat.

"...I fumbled for the light switch at the top of the stairs. Saw the trail of puddles of blood, my father slumped against the wall. He just sat there, staring, propped against the hall wall. I was frozen. I stopped breathing, even. When he didn't move, when I didn't hear him, I gathered all my strength, and moved around him, to my parents' room. I know I did puke, that time, when I opened the door," Deke leaned forward on his knees and crossed his arms, I thought he was going to vomit again, simply from the memory.

"Deke, you don't, you don't, please, you can stop, I'm sorry," I put a hand on his back, feeling the unnatural heat through his sweater, wanting him to be okay.

He shook his head, sitting back again abruptly, taking a deep breath,

"Her head was just, it was just, so violent. There was so much blood. And the room was turned upside down, every drawer ripped apart. I ran out of there, ran to Casey's room. He wasn't there. His bed hadn't even been slept in. He was just a kid, why was he out? Where could he be? It took me six hours to get a hold of him, when he finally answered his phone. By then, the cops wanted to talk to him, everyone needed to talk to him. I'd been out, hundreds of people knew I hadn't been there, couldn't have been there, knew it couldn't have been me,"

I reached for his hand, and he clung to it, the lightning pouring from his fingers, their burn on my hands making the skin feel tight, but the heat wasn't so powerful – they'd only last sparred a day ago. I think the blisters on my hands from Clara's attack were going to scar. I hoped better for my throat.

"Turns out," Deke laughed, dryly, the sound a horror to my ears,

"It turns out, that *Casey* had let it slip to some kids at school, that my mother had recently inherited jewelry from a long lost great aunt; which she had recently gotten appraised, and evidently was worth close to three hundred thousand dollars.

And it turned out, from the long and disturbing court case that followed, that his best friend's older brother decided he needed it. That he would fence the jewelry, keep the money. He and a buddy cut the power, taking out the alarm system. And just broke into my house that night, but my father got in the way. And my mother watched them do it. So they made sure there were no witnesses.

And Casey had absolutely nothing to do with it, except for letting it slip. That's all it took. A wagging tongue and our parents were dead. I know,"

Deke took a deep breath and looked up at the great blue basin over our heads,

"I know it wasn't really his fault. But I needed it to be. I needed someone to take the blame, because those guys shouldn't have been there, they shouldn't have even known. So I took it out on the kid, and then I left, I haven't spoken to him since... I can't...I won't. I threw myself into internships; work, moving up the ladder. I stopped caring about other people, closed off a lot of relationships. People could always count on me to close the deals; because I never let my emotions get in my way,"

He looked at his hands, sparking in the bright light.

"I should've forgiven him. I should've taken care of him; he lost his parents too, that night. But where do I even start?"

I swallowed, roughly, my eyes brimming with unshed tears. It was horrible; it was too horrible for words. But he had told me, he'd let me know, finally, why he felt so strongly about family, why he insisted that Clara and I keep it all together. He didn't want me making the mistakes he had.

I stared out at the parking lot, and the highway beyond, thinking about Reggie, thinking about Clara. We needed each other so badly, so dependently, would anything make us stop talking to each other, completely? This was why Reggie's behavior was so strange. He'd normally never treat us this way. It reaffirmed to me how something was much more terribly wrong than I first had thought.

I could feel Deke's breath, warm on my ear; he'd thrown an arm around me as I had sat, thinking.

"Don't cry, please, I don't, I haven't. Not anymore," he whispered.

I turned to face him; he was so close, so warm in the bright sun.

Why did terrible things have to happen to good people? The dark of his lenses couldn't conceal that he was staring intently at me. A tendril of hair curled down in front of my face, the sun highlighting the red, making it brighter with the refracting gold strands within the dark brown. He tucked it back behind my ear, and I held my breath.

A door slammed beyond, shattering the moment. Clara had stepped out from our room, rubbing her arms, and looking our way. Deke's hands dropped and he turned to look at where my attention was caught.

He blew out a held breath, and rose from the seat, holding a hand out to me. I took it, feeling the reassuring heat, and walked with him back to the room, Clara turning away and heading back inside.

I mentally cursed her.

Chapter 15

Flashbacks

We had gathered our things, checked out of the motel, ate a big lunch, well Clara and I did, anyway, Deke pushing his food around his plate in morose figure eights, and then we waited for nightfall. The last major leg of the trip was across Nevada, and the heat, and the nothingness that it afforded. We figured that a night ride would be best, keeping us and the car cool, and the vibrant and violent light out of their sensitive eyes.

I felt invigorated, and spoiled. I'd had a shower, slept in a bed, had a couple of proper meals in me. I laughed internally at the state of my life that these were now things out of the ordinary.

Clara was restless.

She wandered around in front of where we sat, rubbing her fingers together, and tiny embers jumping from the tips. Deke watched her with narrowed eyes.

"Are you going to be okay in the car, sprout?"

He asked this with a gruff note in his voice.

"How does Reggie know, do you think?"

She ignored Deke's question and stopped her pacing, standing in front of us, and her hands on her hips.

"Know what?" I squinted up at her.

"That we've been coming for him. You've never actually been able to tell him that's what we're doing…and yet he told you not to, and he told you to ditch me," she resumed her pacing.

Deke looked at me sidelong, judging what he should say.

"We think he's connected to you two, somehow. He called, yesterday, when we were at the tattoo parlor, told us everything had changed,"

"He called and you didn't tell me?!"

"He didn't say anything useful, Clara!" I stepped in, backing Deke up.

"But why didn't you tell me?!" Clara was nearing high pitched; Deke and I glanced around at the other frequenters of the park, seeing if anyone was paying undue attention to Clara's hysterics.

"Because it was another stupid useless call from Reggie, Clara, all mysterious and pointless, but he *does* want to meet up, so there's that,"

Clara stared at me, eyes flickering, and the sparks in her eyes became a storm behind her pupils.

"When?"

"He said he'd call,"

"Where?"

"I have to wait for the call, Clara," I tried to hush her, bring her back to reason.

Alternatively, she fumed, debating what to say.

"Honey, your Boston is showing," I told her flatly.

Deke snorted, and Clara's glare switched to him. He immediately shut his mouth, stifling a grin.

Clara huffed and spun away, moving to stomp off down the hill and away from us. Deke rose from the bench fluidly, and grabbed for her wrist, laughing as he did so.

His laugh quickly turned to gasps of pain as he yelped and pulled his hand back, dropping to his knees, and clutching his arm to his chest. I threw myself off the bench and knelt beside him, trying to figure out what was wrong.

"Clara, what'd you do?"

Deke had his eyes closed, hands covering his heart, taking quick and panicked breaths. She glanced down at her wrist, where the smouldering imprints of Deke's fingers burned red. I pulled Deke's hand away from his chest; his fingertips were red and blistered.

"It's just a little burn, Deke, are you okay?"

He gulped, his breathing finally returning to normal, high points of color on his cheeks. He shook his head, and fumbled with his sweater, pulling at it, pulling it off over his head. He pointed at the angry red lines that ran along his fingers, gathered at his wrist, running twisted along the path of his veins all the way up the inside of his arm, continuing up his bicep and under the sleeve of his t-shirt. He looked around feverishly for witnesses and then that too came off over his head. Kneeling there on the ground, shirtless, I could see what he meant.

The angry red path of fire followed up to his shoulder, and blossomed in a twisting nest of burns over his heart. I touched the knot, briefly, and Deke hissed. I had only ever seen pictures of this before. The roping twisted path that burned those who had been struck by lightning. Except he'd only touched Clara.

I helped him back into his shirt and sweater, avoiding looking at Clara, who was sulking a short distance away.

He sat down hard onto the ground and thought carefully,

"I think my heart stopped, for a second there, it was excruciating,"

"She electrocuted you! That's never happened before! Like I know you have this whole, energy thing going on, but you don't normal affect each other like that?"

Deke shrugged, staring off into space. He was gingerly rubbing at the space above his heart.

"Now I know how those guys back in Estes felt,"

His eyes focused on me, cloudy grey quicksilver in the shade.

"You did that to them?"

I blew on his fingertips, trying to calm the blistered skin. He shrugged and looked embarrassed.

Clara had moved on and settled onto a bench a little way away, and sat tapping her foot, legs crossed, and her arms crossed, and refusing to acknowledge us.

"You grew up with *that?*"

He grabbed onto the bench behind him and tried to pull himself up; I latched on to his bicep and helped. When he settled roughly down, he turned to look at me.

"How'd you get away with not being a complete lunatic? Between her, and Reggie, are you the only normal one?"

"I have my moments," I kept my voice low, not wanting Clara to hear us talking about her.

"Yeah but she, she's just, volcanic. All the time, ready to erupt," he shook his head at her.

I nodded in agreement, shrugging at the same time.

"You get used to people, used to their triggers, learn where you can push, so the whole thing doesn't come tumbling down like a tower of cards, she's so strong, but so fragile, it's hard to feel out her puncture points. I will admit though, whatever is wrong with you two, she is even more volatile now than before," I sighed.

Deke leaned back, eyes never leaving Clara's motionless form, miles away even though she was within shouting distance.

"I wish I knew what we had in common, why we both have this curse," his eyes flicked towards me for a moment, flashing in the dappled light coming down through the leaves of the massive tree above our heads.

"If wishes were horses, Deke," I tapped my nose and stood up, shouldering my pack.

He joined me, wincing as he lifted his and Clara's bags. I looked at him hard, always determined to be strong for our sakes. How is it that someone I've known for such a short amount of time could do so much for us?

I waited for him to go speak to her, their words muffled by the sounds of other people enjoying their lives, playing Frisbee, walking dogs, having picnic lunches. I sighed, looking at happiness, the unity, the community of it all.

I checked my watch, wondering how soon we could be off on our way. I ached to get this all resolved. If only so the two of them could go back to their normal lives, be happy.

Deke passed Clara her gear, and she stood up from where she sat. She suddenly surprised him, springing forward and hugging him tight around the middle, barely reaching his shoulder, but knocking him back on his heels anyway. He rested his chin on her head, patting her back, and looked at me.

I smiled.

Clara's apologies were few and far between, and they were something to be treasured, a pearl created from a long time irritation. Acknowledging she was wrong was always the hardest thing to get her to do, but I guess almost killing Deke qualified.

I turned away and headed up the gravel path towards the gates of the park, basking in the sun. Soon we'd be back on the road, hurtling towards the West Coast in our bright red comet, and the secrets it held on its shores.

As per our agreement, as twisted as the terms had become in the overnight and in the morning revelations, I drove the endless stretch of highway that spanned Salt Lake to Reno, where the light itself seemed to have turned red, and the flashing lights, when rising from the desert sand, hypnotized. Gunning across the empty desert, sometimes Deke's hands would twitch in the direction of the shifter, aching to drive the car again, put her through her paces. He knew I saw him do this, and I always rewarded him with a smile and a raised eyebrow.

I'd have gladly turned over the reins to him, if he'd admitted that he threw the poker game.

We passed a sign for Sparks, Nevada, and I laughed. The sound was jarring in the silence of the car. There becomes a point on every road trip, when words can no longer fill the space, and everyone involved just starts to exist, floating internally in their own bubbles.

"You guys would fit right in here," I smiled in the rear view at Clara, who promptly rolled her eyes.

At least, I assumed she did, I might have missed it between the flashes of street light glow.

Deke rubbed at his forearms, slowly and unaware of the flashing embers that were sparking off of his skin.

"Guess we got to get you guys somewhere alone soon, huh?" I made conversation, Deke's head swiveling dreamily towards me.

"Huh?" He blurted out.

I could only imagine that if it had been daylight, I would've seen his pupils constrict. He'd been really far away this time, and I wondered if his mind had been with his brother and the tale he told me this morning.

I reached across the gearbox and placed a hand on the knuckles of his right hand, which were still absently rubbing his left arm. I was rewarded with a violent blue flash between us, a strong static shock piercing the dark of the car. I yipped in response, and pulled my hand back. I didn't react as intensely as I wanted to - I felt I was getting used to the jolts I would get just from casually being near them.

"Oh, that, yeah, Clara? You too?"

He swiveled in his seat to look back at her, and she nodded, rubbing her forefinger and thumb together, cascading power down onto her palm.

"Will you be good, until we get through Reno?"

They both shrugged, and I felt the pressure of responsibility pushing down on me once more. Could these two even try to care about what they were doing? What they were doing to me? What they could do to me, or someone else, if they just stopped caring?

Upon entering the city, Clara and Deke were mesmerized, noses pressed to the glass, as I navigated the throngs of people crowding the sidewalks and stumbling across the streets. It was late, the pedestrians intoxicated and the air was buzzing. Heads turned as we passed by, the car no longer able to hide as it had when we'd driven across the plains and through the empty mountains, void of traffic or really anything to mark the time by. I could feel the rumble of the engine reverberating back at me off the walls and windows that pressed in.

I hoped the doors were locked.

I stopped at a light, as an intense wave of anxiety washed over me, and I was overwhelmed by a crawling sensation up my back, the vibrating sensation in my teeth that always came with completely losing my cool. I kept looking in the rear view mirror at Clara, and Deke beside me, contemplating their rigid forms – unmoving and unresponsive to anything but the mass of people outside.

"Deke, what is it?" I muttered low, trying to attract his attention without any interest from Clara.

When his head finally jerked towards me, I could see his pupils had dilated, full and round and I felt he was seeing right through me.

"Shit,"

I took a quick look at the traffic around, and gunned it forward, slipping between a gap in cars traveling at the cross of the intersection, the sounds of horns blasting around me and adding to the confusion. Pedestrians shrieked and pulled their friends out of the way as I sped through the cross streets, trying to get away from the area.

Most respectable businesses were closed this time of night, bars shooing out the last of the crowd, the stragglers who took their time at last call, and I turned down a darkened side street, devoid of wanderers. The roaring engine echoed here, absent of the muffle of music and voices.

Deke hadn't taken his eyes off me this entire time.

I pulled the car to the curb, twisted the keys, and jumped out of the car, slamming the door in Deke's face as he lunged forward.

My heart pounded as I backed away and saw him scrambling for the handle, it would be mere seconds before he was out and after me. I looked for somewhere to run to, to lock myself inside but only darkened doorways to low-rise apartment buildings surrounded me.

It was then that I realized I'd left Clara in the car, trapped in the backseat.

Deke didn't seem to notice, or care though, as he'd managed to find the handle, and kicked open the door. I could hear Clara screaming at him to stop, suddenly at full volume when the door burst open.

I turned and ran, heart pounding, dodging the cracks in the sidewalk and trying desperately not to trip. One false step could be the end for me.

I could hear his pounding feet behind me, the thud of his sneakers on the pavement mirroring the rapid beating of my heart.

I found a parked car, and veered to the side, suddenly changing direction and putting the bulk of the sedan between Deke and I.

He stopped, dead, and put his hands on the hood, calculating the direction I'd head in, his eyes wild.

Where was Clara?

I was panting hard, not used to sprinting, not for my life, and flashbacks of my nightmares came back to me.

"Deke, don't, don't," I whipped my head around, looking for Clara, hoping she'd come to my rescue, that she wasn't too far gone that she'd understand what was happening, make it stop, as Deke had done for her.

Deke crackled, every pore flaring in the dark street. He leapt up onto the hood, taking steady steps across the bending metal and up over the roof, the leisurely pace of a large cat keeping me paralyzed in my tracks. I shook my head and I backed off, looking for somewhere else to hide.

That was when the engine burned its sound into my ears, accelerating angrily down the street, and I stumbled backwards, allowing the car to pass between Deke and I, grappling for the passenger side door and throwing it open, diving in just as he grabbed for the driver door, Clara behind the wheel. She floored the pedal; smoke spinning from the wheels, wrenching the handle from Deke's grasping hand, and his body rattled along the side of the car as we shot off. I looked back in the side mirror, seeing Deke on the ground, clutching his hand.

"You have to go back; you have to stop him, what if he sees someone else? Goes after them?" I shrieked at Clara.

She was gripping the steering wheel tightly, knuckles white. We'd gone several blocks by now, the lights changing in our favour, and she slammed to a stop.

"Get out, I'm going, I'm going. Hide. Just in case,"

I clutched at her wrist, momentarily, her eyes didn't meet mine, but I was rewarded with a snap of energy, and jumped out of the car, slamming the door. I stood in the center of the abandoned road, and watched her tail lights flare in the distance, devil eyes in the darkness.

I looked for a place to hide, and prayed that Clara wasn't too late.

Too much time had passed. They had to be done by now, they had to be back to their normal selves. I couldn't be abandoned here, they couldn't be hunting me. I was hyperventilating, hidden inside an enormous plastic tube that was part of an immense playground structure I had discovered down a side street. I gripped my knees to my chest, unable to control my breathing. I rocked slightly, straining my ears for any sound, the crunching of gravel under shoe, the call of my name, anything.

Shattering the darkness and the quiet of the neighbourhood, my phone began to ring.

The lilting voices of AC/DC and the opening notes of Thunderstruck felt like they had stopped my heart, and I scrambled to pull it from my pocket.

"Addy,"

Reggie's voice, calm and collected came from the other end as I thumbed the answer key.

I struggled to control my voice,

"Reggie, yeah, not a good time, can't talk right now," my whisper barely controlled into the mouthpiece.

I looked out through the pattern of holes in the sides of the tube, looking for the flash of eyes.

"Sounds like. Are you alright?"

There was a note of concern in his voice I wasn't expecting, not after all the phone calls I'd gotten from him leading up to now.

"No. Yes. I don't know. What do you want Reggie?" I resisted the urge to scream at him.

234

"I assume you're almost here, meet me at Dizzy Moon Pizza, in Half Moon, come at sunset if you can, and come alone,"

"If I live that long," I muttered in response, still frantically twisting my head to see both ends of the tunnel.

"Seriously, Addy, are you ok?" Reggie seemed to be taking my responses more seriously now, an edge to his question.

"Is it Clara?"

"For once, no, just, it's fine. If I can get there I will get there, ok?"

Reggie cleared his throat, and I could tell he wanted to ask more questions about what was going on, but I had already felt I had been too loud, talking too long on the phone, they were sure to find me.

"Be safe," his parting comment rang in my ears, louder than the dial tone that followed.

I thumbed the phone off and struggled with the tears of panic threatening to spill from my eyes.

Deke crouched down in front of the entrance to the tunnel, and I shrieked, throwing myself backwards toward the other exit.

"No, no, no!"

"Hey, Addy, no, no, it's fine, it's me, I promise," he called over my panicked retreat.

He knelt down and waited for me to recover. I collapsed on my back, hand to my heart, and flung an arm over my eyes, breathing shallowly, the air not wanting to fill my lungs.

I could hear him over my wheezing, trying to navigate his tall form into the tunnel, cursing children in the process. I heard his head hit the roof of the curve more than once, a loud thud that reverberated through the thick plastic.

"Shove over, shh, shh, it's fine, move over," I heard his voice quiet and calming.

I shuffled my shoulders and hips sideways as best I could, the tube not quite wide enough for the both of us. He stretched out beside me, warm heat when I hadn't noticed how cold it was in the pre-dawn, hidden inside this playground equipment. I couldn't look at him. This was a nightmare I wasn't willing to see.

He wrapped an arm under my neck, and the other around my shoulder, and pulled me close, rolling me towards him, my face buried in his collar. He quietly shushed me, encouraging me to breathe. He stroked my hair and back, and I slowly felt my pulse return to normal.

"I'm sorry," I could feel the words more than hear them, just the rumble in his chest and throat.

"You promised," I choked out, fresh wave of tears dampening his sweater.

The terror was too raw for his apology. I had thought the attack from Clara had been horrible, but somehow this had been worse. We thought we had beaten it, but we had made a critical error somewhere along the line and I didn't know what to do about it.

He remained voiceless, all of his attention focused on soothing, calming, banishing the chill and the fear of the night.

Chapter 16

Dizzy Moon

We sat in Sacramento, breakfast pushed around our plates, faces white and numb.

I stabbed half-heartedly at my bowl of oatmeal, the thought of anything less bland bringing bile to my throat.

Clara's eyes were red rimmed, as were mine. She sniffed occasionally, her unnatural hunger not even helping her to finish the food she had ordered.

Deke was silent, staring out the window, and it was difficult to see his expression behind the glasses, the bright light shining through the plate glass.

The remainder of the drive here had been quiet, I had relinquished the wheel to Clara, and had chosen to remain in the backseat of the car, alone, unable to meet their eyes, and stared at the bleak scenery around us.

Everything had changed to vast forests of pine trees and scrubby vegetation, and every mile had looked the same, the hills and mountains spanning in every direction.

I figured I had been quiet long enough, we were already starting to get strange looks for our disheveled and heckled appearances, but the complete silence was making some of the other patrons nervous.

"Reggie called. We're to meet. Well, I'm to meet him, tonight, at sunset, alone," I finally confessed.

Clara gaped, startled by the breaking of the quiet.

"Why alone?"

Clara asked, guarded. I glared at her, once, then averted my eyes.

"Probably because he knows what you are, and doesn't want one of you around him," I spooned another mouthful of oatmeal into my mouth, daring her to question my assumption.

Clara leaned forward and hissed, tapping an angry finger on the table,

"Hey, I saved you last night; you could be a little less obnoxious right now,"

"Oh what, now I *owe* you?"

"That's not what, I, ugh!"

She sat back angrily, arms crossed.

Deke looked at Clara, then at me, and then went back to staring out the window.

"Reggie wants just me, deal with it, it wasn't my choice,"

I sat back too, matching her posture. There were flares of pink high on her cheeks, frustration and anger wrestling in her eyes.

"So what are *we* supposed to do?"

She huffed.

I wiped at my face, shaking my head at the table.

"For one thing, pay attention to your little *problems* and make sure they don't get out of control, so that someone doesn't get *hurt*," I gritted through my teeth.

I could see Deke's jaw clench and I didn't regret what I said.

"And find somewhere to stay, so that when we are done with Reggie, I can sleep for a week before I fly my ass back home, and forget about all of this ever happening,"

I ran my hand through my hair uneasily. Deke turned to look at me again. I could see his hands shaking on the table, and he quickly moved them where I couldn't see them anymore.

Clara blustered, no actual words coming from her lips, and then the table was silent once more.

Deke was the first to break the uneasy quiet that had fallen over us.

"We'll do whatever you say, Addy. I know apologies aren't worth the dirt on your boots anymore, but no matter what happens, you know deep down that you need us just as much as we need you, don't ever forget that," he uttered calmly, before rising from the table and straightening his jacket, tapping his finger tips on the table and heading for the exit.

I inhaled deeply and squeezed my eyes shut momentarily, pinching at the bridge of my nose. When I opened them again, Clara was shaking her head,

"You know, if all this with Reggie turns out to be a complete bust, you'll have to forgive at least one of us, you'll be completely alone otherwise," her mouth pressed into a firm line.

"What makes you think I'm not completely alone now?" I pushed my chair back, and followed Deke outside, where he sat quietly on the hood of the car, waiting for us to follow.

"Are you sure you're going to be alright?" Deke looked past me, doubtfully, at the dark windows of the restaurant. I followed his gaze and shrugged.

I looked hard at the concern in his eyes. He'd taken off the glasses, and he squinted up at me. He put a hand on mine where it sat on the sill of the car window, and gave it a small squeeze. His hand was overly warm, but it didn't sear the healing blisters. He looked sad, and he looked like he had more to say. We'd all spent the afternoon in silence, checking into a motel nearby, and had dozed, or read, waiting for sunset. I had been nervous, when I wasn't sleeping I had been pacing, and Clara's nerves had been shot. Deke had offered to drive me here, alone, and I could see how hesitant he was to let me go.

I melted, briefly, wondering about other times and other places where all of this could have easily been very different.

"I'll call you, as soon as I know something," I smiled grimly, and gave his hand one last squeeze.

I stepped back and watched him pull away, the red light of the sunset lighting the windows of the car on fire, the purr of the engine disappearing around the corner with him.

Everything felt very empty in that moment.

I swung back towards the restaurant and contemplated it.

I sighed deeply, and headed between the neighbouring buildings to the alley and parking at the rear.

The door behind Dizzy Moon Pizza was five steps down from ground level. The usual flotsam filled the doorstop area, the kind of things you only find in neglected corners of towns, last year's fall leaves, abandoned paper coffee cups, and a dirty water logged tennis shoe. I could never understand abandoned shoes; I always took note of them – the side of the road, strung up from telephone wires, hidden in ditches and gutters. How does one lose their shoe, and never retrieve it? What terrible thing happened to its owner that they continued on, one barefoot tramping through the elements?

I was clearly delirious. I cautiously moved down the stairs, studying the rust stained metal of the door, the hinges heavy, the handle sticky looking with decay. I could feel the bottom dropping out of my stomach, sickening and dizzy. After all this, what do I even say? What if he isn't even there? I steadied myself, and knocked on the door, firmly, but gently, as flakes of rust scattered down in my knuckles wake.

I looked around, blinking in the sunlight suddenly streaming from between the buildings. The sun was setting, the light a brilliant orange reflecting off the pizza parlor. The solitary cloud that had been casting its gloom had finally scuttled onward. I could hear the traffic steadily passing by from the main road, even at this hour, when most people would have been at home, finishing dinner, putting the kids to bed. I could hear movement, beyond the door, deadbolts sliding back, clicks coming from inside the door itself.

The door opened a crack, a suspicious green-gold eye and the firm curve of a mouth all I could see as I peered through. I blinked at the face staring back at me. It was always vaguely numbing, seeing his face after a long period of time, seeing mine staring back, the jaw more square, the nose longer, the freckles darker, but definitely one and the same. He slammed the door. I rolled my eyes. I knocked again, this time more aggressively, smacking the palm of my hand against the decay.

"Hang on, hang on," I heard Reggie muttering through the metal, could hear him fumbling with another catch and lock.

He pulled the door open wide, and took a half step out. I opened my arms to hug him, but he side stepped my embrace and looked up and down the alley behind me. I took the opportunity in his moment of distraction to study him.

His face was haggard, and had deep purple bruising under his eyes, he looked like he hadn't slept in weeks. His hair, a dark and curly auburn, normally tamed by being short and closely cropped, was heading towards wild and unruly, falling across his forehead and curling against the back of his neck. He was dressed simply, in a worn blue t-shirt and tattered jeans that hung loosely from his frame. He must not have been eating right, or at all.

He chose at that moment to seize me by the elbow and pull me through the door. I hadn't a moment to adjust my eyes to the dim subterranean room beyond before he had a pen flashlight shining directly into my eyes, inspecting one, then the other, the ghost of the light imprinted in my vision.

"What the Hell Reggie, seriously"

I blinked furiously, eyes tearing up. He gave me a quick hug, hard around my ribs, and as I returned it, I could feel how bony his back and shoulders had become. He gripped my shoulders and held me at arm's length, giving me a once over and nodding to himself grimly.

"Thanks for stopping by," he smiled crookedly, turning away from me, shaking his head, muttering under his breath, as he locked the many locks and bolts that lined the entrance door.

He then turned and began heading down a long corridor. It was dimly lit and grimy, the only light coming in through tiny basement windows, half covered in dirt and leaves streaking across the glass. I watched him cautiously, keeping a fair distance between us. Though he seemed skinny and under-fed, he remained confidently tall and broad-backed, posture he had always held no matter what he felt. Mother had never abided poor posture.

One of his hands was clenching and unclenching, whether consciously or not, fingers stretching and curling, seemingly with the flow of his continued muttering as he strode along. We had come to another door, and he rapidly worked through the locks and bolts, at one point pulling a key off a chain he had hidden beneath his shirt collar and inserting it into a lock at the very top of the door frame.

It was then that I noticed the symbols, Deke's symbols, were scrawled and etched fully around the door frame. I glanced around and realized the windows were also marked the same. This was a safe house from the Collectors, and Reggie knew the signs.

He swung open the door, and gestured for me to precede him across the threshold. I shot him a quick glance for reassurance, but he was looking studiously at the floor.

This room was more brightly lit, a bank of desks down the right side, each holding a landline and a computer, all facing the door. Anyone sitting at the computers could see every person who entered this room, and all five of the workspaces were full. To the left was a small kitchenette, and a smattering of mismatched furniture, an overstuffed and stained couch, a pair of garishly coloured armchairs, and an assortment of differently sized dining room chairs, all gathered loosely around milk crates serving as a coffee table. Books lined the wall, a number of bookcases crammed to the breaking point under the heavy tomes. Each of the faces behind the work stations were staring up at me, all similarly hollow-eyed as Reggie, all looking incredibly suspicious, and not the least bit welcoming.

I felt incredibly self-conscious under their direct glare, and looked to Reggie for an explanation. I could see a trace of the old Reggie scrawled across his face, as a hint of a smile curved at his lips. He knew I hated attention, and was clearly savouring the moment. Just like old times.

"Addy, this motley assortment of exhausted looking people, are the rogue Tenders," he swept his hand in a flourish at them.

A scrawny looking blonde woman second from the end raised her eyebrow at Reggie, and returned to her work. The others held my gaze a moment longer, and then flicked back to what they had been doing. A man at the back, tall even from where I could see him, feet up on the desk, had remained on the phone during the entirety of the introduction, speaking quietly and continuing to stare at me. Rogue *Tenders*? I thought; my mind wheeling. But that was what the Collector had called Deke's minder, the woman who had dragged him out of the bar so many weeks ago, the woman who had shown him how to heal when Dezi had attacked. What did he mean? Tenders? The man closest to Reggie stood up and came around the desk, interrupting my thoughts, pushing his glasses further up his nose, and extending a hand towards me.

"Connor, wonderful to meet you," he smiled broadly, eyes lighting up.

He was a little shorter than Reggie, and by default, a little shorter than me, a wrinkled button-up thrown carelessly over a t-shirt and jeans, his sandy hair standing up in all directions, he must have spent a lot of his time thinking, running his hands anxiously through it. He continued looking back and forth between us, and when he determined that Reggie wasn't going to interject, he continued,

"Reggie's been keeping us updated on your progress, we're glad to have you with us,"

He smiled again, toothy. I realized that beneath the tired purple under his eyes, he also had quite the shiner, turning green and mottled beneath the frame of his glasses.

"I'm Reggie's second in command in this little venture," he gestured at the people behind us, who were studiously pretending to ignore our conversation.

Except for the man at the back, who was not even trying to hide his interest in the introductions. I stared at him, trying to focus on the dull ping of familiarity that rang out when I studied him. I suddenly realized what Connor had said,

"Second in command?" I repeated, confused.

Connor nodded vigorously. Reggie sighed and rolled his eyes, and beckoned for us to follow him. At the back of the room was a small door, previously meant for a utilities closet, but as he opened it to let us in, I realized had been converted to a small and cramped office, fitting only three chairs and a desk. The desk was piled high with maps and paperwork, scraps of notes and candy wrappers.

There was no room to get behind the desk on either side, but Reggie deftly climbed with practiced ease, up and over, foot finding the only true bare spot on the desk and settled down into his chair, which rattled against the shelves behind him. Connor took the chair farthest from the door, and gestured for me to sit. When I settled into the seat, Connor and I were so close that our knees knocked, and he fixed me again with his lunatic grin.

Reggie leaned forward on the desk with his elbows, rubbing at his face. I had done the same motion many times over the past few days, and I hadn't realized it was something that we shared.

"So, you're here. Where's Clara?"

He stopped what he was doing abruptly and looked at me dead in the eye. I glanced at Connor and then looked back.

"I left her, with someone, back at the motel, they're safe," I started cautiously. Reggie snorted in response.

"Safe? You think she's safe? You think *they* are safe? You've got a ticking bomb sitting in your room and you think she's safe? You have no idea, Addy, what the Hell is going on here,"

He started shuffling papers on the desk, absently blending them into unorganized piles. He was refusing to meet my eyes, but seemed to be biting back another scathing comment. I stared at him defiantly. He had no idea what I had been through, what we had been through, without him and his team and he was laughing at me?

"Yes, Reggie, she's safe. We marked her, the same as you have around your door, whatever those are, and she's safe. At least as basic a definition as you can have for the word. There have been some hiccups along the way, I won't deny it, but ever since, all we've been doing is trying to find you, and wherever the Hell you had run off to. Clearly you've been hiding from us what it is exactly you're doing here, so if you can cut the crap for two seconds and tell me, just give me some answers, I will take our baby sister out of your hair,"

I finished firmly, sitting back in the chair and crossing my arms. Reggie had gaped when I mentioned the marks, but eyes had grown steely when I mentioned the hiccups, eyes trailing from my throat to my hands, taking in the purple bruising and the angry blisters. He leaned forward in his seat, fingers digging into the edge of the desk.

"I know you know about the marks. And where did you get the marks? Who told you about those? Who *told her*? Let alone how they should be administered?"

He looked incredulously at Connor and then back at me.

Connor shrugged and shook his head. He pulled a small and dog-eared notebook from his shirt pocket and thumbed through it, and then shook his head again and looked to me. I looked at Reggie strangely. Why did it matter? Shouldn't he care if she was safe? That we were safe with him?

"You tell me what's going on here, Reggie, and I'll tell you, alright? Can we make a deal?" I leaned forward in the chair, daring him to make the next move.

He sat back, tapping on the desk. I could see Connor grinning out of the corner of my eye. Maybe he had completely lost it down here.

Reggie's eyes flicked to Connor, then back to me, and he stuttered out,

"Damn it, Connor, stop grinning like a damn fool over there, you'll have to help me fill it in," he sighed.

He pinched the bridge of his nose, the effort of talking was giving him a migraine.

"I'm sorry Reggie, seeing you get put in your place, let alone by someone who makes the same damn faces as you do when you're pissed, is beyond amazing, and I am sure she has the same mean right hook," he snorted, absently waving at his eye and pulled a pen from his pocket and sat with his notebook, patiently waiting. I smiled encouragingly at Connor, he was right about our matching right hooks, and turned back to Reggie.

Reggie took a deep breath,

"Alright, I guess I will start where it all took a turn for the worst. By now, you probably know, we were dead. That vacation was a terrible idea, from start to finish, and the finish, man, it was spectacular,"

My eyes narrowed at his jovial tone, but he only smiled apologetically, and continued,

"I know, I know, it was my idea to go, wasn't it? It doesn't matter. Three other people, actually, died as well. It was a real thunder-banger; no one should have been on the slopes that day. I broke my neck clean, when the snow hit, mangled up my insides pretty bad, didn't have a chance, I was down in those trees, remember? My snowboard had gotten tangled in a snare of bushes when I lost control,"

He was avoiding looking at me now, staring off above my head as he recited this horrible, terrible story.

I shook my head, no, I didn't remember.

"You, well, they figured if they'd gotten to you, maybe ten minutes sooner, you could've been fine, maybe, suffocated in the snow about thirty feet from the edge of the ravine. You could've dropped, too, but you didn't. No one ever would have found you. But they did,"

I shook my head back and forth – I knew his story must be true, but was astonished by how casual he was behaving.

But then again, he'd had time to deal with it, it wasn't new information to him.

"They called Clara, she hit the next flight out of Europe that she could, showed up for the identification, and escorted our bodies home," his jaw was set tightly, a vein under his eye was beginning to throb.

All I could think of was how horrible that must have been for Clara, why hadn't she told me? How could she keep that inside? Why hadn't she called Mother? Did Mother know any of this?

"She was devastated. She went through our funerals, the aftermath. She's a brave little toaster when she really needs to be, and I've always admired that, about Clara. She has focus, you know, when it really matters,"

I nodded. I was stunned. Poor Clara, I couldn't even imagine how she must have felt. How she must still feel, why wouldn't she tell me? Had she been hiding it from me? I realized now, that this could have been a process of over a week. How long were we gone?

"Ten days, that's all she lasted, without us," Reggie took a deep breath and looked me straight in the eye.

My hand went to my mouth to stifle the gasp that tried to escape. Reggie reached out and took the other that had flopped lamely to the desk.

"It's not what you think, she didn't hurt herself, well not the way you're thinking, hey," he patted my hand and then held it tight, reclaiming eye contact, shushing me gently.

He glanced at Connor, who was fixated on him with a hardened gaze. He spoke quietly,

"She did something much, much, infinitely worse,"

Connor nodded and stared down at his book, looking like he'd rather be anywhere else. I held my breath.

"Clara, she sold her soul, in order to bring us back. No memory of it, not for any of us, no idea what had ever happened, just a little trick, a shift in reality really,"

He released my hand and sat back, waiting for me to process what he had said as I gaped at him.

A million questions ran through my head. The most useless one floated to the top and made its way out,

"What?"

Chapter 17

Thunderstorms

Deke yawned and sat back on his stool. They'd managed to find a bar close to where Reggie had insisted Adeline meet him, alone. The lights were dim and the beer was cheap, and that's all that mattered to him. Dark and cheap meant that the locals were keeping to themselves, heads down, and the waitresses weren't too nosy, as long as you kept the orders coming.

They were sitting together at a high table near one of the corners, keeping their backs to the room as much as possible, Clara staring moodily into her beer. The position allowed them to remove their sunglasses without terrifying nearby patrons, the waitress too harried to pay attention. He didn't know Clara very well, but he knew people well enough to know that she was knee-deep to drunk, and steadily sinking, her cheeks a vibrant pink. The alcohol seemed to help deaden the ringing in their ears, the clanging settled to a dull buzz you could almost ignore if you didn't try too hard to think about it. He polished off his glass and checked his watch. Addy had been gone over an hour, and he wasn't sure if he should be worried or not yet.

The waitress cruised past their table, middle-aged and heavily make-upped, her cheeks matching Clara's in vivid colour. She raised a heavily drawn eyebrow and curved their way, pulled by the gravity of an unanswered request.

Clara smiled, and beckoned the waitress lean in. She muttered something into her ear, holding up two fingers, and waggling them for emphasis. The waitress smiled and nodded, flashing Deke a wink, and moved back towards the bar. Deke frowned at Clara. She seemed to be determined to pursue this bender, and he thought under the circumstances this was incredibly unwise.

"Don't you think we should keep our wits about us? What if Addy calls, needs us quick?" Deke quietly asked.

They both glanced at the dark cell phone sitting in the centre of the table. Not a beep or flash had come from it after they let Adeline know where they had gone to wait for her. Clara rolled her eyes, leaning her chin on her hand.

"Deke, Deke, dude, come on. Addy has this, she's gotten our sorry asses this far, she's fine," she drawled out, her I's becoming long and rude in the slur.

Her lips curved up in one corner, crooked, a sly grin plastering her face. She took another gulp of her beer. How many had it been? She flapped her hand at him and leaned forward.

"You, darling, have not met Reggie," she winked and hiccupped.

She giggled at the hiccup, and then seemed to sober momentarily. She brought her voice down to a conspiratorial whisper, so that Deke had to match her lean and incline his head towards her.

"Reggie is a God damned super hero," she suddenly threw her head back and cackled.

Deke didn't see the hilarity of her statement and grinned uneasily, glancing towards the bar to see if they were being watched, unsure what to make of her declaration. It was at that moment that their waitress returned, bearing a tray of four pairs of shot glasses, each holding a different shade of dark liquor. Clara clapped her hands and thanked the waitress profusely, whose smile broadened as she took her leave.

"Clara, don't even think about it," he admonished, giving her a warning look up from under his brows.

He reached for her wrist, but hesitated; afraid their lightning would make an unwelcome appearance when they touched. Memories of the park in Salt Lake City flashed through his head. It wasn't an experience that he wanted to repeat. She leaned forward, smiling ear to ear, and raised the first glass,

"If you don't help me, I will drink these all myself, and then you'll hear *all* about it. Probably from Addy, most definitely from *Reggie*," she clipped at Reggie's name as it came out, biting and sarcastic.

Deke frowned, from what Addy had told him so far, Clara idolized Reggie, this mocking tone was new and he wasn't sure where it was coming from. He looked at the shots again, mentally trying to prepare himself for what inevitably would end badly. He reached for a glass and picked it up gingerly, hesitantly. Clara murmured, barely above the music pouring from the speakers over their heads,

"Four Horsemen are coming for us Deke, bottoms up, freak show," she winked and tossed it back.

She coughed and wiped at her eyes, and sat looking at him, waiting patiently. He sighed, and knocked it back, the warmness spreading down his throat and into his belly, a reassuring weight where once had only been an anxious knot, Johnny Walker taking its place.

Connor cleared his throat, and with a nod from Reggie, took over,

"The Tenders find it easier to deal with their Charges, when the Charges don't know what they've done, cuts out the middle man bargaining, stops them from trying to trade their soul back and get out of the deal," he pushed his glasses up his nose. I stared at him.

What the Hell was he saying?

"You make the deal, reality shifts, you get taken for Conversion, and then you get released. Unsuspecting world gets one more rampaging murderer, Hell gets one more source of incoming souls with every kill," I made a sound in my throat, strangled it, but allowed him to continue.

"With your soul locked down, it's being prepped for Hell, with these horrible and malicious murders. All that you have left is your spark of humanity, so each and every kill is designed to make it weaker and weaker, until finally, you burn out, the Collectors can come for you; take you down and out, hands clean. They just keep making deals; just keep pushing them through, it's like a factory, they're only turning out product," he tapped his pen at the page he had turned to in his book while he was speaking.

"We find on average, most Charges last, maybe, ten weeks? Before they're ready for Harvest, depending on the strength of their soul and the remainder of their humanity,"

Reggie nodded, slowly but disapprovingly at Connor. I looked back and forth between the two. I choked out,

"This is our little *sister* you're talking about?! What is wrong with you?"

I looked to Reggie for any sign of remorse. He didn't look at me. I wasn't sure I liked Connor anymore.

"So what, they're just going to come for her when she's down for the count? That easy?"

I was borderline hysterical. How could Reggie not have told us? Why had he left, when he knew how this was all going to go down? Reggie reached across the desk and grabbed the corner of a large book, water stained, pages browned and dirty, and pulled it over. It looked ancient. He thumbed through until he found what he was looking for. He turned it around and showed me.

"Are these the marks on Clara?"

They were the same as we had marked around the doorframes of my house, the same that Deke had carved into our bodies, and the same they had tattooed back in Boston and I in Salt Lake City. How had he found them? I nodded, waiting.

"Are they just tattooed? Or did you scratch them into her skin as well?"

I nodded again,

"Marked and carved, yes, they look just like that,"

I twisted in my seat, pulling up on my shirt, revealing the marks etched into my body. Both Reggie and Connor jumped.

"What did you say?"

Connor leaned in, taking a better look, while Reggie asked me to say it again. I repeated, eyebrow raised,

"Mark and carve?"

The colour drained from Connor's face, and he flipped rapidly through his tiny notebook. He mumbled as he read to himself from a list I could barely read, scratched down in his book.

"Here," he pointed, showing me the book.

Deacon Masterson, Boston, April 4th.

Deacon? *Deke?*

Clara leaned on Deke heavily, conspiratorially, arm around his shoulders. He hadn't been this drunk in a long time, his head stuffy, and the music beginning to grate on his ears. Clara hadn't stopped at the first round of shots, and he had stopped counting after the fifth or sixth Jose had washed down his throat.

"You know what, Deke, you're good, you're a good guy, and what'd you do, huh? What'd you do to deserve this? Huh?"

Her lips were inches from his ear, but he just didn't have the energy to push her away.

He stared dully into the corner of the bar, head swimming, swaying slightly. She leaned closer, he could actually *feel* her lips touching his ear now, the fine hairs tickling from her breath, and he blinked, trying to keep his eyes open. He knew he hadn't slept much in the past few weeks, if at all, but it had never really hit him this badly until now.

If he were to end up horizontal at this very moment, even to put his head on his folded arms, he'd be down for the count. He settled for trying to concentrate on what Clara was saying.

"I know what I did Deke, I know, I know, I know" her voice contorted into a whine, and she pulled away, lapsing into tears, throwing her head down into her arms.

He couldn't hear her over the music, but he could see her shaking with her sobs. Did she say what he thought she said? She remembered? He exerted what he felt was a great effort, pulled her shoulders towards him, shaking her,

"Look at me, Clara, right now, look at me," she shook her head, his vision doubling and then settling, but she was pulling away from his hands, fighting to get out of his grasp.

Sparks were beginning to glint between his fingers, and he let her go, the sudden absence of his grip as she pulled back causing her to over balance backwards, sprawling on the floor.

He blinked rapidly, too stunned to react, the entirety of the bar staring at them. Deke stumbled to his feet, the ground swaying ominously beneath him, and waved a hand at the other patrons, giving them a thumbs up and flashing what he hoped was a reassuring grin,

"C'mon Clara, c'mon, get up here," he slurred, stooping down and pulling her arm over his shoulder, unsteadily propping her to standing, wavering as he fought to control his and her balance.

The waitress stood by, impatiently, hand on her hip. He could see that their stay had become unwelcome, and he fumbled with his free hand for the cash in his pocket, pressing it into the waitress's hands as he passed by, half carrying Clara as she stumbled along, making their way past staring faces to the door.

"Do you know that name?" Connor asked again.

I suddenly paused, wondering how much I should tell them. Whose side were they on, anyway? I remembered what Reggie had said out in the work area, and ignoring Connor, I pointed at Reggie and asked,

"Rogue Tenders. You said you were Rogue Tenders, what does that mean?"

I crossed my arms again against a sudden chill that ran through my body.

Reggie cleared his throat,

"We were chosen, by Collectors, due to our, well, unique skill set, and we mind the Charges. Make sure they're getting their uh, assignments, following them, make sure they know how to heal, prompt them to kill, we uh, we Tend them until they are ripe for the Collectors to pick 'em,"

I cringed away from him. What was he saying? That he pushed these people towards their final damnation when they've lost their souls? Helped hurry them off to Hell? What kind of monster had my brother become?

"But, we, a small group of us, couldn't do it anymore. It ached, in our hearts, it was so wrong. These people don't deserve to burn, don't deserve to suffer, for a moment of deep-seated need, so we've, well, we've gone off the grid, gone away to where hopefully none of the Collectors or other Tenders can find us, and we have been trying to find a way to help people get away from it," he gestured around at the office and the paperwork strewn across his desk.

They did what?

Reggie seemed nervous now, and kept looking to Connor for reassurance. Connor nodded at him again, only a small smile on his face. Reggie began rolling up his shirt sleeve at the shoulder, and Connor followed suit, shrugging out of his button-down and rolling up his t-shirt sleeve.

They both sported matching tattoos, the same as all of us in the freak show, their skin raised and scarred next to it where they had etched the saviour letters into their skin. Theirs however, were angry red, rather than glittering silver, not healed by the powers that Deke and Clara yielded.

Reggie nodded,

"It was Deacon, wasn't it? He showed you the symbols, didn't he, Addy? Were you travelling with him? Here? Is that who Clara is with right now?"

I flicked my eyes to their tattoos again. I sighed, there was no point in trying to hide it. Connor evidently had a list of some sort, of who knew about the marks, and I couldn't get away from it. I nodded. Reggie grinned triumphantly, Connor's face mirroring his response.

"I knew it! Reggie, do you know what this means?"

Connor leapt up and squeezed past my chair, and quickly left the room, the frame rattling slightly when he closed the door behind him. I could hear excited chatter from the room beyond, a number of voices calling over each other to be heard. Reggie's face returned to its former seriousness, I could practically hear the gears whirring as he thought about what to say next.

"Reggie, how do you know who Deke is?" I asked, carefully, studying his face.

He shrugged non-committedly, and hesitated. I could see his hand was still spasming, clutching and releasing the edge of the desk. He hid it well, but I found it distracting, what had caused it?

He saw where I was looking, not really at his face. He held his hand in front of him, watching it tremble slightly, finger tips itching.

"Sometimes, when deals are made, to bring people back, the forces of darkness aren't quite adept at... putting the broken things back together again. You can only fix something so many ways before the edges don't quite meet up anymore, haven't you noticed anything different about yourself since you've been back?"

A sudden realization crossed my mind. I'd been a stumbling fool, tripping, slipping, and accidentally cutting myself. I'd never been that way. I'd always been graceful. I had assumed it had something to do with Deke or Clara, and while it did have something to do with Clara, it wasn't in the way that I thought. I frowned and rubbed my face. This was all getting out of control. Who could ever believe all this?

"But if they change things, put them back to the way they were, why were the articles online? Why do I have an obituary? Why were we able to find out all about dying?"

"Well there's the thing. They aren't very good at this. They've been doing it for thousands for years, but in all, the story telling of death in a permanent way, on the Internet, is relatively new. Granting a soul's wish is just a stop-gap before the Charge dies. It's not that we didn't die, that never changed. We just are no longer dead. Have you tried contacting work lately? They just never know you ever even existed,"

The thought struck me hard. I hadn't been at work. I hadn't even thought of work. What had I even been doing this whole time? How was I going to put my life back together?

I took a steadying breath. One problem at a time. I turned back to the problem at hand.

"So tell me, Reggie, please. How do you know Deke?"

"I don't, not really," he began.

Deke pulled and guided Clara outside of the bar. She was stumbling and maniacally wavering between two extremes, sobbing and crying "I know" and just as quickly lapsing into laughing, even cackling, and he wasn't sure which frightened him more.

The air had grown close, and heavy with static. A chill wind was kicking and whirling by, the scent of rain thick on it. They had made it halfway down the street when she pulled away from him, catching herself against the rough brick of the building and scuffing her hands. She felt her way along to the corner, and moved into the dark shadows of the alley. He removed his glasses and followed her. The shadows in the alley were deep, and he'd need every extra sense he had. He didn't know what she was doing, where she was going, and he wish he was sober enough to get a straight answer out of her. What did she remember? Would she remember again, once she had dried up?

He debated calling Addy, get her to come save him from her sister and her drunken antics. It seemed that the only logical solution right now would be to just keep her safe as he could. She had drunk him under the table, and he was at a loss for dealing with her hysterics. He blinked, trying to adjust his eyes to the sudden darkness, leaning heavily against the wall. There she was. Clara was propped up against the wall herself, head back, staring up at the sky peeking between the rooftops of the two buildings. She had gone strangely quiet. Her eyes were reflecting some far off light in their mirrored irises.

"Deke," she said softly, low in her throat.

He could barely hear her from where he was standing. He waited patiently for her to continue, his brain still warm and blanketed, the ringing quieted from the effects of the alcohol, but deep down he knew this was too important to forget, and focused on her voice.

"They were dead, Deke. They left me, they left me with *her*," she gritted her teeth, pounding a fist into the brick against her back.

Her skin was beginning to glow, low levels of electricity snapping across her arms, cascading down her neck. Deke glanced nervously to the entrance of the alley. All it would take was one person, the wrong person, to look down the alley and see her. Her eyes caught his, pleading. She inhaled deeply, staring back up at the sky. Deke moved closer, making soft shushing noises, what he only imagined you'd use on a skittish horse or a frightened dog, trying to sooth her so she wouldn't attract any attention.

Stumbling drunk was one thing; lighting up a back alley with her own body was completely different. She wiped at her face, a strange keening sound was escaping her, what she wanted to say was too terrible to form into words.

"Clara, tell me, just tell me, we'll make it better," she focused on him again, eyes flashing, the storm behind them flickered; he paused his hushing, stopped moving towards her, afraid of being hit with the heart-stopping flare she had attacked him with in Salt Lake City.

"I gave it all up, to get them back, I needed them, I needed them *here, here with me,*" her lip trembled, tears running down her face, reflecting the glittering from her eyes.

She was so scared, just a scared little girl, and his heart was breaking for her.

"What'd you give up, Clara? What'd you do?"

He moved closer, mere inches away, trying to get her to focus on what she was telling him, rather than letting her emotions take over the situation.

When he kept her talking, she focused on her words and the lightning faded.

Clara whispered,

"I gave them my soul,"

"You're joking," I looked at Reggie incredulously.

He smiled grimly in response, and then tapped the side of his nose. It was our sign, as kids, for dead serious, when a story seemed too fantastical for words, and Mother had told us to quit playing around. How many silent cues did we have? How many inside jokes, secret codes? And now all of this, on top of everything, Reggie, was psychic.

He had been, for years, and the tumblers in my head slowly fell into place.

Every game of hide and seek, no matter where I hid, he found me quickly and easily. The times he had shown up at my dorm room, coffees in hand, late at night, when I was close to the breaking point over exams, or boys, or Mother. He never had to be called, never needed to be asked. Sometimes he would just absently leave the house and come back with a weeping Clara, who had fallen from her bike several blocks away, or knocked her head on the monkey bars at the park down the street.

And not too long ago, he was recruited by the East coast faction of the Tenders for his connection to the fresh Charges in the area. The Tenders, as a group, were the voices in the heads of hundreds of people, just like Deke, just like Clara, that convinced them to kill. And they could do it from anywhere, from work, the park, the comfort of their own bed. They just waited for the signs, and off they went, adding their overwhelming voices until their broke their Charge, and they were ready for harvest.

Until the accident happened, and Reggie could finally be free.

His death had broken his connection with the Collectors long enough for him to get the tattoo and leave the field, but he couldn't just leave these people to suffer with their uncontrollable powers.

Reggie was sitting on the edge of the desk now, on my side, looking at me carefully. It was too much for me to take in, too many questions fought on the tip of my tongue.

"Before I left, to come out here, I contacted as many people as I could, gauging interest, relaying them the consequences. There are so many Tenders, they didn't notice most of us going missing, at first, but here we all are, fighting what we can only hope is the good fight," he smiled wearily.

"Deacon, Deke as you call him, we had gotten his name from a mole we have who is still working with the Tenders in Boston, Deke was incredibly strong, working incredibly fast, and had tangible feelings of guilt, we could all feel it even from all the way out here. The mole thought if it was going to work for anybody, it'd have to work for him. We figured he was a prime candidate for our new program. That we could apply what we knew had saved us from the Collectors and the Tenders, and see if it affected someone who had already gone through Conversion, and a rough one at that,"

I beamed. It all made sense now. Reggie had orchestrated, somehow, Deke's escape from the life he had been leading. He had been tracking our progress, through me, using his psychic powers, until Salt Lake City. Once I had gotten the flirty red head to tattoo the last half of the spell onto my body, the signal cut out, and he had had to call me to reconnect.

"How'd you do it Reggie? How did you get the message to him?"

Reggie's face clouded.

He frowned and then bit his lip. His eyes unfocused and his breathing became rapid. His whole body became rigid where he sat, the hand spasm becoming more pronounced, a spider on the desk, drumming a staccato rhythm. I held my breath, watching as his pupils dilated, the green entirely gone. I gripped his arm, afraid that he would take a tumble and hit his head on the desk. As quickly as it had started, whatever it was, a mere half a moment later, it stopped. He took a deep breath and blinked a couple times, focusing on me once again. He patted my shoulder, ignoring the concern in my eyes.

"Sorry, duty calls. How about you come, meet the rest of the team first, and we'll talk more in a bit? I know this is a lot to take in, and I for one, could use a drink,"

I mentally staggered at his change in behavior, and the abrupt change in subject. I wanted to know, needed to know, so many things. Reggie saving Deke, had saved Clara, and he hadn't even known it would happen.

And did he know about their power buildup? Did he know they weren't actually cured? Did he know that the urge to kill came back, if they weren't constantly vigilant? Was the seizure-like episode he had gone through moments ago part of being psychic, being a Tender, or a side effect of coming back from the dead? How did Clara sell her soul? *Who* did she sell her soul *to? How could she have sold her soul for us? How could my little sister do this for us?* I think Reggie and Deke *and* Clara needed to have a long, tough discussion.

Reggie was already out the door, smoothing down his t-shirt, and running his fingers through his hair.

The room beyond was still all aflutter, but I could tell that the mood was no longer celebratory – everyone was at their work stations, rapidly keying at their computers, phones to their ears. The tall man I had noticed before was the only one not reacting to the situation, and had turned in his chair, fingers together, as Reggie entered into the room. He gave Reggie a small nod, eyes flicking to me and back again.

Reggie approached him, looking grim,

"Addy, this is Mateo, he's the one undercover in the Boston faction, I mentioned earlier. Mateo, this is my sister," Mateo extended a long hand, dark eyes flashing.

Upon closer inspection, he looked to be of Latin descent, towering over both myself and Reggie, all dark hair, and deeply tanned skin. The uneasy feeling that I'd seen him somewhere before washed over me once again.

He was coiled as tightly as a spring, the extension of friendship offered by the hand not quite reflected anywhere else in his demeanor. His hand was warm and dry; he didn't seem to have been bothered by the frenzy that had stirred up the rest of the room.

In fact, where everyone else looked haggard, too-thin, too-tired, rumpled and strained, Mateo was the perfect impression of undisturbed, clad in a finely tailored dress shirt, open at the collar, dark jeans, and what Clara would only have described as shit-kicker boots – no doubt steel-toed and heavy.

It was then that I noticed the holster at his hip, the badge clipped next to it shining, and I became intensely disturbed as to the depth of personnel the Tenders recruited from. Mateo's eyes strayed to where my gaze was being held, and he broke out an even white smile,

"Boston PD," he nodded slightly.

My blood ran cold, and I was certain my heart skipped a beat.

Reggie had gotten Deke's name from his informant in Boston.

Mateo must be the informant from Boston. Was that why he looked familiar?

Deke was wanted by Boston Police, was this the man who had tipped off the FBI when we bailed from the state of Massachusetts? Had he used his psychic abilities to track where Deke had been?

I plastered what I only hoped could be interpreted as a genuine smile on my face and nodded in response.

Mateo turned back to Reggie, and I felt a physical sensation of being dismissed.

"I trust you heard? We haven't got enough recruits for this, do you think they know?"

I could detect only a slight note of concern, in an otherwise clipped and business-like manner. Reggie scratched at his scruff, eyes passing over the remainder of his team.

"What's happening? Reggie?" I put a hand on his arm.

"I think I need that drink," he responded, tiredly.

Deke could only stare at Clara. Thunder was beginning to rumble in the distance, lightning cracking just outside of town. The rain would be here soon, you could feel it, heavy and damp in the area, suffocating.

Her eyes were dry now; her admission had lifted the heavy weight from her shoulders. She still avoided his eye contact, still clung to the wall, determined it support her for her decision many weeks ago.

Did this mean that selling her soul, made her like this? Had he committed the same crime, the ultimate sin against his own person, turning him into this predator, this unhuman thing? Why couldn't he remember? He looked down at his hands, which had started to flicker and glow, steadily intensifying crackles of electricity scrawling across his skin. They reflected in his strange eyes, the irises liquid in the fast approaching storm.

The rain came down, suddenly, hard, and unrelenting, pounding against their heads. Steam rose from their skin, their clothes becoming drenched, slick and clinging. It thundered on the road, cascaded from eaves, the whole world turning into a static grey haze. They tilted their faces upwards to the heavens in wonder, basking in the cooling shower, their bare skin licked with the tongues of blue flame they no longer bothered trying to control. Their glow filled the dark alley; everything tinted blue, strange shadows flickering.

Thunder reverberated in their bones, the storm wickedly churning. Deke could feel the electricity in the air, could feel his body absorbing the charge, every nerve ending tingling. He now agreed with what Adeline had said, back at the campsite, so long ago, when he had pulled her close after her nightmare.

He felt *infinite.*

He looked down at Clara, could see her focusing on him, rain running in rivulets down her face, silver eyes sparkling with lights and rain and tears, lightning bolts refracting in her irises. Everything was incandescent in the center of the roaring skies, the wind whipping into frenzy down the alley, no breaks in the flashing, the storm a growling predator, stalking the air around them. Rain dripped from his hair into his eyes, it ran down his back, between his shoulder blades, finger tips of water coursing into his hemlines, teasing at his bare skin, soaking rapidly into his shoes.

Clara chose that moment to step forward, rising up onto her toes, curling one hand around the nape of his neck, the other pulling at his sweater and pulling him close. Her lips were on his, the electricity between them snapping and cracking where they touched, fingers of blue flames spreading into the atmosphere, intensifying.

He responded back in kind, the chills running through and across his body over-powering. Goosebumps rose across their skin as he tangled both his hands into her hair, pressing hard against her, pushing her up against the brick. Her hands skimmed his back, holding him tighter, fingernails digging into his flesh.

He paused, gasping for air; Clara hungrily planting kisses along his jaw line and down his throat. His hands found her face and pulled her back to his mouth, a gentle, teasing, nibble at her lips. He took another deep breath. He opened his eyes and stumbled back slightly, and Clara stared right back at him, eyes wide and stunned. He wasn't prepared for what he saw.

Green eyes stared back at him, and Clara gasped, seeing baby blue.

Chapter 18

Tell It Like It Is

Reggie; armed with a distinctly caramel coloured rye and cola, light on the cola, sat down heavily into one of the overstuffed sofas, and settled his glass on the milk crate. He leaned back and crossed his booted feet, staring at his assembled team. I perched nervously on the edge of a dark wood dining chair, and waited patiently for him to speak.

Connor sat on Reggie's right, the thin looking blond, who Reggie had introduced as Stella on his left. Mateo sat across from me on another dining chair, long frame folded over his lap, elbows resting on knees, long fingers folded together.

According to Connor, the remaining two members were Rick and Julia, a compact and well-muscled man of Asian descent, and a young woman, barely older than Clara, probably and easily five years my junior, with an astonishing shock of deep purple hair plaited into two thick braids down her back.

They all looked anxious, but they all waited patiently for Reggie to speak.

"As you know, thanks to Adeline here, we have discovered that we were successful in two of our Boston missions, one, to successfully neutralize a Charge, and two, to successfully convert an Initiator to our own devices, who, obviously and regretfully, was lost in the process, but I only hope now, she is at peace,"

Most of the group nodded in agreement, solemnly. Mateo and Rick both crossed themselves, muttering under their breath. Reggie opened his mouth to continue, but I interrupted,

"I wouldn't say neutralized, guys, sorry," I said quietly.

All eyes turned to look at me; I could tell they were stunned by the interruption. I felt nauseous under their gaze, but knew it had to be said. I placed a scarred hand gently on my throat,

"Deke and Clara, they aren't neutralized. They just don't hear the voices anymore. They do, however, continue to have a slow increase in negative energy, until it, uh, releases itself. Clara attacked me, Reggie, *after* receiving the tattoo, violently, and unpredictably. But we did find out, through Deke trying to save me from her attack, that they can release that energy, two Charges, if they spar and tire themselves out. You know, like overusing an outlet, just shorts everything out, blows their fuse. I travelled across the country with the two of them, and it was the only way I could feel safe, unless they forget,"

I could see pity in Stella's eyes, Mateo's reaction blank and unreadable. Rick leaned forward and muttered into Connor's ear, who nodded in response. Reggie stared at the pair of them briefly, a strange look passing over his eyes.

"I, I, uh, I do think it's a step in the right direction though, towards fixing them," I finished, hesitantly.

I felt I had suddenly undermined the work they had tried so hard to develop. All was silent as everyone considered this privately.

"What's an Initiator?" I asked the room, looking from face to face, trying to break the awkward silence. Rick took the spotlight,

"They can be anyone really, just like us, you know, psychic. The really good ones, they're usually lawyers, but this collection of Tenders on the East Coast have one or two priests, and many, many bartenders. They infiltrate where they can, people who are wonderful listeners, people who are practically paid to do it. They listen to what a person wants when they are most vulnerable, most likely to say what they want most in life, most likely to give the honest truth in what they'd give to have for what they don't,"

I nodded, something suddenly clicking.

"Dezi, you controlled Dezi, to give Deke that information down by the ocean, didn't you, how, how did that happen? Did you kill Dezi? Did you throw her from the wharf once you were done with her? Did she really mean so little to you, that she was so easy to sacrifice?"

Rick nodded slowly, lips pressed into a grim line.

"Yes, I know how it sounds, and you're absolutely right. Once upon a time, many, many years ago, Dezilyn Pritchard was a woman, who lived and breathed and loved and laughed, somewhere in North Dakota, but certainly not in this decade. Initiators are well, I have to say, they aren't really alive. They are dead, reanimated, controlled by Collectors to listen to the deepest wants and desires of their targets, and get them to sign on the dotted line. They just have to say the right words, and to be honest, after enough bourbon, you can get almost anyone to say anything. The creature that took over Dezi alone put away close to three hundred Charges, from start to finish," I gaped at him.

He took my stunned silence as permission to continue,

"Once they say the, excuse the term, 'magic words', the call goes out for local Tender in the area to take over, they make the contact, their heart's desire is miraculously granted, then they abduct them for Conversion, wipe their memory, and release them back into the wild. They've been marked with the sign of the Collectors, so then we're off to the races to commit the mayhem and chaos we instruct them to do,"

Reggie cleared his throat,

"In this case, we used Dezi, pushed out her Collector that was squatting inside her brain, and took control, briefly, for as long as we could. It was rough, and it can't take too long, the Collector is the only thing truly keeping the body from bottoming out, in the end,"

"The finger prints? The ones burned? Are those the signs of the Collectors?" I traced my collarbone.

Rick looked surprised, but it was Mateo who stared grimly into space, and began speaking,

"One and the same, each one unique to each Collector, they lay claim to them, possessions. They have no respect for the sanctity of humanity, of our souls," his eyes hardened.

"How could you do it? How could you agree to become a Tender?"

I blurted out. It was all fine and heroic that they were attempting to use their skills for good, that they had acknowledged what was so horribly and terribly wrong, but how does one even begin? How could anyone be so twisted? How could my own brother be so cruel?

Rick, started the ensuing confessions, each one has horrible as the next, tales of death and bloodshed and mayhem, threats to their families lives, of the blackmail held against them so that they'd continue to perform their wicked deeds in the name of gathering souls.

"Who did this to you all?" I barely whispered.

"The Collectors," Reggie sighed.

Deke tentatively stroked Clara's face, running his hand gently along the curves, thumb tracing her lips, staring into her brilliantly green eyes. He'd never seen them this way, and he was astonished. The rain had since stopped; the storm had moved onward, the rumblings still coming long and low in the distance. They were drenched, through and through, and Deke was acutely aware of every inch of his body that pinned Clara to the alley wall, every flicker of electricity that snapped between them, low and soft aches against the abnormal heat of their skin.

They weren't cured, far from it, but something was exquisitely different.

He realized what it was.

It was the complete and utter silence in his head, no ringing, clanging, shrieking or banging.

He was left alone, with just his own thoughts, desperate and alone, tinny sounding in his own brain after struggling for so long with the turmoil in his head.

Clara smiled, she was experiencing it too, and a weight had lifted from behind her eyes, in the curve of her shoulders. She gently touched the marks on his collarbone, just above the neckline of his rain-drenched t-shirt, and moved forward again for another long and deep kiss, static crackling between their lips.

Mateo pursed his lips, staring grimly at the assembly as he relayed the current situation.

A sudden influx of Conversions had happened here in California, near to this ragtag and hastily thrown together base of operations, and they were being drawn to Half Moon Bay. An overnight Conversion of five or six was normal in a major metropolitan area, where the vast number of population could easily hide the discrepancies of absences and murders. But this was eight, and this was around Half Moon Bay, a tiny city of only eleven thousand people. A kill streak here was bound to attract authorities of multiple levels of government, and he was debating if and when he could step in to prevent an onslaught of attention on the area.

Mateo had heard the call for additional Tenders come through, and had duly informed the marked and carved on his team, and he had communicated silently to Reggie when he had been in the office with Adeline. The strange symbols on their bodies blocked Tenders and Collectors alike from connecting with them, but not at close range. Regular everyday people however, were a completely different story. Any one of them could peer into the thoughts of any person if they concentrated hard enough.

They could all communicate silently if they wished, but Mateo was by far the strongest, as he remained unmarked, aside from a small crossbones tattoo on his shoulder, and an ugly looking scar running rampant from shoulder blade to kidney, sustained from a knife fight with a perp he didn't have an advantage against. He listened in on the conversations of the Tenders, half-heartedly and occasionally having to contribute, to waylay suspicion, and kept to himself as much as he could.

The question was, why were there so many fresh Charges, and why were they all here? They couldn't possibly know what he knew. How did *she* find out? And what were they going to do about it?

Reggie sipped moodily at his drink, swirling the ice in the glass.

Are you going to tell her?

Mateo trickled into Reggie's brain, his mind voice an octave lower than his real voice, and always sickly syrupy. Reggie's arms and shoulders stiffened slightly in response to the invasion. He was better at hiding it when he was simply lounging on a chair.

Reggie's eyes flicked to Mateo, who was studiously staring at the ceiling.

Not until I have to.

She already knows too much, you know this is going to blow up right in your face, Reggie. Mateo chided carefully.

He had known Reggie for a very long time, and it was only a recent development that required he stay off of Reggie's bad side. He had returned from the grave incredibly angry, Mateo knew something was broken inside, and he was prone to a violence he never even would have considered before that fateful accident. Mateo had been on the wrong end of it, many a time, and he only thanked God that he was bigger and stronger than his renegade leader, and that fact alone waylaid the worst of his wrath. Connor wasn't so lucky.

The rest of them hadn't come back as shells of their former selves, though he knew most of the team still had nightmares sometimes about the drownings. It took their death, however temporary, to break the connection, and it was the quickest solution they could come to in a short period of time, and an easy sacrifice when it meant they could be free from the guilt and the pain of what they were doing.

They didn't manage to revive everyone though, and sometimes those accidents weighed more heavily on him than anything else. It boiled down to seconds you didn't know you had to steal, the moments when any single heartbeat could make or break the victim.

He debated pushing Reggie, getting Reggie to confess everything, every last detail, but it wasn't the right time. Not for any of them.

The phone on the nightstand finally buzzed, heralding news from Adeline. Deke winced, startling awake in the sudden glare in the darkened room, his head already pounding, and his tongue feeling heavy and sticky against the roof of his very dry mouth. He picked up the phone and checked the display, eyes narrowed against the light.

The clock read that several hours had passed since she had left to find Reggie. He didn't realize it had been so long, and his heart skipped a beat, had he really been so negligent? What if something had happened, what if she had needed him? What if Reggie had turned out to be more than one or two screws loose? He shook his head, feeling his brains rattling about in his skull. Getting drunk right now was quite possibly the worst idea he had ever had, and unfortunately, he was still feeling it, the edges of everything softly blurred and numb in the late night.

He thumbed open the message and squinted at it, trying to decipher the dancing letters in front of him.

Meet me at Dizzy Moon, rear doors, 3am. Bring Clara.

Bring Clara? He mused.

As if Clara would stay anywhere she was told to, if Addy had directed him *not* to bring her. He closed down the phone, bringing back the blessed darkness, and laid it down on the nightstand softly. He squeezed his eyes shut, willing his head to ease up on its incessant knocking and clanging. He had an hour to kill, figuratively of course, before he had to meet Addy (*with Clara*) at the restaurant several blocks away. It must be closed by now, there was no way it was open this late, not in a cow-poke town like this one.

Something niggled at his brain, his mind still trying to do backstrokes through the muddy swamp that the Four Horsemen, Jim, John, Jack, and Jose themselves had created.

(*With Clara*)

Shit.

It was at that moment that the hand ran lightly up his body, a slow glide of sparks flickering in the dark, from navel to chest, warm and fragrant; the smell of rain suddenly assaulted his nostrils and memory from the piles of wet clothing strewn around the room.

Shit.

(*With Clara*)

The last of the effects of the liquor peeled from his brain, and he was wide awake as effectually as being doused in ice water.

He rolled away from her touch, over correcting, and ending up falling out of the bed, hitting hard on his knees on the motel floor. He stood up shakily, Clara propping herself up on her elbow, wondering what the Hell he was getting up to. His eyes grazed across her curving form as she held the blanket loosely to her chest. He rubbed his face vigorously with both hands and inhaled deeply, and stuttered,

"Um, so, uh, Addy needs us to meet her, I uh, I think Reggie is good to see us," Clara winced at Adeline's name, and threw herself back onto the bed with a huff of air.

Deke chose her distraction as the perfect moment to escape to the adjoining bathroom. He cranked the taps and splashed water on his face, what felt like great gallons of it, and drank as many more.

Shit.

He finished patting his face with the hand towel, sighing into it. He pulled the towel away and looked hard at himself.

His eyes were silver again; molten in the strange motel fluorescents, absolutely not the eyes he was born with. He blinked, rapidly, inspecting them from all angles. But the mirror wasn't lying.

Whatever had happened in that alley, out in that storm, it wasn't permanent. He threw the towel down into the sink, and stomped back into the room. Clara hadn't moved any more than to prop herself into a sitting position against the headboard, knees to her chest. He realized he could see her doing this, despite the room being in complete darkness. The powers had come back. He saw her pupils flash in the dark, glowing and predatory, and knew she was thinking the exact same thing,

What the Hell had happened?

The air felt heavy with words unsaid.

A man could suffocate, he thought. He rubbed the back of his neck, anxiously, wincing at the flare of heat and static. He moved to the window, peeking out between the curtains. The storm had long passed, and the moon had risen. Several dark shapes stood silhouetted in intervals among the darker shadows of neighbouring buildings. Deke frowned and hid behind the edge of the window, peering through a slit in the curtains.

"Clara, come here," he whispered, barely a hair above breathless.

She came to the window, padding barefoot on the carpet, gingerly tip-toeing around their sopping clothes, wrapped in the sheet she had pulled tiredly from the bed, and looked out to where he pointed.

"What are they?" She whispered, breath fogging up the glass.

He stared, hard, seeing subtle movements, heads turning slowly, seeming to be picking up scents on the air in the gently wafting breezes. When he saw the glint of their eyes, reflecting the moonlight, he realized exactly what they were.

They were different, just like them, cursed, silver eyes flashing, and they were surrounding the front of the motel, waiting and watching. Deke highly doubted they had had any recent trips to the tattoo parlor. He slowly backed away from the window,

"I think they're hunting us, Clara, like we used to, back in Boston," he knelt by his backpack, trying to calm his breathing, pulling out dry clothes, quickly pulling the t-shirt over his head, buttoning his jeans as he paced the room, retrieving his hoodie from the chair, and pocketing his switch blade.

Clara followed suit, hunting down her dry clothes and dressing quickly. She waited patiently by the door, watching as Deke gathered Adeline's things into her pack, and shouldered both of their bags. He checked the window again, but they hadn't moved, motionless in the dark, his only tip-off to their inherent malice was the glint of their eyes.

They couldn't go out the front door, they'd be instantly exposed, face full of the moonlight, probably blinded, and if they were even half as fast as Deke was at his full strength, they'd be on them in a heartbeat.

Deke tilted his head towards the bathroom, and Clara understood, following him quickly and quietly. He slid open the window, and stuck his head out, thankful that they were on the first floor. The broken and weedy concrete below would have been no soft landing if they had to jump any farther. The street intersecting the rear of the motel was well lit, small suburban homes and well-manicured lawns stretching for a good mile.

He couldn't see any strange forms hiding in the few shadows cast by parked cars and the odd shrub. He gestured for Clara to go before him, as they tried to make minimal noise. She dropped her bag out of the window, and stuck her head out, judging the angle of the drop. She put a foot on the toilet, another on the sink, until she had moved herself up to the height of the window sill, and pushed her legs through, sitting down on the edge, feet dangling. She glanced back at him and he nodded, before she pushed herself off the edge and dropped lightly to the ground.

Deke hesitated before following her. He locked the bathroom door, if they came in now, it would give them an extra second before they broke down the door. He hauled himself through the window after Clara, landing carefully to a crouch amongst the weeds.

They moved off hurriedly, keeping to the shadows of the houses lining the street, occasionally triggering a half-asleep and wary dog from inside, but the barks faded quickly as they ran. When they had escaped suburbia, and reached the main street running through town, they slowed, carefully looking for any signs of the shadowy figures from outside the motel room. Only a few cars were even out at this hour, the moon high and very round, perfectly lighting their way.

He checked the phone for the time; they had only about ten minutes left before they'd be facing Adeline and her brother. Given the very recent events

(With Clara)

He wasn't sure what to say, or do. He wasn't sure why their eyes had changed to normal, at that moment, with her. He wasn't sure why he had even responded to her advances as he had. He was adult enough to know he couldn't blame it all on the alcohol. That she couldn't blame it all on being emotional and taking solace in the situation, and in him. And what about the fact that she rediscovered she had sold her soul? What did that make her? What did that make him? It was making his head throb worse to think about. And could she stop looking at him like that?

Clara was throwing sidelong glances at Deke, the urge to speak bubbling up in her throat, washing away like bile when she thought about what she was actually going to say.

But then they were there, and they were knocking on the door, Clara a half step behind Deke's shoulder, anxiously wanting to reach for the sleeve of his sweater, needing comfort to know that she wasn't going crazy, that something, for a very short amount of time, had changed, and that maybe they weren't as doomed as they thought.

But if Deke's reaction when he finally realized what had happened was any indication, she wasn't holding her breath that he'd find his answers with her. As the locks behind the door tumbled, she continued furtively glancing around for any sign of being followed.

The door swung wide open, and two men stood on the other side, both holding formidable looking firearms, and both looking on the wrong side of scared. Deke held his hands up, palms out, hoping to look as helpless as possible. The shorter one on the right turned to the tall and dark haired man on the left and raised an eyebrow. The taller one nodded, lowering his firearm, but kept it angled down at his side, preparing for any trouble they might give them. The shorter one produced a penlight from his pocket, and gave them a cursory sweep across their eyes. He didn't have to look hard, as the metallic sheen of their irises picked up the light brilliantly in the dark. He frowned, and took a step back, half-cocking his head towards the other man.

"Show us the tattoos," the tall man said, voice low, a trace of a Hispanic accent curling his words.

Deke glanced at Clara, and then pulled his shirt up past the waist band of his jeans, twisting for them in the light of the flashlight, scars glittering between the sharp angles of his hip bones.

Clara turned her back to them, and Deke brushed her hair aside from her neck, the brief contact spilling electricity through the dark, chills running down Clara's spine. He pulled the back of the collar of her shirt and sweater aside, allowing them to see the tattoo across her shoulder blade. Clara turned back, crossing her arms across her chest, waiting for their verdict.

Tall man nodded, and gestured with his gun for them to enter, following them down the dimly lit hallway while the other gunman fastened the locks behind them. Deke resisted the urge to turn and run away, despite his greater instincts. There was nowhere to go, and besides, Reggie and Adeline were down here, waiting, with quite possibly every answer he could ever need.

According to Clara, Reggie *was* a superhero after all.

Chapter 19

Confessions

I waited nervously. I was beyond over tired, but there was no way I was going to sleep. I couldn't seem to figure out where to hold my hands, how to hang my arms. I was jittering with excitement and Reggie's extra strong brew. When Reggie had finally realized the time, he had switched to coffee and prompted me to put out the call.

He wanted the two of them as close as possible in light of the news about the influx of Charges. Until they knew why the Charges were here, they couldn't assume anyone would be safe. Mateo and Rick could handle one or two on their own, but Reggie wasn't fond of the idea of the entire team trying to take on close to double their numbers, with each only having half the strength of a new Charge. Julia had been hard pressed to be convinced that they would even be safe with Deke and Clara between their four walls, but I had won her over eventually. Deke wasn't hard to like.

The door to the base of operations swung inward, and Deke stood in the doorway, blinking hard in the bright light of the office. He looked overwhelmed, and the colour in his face drained as he looked around the room. Reggie leaned against the desk next to me, arms crossed over his chest, booted feet crossed at the ankles. He looked the picture of calm and collective, but I knew it was all for show. I could see the index finger of his spasming hand tapping furiously against his bicep, the only movement he made at their arrival.

Deke stepped in, and Clara moved in behind him, keeping half a step behind his shoulder, using him as a shield from the light. Mateo and Rick moved in with them, carefully locking the door, and crossed over to our side, a team of seven standing against their pitiful two.

"Well," Reggie started, stepping forward, and standing in the yawning wide open space between Deke and I, hands behind his back at parade rest.

It struck me again how thin he was, how sharply angled everything that made him Reggie, made him my twin, had become. I waited for his face to soften, waited for him to greet Clara like the big brother he was, how he had always been to her, but it never came. Instead, he looked bitterly grim, he had an unpleasant task to accomplish and no way of talking himself out of it.

Clara's face that had been hopeful when she finally saw Reggie had become shuttered and grim. Deke's eyes flicked between Reggie and me, and then scanned the remaining people in the room. Reggie launched fully into it,

"Clara, this is a fuckin' doozy of a shit storm you've gotten yourself into this time, you couldn't just, just leave it alone, huh?" His voice faltered as he saw her eyes begin to brim with tears. He swallowed roughly and continued,

"No, no crying. You couldn't leave well enough alone, and now once again, I'm trying to clean it up. We are going to deal with this, like adults, we're going to tell you, and

Deacon here what is what, we're going to deal, with this shit that's going on right now, that's coming down on us hard," he glanced at Mateo, who inclined his head.

"And then, you're out of here," he folded his arms again, studiously ignoring the tears that had begun to stream down her face.

Deke put a supportive arm around her shoulders, and she turned into him, hair hiding her face.

"Reggie," I called his name flatly, willing him to look at me.

He couldn't behave this way, not now, not ever. He wouldn't look at me. I could tell he was connecting with others in the room, using the pause as a distraction that he was doing so.

"Reggie, if you're going to say something, say it *out loud*," I chastised him.

He threw back his head and sighed impatiently, and looked towards Mateo,

"You're right, we shouldn't have told her,"

Mateo grinned and shrugged, Connor blushing down at his shoes, Stella and Julia looking anxiously between each other, evidently having an intense discussion behind our backs.

Deke's face contorted with confusion, and I could see he was getting worked up, that absent calm before the storm radiating out from him, the air being slowly sucked from the room, his fingertips sparking. I moved toward him, to explain, but he took a half step back, frowning.

I cleared my throat, and turned back to Reggie,

"Reggie, can you please take Deke into your office, explain to him what you told me? I want to speak with Clara, without you,"

Reggie looked taken a back, as if I had told him his job was to fish a snake out from beneath the shelves in his office.

"Reggie, you ass, he's safe, go, please?"

I moved towards Deke and Clara, actively putting my back to the rumbling storm that was masquerading as Mr. Deacon Masterson himself.

I pulled Clara away from his reassuring arm, steering her towards the overstuffed couch, pushing through the awkward line of ex-Tenders that jumped back from out of her way like they had been electrocuted, and sat her down next to me.

Reggie squared his shoulders, straightening to a more impressive height, and gestured for Deke to follow him. The gang parted this time, keeping a careful distance away from them, Rick visibly squaring up Deke as he passed, Mateo finally holstering his weapon.

Connor looked to Stella and Julia, and tilted his head. They moved in unison towards another door at the back of the room I hadn't noticed previously, and made their way through, Connor taking one last long and hard look at me before closing the door.

Mateo settled back into his desk chair and picked up the phone, turning his back to the room. Rick made himself scarce. I wasn't sure where he went to, but I definitely didn't care. It's amazing the change in people, when you throw a lion amongst the sheep.

I turned to Clara, who had dried her eyes, and now stared stonily at Mateo's back.

"I'm sorry about that, I didn't think he'd react that way, he seemed fine with it, until the moment you walked in, I don't know what happened," I apologized, not knowing why exactly I did it.

It wasn't my fault that Reggie decided to act cruelly. Clara shrugged, only half listening. I took her silence as an invitation to continue,

"Reggie was the one who sent the marks to Deke. He's the reason Deke is safe now, and why you're safe now too," her eyes flicked to me, and lit up momentarily, the irises catching at the bright light, reflecting deep silver pools.

She pulled her glasses out and tilted them at me; I nodded, allowing her to return them to her face.

"Addy, I uh, I know, now, where I went wrong," she started, blowing out her cheeks and focusing on Mateo, avoiding my eyes.

I grabbed her wrist, a shrill note of shock rising to my lips, when a sudden crashing commotion from Reggie's office caught our attention, Mateo shooting to his feet, one hand on his revolver, the other gesturing for us to stay where we were seated.

He proceeded towards the door rapidly, listening to the sound of raised voices of Reggie and Deke, their words blurred through the heavy door. Something or someone was thrown violently against the wall, the glasses rattling in the kitchen cupboards. Mateo didn't enter the office, but waited patiently, gun at the ready.

After a moment of silence, where he listened overly intently, though the raised voices had settled, he holstered the gun, chuckling to himself, and shaking his head. He winked at Clara and then sat back in his chair, busily distracting himself with papers on his desk.

I pulled on Clara's wrist, which I had just realized was still in my hand, I could feel the heat rising, making the blisters sting.

"What do you mean, you know? How do you know? What suddenly changed? You remember?"

"We, we got drunk, Addy, waiting for you. And the more I drank, the more I remembered, I felt like I was pushing aside a wall, in my brain, you know … I could barely stand up anymore, but I remembered, I remembered everything," she put her face in her hands, shaking her head.

Mateo had swiveled in his chair, making no effort to pretend he wasn't listening.

"The funerals? The bargain?" I asked, and Clara nodded, still hiding her face.

Mateo rolled his chair closer, elbows on knees. I shook my head at him but he shushed me. I glowered at him in response, but he took it in stride,

"Clara, help me out here, I need to know something very, very important," Mateo paused, waiting for her to respond.

When she didn't, he pushed,

"Clara, you gotta tell me, do you remember what your Tender looked like? Did they ever give you a name? Anything we can go on?"

Clara raised her head and looked directly at him. Mateo's gaze softened, and she hesitated, and then shook her head, defeated. Mateo's head dropped between his hands, and he rubbed his eyes.

"Alright, alright, never mind," he swiveled in his seat and headed back to his computer, mission evidently a failure.

Reggie stared stonily at Deke. He wasn't sorry that he punched him. He was even less sorry because Deke hadn't even flinched, and his hand was on fire, the small bones feeling fragile and bruised. He certainly wasn't sorry, as he watched the bruising along Deke's cheekbone swell up, because of the way Deke didn't even bother to gingerly inspect the small cut on his face where Reggie's class ring had bit into his skin.

Deke stared right back at him, silver eyes flashing, sleeves pulled up to show his landmark scars, arms crossed, feet up on the desk. How Reggie hated that.

But that was Reggie's punishment, now wasn't it? He had made the mistake, of taking a little look, of unlocking the door and trying to sneak into Deke's mind. The flashes he had seen, silhouettes against the lightning, the curve of a hip beneath the sheets, the salty taste of sweat and the heady scent of ozone. He had reacted before he had thought about it, throwing Deke up against the wall and hooking him one, Deke protesting and playing innocent until he realized what Reggie had done, what Reggie was capable of doing.

Reggie shuddered again and shook his head, prompting a curve of the corner of Deke's mouth, just a flicker, thinking about what Reggie had seen. Reggie had sent a brief message to Mateo, who had been assaulting his brain since the ruckus first started, and put a leash back on that particular guard dog.

"Well, now that we have that settled," Deke cleared his throat.

Reggie continued his tale, a condensed version of what he had told Adeline. Explained how the ex-Tenders had controlled Dezi, with their minds, directed her to him, as she had a connection with him, being his Initiator, she could track him down. Made her scrawl out the words, hoped they would be used, interpreted, every motion an incredible feat for even the collective of the group.

She wasn't human anymore; they didn't feel bad about abruptly tossing her into the ocean. In the back of Deke's mind, he knew they were right, though it was difficult to swallow Dezi's betrayal for his soul. He had to take solace in the fact that he'd never known the real Dezi.

"And then here we are, you're our first free Charge, in the flesh, we're blind out here, doing what we can, just hoping it makes a difference, and maybe one day, we'll figure out how to release your soul from contract, get you back to normal,"

Reggie finished. Deke had relaxed, visibly, over this extended distraction of conversation; he could feel the charge settling under his skin, his body no longer crawling beneath his clothes.

"Can I show you something, without you punching me again, you overly-protective maniacal big brother that you are?"

Reggie raised an eyebrow.

"Just tell me when to start and when to stop. I'd rather douse my eyes in bleach than see any of that again,"

He rubbed his face and waited. Deke concentrated, hard, on the alley, the thunder storm, the kiss. Reggie had closed his eyes, though Deke could see them moving below the lids. Reggie's face grimaced. Deke chuckled, and focused; remembering the heat and the steam, the sizzle of the skin, of opening his eyes, staring into Clara's. The brilliant matching green to Adeline and, as Reggie's eyes shot open in horror and confusion, an exact match to his as well.

"Shit," Reggie mouthed.

There was another scuffle, the door to the office yanked open, Clara and I on our feet, watching in shock. Reggie yelped as Deke tackled him around the knees, pinning him. Reggie rocked, rolling Deke off and scrambled to his feet. Mateo moved in, lithe as a panther, looking for an opportunity to get in between the two as they fought. I raced over, pushing a hand on Mateo's chest, pushing him back as he reached for his weapon. I managed to slip a shoulder in between Deke and Reggie, facing Deke, wary of any change in his demeanor that would indicate he'd flipped to the dark side again.

But it was just Deke, no predatory curve to his shoulders, his hair roughed up, and a bruise swelling around his eye from a punch I hadn't seen land. I looked over my shoulder at Reggie, still firmly gripping the collar of Mateo's shirt.

"Reggie, seriously, what the Hell did you say to him, did you hit him?"

Reggie's penchant for getting people right wickedly mad at him had always been his strong suit – but this was getting to be unreal. Reggie gaped at me for a minute, as I stood knee deep in the middle of a fog of testosterone, having thrown myself directly into three lines of fire. Deke positively crackled, and Mateo took a step back, shaking his collar from my suddenly released grasp.

Reggie's eyes flicked to Deke, concentrating hard, and then he suddenly exhaled, laughing. Mateo also began laughing and I stared at them all in confusion. Deke looked down at the floor, blushing up to his ears and around his hairline. I swung to Clara, who stared at the lot of them, her lips pressed into a thin line. I guess Clara didn't know what was funny either, and I slowly backed out of their circle.

"Are we all good? Is everybody all good? Care to share with the class what's so funny?"

I asked the general room, realizing that Connor was poking his head around the door he had disappeared to previously. Reggie shook his head, still chuckling softly, and headed for Connor, who withdrew from his post and slipped back inside to where he had come from.

"Clara, care to come with me?"

He beckoned, smiling at her, a note of his old caring personality inflecting his tone. Clara stared at me in this sudden change in attitude, and hesitantly moved toward him.

Reggie looked directly at me,

"You stay, and you too Deke, take care of your business, man, make it easier on all of us. And Mateo? Don't be a knob. Go grab coffees or something, make yourself useful," he winked and closed the door behind him.

Deke had relaxed to a simmer, but still seemed uncharacteristically jumpy. It made me think back to when we had first met, when he had been terrified and on the run, hiding in my home. I reached out to touch his arm, hoping it would bring him down a notch, but he flinched away from my hand.

Mateo shook his head and scoffed, throwing on his jacket and heading out of the entrance door, the locks clicking and tumbling behind him. Deke and I were left alone, and I sat down on the couch and waited expectantly for him to fill me in on his opinions of what Reggie had told him.

He sat awkwardly on the edge of the couch, suddenly all gangly joints and wrong angles. He scratched at what was rapidly becoming a beard, dark even against his tanned skin.

"Sorry about Dezi," I broke the ice, and he smiled wistfully in response.

"Sorry about Clara," he replied.

"Well, it was a decision she made, she doesn't tend to think about long term consequences, you know,"

"I'm getting to see that, more and more,"

"But hey, I get to still be here, so I guess that's a plus," I smiled.

Deke's face clouded, and he turned his eyes away from me.

"Sorry about Clara," he turned back to stare directly at me.

"Yeah, I get that, we're dealing with it, right? Reggie's got all this going on, with the psychic stuff, and he's going to find a way to help you, and Clara, he's got this,"

"No, Addy, you don't get it," he turned away from me, putting his head in his hands and furiously scuffing them through his hair, sparks flying.

I put a hand on his shoulder, hesitantly, and this time, he didn't flinch away. He turned and looked at me, head still in his hands.

"Clara, she remembered, everything that happened, she was very, very drunk. I practically had to carry her out, but I was barely standing either, Hell, I think I'm still drunk, certainly not feeling this good ol' work of Reggie," he gently touched his face, a half-hissing wince coming out of him as he skimmed the broken skin.

"Yeah, she told me that, that she'd thrown a bender. She didn't mention you'd joined her," I cocked my head at him, grinning, realizing how blood-shot his eyes were beyond the silver.

But I was confused by what he was getting at. He threw his head back, staring at the ceiling and exhaling loudly. He groaned,

"Why are you making this so difficult," he sighed again, shaking his head at the pipes that lined the ceiling under the restaurant.

I was dumbfounded. What was I making difficult?

"Reggie and I fought, in the office, once, because he found out some information that was downright disturbing to him, and decided to deck me for it. We fought out here, a second time, because he was going to blab it out to you, because he thought you knew already, and I couldn't have it come from him, I just couldn't. That's not fair to anyone," he fidgeted back to upright, and turned on the couch to focus his body directly towards me.

I reached out to touch his swollen cheek, and Deke flushed again.

"Yeah well, Reggie's an asshole, I'm sure it wasn't worth it, half the guys in here have black eyes because of him, he's a loose cannon," I smiled, hoping it looked encouraging.

"Clara, and I, we, uh, yeah," he pressed his hands together and then exploded them outward in some bizarre gesture.

"You, huh?" I cocked my head at him again, confused by his waggling fingers. He muttered under his breath.

"What? Come on Deke, spit it out, stop being weird,"

Deke rewarded me with a hang dog look of shame,

"I slept with your sister," he exhaled in one quick breath, and then leaned back away from me, wincing.

I stared at him.

Clara stared through the bars at the man sitting cross legged on the floor of the jail cell. Occasionally the man would roll his head on his neck, stretching out the kinks, and would grin at her, eyes glinting quicksilver in the dim light.

Occasionally he would snicker, and the sound drilled chills down her neck. Reggie stood close by, watching carefully. He had told her about what he knew; that he'd caught the images from Deke. He told her that he knew what had happened between them. She'd caught the bemused glint in his eye, but when he'd pressed about their eyes changing back to normal, about the absence of the ringing, she could only shrug, she had no answers. He had seemed disappointed then, and she hoped it was only for the lack of information.

"We caught him, up in San Francisco, a couple of days ago, it was like trying to pin a rabid pit bull. We've got him tranq'd up; cell is carved up to keep the Tenders out of his head. We were waiting to see how Deke fared, marking his body, before we took a shot on this guy. Deke's a kitten compared to what I've seen this guy do. Almost bit a chunk of Rick clean off," Reggie grimaced.

Clara tilted her head, something about him seemed awfully familiar, but she couldn't quite place it. She looked at Reggie, admonishing him with her voice,

"You know, Reggie, we weren't wild animals, stirred up into a blood-thirsty frenzy. You were a Tender. You know how it works. No killing unless we're compelled to,"

"Yeah, well, I don't think any of the other Tenders were leaving this guy alone, maybe he was Mr. Clean in another life and needed that soul dirtied up nice and good, before he'd be worth anything Down Below,"

The capitalization stood out in his voice. No need to explain where he meant. Julia came down the hall stripped down to her tank top and jeans, and stopped on the other side of Reggie, hands clad in latex gloves.

"Table's ready when you are, Reg," she snapped the wrist of one of her gloves and moved off farther down the corridor.

Reggie shot her a grateful smile and nodded.

He turned back to Clara,

"If this works, and you're right about the other Charges hunting you down in this last Conversion, we'll hopefully have one more good guy with super powers on our side,"

Reggie raised the tranquilizer gun he held in both hands, aimed it at the caged man, and pulled the trigger, the crack echoing down the cement walls.

Seven seconds later, the man slumped to the ground, head smacking hard against the concrete.

Mateo moved slowly, shadow to shadow, keeping the Charges that stood motionless in the parking lot behind the pizza place in view. It was giving him some seriously strange vibes, he'd never seen Charges still, even when they were briefly released from killing; they were usually spastic, twitchy, endless fidgets. But these ones, they just lurked. He stifled a shudder and crept carefully onward. Once he'd reached the mouth of the alley that led back to the main road, he paused, grey light slowly filtering over the horizon.

Mateo.

The voice prodded lightly at his forebrain, and he looked around for the source. He saw the flare of a cigarette coming from the shadow under a fire escape, and moved towards it.

Rick nodded at him when his eyes adjusted enough to see who it was, and they both turned to look at the crowd in the parking lot.

Weird, huh?

If I hadn't seen it with my own eyes I wouldn't have believed it.

Deke said they'd been waiting outside the hotel.

And they followed them here? How did they find them? I thought they were marked?

Just because they can't sense them, psychically, doesn't mean they can't hunt them, sight, sound; smell, I'm sure they can follow the electricity. You get that ozone coming off them, especially when they're upset...

Rick nodded again, taking one last drag, throwing the butt down and grinding it out with his heel. Mateo watched the smoke drift skyward against the fading stars, the sky a clean slate after the storm.

Think they'll be fine if we go?

Yeah. Nothing is getting through those spells.

Rick shrugged and turned away towards the main street, buttoning his coat as he went. The pre-dawn air was chillier than normal, damp after the rain. He wasn't sure how he felt about all the siblings under one roof; one an ex-Tender, one a Charge on a leash, and one, presumably, only human. But if Connor was right about anything, all of it was hereditary, and Adeline was bound to pop with some sort of extraordinary sense before the day was up, especially with all the other influences around her, he'd put all his money on it.

Mateo took one last look at the silent assembly and zipped up his windbreaker, adjusting the hem for the bulk of the gun, falling into step with Rick.

Julia swabbed away at the blood pooling in the shallow cuts she was making in the skin of S.F. She had the marks memorized by now, knew every notch and slice. She had been designated by the team as the tattoo artist for the marks, given her life skills before the Tenders, but she could never get used to the scarring process of the spell.

It still turned her stomach. She had already tattooed S.F; that had been a piece of cake.

But then, how hard could it be, when he was bound and gagged and unconscious on her table? Her mind briefly went back to the night shifts, the rowdy college boys trying to make a point, something to prove in the pain of an undoubtedly tacky barbed wire or tribal cuff tattoo. She wiped her lilac bangs from her eyes, dabbing at the sweat on her forehead. She stepped back, craned her head at her handiwork. Reggie stepped forward and studied the marks as well. Any slight stroke out of line could be fundamentally disastrous. S.F stirred, eyes blinking open, his face squished against the stainless steel table. Reggie gently squeezed Julia's elbow, and pulled her back a half step,

"Hey San Fran, willing to talk to us now?"

Clara stared at S.F nervously. This would prove her and Deke weren't a fluke, that this was a working solution and not a half-formed dream or wishful thinking. S.F blinked slowly, nodded slightly. Reggie moved forward, using his switchblade to deftly cut the gag. Reggie gestured for Julia, and together, they seized him by the shoulders and turned him over, helping him to sit up.

"We aren't going to untie you, alright? Just until we get some answers," S.F nodded again, eyes flashing in the bright over heads, squinting in the light.

When his eyes locked on Clara's, and he saw her matching glowing irises, confusion swept his face.

"Who's she?"

His voice sounded raw and hoarse. Clara stepped back and looked frightfully at Reggie.

"Never you mind who she is. I'm going to ask the questions," Reggie patted him on the shoulder.

Julia swung around a rolling desk chair and pushed it at Reggie, who flipped it around backwards, straddling it in front of S.F, arms resting lightly on the back support, switchblade hanging loosely in his fingertips.

"We're hoping, as of this point; that your nightmare is over. We hope that we've stopped the voices in your head, and that you'll be able to carry on, as best you can,"

Reggie continued. S.F looked fearful, and turned away, staring hard at the floor. Reggie took a breath, and started to speak, but Clara interrupted,

"You could hear it, couldn't you, until Reggie came over?" S.F slowly looked across to her, and fixed her with a strange look.

She felt he was looking right through her. He nodded slowly, and she gave him a reassuring smile. She placed a hand on Reggie's shoulder and squeezed. She moved closer to S.F, studying his face, the horrible feeling that he looked familiar to her tensing her shoulders,

"I'm like you, I hunted like you, and I've been through the same as you. I was marked, I was carved, and now, I'm me. Except when I am near another one of us, then the ringing starts. It goes away, around certain people. I only know of two people so far that cancel us out. Reggie is one. My sister is the other. She's here somewhere too. You can trust us, and we need your help, there are more of us, out there, and they are hunting us down, they aren't marked, so we won't be safe for long. Do you understand?"

He licked his lips and shifted his shoulder, wincing at the pain from Julia's work.

Clara moved forward and placed her hand on S.F's shoulder, palming the cuts that scored his skin. Reggie had made a half-start attempt to stop her from getting closer, but she waved him off. She muttered a few words, and S.F hissed through his teeth as she felt the charge running through her arm. She pulled her hand away, revealing the sparkling hieroglyphics her powers left in his wound. She thought Reggie's eyes were going to bug out of his head, and Julia stepped in close, studying Clara's handiwork.

"This is remarkable, when did you figure out you could do this?" Julia was in awe of the intricate silver threading, a compliment to the fresh tattoo.

"You gotta show me how to do that," S.F gulped, looking up at her in awe.

It was then Clara realized he was unmarked, his long and muscular torso bare, not a scar on him, anywhere that she could see.

If he had truly been as active with the Tenders as Reggie had claimed, he must have always come out an uninjured winner. Her mind went back to the moments she had shared with Deke, when she had explored every scar that glittered across his lean frame. She shook her head,

"A friend showed me, he's really been through the ringer... his Tender showed him how, so he showed me," Clara explained to the room.

S.F looked confused by what she was saying, but she knew that Reggie had a lot to fill him in on. Reggie leaned forward against the chair,

"So, San Fran, do you have a name? We can get you all caught up, if we start from there,"

Stella entered the room, door banging against the bare stone walls, and took a long look at Julia. Julia's head raised up, tilted towards Stella, and then she quickly rose and left the room. Reggie suddenly reacted, throwing himself back as if he had been hit, wincing in the rolling chair. He sprung up, knocking the chair across the room, rolling on the uneven basement floor, and followed out the door, leaving Clara alone with S.F. He looked at her worriedly, unease flashing in his glittering eyes,

"Where did they all run off to?"

"Oh, well, the lot of them are all psychic. Not a lot of talking going on around here. Not out loud at least. I can't ever seem to get a handle on what's going on, so you aren't alone," she smiled reassuringly. She figured she might as well get information out of him for Reggie in the meantime.

"Alright, so, where were we, your name? Do you remember?"

S.F frowned, seeming to go inside his head for a moment, brow wrinkling, eyes seemingly searching for where he had filed the information away for later, not sure where to find it.

"Casey," he suddenly blurted; a look of triumph on his face. Clara nodded and smiled. His eyes searched her face for a moment, and then a smile lit him up,

"Casey Masterson,"

Clara's jaw dropped. Now she knew why he looked so familiar.

Chapter 20

Come Out and Play

"**What do you mean, she's gone?**" Reggie screamed at Deke, his face red, his twitching hand becoming more pronounced and spastic. Julia and Stella awkwardly stood by the kitchenette, coffees in hand, watching Reggie and Deke circle the makeshift living room. Julia looked worriedly at Stella,

What if they start fighting? What are we going to do about it?

Adeline stopped Deacon and Reginald and Mateo earlier, I'm sure we could handle it.

Yeah but Adeline isn't afraid of Deke. And she doesn't know Mateo.

What, are you afraid of Deke?

Stella put her arm around Julia's shoulder. The younger woman was shaking slightly, and Stella tightened her grip.

I don't know what I'd do, if something happened to Reggie.

I know honey, I know.

Deke's eyes flashed as he moved behind the couch, none too subtly putting its overstuffed bulk between him and the Reggie he needed to defuse. It had to be some sort of record, getting Reggie spitting mad three times in such a short amount of time. He'd have to ask Connor, or Addy, if she ever spoke to him again.

"I'm telling you, Reggie, I told her, I told her and she split, man, I wasn't going to chase after her, she was losing her mind," he held his hands out low, patting down the air, urging the sparks that glittered on his fingertips to stay calm. He knew that causing a lightning show would only increase the tension in the room and he was not willing to take a chance hurting any of them. Reggie's eyes flicked to Deke's hands, eyes widening.

"You should have stopped her! They are out there, and who's to say they won't go after her? We don't know if the Tenders controlling them know who she is, or know who I am, and what are you going to do if they take her; or worse? We can barely stand up to them as it is!"

Reggie angrily ran his hands through his dark curls, clutching his head and turning away from Deke. Reggie swore loudly and stomped to the other side of the room, every inch of his body tensed, hands on his hips now, angrily staring up at the ceiling and muttering. Deke looked at Stella and Julia and shrugged his shoulders, eyes flicking to Reggie and back again. Julia continued looking worried, but Stella fixed him with a wolfish smile, all teeth and no compassion.

"I'm impressed, Charge. You'll be getting the whole Byrne clan coming down on your head, you keep this up,"

Deke studied her, hearing the malice in her voice and not sure what he did to deserve it, offended by what she had called him.

Julia moved over to Reggie, resting a hand on his trembling shoulder blade, speaking to him quietly. He sighed and visibly relaxed. He looked down at his twitching hand, stilling it with the other. Julia went up on tip toe, impressively high for her diminutive height against Reggie's, and gave him a quick kiss on the cheek.

Well, actions speak louder than words, Deke thought. He looked back at Stella who was still studying him with a predatory glare. He narrowed his eyes, willing her to try something, anything, because after all he'd been through since getting here, he wasn't against putting her in her place.

Normally, he'd be horrified by the thought, but there was something about the hard glint in her eyes, and the way she held her whip-thin and angular frame that offered no apologies. By this time, the rivulets of electricity had ceased, the curls had darkened from his hands. He was slowly getting an easier time of controlling them, as time went on, and for that point, he was glad. Julia had done her duty, the toxic tension of the room diminished as Reggie returned to the conversation.

His emerald eyes still flashed, but the corners had softened. Deke let out a deep breath and watching him carefully.

"Did she say where she was going? What she was doing? She's in a strange place all alone. She wouldn't be dumb enough to go back to the motel, would she?"

Reggie crossed his arms and asked the questions sullenly.

Deke wasn't sure what Julia had said to him, but she had certainly put him in his place, whether he liked it or not.

"As I said, Reggie, I've got no clue, you've known her longer than I have, I don't know her well enough to know what she does when she's hurt, or angry. God knows, I dealt enough with those emotions the entire way here but I know I was only just scratching the surface, especially between those two,"

Deke was indignant, but to Reggie, he looked pathetic. This man strolls into his sisters' lives, ruins everything, when Clara was already doing a damn fine job of it, helps them to drag themselves across the entire country, and now, was tearing the two of them apart, and expecting Reggie's sympathy. He'd knock Deke out on his ass if he thought it would help. But he needed all the help he could get and he couldn't waste it all on the emotions of his sisters.

"Can't you just?"

Deke tapped his head and waved out at the basement ceiling. Reggie shook his head and rolled his eyes.

"She's marked, remember? That's why I had to resort to cell phones," Reggie replied flatly, then continued,

"I'm going to ask Clara what she thinks; maybe she'll be less useless. Stella? Let me know the second that Rick and Mateo come back, we'll need them out looking for her,"

Stella nodded, glaring at the back of Deke's head.

Deke felt helpless. No one here trusted him, and no one believed he could be helpful for anything except fighting.

Truthfully, he'd already gotten into two physical altercations and multiple verbal arguments so far, but it wasn't his fault. Everyone was wound too tight. He was the one with the supposed murderous and rampaging streak, and yet everyone else was satisfied with taking out their sores on him. And he'd told her he was sorry. And he was, so very, very sorry. He'd take it all back in a heartbeat if he could.

Reggie turned towards the door that led to the cells beyond, but the door was already swinging open, Clara standing pale and drawn on the other side, eyes searching for Deke. Clara took in the room, men angling awkwardly away from each other, Julia looking eerily composed, Stella murderous.

She'd heard Reggie from the other room, his voice echoing down the hall, causing her to cringe. She guessed the cause of the disagreement, there was no doubting that Addy had run off. Clara knew that she would. She'd been afraid of it every moment since she'd shaken the cobwebs from her head and thought hard on what she'd done. It was the Byrnes solution for everything – run. Run far, run fast, and don't look back. Clara entered the room, all eyes on her, waiting for her to speak.

Four pair of eyes, were all suddenly reflecting the seriousness of her demeanor, the angle of her posture, and it was evident that something important needed to be said. She could feel the thunderheads rolling off of Deke once more, the tension in his face. Did he know? Did he know who they had here? Did he even know he was alive? She squared her jaw and raised her chin, her silver eyes lancing into his. She only had to say one word, and it destroyed him, the bottom falling out of his stomach and his head whirling around him. The walls felt like they were pushing in, the floor dropping below, a tidal wave of emotion hitting him soundly in the throat,

"Casey,"

Mateo looked tired. He knew it, he could feel it, and he could see it reflected back at him in the plate glass window of the diner he stared out of, finger tips of red dawn smearing themselves across the horizon. Rick looked no worse for wear, still young and exuberant, late nights and early mornings were still a decade ahead of him, maybe longer.

Rick was scratching absently at the tattooed sleeve that ran up his forearm, the marks they all bore intermingling with a stunning green serpent, the scars running up its scaly back.

Some of the work Julia could do, outside of what the team needed from her, was truly stunning.

Sometimes Mateo wished that he could be one of them, one of the marked, innocent of the Tenders beckoning, that he could focus all his time and energy on pulling in Charges and working on finding a cure for them. Rick seemed to have a different idea.

"You know, sometimes, I wish I could still hear what was going on, from them, have a better idea. Feel like I'm sitting in the dark, man, a sitting duck," Rick muttered, turning his attention to the sugar spoon on table in front of his coffee, twirling it in his long fingers.

Mateo shook his head at him, slowly,

"It's radio silence right now, I don't know if they're congregating somewhere, talking this out in person, but nothing is coming across. I think they know there's a mole in their system,"

Rick looked taken aback,

"Did you tell Reggie this? Connor? They should know that you're shut out,"

Mateo shrugged and turned his lanky form on the bench of the booth, resting his shoulders against the glass and stretching out, crossed boots hanging over the end.

"They've got enough on their plate right now, they've-"

Mateo winced, clutching at his temples, knocking his cup over with his elbow, spilling hot coffee across the expanse towards Rick.

"Frig, tell me you heard that,"

Mateo pinched at the bridge of his nose, blinking rapidly, fumbling for napkins in the dispenser, dabbing at the sudden nosebleed he was experiencing. Rick gaped at him, and handed him more napkins, practically upturning the dispenser to curb the flow of coffee that had inched its way steadily towards him across the scarred table. Mateo opened his eyes and glanced at Rick, who shook his head fervently.

"Damn," he tipped his head back, still pinching his nose and slid from the bench to standing, fumbling for their mess of napkins, bunching them in his hand and heading for the door.

Rick followed him, bewildered,

"Mateo, stop, stop for a minute, what's going on?"

The door chimed as Mateo elbowed his way out past the younger man, checking for his gun under his jacket.

"Have you got your gun? Knife? Anything?"

Mateo was on the move, firing off questions with loping long strides, boots thudding along the street.

"Yes, but Mateo, wait, MATEO!" Rick grabbed at the sleeve of Mateo's jacket roughly, pulling him aside.

He was taken aback by the glint in Mateo's eyes, the stony glare he received when Mateo finally released the napkins he had still been clutching to his face.

"Will you tell me what's happening so I don't know, I don't go in blind? What the Hell has gotten into you?"

Mateo pulled his sleeve abruptly from Rick's grasp, looking around urgently before pulling him aside.

"You really didn't hear it? How is that even possible?"

Mateo looked down at Rick, searching his face.

"That's what I've been trying..." Rick faltered as Mateo rocked back again against the brick of the building next to them, clutching at his hair.

Rick grasped his shoulder, steadying him, looking around for anyone to see what was happening. The streets were still empty at this hour, still too early for anyone to be heading off to work. Mateo fumbled along the wall, fresh blood dripping from his nose.

"Adeline. Something is wrong. She's, she's screaming, in my head,"

Rick reacted to Mateo's confession, panicked, looking around for any sign of her.

Mateo bent his long frame over at the knees, leaning against the wall, waiting for the dizzying pain to stop, hoping that his nose would cease bleeding. He'd never experienced as powerful a transmission as this; most of the voices in his head were nudgings, gentle, a softly prodding finger and a quiet message. Adeline was cutting, a knife, deep, right through his nerve endings. He guessed now that he was right, that she wouldn't be the only Byrne without powers. This made everything much more complicated.

"Well we have to find her? Do the others know? I thought she was with them?" Rick asked anxiously, waiting for Mateo to buckle down and give him direction.

Mateo scoffed, briefly, a gurgling noise that mixed with the blood that was running down his throat.

"Deke had a confession to make, I don't think Adeline took it too well," he grimaced.

Mateo staggered forward,

"I think she's this way, come on, you'll have to try, to get through to Reggie, I can't right now, it hurts, everything hurts," he winced at the fire spreading through his skull, barely able to form the words. Rick shook his head and pulled out his phone,

"No way I'm trying that, look, sit down, you look like you just broke something, no, sit,"

Mateo tried to veer away, but Rick grabbed his upper arm firmly, phone to ear as it dialed through, and pushed Mateo down on the edge of a cement planter, still empty from the passing winter.

He could see Mateo trembling, and he knew that their interim rock star was hurting a lot more than he was letting on. If he had tried manhandling him any other day, he'd have needed more than two hands, and probably would've ended up with a broken wrist for the trouble.

"Yo, Reggie, yeah? Yeah, he got a full hit of it. Yeah? Really? Shit, no I'm fine, she must be by you guys," Mateo stared incredulously at Rick, hearing only half of the conversation, watching as Rick's face transformed with each new revelation.

"Yeah, probably, good idea," Rick looked directly at Mateo, and then turned away,

"Alright, yeah, see you guys there then," he thumbed off the phone and turned back to Mateo, who was alternately looking concerned, and shooting him daggers.

"Adeline ran off; just like you said. Something Deke did. They heard her, knocked them back pretty bad, but it looks like you're the only one who got hit that hard. Since they got it, and I didn't, we are assuming she's off to the east somewhere, they want us to come back there first, and not go running off," he grabbed Mateo again as he tried to hobble off and forced him back to sitting,

"Not, *running off* Mateo, half-cocked and no plan, ok?" He looked directly into Mateo's eyes, could see the cop in them trying desperately to spring into action,

"Grab me again, kid, I swear to God," Mateo gritted his teeth, leaning on his knee, running a hand through his hair.

"God ain't in this right now, so you need to just relax, we'll get her,"

Mateo shook his head.

"You didn't hear her Rick, something awful is happening,"

"Yeah, I can see that," he squeezed Mateo's shoulder, and started off towards the base, hearing Mateo groan as he staggered to his feet and followed after him.

Deke stood in the doorway, staring. He couldn't help it. His feet were frozen where he stood, his knees locked, fighting against his will. The face looking back at him, the glaring silver eyes that should have been a searing cobalt blue, they were like looking into the deep rivers of the past.

Time flowed differently, in this moment, eddies catching his memories, tossing them back at him, flotsam on the shore. They were staring down that same nose at each other, mirrored in the high cheekbones, their father's face, the one that they shared, fixing each other with an odd look of love and bitter contempt.

Where Deke was lean, a runner in a previous life, Casey was a whip, muscled, but in that angular fashion of snowboarders and skaters. Moments of history passed by, each thinking of what went wrong.

They both had their arms crossed, Deke standing, Casey still sitting on the metal table where Julia had tattooed him, the pain still dully thudding deep in his muscle.

Deke could feel the energy in the room crackling, a thunderstorm brewing between them. He knew Casey was only freshly tattooed, that he shouldn't be a problem, yet, but he didn't know how strong Casey was, or could be. The truth was, no one could know anything, and it was all too new, too much for anyone to really know.

He was hesitant of crossing the threshold; of starting this conversation again. He was hesitant of going back, to that place, so many years ago, that he'd only just started thinking he could forget. But first, of many questions, he needed to know, *did Casey know why he changed?*

"So, sold your soul, huh? Why am I not surprised?" Deke started, taking that last step into the room, closing the door behind him, and any chance on delaying this conversation. Casey wanted a piece of him?

Bring it on.

Casey looked startled, whether at the sudden aggressive tactic, or the question, Deke couldn't be certain.

"What do you mean?" he wavered, eyeing Deke carefully, wary, sizing up their differences, wondering if it had been long enough.

"Don't play dumb with me, Casey, you know that's why you are what you are now," he pushed his hands into his pockets, the motion casual, but the reasons were less than benign. He was grasping at his knife, keeping it at the ready. Casey's eyes narrowed.

"If that's true, you did too. What was worth it to you, Deke? Have you figured that out?"

Deke slowly pulled the chair Reggie had vacated earlier closer to him, sitting down carefully, maintaining a strategic distance between them.

He leaned forward, pushing up the arms of his sleeves, revealing his scars.

Casey's eyes flicked to them, momentarily, and then back to Deke's.

"Your little girlfriend, showed me you could do that, I'm impressed,"

"Don't,"

Casey's lip curled into a sneer, his eyes glittering with barely contained wrath.

"You don't scare me Deke, not anymore," Casey matched his lean, folding his hands at his knees.

"I'm not here to scare you. I'm here to understand what you did, why you are here, how you managed to be the most violent Charge this team has ever encountered, seems like more than a coincidence, that we'd both end up the same way," Deke reasoned, sitting back.

Casey merely stared at him, the predator inside him swimming just below the surface, a sensation of another being looking out through Casey's eyes. This wasn't him - this attitude, this posturing, he had a distinct impression that something else was inside him, using Casey as a mask.

Deke shuddered.

"Why'd you do it Casey, what could you possibly gain?"

Casey grinned, eerily, toothily. His head lolled on his neck,

"You, stupid,"

Deke shook his head. What could Casey possibly want with him, after all this time?

"We knew the only way to get to you, was through her, but you shut us out Deke, you closed the door," Casey had gone rigid, his eyes rolling upwards.

The voice coming from him was too deep, too rasping, to be Casey. Deke was startled backwards, entirely uncertain of what was happening. Casey's skin began to crackle, lightning fissuring from pores, leaping from his fingertips, sparking around his head.

"We have her now, Deke, so come and play," Casey's head lowered, level with Deke's.

He swore, for a moment, as the lighting in the basement flickered, in the glow from Casey's skin, the glistening shadows of pointed teeth flashed across his mouth, the whites of his eyes reflecting the lightning. Deke grabbed at Casey's shoulders, shaking him,

"What the Hell are you doing in my brother? Get out!"

The voice cackled once,

"We have her, Deke, we have her, Deke, we have her, Deke, come to where the dead play, come and play, come and play," the horrible voice issued its taunt, over and over again, Deke furious.

His own hands began to spark in response, vivid and angry. Where his hand clamped down on the marks on Casey's arm, he felt a strong jolt run up his arm and back down, a blinding flash striking his vision. A shrieking wind filled the room, scattering paperwork and knocking down books. A loud crack resounded across the ceiling, echoing in Deke's ears.

Casey crumpled to the table.

The site of where Deke had held him sizzled, his grip burnt into Casey's flesh.

"Shit,"

All thoughts of their estranged relationship and the subsequent anger briefly fled Deke's mind as he knelt down to table level, shaking Casey's prone form, trying to stir him awake.

It hadn't been Casey. It hadn't been Casey at all. If he had known, if he had known the Collectors could do that, what would he have done differently? Who knew they could possess people, even with the marks?

Casey's eyelids fluttered, a dull groan escaping his lips.

"Deke?" he mouthed, struggling to form the word.

Deke nodded, rising from where he knelt to give him room to struggle back up to sitting. Casey had visibly cringed when he had looked into Deke's eyes.

Did he know what the strange eyes meant for them? They were now in an even stranger position than before. What did Casey know? How much *could* he know? When had the Collector taken over?

Casey clamped a hand to the burn on his shoulder, hissing as his fingers touched the enflamed flesh, the raw tattoo and the silver symbols. He didn't want to meet Deke's eyes again, wouldn't look him in the face. Whether it was guilt, or embarrassment, or fear, Deke didn't know.

"Casey, I know this is difficult, and this has been like a terrible bad dream for you, for both of us really, but you have to tell me what you know about what's going on here," Deke sat back down on the chair, suddenly feeling his years.

Feeling all the time that was slipping past him, all the time he had spent on being someone he wasn't. The last thing he needed right now, was this reminder, his little brother, the one person he had turned his back on from his old life that he never should have abandoned, coming forward and becoming a part of this destruction.

Casey wrapped his arms around himself, not from the cold; they didn't feel that anymore - but from recollection.

"They told me you were dead," he raised his molten eyes, finally, staring straight at Deke.

"Who told you?" Deke leaned forward.

"These men, they came to the door, couple weeks ago. They looked military. You know, all black, flak vests, the works. They told me that they'd taken you away, that you were theirs now. I didn't believe them, I didn't believe them at all, I swear,"

Deke grimaced and nodded for him to continue. There was only one group of armed men he'd come across, ever, in his life, and he would bet his life, or whatever you'd call the scrap that was left, that he knew exactly who sent them Casey's way.

"They showed me pictures, of Aaron, of what was done to him, because he got in the way," Deke shuddered at the thought.

He hadn't even had a moment, in a very long time, to think about what he'd done to that poor kid; just a roommate at the wrong time, wrong place in Deke's life. What would Casey do, if he knew that the Collectors hadn't done that to Aaron? That it had been Deke's fault all along?

"They said they'd be back, when they needed me, that the moment I saw them, I'd better know that you were gone, and there was only one way to ever get you back,"

Casey rubbed at his face, in disbelief, as he recited the tale he had lived, experienced, and still didn't understand.

Did they know he was going to break free of their control? Did they anticipate it? Plot against it, using his brother as leverage in their weird twisted game?

"So you made a trade?" Deke asked hesitantly, settling back in the chair.

Casey made a half-hearted shrug, staring off at the ceiling,

"I didn't think it was real, Deke, I just figured, if I played along with their game, they'd let me go, that it was all some sort of horrible joke, or something to do with one of your cases, trying to fix the results of a trial or something," Casey deflated, kicking his feet that dangled above the floor where he sat.

"Casey, I was *never* a criminal lawyer, I work, worked - on corporate mergers, what on earth would brutally assaulting and murdering Aaron, or anyone else for that matter, have to do with that?"

He rubbed his fingers through his hair, sparks flying. Casey looked at him oddly.

"How would I know that, Deke, when was the last time you were home? Picked up the phone?"

Deke stopped what he was doing, and shook his finger in Casey's direction,

"Don't, don't even go there, you know I had to leave,"

Casey scoffed. Deke bit back the words he shouldn't say, and continued,

"Anyway, that isn't the point. Point is, you played with fire, thought it was some strange awful joke, and now, coincidently, we are now in the same boat, despite the fact that it's been close to seven years since I've even laid eyes on you. I assume you know the basic rules of the game so far?"

Casey stared at him hard, absently tracing his fingers along the assorted marks on his arm.

"Sell your soul, kill the chosen, purge your humanity, go to Hell, and do not collect $200. Use the Charge to your advantage; don't get dead before you're ready," he recited.

Deke was taken aback.

"How do you know all that, how did they tell you?"

Casey shrugged.

"She told me you wouldn't come back, that I wouldn't find you, unless I did it right. Did as I was told,"

"She?"

"Some foxy looking woman, smoking body, golden eyes, she was a snake made human, if you ask me," Casey shook his head, trying to clear his brain of the smoke obscuring his thoughts..

In essence, that was what she was, their Tender. Smoke and mirrors vilified.

Casey pulled his legs up onto the table, sitting cross legged, straight-backed and pensive, rubbing his temples.

"What on earth is that God-awful ringing? I can't make it stop, it's coming from inside my head, and it's brutal,"

Deke grimaced.

"It's a side effect of you and I being near to each other, how we know we are around other Charges. I thought at first, it was bells, the first time I heard it, but now I feel like it's feedback, you know, when you get a microphone too close to a speaker? Signals crossing or something,"

Casey looked revolted, scratching at the stubble on his face.

Casey had changed so much since the last time he had seen him. Seven years was a long time. He'd grown a head taller, filled out; his stubble shadowing what could easily become a full beard, rather than the spottiness of adolescence. Deke had to keep reminding himself that though Casey was his kid brother, he wasn't a child anymore.

Deke realized with a jolt that aside from what had happened in the past few hours, Casey was entirely unscarred. Reggie had said Casey was incredibly violent prior to capture, and yet he didn't have a mark on him. Deke became incredibly aware of himself and the damage he and others had done, the scars crisscrossing his arms and torso.

"I think we had the same Tender, you and I, though for different reasons, she wanted you to lure me, find me, bring me out here, though, she did a piss-poor job of it, if you ask me, seeing as how I didn't even know you were down here, until Clara came out to tell me,"

Casey cocked his head to the side.

"Was that the blonde? She was the one who came to talk to us? The Collector let me up, then, gave me control. He didn't know my name. I tried to warn her, but she left, and then he came back, squashed me down, I was only able to watch," an involuntary shiver ran through him.

"Did you notice when Reggie was here, that the ringing went away?"

Casey raised a hand above his head,

"Yey high? Red hair? Coiled just a little too tight? Yeah everything was fine, until he left, she's the only one like me I had ever seen, until you showed yourself in here, what does it all mean?"

Deke shrugged, sighed, deflated. That was the question of his life, what *did* it all mean?

"The only thing that Reggie and Addy have in common, and they both make the ringing go away, mind you, is that they were Clara's bargain. They're the reason she sold her soul. I don't know why it makes them different, or what they are beneath it all, but they seem to fix a lot of this, they cancel it out, when they're around," Deke made a vague gesture around his face.

In that split second Deke knew the mistake he had made. He'd heard it in his voice, the softened pause after he said Addy's name.

They'd been wasting their time here.

The Collector had said the only way to get to him was through her - and Deke had shut the door. Adeline had been the only tool that the Collectors had, they had invaded her dreams, hunted her down while she slept, and Deke had made sure that they could no longer find her. After Addy had received her tattoo, causing radio silence, the Collectors had returned to capture and use Casey, in order to get back at Deke.

They wanted him. They wanted him to come and play, come play where the dead play. They weren't going to give up on reclaiming him.

And they had their bargaining chip.

Chapter 21

Purissima

"Good, you're here,"

Reggie commented angrily, looking up as Mateo burst through the basement door, Rick in close step behind him. Mateo looked like he'd been through Hell, the color drained from his face, his normally crisp shirt spattered with droplets of blood. He swayed on his feet, surveying the scene before him.

Julia was sitting primly on one of the couches, handkerchief pressed to her face, held tilted back to stem the blood. Reggie sat close by her, massaging his temples, one of his eyes had gone bloodshot.

Stella looked unaffected, though relatively more green than was normal. Connor was sitting on the floor, back against the cupboards, cradling a glass of water to his forehead.

Clara looked numb, shaking quietly in her seat at Connor's desk.

Deke chose that moment to enter through the door at the back of the room, the Charge labelled S.F close behind him. Mateo reached for his gun, but Reggie waved him off.

332

"Been a lot of revelations here, Mateo, since you were gone,"

Mateo's eyes slid to Clara, waiting, breath bated. Was it now that all will be revealed? Was he right?

Reggie's look shut him down. Reggie knew what Mateo was thinking without even having to check in.

Mateo realized S.F was staring at Rick, concern bubbling behind his eyes.

Deke had slid S.F slightly behind him when Mateo had reached for his gun, and he suddenly saw the similarities between them, in posture, in face, in build. And with the matching mirrored irises, it wasn't hard to see the resemblance they'd all missed when Deke had first appeared.

"You're brothers," he stuttered, and all eyes turned toward Mateo.

Reggie nodded his head, and waved it away. Mateo had a hundred questions; he needed to know what they knew. Reggie stared him down though; the audience of the room was too intent, too interested, they couldn't share what they knew, not yet.

"Rick, I need you to stay here, Mateo, can you walk? You'll need to move fast," Reggie questioned, calmly, rising to stand in front of them all.

Mateo straightened up, tried to ignoring the rushing in his head, knowing that behind the rigid question was genuine concern for his well-being,

"As always, for a Byrne," he tipped a mock salute, and Reggie's mouth creased into a thin line.

"You know where you have to go, what I need you to do, right?" Reggie asked, seriously, staring hard at Mateo.

They didn't dare use their telepathy, all their heads felt exposed, open nerves rubbed raw.

Mateo nodded, casting another curious glance at S.F and Deke, and retreated the way he came. He raced as fast as his unsteady legs would take him, unbuckling the locks at the door, praying that Addy would be exactly where he thought she was.

"Since when did we let Gnasher out of his cage?"

Rick gestured at Casey. Rick had been tempted to go with Mateo, no one else was going to look after him and he was running himself ragged. The man was almost old enough to be their father and he treated them all as such. Always putting this ragtag group of kids, really, ahead of himself. Who knew what the cost would be, one of these days? Casey shrunk back, looking apologetic. Deke strode forward,

"Since Reggie's girlfriend here bagged and tagged him with the marks, so don't worry about it *Rick*,"

Rick huffed, angrily, eye-balling Casey's guilt-ridden face, not trusting it for what it was. Deke waited for an angry retort from Rick, but none came. When he was satisfied that Rick would stay shut up, he continued,

"Now that that is settled, Reggie, what can we do? You've got three Charges on your hands now; we've got to be worth something,"

Reggie nodded, making sure that Rick and Casey were now of an understanding. It was obvious that Rick was hesitant – Casey *had* tried to literally take a bite out of him – and he had the nineteen stitches under his collar to prove it.

"Where did the Collector say they'd taken her?"

"Where the dead play. He just kept saying that, over and over again, does it mean anything? Cemetery? Can't be that many in Half Moon, could there?"

Deke looked around as everyone rose up from where they had been sprawling, straightening stiff limbs and looking between each other anxiously. Reggie rubbed at his face, running his hands anxiously through his hair.

"Purissima," Reggie put his hands on his hips and sighed.

Connor spoke up,

"You always figured we'd end up there, Reggie," Connor looked exhausted, skin pale beneath his black and blue eye, but there was a hopeful gleam behind his glasses that Deke didn't know what to make of.

Casey moved over to sit on the desk next to Clara. Even to the uninitiated of the group, it was obvious where loyalty lines lay – Charges with Charges. Deke raised an eyebrow at Clara, who returned his gaze numbly. He desperately wanted to comfort her, but there was a chasm between them now. Everything was going horribly wrong.

"Purissima was an old town not far south of here. It struggled, in the 1800's, to claim its space, to grow, to prosper, like all towns back then, dealing with swinging pendulums of drought and floods. Come 1868, homesteader John Purcell deeded his property to create the Purissima Cemetery - but before it could become hallowed ground, a farm hand tired of struggling through the chaos of the West went to the center of it all and called for the Devil to come save him, offering up the souls of the villagers in return," Connor recited.

"Problem is, he figured the Devil would just take the souls, leave 'em for dead. But he doesn't play like that. He took this opportunity to Convert them, and send his children on their merry way to cause destruction and mayhem where ever they roamed, until they burnt up and his Collectors could have them. By the 1930s, there was no one left, and even the buildings were on their way out," Stella caught up to where Connor dropped off, an icy edge to her tone.

"And now, Purissima is a ghost town, nothing left of it actually, except the cemetery. General idea is that the Devil preserved it, a kind of homecoming location for all the energy of Converted souls," Connor pushed up his glasses, wincing where his finger caught his black eye.

"Is that why you guys chose to settle here? To be close to the energy?" Clara asked, looking back and forth between Connor and Reggie.

Connor nodded, while Reggie looked away from her gaze, staring down at the floor. From the expression on his and Rick's face, they looked to be in private discussion during this story time.

"So, we can pretty much guarantee, if the Collector that was possessing Casey told you that they're keeping Addy where the dead play, it's going to be there,"

Reggie moved over to the large metal cabinet behind the desks, pulling another key from under his shirt and unlocked it. He pulled the double doors open wide and studied the contents.

Deke moved forward, staring in awe at what it held.

The vast arsenal inside was completely unexpected when you considered who in the room would be employed to use it. None of them were truly cold blooded killers, but the fact that they'd be taking down Charges – other people with blood on their hands they couldn't control – people that could be saved if only they would be marked – sent chills down Deke's spine. And he was certain that Clara and Casey would feel the same.

Reggie handled the distribution, with routine checks of slides and safeties, locks, ties, and ammunition quickly following. Deke's head spun, Clara looked ill. He looked down at the gun that had been pressed into his hand; what was he doing? He was a lawyer, how did it all come to this? He choked back a wave of nausea, thinking back to his father's unseeing eyes staring up at him. He nearly dropped the gun.

Julia came up, eyes gentle and vividly blue, and placed a hand on his. She jumped, briefly, as the shock passed through her arm, but didn't let go until he had returned her smile.

She proceeded to give him a short tutorial, speaking low, passing glances to Reggie's tense back as he continued on his way, and handing out the tools of mayhem and destruction they would need to even stand a chance.

Casey watched on with interest. Reggie hadn't provided him with a gun, but rather had handed over a wicked looking dagger. Deke hadn't heard what Reggie had said, but a dark and troubled look had passed over Casey's face and Deke needed to know what had caused that reaction in his brother.

But questions could wait for later.

Reggie pulled a long coat from the rack by the door and shrugged into it, concealing the holsters he had donned and the guns they held.

Deke thought he looked older now – too worn around the edges, too tired for his age. The hand spasm was hidden by the sleeves of his coat, but Deke could catch the ticking running up his elbow as he surveyed the motley assortment of life-or-death followers that prepared for what could quite rightly be their ends.

Reggie's gaze moved to focus on Clara, and it hardened. Deke realized they hadn't actually had a chance to talk – to explain, there had been no time for Clara to try to fix what was wrong between her and her idol.

Clara's face spoke volumes though, and his heart broke for her.

As wrong as it was, what she did, as much as Reggie never would have asked her to do it for him, not in a million years, she only could have done it out of love, right?

Reggie couldn't hold that against her, not forever, they'd have to make up eventually. Otherwise, what would the point be?

It bothered him though, as he still didn't remember why he had done it, what he'd given up to become what he was today, what could he possibly have told Dezi, that she would've flipped him for Conversion?

Deke studied the back of Casey's head, Julia had moved on to him, speaking quietly, briefly touching his arm where his new assortment of scars lay and smiling encouragingly.

Was it Casey? Did he finally realize that Casey was all he had left in the world, and that he'd do anything to fix the animosity between them? That couldn't be it – he could still feel the anger burning holes in the back of his skull, the desire to rage at the universe when he thought about what Casey had contributed towards his parents' deaths.

It was obvious why Casey had given up his soul, Deke's Tender had come to him explicitly with the intention of tricking Casey into giving it up to rescue Deke, when in all honesty – they were only using him because they were so alike; guilt-ridden, vulnerable, and utterly vicious. They had no intention of letting Deke know what his brother was doing out in San Francisco, they simply were increasing their efficiencies coast-to-coast.

Deke resisted the urge to fling the gun at the wall in anger. Unbidden, his skin had begun to spark, Clara and Casey swiveling towards him as the smell of ozone filled the air.

"Deke," Clara warned, moving close to him.

Her eyes flickered, he could see that she was barely reining in her power too, and now he understood the tremble to her lips.

"Don't touch him Clara, we'll need it, against the other Charges, don't need you blowing up the bug zapper before we get out there," Reggie called across the room.

"What happens if it overpowers us before it gets there, huh Reggie? You and your whole team will be right in the way, and this whole thing will blow up right in your face,"

Reggie cracked open his shotgun, checking the rounds, before slamming it closed.

"He's a loaded gun Clara, you too. Just gotta point you in the right direction and shoot," he tipped his fingers in a mock salute, and then spun around, gesturing for his motley crew to follow.

Reggie and Mateo had discussed this a thousand times before. They had discussed it well before Reggie's death – they had discussed years before Reggie ever officially became a Tender.

They knew exactly who would take Adeline if Reggie ever rebelled. They simply would have to wait for all the pieces to slide into place once Reggie escaped the Tenders. There was a certain inevitability to the situation that they never would have been able to work around. When you worked against a common enemy this strong, this predictable, it was only a matter of time before the walls crumbled around them.

It was why Mateo had Addy's house watched. It was why only he knew that Deacon Masterson, their first attempt at saving a Charge, and gone to Adeline's house that night, that he had followed Clara. Mateo had spent every moment since trying to understand why. They hadn't known Charges could sense each other, not until now. But he was relieved the stars had aligned how they had – that Deke had found Clara and that Addy had figured out the marks.

She'd always been so smart.

It was true, that Mateo had sent out the bulletin for Deke's crimes before flying out to join Reggie. But it was the only way to pull sightings in from across the U.S, to track more carefully where they were, and how soon they'd be here, especially once Addy realized she needed to be marked too.

Mateo just wished that Reggie could have set aside his anger, and told Addy sooner what was what, he wasn't protecting her anymore by not telling her the truth. Normally, he'd agree that the truth was dangerous – but now it was the only thing that could have kept her safe.

He just needed her to be safe. It wasn't fair.

Mateo put his head between his knees, needing another rest, head pounding, just needing another moment to stop, and think, back to when he had realized he needed to be there for her, for them all.

Mateo had held the tiny baby in his arms, so many *years ago; it was this darling little girl who had the whole* world in front of her. He had wondered at her fingers, the tiny grasp around his thumb. Her twin lay in the crib below, gurgling, smiling up with tiny emerald eyes and long lashes.

They were the splitting image of their mother and he had cringed at the thought of their future with her.

He had only just been introduced to this strange new world, and it had become a terror he only could have imagined, and yet here he was, still.

Levina Byrne had come to him, a year previously, inviting him to join the Tenders. She had explained it as a great honor, a holy mission to cleanse the world of evil.

He had believed her, at first, believed in his powers, and it was the only thing that had kept him that year; the idea that he was doing right. Then he had found out why these babies were born.

He had found out that they were needed for their powers, to continue a long line of powerful psychics among the Tenders. The whole truth had unraveled after that. All the innocence lost, the lives thrown to the wayside time after time; and for what? This was all because Hell wanted more souls? He had regretted every moment he had helped them with their mission. But he couldn't leave the fold. Not now.

He had wandered to the window, Adeline cooing in his arms, and looked out at the sunset beyond. The shadows were dusky, the air a bright beautiful orange. A storm brewed on the horizon, dark clouds and vivid lightning.

He remembered the feeling of tension, that crackling underbelly of fear he felt every time he looked down at her. No one else was going to watch out for them, no one else was going to make sure they got out of this alive.

So he would.

Mateo was stunned out of his reverie by another skull splitting scream, pulled violently back to present time.

He had paused, leaning against a fence post several blocks to the east of the bunker to gather his thoughts, dabbing at his trickling nose. The images had flooded into his head, unbidden from that night so many years ago when he had made a promise to a tiny little girl and her twin brother.

He'd barely been beyond a child himself, still young to the ways of the world, but already so far outside of innocence, once the Collectors had gotten their claws into him.

Thoughts raced past, following the scream that ran through Mateo's head. They had found out where she was. They had found out who she was. Levina had found out that Mateo had been harboring the one person she wanted most, and she was taking it out on Addy.

He cringed. He had hoped that Clara hadn't known who her Tender really was. But something told him she had been lying to him, and hadn't wanted to say anything in front of Adeline.

Why had it all gone so horribly wrong when Reggie and Addy died? Clara had been inconsolable. Mateo knew how deeply injured she was, because he had tried to help her.

He had flown with her, to Whistler, held her hand while she made the identification. He had helped her escort the bodies back to Boston. He had tried so very hard to make her understand; to help her make the right decision. He needed her to make the decision that left their cold and broken bodies in the ground. It was what Reggie would have wanted. It was what Adeline could have handled.

But Clara had been fragile, a little bird with brittle bones, too many years of harsh words and wrong decisions. She couldn't handle knowing what Reggie was, what Reggie had been. She couldn't handle being all alone with *her*, the one who had forced Reggie into it all to begin with, the moment his powers started expanding. To top it all off, Clara couldn't handle knowing that she could change it all; that it was in her power to make it like it never ever happened.

Wouldn't you? If you knew the only people you loved in the world, and the one person who knew the truth, were gone, forever, and you could *change that, bring them back to life - wouldn't you?*

He just wished Clara hadn't gone to her. If Clara had come to him first, he could have helped her, helped her find a different Tender. He could have helped her smuggle away, away from that awful, evil woman, try to live a normal life until they could find a way to get her soul back. But instead, Clara had chosen to forget him. Forget what she had done, to do it all the hard way. It was easier for her. She didn't have to deal with the pain of losing them anymore, as he did every day since.

It had cut him to the core, knowing that Clara would so willingly give them all up.

Now, Adeline was in danger, all these Collectors and Charges that were coming down on their heads; putting Adeline in danger of finally learning the truth about her family. And the secrets that Reggie had kept for too many years.

These were secrets that would have died with Reggie, if only Clara had been strong enough.

Chapter 22

Mother Dearest

I hadn't realized there would be so many of them. I just needed to get outside, to get air, to get out of this web of lies and deceits that just kept growing around me.

Why did everyone feel the need to lie to me?

Reggie had never told me the truth, until now. Did he honestly believe me so fragile? Everything I'd ever known about him was twisted. Clara couldn't tell me the truth, because she'd been forced to forget – but she'd been living with me alive every day, and I'd never known the difference.

And now Deke, the one person I'd trust with my life and he'd gone and done *that*. *And Clara couldn't tell me that either.*

What was I supposed to do?

I sat down on the curb, the blood red fingertips of the sun finally rising above the horizon, the light weak and oddly pink.

They were so very quiet; I didn't look up until it was too late.

A dozen hands grabbed me, eyes glinting, silver spun in the strange light, men and women, Charges, pinning my arms at my sides. When their hands touched me, I burned, and I took a deep breath, and I screamed, long and loud. They let go of their hold, grasping their heads and buckling.

The scream echoed long after I stopped, bouncing off the walls in an unearthly rhythm.

I scrabbled backwards, reaching for the handle of the door, desperately trying to pull myself inside, when they advanced towards me again, each gripping a limb tightly.

Deke's Tender appeared in front of my eyes before I could scream once more, just as he had described her, dark flowing hair and glittering golden eyes. She smiled, wolfishly, and snapped her fingers.

The seconds as they ticked by burned me to the core, every bone, every muscle, every organ, and every nerve on fire.

I screamed again, but it was lost in the darkness where pain held my hand, pulling me down.

I gasped, the pain ceasing, and realized I was no longer anywhere near Dizzy Moon. I lay on hardwood floor, gazing up at a plaster ceiling, an elegant glass light fixture hanging down above my head. I winced in the soft light, my head splitting open.

"Are you finished?" Deke's Tender appeared in my field of vision, the wafting smell of lilies following her move.

"Lilies," I wheezed, clutching at my forehead.

She turned away, speaking to someone on the other side of the room.

"First, she screams incessantly for half an hour, now she's questioning me about my perfume choices," she shook her head and clucked her tongue at me.

I rolled over onto my stomach, anxiously trying to clamber to my feet. Having her stand over my head was dizzying, the golden eyes hypnotic. I only made it to my knees before the nausea became overwhelming.

She stood before me, tall, straight-backed, arms crossed; face an expression of cold disinterest, and seething hatred.

Something tickled my brain, a thought, or a memory, it trickled down my spine and I struggled to grab hold of it.

She took several steps forward, rapid and imperceptible, and stooped down, grabbing my chin, turning my head, and staring at my eyes. I tried to pull away but her grasp was iron tight, I could feel her dark red nails nearly piercing my skin.

"I know, you remember, I know it's in there, somewhere, Adeline," she hissed.

The way my name curled around her tongue, combined with the overwhelming scent of dusky flowers served to knock the sense back into my brain.

I understood now, what Deke had smelled back at the cottage, understood what caused the predator to raise its evil head deep inside him. I had taken a nap in her room; I had lain for hours in this scent. And he had known.

She released my face, and took a step back, smiling.

"There she is, clever girl," she whispered, low and sultry, a pout grazing her lips.

She looked back at the shadowy corner once more, a low growl rising in return from the emptiness.

"Mother?" I whispered.

She smiled, toothily.

"How?" I shuddered, cold against the floor.

She tapped a finger against her arm, impatiently, debating how much I needed to know.

"First off," she wiped at her arms, first left, then right, straightened her shoulders, and snapped.

Her hair began to shorten, curl, and lighten, rising to just above her shoulders, falling in fat red ringlets. Her skin slowly transitioned to a creamy unmarked white from warm coffee. Her eyes widened, and the hypnotic gold slid towards a deep stormy green, the color of broken bottles stirred up in the sand, pounded to round edges. Her lips grew fuller, Clara's mouth, and she fixed me with an even white grin, wolf's teeth in a rosy smile. Mother as I knew her, always had known her, now stood defiantly in front of me.

"Better?"

I cringed back away from her – what was she?

"I make dreams come true, Adeline," she responded softly to the question I didn't ask out loud.

I didn't answer, I could only stare. What had my life been? What was I?

"You're of ancient people, Adeline, we keep everything running smoothly, make sure that the Kingdom has souls, by making sure the people up here have their hearts desires, it is a glorious and noble purpose," she straightened her collar, the cold look still in her eye.

"You damn people to Hell!" I accused, lip trembling.

I didn't feel that I was in control of my own body anymore, shaking with rage.

"True, but for one shining moment, those people are infinitely happier. They wouldn't do it if they didn't believe it was worth it, would they?"

"You trick them!"

"Yes, I do. But it fulfills them! They experience their hearts desire. How else to draw on their spark of humanity? How else to charge them up, so we can burn them out? Stars burn brightest before they die, Adeline. We need souls, and they give them to us,"

"But why would you let Clara do it? How could you? She's your daughter, we are your children! Are you really that heartless? Did you force Reggie into the fold? Make him become as heartless and murderous as you? Don't you think he'd rather have died?"

"Souls are souls, Adeline. I haven't lived this long, been this successful, to let your opinion of family get in my way. I see opportunities, and I take them, your father was one of them,"

My heart dropped like a stone, my throat closing around the scream of rage I would not give her the satisfaction of hearing.

"Then why are we even here? Why did you even bother?" I raged.

"The hope that some of you, maybe even all of you, would be like me; would have the power, be committed to the cause as deeply as I am. We needed you to continue on the long illustrious line of Tenders. What else would the point be?"

There was nothing inside of her that wanted us, needed us, or loved us. The reality of our lives was that we only existed to be wielded, and the idea relentlessly pummeling at my brain. And Reggie had known, Reggie had known it all, for years, and he never told me.

"And now, I have you, and Deacon will come. He will come for you, as he must, and if I'm lucky, so will that entire gang of disobedient miscreants and their feeble attempts to pull down this machine, mere grit in the massive cogs that have been turning for centuries. We'll cut them down, drag them out. Destroy those silly symbols and get Deacon and Ellaclara to do what they do best. Harvest me innocent souls, until they burn up. And then everything will be back to the way it was. Reginald will behave as a true Tender, if it's the last thing he does,"

I stared at her in horror, at the monster in Mother's mask I could now see clearly.

She smiled.

"I could never let my best Charge go, Adeline. He was relentless, guilt driven, perfection, and I need him to finish what he was Converted to do, it was just lucky for me that he found you, you always did feed the power,"

"I did what?" An intense shudder passed through my body, a realization of the total exhaustion I had been experiencing.

"You and Reginald, twins, powers split when you were born. I always told you Reginald was the better half, psychic, all-knowing, but what I didn't realize, until much later, was that he was drawing on you, on your latent power, and so could the Charges. They feed off it, absorb it. All this time with Deacon and Ellaclara, and didn't you feel it? They can only gather so much, through storms and electronics and static, but with you; they could go on for years longer than a regular Charge, we would never have to surrender them to the Collectors until we were ready,"

I was at a loss for words, realizing that every moment in our journey, when I had thought I was feeling too tired, too exhausted beyond necessity, they had actually been draining me. When Deke had gripped me tight at the Estes camp site, our powers were colliding. No wonder they both needed to spar so quickly, trapped in the car with me for hours at a time. No wonder Reggie had always crashed at my place during his weeks of depression. He'd needed to recharge, he needed to be near to me.

And it was no wonder Reggie had run off to California, as far away from me as possible.

He didn't want me to know.

He didn't want to use me anymore.

I pounded the hardwood floor beneath my fingers, shaking my head.

Mother raised a carefully arched eyebrow at me.

"Come, Adeline, get off the floor, there is work to do before Deacon comes to find you. He won't be expecting us here; it isn't where we told him to meet. No use using your tantrums on me, you know they never worked,"

I looked up at her with utter disgust.

A knocking came from the trim of the entry way behind me; I flinched and turned toward the sound, Mother looking up at the new arrival.

She smiled, as I gaped.

"Ah, yes, Mateo, do come in. This must be strange for you, since she hasn't the slightest idea who you are,"

Mateo inclined his head slightly, the closest he'd ever get to actually bowing in her presence. My eyes were wide and wild, I knew, and my head spun with this new revelation. Did Reggie know Mateo was playing both sides?

Mother nodded in return, and gestured toward me, before spinning on her stiletto heel and heading towards the passage beyond. Mateo stooped and grabbed me under the arm, roughly pulling me off the cold floor. I squirmed in his grasp, trying to twist out of his hold.

"You asshole, you lying, conniving, how could you," I hissed through my teeth, trying to break free.

"Shh, listen, hey, stop,"

I clocked him directly in the chin, and he grabbed my wrists, holding them tightly behind me.

"I don't have time to explain right now, I'm trying to *save* you, if you'd just stop *fighting* me,"

I roughly pulled forward again, but he held my wrists tight, and pushed me ahead of him, frog marching me after Mother.

My head whirled. What was Mateo saying?

He pushed me down a dark hallway, elegant and expensive paintings lining the dove grey walls, the dark wood floors shining. Mother's heels clicked as she travelled before us, a foreboding sound in the otherwise silent house. The cloying smell of lilies covered everything; the stench was enough to make me retch. It crawled down your throat that scent, and it made me want to claw out my eyes. How had I grown up with this?

She came to a stop before a dark mahogany door, and consulted her watch. Mateo waited patiently, still grasping my wrists, and she smiled at him. She began to transform once more, a reverse to the revelation from earlier, the hair darkening, lengthening, curling, her skin changing back to the rich café au lait it had been when she appeared, her eyes becoming almond shaped and the strange gold color reappeared, flashing in the dimness. She straightened the cuffs of her shirt, dusting invisible lint from her pants, and inclined her head towards the door.

"Take her in there, for now Mateo, keep an eye on her. You know her as well as I do, she's a tricky little minx and she's sure to find a way out, or a way to contact Reginald, if you don't watch her carefully," she instructed him, turning those strange snake eyes towards me. Mateo nodded in agreement,

"Yes, I know whose blood she is," he offered a sardonic smile in accompaniment.

354

Mother laughed, a tinkling sound, light and flirtatious. She turned away again, wiggling her fingers over her shoulder as she left. Mateo let go of me with one arm, looking hurriedly around the dark hall, and then opened the door, pushing me inside the pitch-black room ahead of him.

When he had closed the door behind him, flicking on the light switch nearby, I whirled on him, beating my fists against his chest.

"What the Hell is going on Mateo, why are you here? Do you work for her? Did you double-cross Reggie?"

Mateo leaned his tall frame tiredly back against the door, hands held up in surrender, waiting for me to realize he was wearing his bulletproof vest – and that my hands already felt beaten and bruised from my assault on him. They were sure to be black and blue by morning; if I lived that long.

I stepped back, waiting for answers, waiting for him to confess everything.

"Mi mariposa loca," he murmured under his breath, admonishing me in Spanish.

Those words, I recognized them. I could remember that voice, whispering to me in the dark, the lilting cadence, the rolling of the tongue.

I would wake up, with nightmares, screaming. I couldn't have been more than six. Most nights, Reggie would gently crawl over from his side of the room; snuggle tightly up against me, waiting for me to be alright. But there were nights... I could almost catch them, the memories flitting away, tiny fireflies of remembrance. The smell of sandalwood, of being picked up in the dark. Of being cradled until I slept; the whispers, comforting in the dark, the words foreign to me.

"What did you say?"

"My crazy butterfly," he smiled grimly, half flinching, waiting for something.

"You, you were there, weren't you?" I stared at him, mouth agape, seeing him with different eyes.

"Always,"

The past came rushing back to me, all the memories, brutal and complicated. Everything I'd ever remembered that was good, caring, loving, memories of my Mother and the moments when she was ours.

It was never her.

It was Mateo, always Mateo. He was the one who comforted us when we cried. He was the one who had taken us to Yellowstone. He was the one who had taught us to swim, to ride bicycles, had sat at Mother's kitchen table, teaching us our alphabet.

All the memories hit me hard, the reality of it all shifting back to the truth, Mother erased, and I staggered.

"Did Clara make us forget? Was it part of her deal?"

Mateo's hands lowered, I could see them shaking, clenched now.

He nodded.

"Oh, Mateo,"

I stepped forward, bridging the gap between us, the forgotten years, the damaged chasm where everything had been lost, and clung to him, tears dampening his dress shirt, and he squeezed me just as tightly back, muttering Spanish into my hair.

He held me out at arm's length, and stroked my hair, tears brimming in his eyes.

"I hoped that eventually, you would remember me again, the reality the Collectors construct is fragile, flimsy at best, I knew it could be broken,"

A clock chimed in the hallway, and Mateo froze, counting the beats.

"We don't have much time, I don't think I can get you out of here, not before they notice, especially with those great invisible bastard dogs wandering the grounds, but I will do everything I can to get you away, once we are out at Purissima, it is where she expects them all to find her,"

"What is Purissima?" I asked as Mateo rushed to the window, looking out between the curtains and then turning back to me.

He stooped down and pulled a knife in a carbon holster from his boot, passing it to me.

"Put this, at your back, in the top of your pants, just there, your shirt should hide it," I did as I was told.

He checked the corridor, only opening the door a brief crack and then closing it with a soft whisper.

"Purissima is where it all started, it's a ghost town now, and nothing is left but weeds. But the old cemetery is still there, lost among the trees, she's amassing the new Charges there, she will stop at nothing to bring Deke to heel, Reggie too, I hope in the distraction I can get you out of there,"

"But, what about Reggie? What about Deke? What about Clara? Aren't we going to save them too?"

He looked searchingly into my eyes, and I saw the defeat in them. He took me by the shoulders, lowering his face to my level,

"Reggie agreed, years ago, that if it was him or you, I get you out first, and Clara well, she made her bed, and I will only help her once you are safe,"

I looked at him, aghast.

He looked away, sighing heavily.

"I know, it isn't what you want to hear, but you have a brother that never wanted to live again, and a sister who already gave her life for you, and you have to understand – they are both broken, and even if you were all to survive this, they would never be the same, one day or another, you're going to have to go on without them,"

"That's your advice, Mateo? You've been with us our entire lives, loved us, protected us, and saved us as well as you could, and your advice is to just let them go?"

He jerked back as if I had struck him.

His brown eyes widened, and he looked to struggle with what he wanted to say.

"Addy, my heart broke, when I heard the news. After all I had done for you, and all you three were to me, to find out that you had both died? Cold, alone, crushed under millions of tons of snow? That even if I had been there, there was nothing I could have done to save you? I made my peace, and tried to convince Clara otherwise. I tried so damn hard, but you know her!"

I could feel my heart shattering for him, as he continued,

"She went behind my back, went to your mother, and your mother made her promise that part of the deal was that I couldn't know any of you anymore. I think she may have suspected I'd fallen short of the flock, that I couldn't do it, couldn't be a Tender anymore. Do you know what that does to a person? Losing someone, completely, that you've loved since the day they were born, only to have them come back to you, but never to know you? Can you honestly know how that feels? I tell you, Addy, I tell you to let them go, because I know you will survive, as I did, as I had to,"

My face screwed up at his speech, I tried to choke back the tears, this man who'd seen me cry a thousand times, and now I didn't want him to see?

I turned away from him, and felt his warm hand on my shoulder.

"I'll try, Addy, but I am only me, and there are so many of them, and she is so strong, your Mother, she isn't human, but I promise only my best,"

I inhaled deeply, the weight of the past few hours heavy on my shoulders, and patted his hand. I turned to face him, my mentor, my protector, buried in the sands of time and memories, hidden from my reality and stripped from my brain,

"What do I do?"

"Why is this town so empty?" Clara asked quietly, a half step behind Deke. They were traveling, single file, through the streets, weapons carefully hidden in pockets and holsters and under jackets. It was a strange enough group to see, in the middle of the day, but shortly after dawn?

Any one person would have stood out, but together, three woman and five men, three of which had strange silver eyes and sparking fingers were definitely more than unusual.

She avoided touching Deke, as per Reggie's instructions, which the more she thought about, had sounded like a threat.

But she really wanted to. She really wanted to grab his hand, pull him aside, and make him talk. She needed to. She needed to know what he felt, why it had happened. Maybe she had been jealous, maybe she had been selfish, and maybe she had needed the comfort.

All those excuses, accusations, they made sense to her. At the bottom of it all, in the deep dark place where she acted out, those excuses were acceptable. But Deke didn't seem the type, didn't seem the type to have given into her so easily, especially when Addy's name was always so close on his lips. She shook her head, thinking all these things to herself, watching the sun rise over the town.

Reggie, a couple of beats ahead of her, Connor and Julia flanking him, seemed to be pondering a response to her question.

"This city is perched precariously close to a place of great evil, sometimes I think they just know, when it's better to just stay inside, you guys exude a lot of negative energy you know, so you can just imagine what it feels like to live somewhere that's been absorbing it for the better part of a century," he explained, over his shoulder, still wary and watching the shadows.

"Why would anyone want to stay here, then?"

She asked curiously, feeling that a hundred eyes were watching her through the cracks in curtains, behind closed doors.

Reggie looked at Julia, who winked at him and turned back to Clara.

"The surfing is legendary," she smiled and shrugged, and turned back to her careful strides.

Clara was dumbfounded, and shook her head. The group remained silent, but that didn't mean they weren't communicating. As far as Clara knew, they could be having intense discussions about the three of them, and they'd never know. She glanced back at Rick, who was bringing up the rear, and he raised an eyebrow at her.

Maybe she did know. The lot of them had terrible poker faces.

Casey and Deke were muttering between each other, keeping their voices low and their heads together, careful not to bump into each other. This meant the Charges were effectively pinned between the two groups of Tenders as they marched onward. Clara's skin crawled when she thought about Addy, where she was, and what could be happening to her. She must be so scared, Clara thought.

Well, I'm scared too, she admitted to herself.

She had known, the second she saw Mateo, saw him with Reggie, that this was all on the path of a slow burn to a bitter end. Mother was going to be so mad.

"Do they have to smile at me like that?" I cringed, looking up and down the line of gathered Collectors.

They were all tall, dressed finely, and all had the same pointed teeth, filling their mouths to the brim, lips torn and mangled. They looked like they could have been anyone off the street, unless you looked at their mouths. Or took a second look at the mass of chains they each held, much too heavy for a normal man.

Mateo held my elbow loosely, giving the semblance of total control to anyone watching. It also gave us the added benefit of standing close enough together to speak without being overheard.

"Sorry to burst your bubble, but that's just how they look," Mateo muttered softly in response.

I shuddered.

Amidst the Collectors, I could hear heavy footfalls, any number of the invisible hounds stalking amongst the grass, scattering birds that were hiding carefully under camouflage. Occasionally, they fought, the whines and growls coming out of the thin air, and one would quiet, whimpering.

"Have you ever actually seen one? They're dogs right?" I whispered over my shoulder.

Mateo chuckled in response.

"Sure,"

I didn't take that in any reassuring way whatsoever.

"So can these guys... you know...die?" I coughed out, tripping over the word.

I didn't relish the thought of having to kill anyone, or anything, but if it came down to it, it'd be important to know if it was worth bothering to try; especially if they tried to touch any of my family.

Sure, I was livid at Reggie, for keeping secrets, for hiding what Mother was and that Clara had brought us back, for running away to the other side of the country, abandoning us.

Sure, I was outraged at Clara, for deciding for me, if I should continue living, for making that decision without my knowledge.

And of course, I was mad at her, for Deke. I couldn't even process that right now, couldn't even fathom how it had happened. Or even why it had happened. All I knew was it hurt. I didn't have a claim to him, I knew that, but I thought he had felt differently. I thought maybe there had been something there.

I guess I was wrong. But, all in all, I still loved them, and I would still destroy anything that came between me and the people I loved.

Mateo shifted, bringing my attention back to the task at hand.

"Collectors don't die. You can't die when you aren't alive, same with the *dogs*. But the Collectors, unlike the Charges, can't touch you unless they're supposed to. They're just here for show, really. Scare the Hell out of most people, since Charges look normal until they're coming at you."

"You don't need to remind me about that," I said quietly.

Mateo's grip tightened slightly. I had told him about what had happened in Ohio, and later in Reno. The look in his eyes had broken my heart. My eyes rose to where Mother paced at the top of the hill, the broken teeth of the remaining gravestones scattered about her, rising from the brambles and vines in concentric circles.

The sun pierced the trees, rising up over the tops of the dense branches, scattering the light, dappled across the grass and weeds.

The heat was rising around us, the vegetation steaming, everything was becoming sticky, and yet my clothes felt clammy, it was so cold in the presence of the Collectors. It made me wonder, if they had been following me closer than I thought, all through this cross country trip. It made a lot of the moments when the chill was unnatural make more sense.

"What is she doing?" I cleared my throat, hoping she didn't hear me.

"She's communicating with a lot of Tenders right now, the ones controlling all the Charges prowling around out here, making sure they know to wait for her word, before they sic them on anyone," he slowly tilted his head towards the depths of the forest.

I could see the silhouettes of numerous figures amongst the trees, maybe six or seven, their eyes flashing in the sunlight.

"You can hear her?"

"Of course,"

"So does that mean that Reggie and the rest of them can hear?"

"Only if they're close enough, and we've got a horseshoe up our asses,"

"What are the chances we'd be that lucky?"

Mateo shrugged, watching Mother carefully, as his entire plan hinged on whether or not she was paying attention once Reggie showed up. We had both agreed, that according to her, I was secondary in any plan she had. I just didn't have the worth of Reggie or Clara, and especially Deke, and my relegation to simply bait was the only thing working in my favor. It was a careful waiting game.

Mateo had just hoped that Reggie wouldn't make her wait too long.

I agreed.

Mother gestured for Mateo to bring me over. I stared at this strange creature whose form Mother assumed. I still couldn't figure out how she did it – and Mateo hadn't offered to explain. He merely told me that she wasn't human – and anything else would be just too much to consider.

But after seeing the Collectors and feeling the warm breath of their beasts of Hell on my face, invisible and deadly, I was willing to believe anything.

"Hello, Adeline, keeping well?"

She smiled, the sunlight making her golden eyes glow. I rolled my eyes, and tried to pull my elbow out of Mateo's grasp.

"Reggie's not going to let you do anything to him, or Clara, you know that right?"

Her eyes narrowed at my use of their names, and I felt the cold eyes of the row of Collectors turn towards me.

"It must be hard, having so much faith in people that have hurt you so badly," she drummed her nails against her chin, arms crossed, looking at me with tilted head.

"Nothing as so bad as learning someone you called Mother is responsible for the damnation of thousands, including her own children," I spat back at her.

She chuckled in response, and I resisted the urge to claw her eyes out. The knife in my waistband was so close to my hand, if only Mateo would let me go, momentarily.

Mateo squeezed my elbow gently in warning. I assumed he could see what I was thinking, so I consciously tried to make my mind go blank.

"Mateo, darling, would you mind going and telling the Collectors we'll need them out of the sightline, if we're going to have any chance that the lot of them will all come up here?" She asked primly.

I could feel Mateo's involuntary shudder and winced internally for him.

He released my arm and headed back down the knoll, leaning back into the abrupt slope, sliding on the grass and crawling weeds. He remained stiff-backed, alert and wary as he approached them. They couldn't, nor wouldn't hurt him, but they were intimidating and terrifying to behold.

"I'm growing tired of this waiting game, it's time we gave them some encouragement, don't you think?"

I barely had time to react, let alone step away from her grasp, before she had latched onto my forearm, setting every nerve on fire. I screamed, once again, inside and out, every cell of my body shrieking. Through the fog of pain, I could see Mateo stumbling, the effect of my cry hobbling him as he struggled to return back up the hill.

She released my arm, and stepped back, a pleased smile stretching across her features. I crumpled to my knees, discarded and exhausted.

"Wonderful. I knew that latent power could come in handy for something, there's not a Tender or psychic within a hundred miles that couldn't hear that,"

Mateo had finally made his way back after the Collectors had drifted off into the trees, wordlessly, bloody grins smiling. He was wiping a drop of blood from under his nose, the red smearing across the back of his hand.

"Levina, was that truly necessary?" Mateo chastened softly, eyes torn between concern for me and pretending to remain the good little soldier she expected him to be.

Her only response was a gentle laugh and the flexing of her fingers as she reached for me one more time.

Chapter 23

Showdown

Deke cringed as the scream echoed through their ears once more. Even he could hear them now, after being spared from the explosive reaction in the basement when Addy had first run off. But it sounded muffled, underwater, far off and faint.

The rest had stumbled, some falling to their knees, trying to hold up against the assault on their minds. Reggie was tense and shaking, trying to remain steady in the face of the obvious pain of his sister, Julia, ever vigilant at his elbow, trying to keep him calm. Clara had gone pale, lost in thought, and had only snapped out of her reverie once the first scream had rippled through them.

They were collected in the ditch, just outside the road that turned off towards the remnants of the cemetery, trying to formulate a game plan for once they'd made it through the woods.

Birds tweeted at each other innocently, the occasional car blowing by, not slowing or caring for the strange group of people assembled on the side of the road. They'd scared a deer out of hiding about a half mile back, it had frantically side-stepped along the road before bounding across in a blur of beige and white.

The world seemed to be holding its breath in the presence of the other worldly forces beyond the line of trees. Whether or not it ever exhaled - and what it would take to release the pressure, had yet to be seen.

Deke rubbed his hands together anxiously, the embers flying from his fingers, and he splayed out his hands, staring at them. He was getting worried about how much longer he'd be here for, how much longer before he'd be out of control. He could only remember the absolute terror on Addy's face, how she had run from him, hid from *him*, the one person he'd promised he'd never hurt. And he had, twice.

How could he let her down so badly, when all she had done this whole time was give up everything for him? That she had just dropped her entire life, just to help him? A complete stranger?

His mind went back to comforting her, hidden in the playground equipment, how she had needed his closeness even after losing her mind with fear because of *him*.

How he'd been the only thing that could have made it right again; he didn't think even Clara or Reggie could have laid claim to the same. He resisted the urge to kick at a nearby rock, watched the tendrils of lightning increase in their intensity, rocketing up and down his arms. He took a deep breath and held it.

If he ever saw her again, if he ever got her back, if they lived through this, he would make it up to her. She needed to know how sorry he was.

Connor, Reggie, and Rick were in intense discussions with Stella, they must have realized that the screaming was done, as of now, and were working through possible scenarios hurriedly.

Julia sat with Casey, and they continued to talk. Deke wished he wasn't such a coward, that he was the one with his brother. But there were more important conversations to be had at the moment. He tilted his head at Clara, gesturing to a fallen tree that had plummeted lifeless into the ditch years ago and she nodded slowly, studying him warily.

They sat carefully, careful not to touch, careful not to sit too close. This taboo seemed to increase the tension, for after a week of preternatural closeness, and their recent entanglement, it seemed an impossible feat to comfort and explain with only words.

"Clara, I-," he turned towards her, barely shuffling back slightly to prevent their knees from knocking but she immediately began shaking her head, avoiding his eyes.

"Nuh, uh, no, Deke, I need you to listen to me, ok?"

Her eyes remained on Reggie, ignoring Deke's quick intake of breath at her admonishment.

"Addy told me what you said, back in Salt Lake City. About how you'd just, just let everything go to Hell because it was your last pit stop anyway, and why the Hell not, right?" Deke nodded, slowly.

She rubbed at her forehead, realizing that the discussions of the group in front of them were quickly coming to a close. Time was running out, and there was just too much to say.

"You were right, absolutely right. I threw caution to the wind. I just... wanted it all, I was so out of control this entire time. You know, you've been along with us, this whole way, done everything you can, mending fences, keeping us safe, you've been the glue holding us together," she finally looked at him, silver eyes filling to the brim, glistening in the bright morning light.

She must have been in agony in the glare, but this was important, she needed to see him. And he needed to see her.

"But...through it all, no matter what happens, or has, in fact, happened," she cleared her throat, passing a hand over her brow.

"I've known that you've never been mine. You and Addy, there's something, not sure what, I'm not even sure if it'll ever be more, but I've seen the way she looks at you, I've seen the way your body language changes when she's close. I've heard the way you say her name. Hell, you guys fucking glow when you touch. You couldn't see it that night in Reno, but your presence just, it filled that tunnel. I was watching you, and I've never seen anything like it. You've been through the fire, you two, with me tagging along, and I thought... hoped, I had a claim to a part of it too. It was a stupid thing, and it happened, but I'm not stupid, Deke," she smiled, quietly, tiny twists at the corners of her full lips.

"Clara, it's not-," Deke started, hesitantly, head buzzing with what she was saying.

She shushed him, quietly, realizing that Reggie was approaching them.

"Deke, just never let her down again, alright?"

The smile cranked up another notch, and she let out a laugh nervously, before turning her full attention off of him, demeanor changing to serious and fully obedient in the presence of her older brother.

Deke would always marvel at her in that moment, that bright light sparkling off her hair, her white smile, and her glistening molten eyes.

How much more would this girl give up for her family?

Who would ever provide her with the happiness she so desperately deserved in return?

The whole team, as Deke was now calling their collective, stood fanned around Reggie, a half circle surrounding where Deke and Clara sat, Casey a half step back from everyone, still unsure of his place or position, still crippled by the memories of San Francisco that haunted his eyes.

"We're going straight up the path, right up the middle; keep all the eyes on us. She'll have Addy front and center, guaranteed, but I bet you the Charges will be lurking in the woods. You guys go after them, use your speed to your advantage, only buzz them out at last resort, you've got guns, they're really only people – so use them," Reggie explained.

Clara gulped.

Something ticked in Deke's brain.

"Wait a minute, *SHE?*"

He stood up angrily, the ring suddenly seeming close and accusing. A thunderbolt of panic seemed to hit Clara; she was shaking her head fervently at Reggie. Several heartbeats passed, the seconds ticking away. Deke's eyes narrowed. They weren't sidestepping this. Not now, not ever.

"Who has Addy? And how do you know who they are?"

The Tenders all seemed to be holding their breath, while Clara looked on the verge of a full-on panic attack.

"Didn't she tell you? Not much for pillow talk, huh, sis?" Reggie's eyes focused angrily on Clara.

Deke took a furious step towards Reggie.

Screw needing his energy for the fight ahead. He'd fight Reggie now, just to get the truth out of him. He relished the thought of finally shocking this asshole back on his ass. Whoever had Addy was hurting her, and Reggie knew who it was this whole time?

"Your Tender, Clara's Tender, and I can only assume Casey's Tender, is our Mother, and I use that term loosely," Reggie confessed flatly.

Deke swore he saw stars, the revelation would have knocked him flat back onto the log behind his knees, but he took a deep breath and steadied himself. Deke stuttered for words, trying to grasp exactly what this meant.

"Don't hurt yourself, Deke," Reggie cleared his throat.

Casey's head was whipping back and forth between Reggie and Deke, trying to absorb what was being said.

"How do you know?" Deke gulped, looking at Clara for answers.

"Why she sold her soul wasn't the only thing Clara remembered last night, Deke, and I've known the truth for years. How do you think I got roped into this? I knew it must be true though, once you so vehemently described that awful smell, those lilies,"

An intense look of disgust crossed his face, a muscle memory, reflex at this point.

That moment with Addy in their cottage filled Deke's brain, the smell in her hair. She'd slept in her mother's room. He'd known, deep down, that he recognized it, and it had unsettled him, drove him close to crazy, but he didn't until this second know why.

Clara wouldn't meet his eyes.

"But don't worry about us, Deke, this has been a long time coming, and there won't be any feelings getting in the way of what needs getting done," Reggie smiled grimly.

Deke was still reeling. But what was she? What were they? Were any of them actually considered human?

A ripple of smirks and quiet snorts went through the crew.

GET OUT OF MY HEAD! He shrieked internally.

"No worries Deke, the Byrnes, well, we're human enough, where it counts. She, on the other hand, I don't even know. But the face she showed you isn't her true form, neither is the face that raised us. She's something else completely, something from the deep and dark and twisted. From the readings we've done, from the books we've stolen from her private collection, I'm fairly certain she's the creature that made the original deal on this ground with John Purcell over a hundred years ago in the name of the Devil, but that's just our guess," Reggie rested the stock of the rifle he carried on the ground.

He looked at the gathered group, and took a deep steadying breath.

"We're Tenders, so don't worry about the Collectors. You know as well as I do they can only touch Charges. Ready Charges at that, and I think the three of you should be good," his eyes passed over Casey, Deke and Clara, resting on Clara's strangely hopeful face.

Deke looked at everyone, and asked the question no one had brought to their lips.

"But what happens once we find Addy? How exactly do we get her back from your mother?"

Reggie fixed him with his intense gaze, they were Addy's eyes, staring right through Deke.

"Just leave it up to me," he smiled grimly, swinging the rifle up onto his shoulder and nodding his head in the direction of the forest.

No more words were said. Everyone followed into the dark and tangled brambles of the underbrush, Reggie's group heading toward the brightened dirt path, hot in the sun, the rest moving off between the trees.

And it was the last moment that anything went right.

Clara's heart pounded. The forest was eerily quiet, the dappling sun and shadows blurring together in the wake of the unshed tears of her eyes. She held her gun at the ready, down and to the side the way that Julia had showed her. Deke and Casey had long ago fanned off to the right, heading towards the west side of the clearing she could spot far ahead through the trees.

Occasionally, the sharp report of a pistol would come echoing through the woods at her, and she would jump, scared, wondering when it would be coming for her.

She wanted to cry. She wanted to curl up at the base of a tree, just hide; she didn't want to be brave anymore. She felt like a child, cold and uncertain, her stomach in her throat. All those nights, when she'd been hunting, in the dark, even though she hadn't been in control, she hadn't been afraid. They didn't let her be afraid. Now the fear that crawled up her back threatened to consume her entirely.

She wiped her nose with the back of her hand, conscious of the gun in her grip.

She wished Mateo was here. He'd know what to say, what to do. He'd comfort her. Hell, he'd take care of it for her. He'd tell her to go home, and that he would look after it. She hoped he'd found Addy. He was the only one who'd ever made things right.

Reggie felt more exposed now that Deke and Casey had split from their group. He hadn't realized the comfort he had felt having their crackling and spitting energy close by. They were something he knew, something he could deal with. They had the speed and the adrenaline he needed to protect the group; to protect Julia. His gaze swung her way, his brave little warrior, so tiny, so much stronger than he.

Everyone had their rock, but Julia was a mountain, and he'd do anything for her. He'd begged her to stay back; he didn't want Mother to see her. He didn't want Mother to *know* that someone was in his life, that someone other than her was important; because she'd use her against him.

But if all went as he believed it would, it wouldn't matter anymore. The four of them were propped against a hillock, surveying the scene in front of them. Rick had run off, flanking the left. Guns were his thing. Danger was his thing. The guy was an adrenaline junkie, addicted to extreme sports and hunting and racing, fast cars and death-defying stunts. Reggie hadn't had to tell him twice.

He figured Rick was also anxious about his mentor, Mateo, and needed to get him in his line of sight.

Reggie accepted this.

Mateo had raised him and his sisters, knew everything about them, taught them everything he knew.

It took a long time for them to build that relationship back up, after Clara's little indiscretion, but it had happened. But Addy ranked over Mateo, and Mateo knew that. Reggie had made him promise. He knew now, the only way out was dead. He didn't need the reminder.

His head turned to Julia again, and she smiled, brilliant eyes taking him in, her soft and minty smell light in his nose. He wrapped an arm around her and pulled her close, kissing her deeply, tasting the metallic twang of her piercing on his lips.

Rick stood over the Charge, an older woman; dark hair streaked with grey, watching as the red stain on the chest of her shirt expanded slowly, the scent of the gunshot fading in the air. Her eyes were wide and unseeing, bright silver and rimmed with blue. He could hear his blood thudding in his ears, and took a deep steadying breath.

One down.

"Our guests are here," Levina smiled, rising from **where** she had been sitting primly on the edge of one of the few standing gravestones.

She stared off into the distance for a moment, focused on the distant path that entered the clearing, and then turned towards me.

She pointed with her fingers,

"Four there," she pointed to the right of the path's entrance.

"One there," she turned her finger to the right.

"And let's see... ah yes, my lovely boys, the Mastersons, and of course, Ellaclara," she swung her hand in a wave towards the left, off into the trees.

The Mastersons? I thought.

Wait.

Casey? He was here?

How? Where? My head spun. Where did Casey come from? My brain tripped back to the phone call from Reggie, when we had been in Salt Lake City, his muffled raving about tranquilizers. It couldn't have been, could it?

Levina took two steps forward, gesturing Mateo to bring me forward also. He whispered a quiet apology in my ear, and pressed me forward.

"Reginald, darling, I know you are out there, you and Deacon, we can make this easy, if you just come out and play now, don't cause any more trouble for your Mother," she called loudly out at the ring of trees.

Everything had gone eerily quiet, no sounds echoing around the meadow. I didn't know where the Collectors had gone to, and if the hounds were wandering, hunting the forests for Reggie and his team, they were silent.

I resisted the urge to scream out, to tell them to go, to leave me to her. What was the worst that could happen to me? What was the worst that could happen if Reggie surrendered; or even if Deke surrendered? They'd figure something out, right?

I shuddered in response. This wasn't going to end well, no matter how much careful planning had gone into it. Reggie wasn't exactly known for his foresight; his game plan of act first, ask later had gotten him into more than one fight he couldn't win as a teenager.

"Deke, no, don't do it, don't listen to her,"

Casey grabbed at the front of Deke's shirt, shaking him.

"Casey, I have to, there's no other way," Deke yanked his collar from Casey's grip.

Casey's eyes searched his, wanting him to agree, wanting him to stay. He'd only just gotten his brother back, and now he was throwing himself to a madwoman; a madwoman who wasn't technically even a woman. What world had he gotten himself wrapped into?

"Deke, please, don't do this to me," Casey pleaded.

He was no longer beyond begging. If he'd only begged sooner – years ago, maybe they wouldn't be in this mess today.

Deke wanted to hug him, wanted to let him know it would be alright. But he couldn't in his right mind make another promise he couldn't keep.

Casey whispered, sullenly,

"Don't leave me alone again,"

Deke sighed, studied Casey's face. Yes, he had grown up; too much, too fast, alone for too long.

A small noise hitched in Casey's chest, a sob he didn't want to let Deke hear.

That one small sound from Casey suddenly burst through the cloud that Deke's shift in reality had wrapped around his brain in a cold fog. It was all it took. He remembered what he'd given his soul up for. A small murmur escaped him, whether a whimper or a laugh, he'd never remember in the brightness of his sudden realization.

He had wished that Casey wouldn't hate him anymore for abandoning him. All of Deke's own anger, he'd kept –

because it was anger at himself for doing the wrong thing. All he'd wanted was his brother to remember he still loved him.

And now he was doing it all over again.

"Casey, I promise I'll be back for you, this isn't ending here," he clutched the thick leather of the shoulder of Casey's borrowed jacket.

Casey resisted the urge to grasp his hand, his lip trembling.

Deke, stricken deep down into his heart, gave him one last smile, and hurriedly turned away, pushing his way out of the underbrush and into the clearing.

I could see Mother was getting impatient. Her jaw tightened ominously.

A flurry of movement came from the trees to our left; Deke manhandled his way through the thick underbrush, silently approaching the foot of the hillock. He had shadows under his eyes, his clothes were roughed up, and he was brandishing a gun. On top of it all, his skin crackled and flared, sending off embers in all directions as he gazed up at Mother at the top of the hill. Our eyes met, once, and then he slid all of his attention back to her.

"What is that asshole doing?" Reggie blurted out, watching Deke from across the field from their hiding spots.

Connor shook his head in response. Stella had disappeared to find Rick moments before, itching for a fight.

A voice, high and lilting, a touch of an accent, caressed across his front brain, deep inside his head,

"Come here, Reginald, come out, come out, I know you're here,"

Reggie felt a chill run down his spine. Similarly, Julia and Connor shivered on either side of him.

"She knows you're close enough," Connor shrieked, his voice barely a notch below only dogs hearing.

"Connor, you know damn well she knows exactly where every one of us is right now," Julia muttered across Reggie's neck at him.

Twigs snapped behind them, a low growl issuing from seemingly thin air.

Reggie rolled around onto his back, swinging the rifle around and fired off a shot into the trees. He was rewarded with a loud yelp and thud. He hoped he had killed it, and not merely enraged it or its friends.

He paused, listening carefully.

Another sharp report came from the direction Stella had run, and then another, and another. Connor moved to get up and run towards the sound, but Reggie stopped him, grabbing onto his wrist.

Connor yanked his hand away from Reggie and looked at him hard.

I need you to watch after Julia

Reggie, no, you're not asking me to do that

Yes, I am, you promise me she gets out of here

I'm coming with you

Don't make me hit you again in your big dumb head, Connor. Do what I ask you to, ok?

Connor's eyes searched Reggie's one more time, before he conceded, the defiant fire burning out in him. He pushed his glasses up his nose, his shoulders slumping.

After how many years that Reggie had taken care of him, it was the least he could do in return.

Reggie ran one of Julia's thick purple plaits through his hand, and smiled, cupping her head and kissing her once more, quickly and with determination.

He pulled himself up and over the ridge they'd been kneeling behind, and headed out into the brilliant sunshine, tall, posture straight, head held high.

Reggie was never going to be afraid of Levina again, he would make her damn sure of it.

He caught sight of a couple of Collectors, lurking in his sightline just along the edges of the trees. They seemed to have been attracted by the shooting of the hound, though they didn't speak. The odd rushing sound of wind and the strange refracting of light just behind them signified that their portals were mostly closed; no one was around worth tearing through time and space. Not just yet, anyway.

"Ah, boys, come a little closer," Levina drawled, gesturing out with both hands, palms up, gesturing for their approach.

Reggie and Deke stood still where they had entered the glade, a couple hundred feet apart, staring up at where she stood. Reggie tipped his head slightly at Deke, who nodded in return. With an exaggerated sigh of frustration, Levina gestured again, this time, their bodies reacted limply, puppets on strings, rising awkwardly up into the air, feet dragging, pinched by invisible grips on their shoulders.

She gestured again, and they slowly dragged forward, struggling against invisible bonds, guns dropping into the grass from their grasping hands.

Reggie struggled to yell, to shout, to threaten, to swear bloody curse words but nothing would whisper through his suddenly silent throat. Deke appeared to be trying the same thing, straining himself, face turning sullenly red. However, the more they struggled, the tighter the hand squeezed, feeling their bones clicking together in an invisible vice.

Once they had reached the top of the hill, brambles brushing the bottoms of their feet, Levina released them, dropping them hard onto the ground, legs buckling beneath them.

Reggie sat on the ground, livid, fuming, and waiting for her to make her next move. He looked at Addy, rigidly standing next to Mateo, worry in her eyes. She didn't look scared. He had never seen her downright scared, never seen her terrified. She was always the calm one. The organized one. If she'd had his powers, none of this ever would have happened. He hoped between her and Mateo that they had a game plan, which they would use anything he'd do as a distraction to their advantage when the moment came.

He wished in that moment, that he'd had a chance to explain everything.

Would they still be here, in this place, if he had?

I studied Reggie and Deke, now mere feet away from where I stood with Mateo, and I hoped they were okay. They didn't look any worse for wear, hadn't been injured by the gunshots I'd heard, ringing out from the trees. I wondered where Casey was, wondered what their plan was. I wondered if any of us were getting out of this alive.

Deke's eyes met mine, wincing against the glare and heat of the bright noonday sun. He must have been in agony, but he didn't want to let it show. I brought my hand up, slowly, as if to scratch my face, and silently tapped the side of my nose. For a split second, his concern flashed away, a trace of smile turned up the corner of his mouth. And then his attention was back onto Levina.

"Why must you test my patience, Reginald?"

Levina rolled her eyes. Reggie had been trying to fight his way to his feet, exaggerating every motion struggling against a harsh current.

"Don't fight with her Reggie, it'll just make it worse," Mateo muttered under his breath.

Levina turned to look at Mateo, daggers in her eyes. A moment of realization hit her, and she turned back towards Reggie.

"I see what you've done, Reginald, I see that you've tried to turn my most faithful against me, again. By now I am sure you know that it was part of the deal Clara made with me. But I see that the two of you have become reacquainted. No matter, he can't prevent what will happen from happening," she smiled, venomous.

"How could you let Clara make a deal? Do you feel nothing?" Reggie hoarsely called up to where she stood.

She had finally released his vocal cords, and they sounded strained, taut.

"Darling, you've been involved in this long enough to know better, it's all about the deals, and the souls, nothing is more important," she strode up to where he remained kneeling, and looked down at him, a steadily rising wind whipping her hair around her face.

She looked up pointedly to the sky – the wind was rushing in whirling dervishes, scattering loose leaves and dust into the air. Dark and swollen clouds were gathering on the horizon. There was soon to be a severe storm crashing down on them, the static in the air raising the hair on their arms. The dull groan of thunder reached their ears, deep and full in the distance.

It was then I noticed Rick, rising out of the tall grass on the far side of the hill. A trickle of blood ran down his temple, a scrape across his cheek. I tried to catch his attention, I tried to shake my head, and I would have screamed if I thought it would have made a difference.

But he strode quickly, defiantly, with purpose, towards Levina, arm raised, pistol at the ready, aiming for the back of her skull. He was mere feet away from her, when I could see her smile in reaction, teeth glaringly white and pointed, golden eyes flashing.

She raised an arm, and made a shooing motion, dismissing a rather obnoxious fly.

Rick was picked up, clear off his feet, and sent tumbling backwards far off to where he had climbed from, his body tossed like a ragdoll to where he fell outside of my sightline down the side of the hill.

Unexpectedly, Clara had rose out of the grass at the same time, hurtling through the air sideways and landing hard against a barely standing gravestone, her arm cracking mightily with the force of the impact, and her scream wrenched through the air. It was then that all went quiet, not even a whimper from her, and no sign of Rick.

I thrashed against the suddenly tight grip of Mateo, he wouldn't let me go, wouldn't let me run to her, wouldn't let me see. He wrapped his arms around me as I struggled, flailed, I tried elbowing him in the face, the side, I needed to see Clara, I needed to make sure she was alright.

Deke had the same idea, but he struggled against an invisible captor, his skin glowing and flashing with unrestrained reserves of power. I could see him losing focus from here – I could see the predator rising to the surface, his pupils expanding. I could see that if there was one faint moment of misguided relaxation on Levina's part, he would be at her throat.

"There's the Deacon I wanted to see,"

Levina grinned maniacally, relishing in watching his face curl into a snarl, and the lightning crackling along his fingers.

I was horrified, yet enthralled. This was the creature hiding deep inside, the one that lived in all the Charges, feeding on the energy, obeying the orders from the Tenders.

It was Deke, yet not, the features hardened, twisted, unnatural. I could see his pupils had widened to the point of complete dilation, not even a rim of silver remained.

Reggie looked on in horror. He wasn't even trying to fight against Levina anymore, every muscle tensed for the moment she let him go. I had an idea of where Levina was going with this. She was riling up the both of them to the point of no return, until she could be sure that Deke was an absolute threat.

"So Reginald, I will give you a choice now," she crouched in front of Reggie, and absently stroked his cheek.

He cringed back from her touch in response. I could barely hear her from where I had collapsed against Mateo, panting, exhausted from trying to thrash away from him. He still hadn't loosened his hold.

"Join us, join me, once more, and we'll remove those silly marks. We'll turn you back onto the path of the True Mission. Or I release your new little best friend here, and see what order he chooses your precious sisters to die in. Or perhaps, he'll choose Mateo first, what do you think?"

Reggie's eyes briefly flicked towards the snarling face of Deke, and then to me.

"Reggie, don't do it! Don't give in to her, it's not worth it, we're not worth it, don't go back to her!" I screamed, renewing the struggle against Mateo, who firmly clamped a hand over my mouth.

He pulled me backwards, staggering away from the peak of the hill, hauling me away from seeing where Clara lay, farther away from the twitching and violently clawing Deke, only restrained by the will of Levina.

I could barely hear what Levina said next, Reggie's voice carrying in the wind and maelstrom surrounding us, echoing in my head more than in my ears,

"I'll never join you again, Levina, it will never happen, I would rather die. Just take my soul as payment, take it, take it for Addy, let her go, just let her leave, she's no good to you without me, without Deke, she would rather die, so please, just let her go,"

I know I screamed, though I didn't hear it in the rising shriek of wind, but I know I screamed. I heard Levina's joyful cackle above the chaos, and the sky tore apart, the sudden rain thundering down on our heads.

"You think there's hope. You think you can change, change back, once you make a deal, don't you? It can't be reversed darling, but say the words, and it's mine," she wrapped her hand around his throat, pulling him to his feet, holding him high above her head, he struggled and kicked, feet trying to find purchase in the air.

I didn't hear the words with my own ears, but I knew what he said. Levina made sure the images flashed in my brain, over and over, surely to drive me mad.

Reggie's face, dripping with rain, water pouring down Levina's arm, soaking into her shirt sleeve. Reggie's eyes fading, regret buried deep in them, their vibrant green no longer flashing.

He croaked out,

"I give my soul for Addy to escape you,"

Levina cackled once more, her grinning teeth growing ever more pointed. She uttered only one word,

"Deal,"

And with that final word, my world came crashing down around me. It seemed so simple, such a simple tiny action, a slight twist of her hand.

But I hadn't known, had never known, she was so strong. Psychic energy, magic, whatever was used, there was no way that the damage she then inflicted on Reggie's body could have been performed in any other way, so rapidly, so exquisitely, so deadly.

Reggie's head twisted violently to the side, too far, too fast, a loud cracking sounding across the meadow, and then each, and every, single bone in his body followed, in rapid succession and in horrifying detail. I watched, as the card tower crumbled, collapsing ever downward, the snapping of his bones ringing in my ears.

Mateo grasped my shoulders and turned me towards him, trying to cover my ears, to smother the sound, pushing my head into his chest. I couldn't even cry, I couldn't even think of what was happening, what I'd seen, every molecule in my body suspended in disbelief, every nerve screaming that it wasn't happening. I was screaming into his collarbone, muffled by his vest, drenched by the rain.

Mateo's grip loosened, and I turned back, needing to see, needing to understand. All I saw was Levina flicking her hand, tossing Reggie's broken body away from her, just a discarded toy, just a useless weapon, unimportant and unwanted.

Thunder roared overhead, lighting crashing and crackling around us. The sky was so dark, so menacing, purple and bruised.

Deke was shaking, violently, glowing ever brighter. The storm was doing something to him, and it must be doing something to all the Charges, if there were any left, hiding somewhere in the woods.

Levina stood over him, glaring down at his shuddering,

"And how about you, Deacon? Ready to do what you were born to do?" She shouted over the raging storm.

She turned away from him, and pointed towards me,

"And go,"

Deke sagged momentarily, relaxing against the sudden release of tension, and then sprung to his feet. Whatever Levina's plan had been, Deke hadn't received the memo. Maybe it was part of Reggie's deal, but Deke didn't spring towards me.

Deke lunged directly at Levina's waist, tackling her to the ground in a moment of unexpected violence. Deke straddled her as she twisted in his grasp, and his hands reached for her throat, his grip slipping on her neck in the pouring rain.

I lunged forward, wanting to help, but Mateo looped an arm around my waist, leaning forward and yelling into my ear over the storm,

"This is our chance, we have to go, we have to go now, once he's done with her, he'll come for us,"

I shook my head and continued fighting, needing to see.

Levina placed a hand on Deke's chest, even as her face turned purple, and abruptly tore Deke away from her, sending him plummeting back down the hill from where he had arrived, smashing headlong into a headstone obscured by the high grass.

A shrieking scream came from the treeline, and a young man came racing from out of the forest, dark haired and tall, angular, eyes flaring in the brilliant flashes of lightning.

"Casey!" I screamed, hoping to attract his attention, to prevent him from attacking Levina.

If Deke had no chance, there wasn't any way in Hell that Casey could do anything more.

There was a brief hesitation in the direction he headed, a faltering as he heard his name. He didn't know who I was, he didn't know why I knew his name, but it was in that second he had realized his mistake.

A Collector appeared between Casey's advancing form and where Levina stood, poised on the hilltop, waiting for the younger Masterson to come for her. If I hadn't been staring directly where the Collector has appeared, I would have assumed he arrived in a bolt of lightning, the rushing and tumultuous portal opening wide behind him, a sneer crossing his face.

Lifting the chains in front of him, the Collector suddenly threw them, as if they weighed no more than a small bit of rope, directly at Casey, and where they touched him, they wrapped, tight, alive, a metallic snake, a metal constrictor around his arms and legs and chest, pulling tighter and tighter.

The Collector snarled, smiling, the end of chain that remained in his hand heavy, and he pulled, tugging Casey towards him. Casey screamed, the chains cutting into him, skin bulging and straining against the links.

I looked on in horror, watching as the tethered and bound little brother of Deke was dragged, kicking and screaming along the muddy ground, the weeds and thorns tearing at his clothes and hair and skin.

Deke rose up, staggering, collecting himself, hand to his head, and his eyes lit onto Casey. My heart broke, at the look of utter defeat that crossed his face, even in his frenzied state as he saw his brother being dragged towards Hell.

Levina's eyes lit up as she saw Deke struggling to climb up the hill towards her. I could see she took joy in this, in the heartbreak of others. She was a monster I would destroy, when I had my chance.

She let him get close to her, so close, gazing at him with her golden eyes, a thrilled look of success in her face.

When he lunged for her once more, she gripped his reaching forearm, his scars glinting in the effervescence of the storm, and he howled in pain. Whatever it was that she had done to me, on numerous occasions, whatever it was that she did that rippled pain through every square inch of your body, she unleashed fully on him, until he collapsed, panting at her feet, tears pouring down his face.

It was then that I noticed Clara, struggling around the headstones, and I could feel Mateo tightening his grip, still trying to pull me away, trying to let me take my chance to live, trying to convince me that I couldn't let Reggie's death be for nothing.

I wouldn't listen. His words flowed over and through me and in and out of my forebrain in a steady stream.

I denied them all.

This was ending here.

I wasn't running.

Clara climbed steadily along the ridge behind Mother, fingers digging into the grass, pulling herself along with one arm, the other, so twisted and broken and held against her body as tightly as she could. Her feet were having problems catching themselves in the wet grass; I could see her sliding backwards every few feet, the steep incline holding her down. She was glowing and crackling, entire body charged and sparking, a bright white light. I didn't know how Levina couldn't see her, the stark contrast in darkened stormy skies setting stark shadows across the trees. Maybe she couldn't see, for how brightly that Deke now burned.

Deke wheezed where he lay at Mother's feet, gasping for air under her foot that now rested on his throat, his face bloody and dripping, the wound on his temple from his headlong descent into the headstone still oozing, his skin flickering white lightning across his entire body. The wind howled, whipping leaves and dust in dizzying maelstrom around the three of them. Levina stared down at him, malevolent, hatred burning in her eyes. She was unaffected by the heat and the electricity he was generating, immune to his powers, so much less than her own.

"You should've stayed down, dog, and taken what you deserve, no one fights against me," she growled down at him, an eye on the Collector who had succeeded in pulling Casey up to his knees, a hand wrapped tightly in the chains that bound him impossibly tight.

Deke weakly grasped her ankle, trying to pull her away, but it was to no avail. He hadn't yet noticed Clara, squirming her way slowly towards him, the tears running down her face. I fought once more, struggling against Mateo, his arms held tightly across my body, pinning my hands down, keeping a wide stance so that I wouldn't topple us both to the ground. I kicked down on his in-sole, stamping as hard as I could, and he exhaled sharply, leaning forward, mouth pressed to my ear, uttering swears and threats in rapid Spanish, only an occasional word piercing my understanding.

But he had finally given me the moment I had needed, I had finally wore him down, his arms had loosened when he had reacted, and I forced myself forward once again, ripping free of his grasp, stumbling forward towards the hillock. I headed directly for Clara, running to her in a desperate flurry.

I realized at that moment, that Clara had reached out to Deke, sliding a half step back, and then flopping forward, hand reaching, desperately, clawing towards him. Deke's eyes were fixed, staring at me, slowly dimming, and the fire that flashed behind them fading quickly, the fight washing out of his face. He smiled, slowly, defeated, eyes closing.

"Clara, no!" I screamed, but she lunged forward once more anyway, grasping Deke's outstretched hand where he lay.

Levina turned awkwardly at the same moment, finally realizing her daughter lay sprawled behind her, and shrieked out a high pitched howl, but it was too late.

The instant Deke and Clara's hands connected, a blindingly white flash erupted between them, swallowing the entire scene, lightning and thunder rolled into one, the intense heat expanding outward, an atomic bomb. A rolling bang followed the explosion, rippling outward, creating another flash, cracking whip-quick through the air, and the subsequent explosion threw me backwards, landing hard against Mateo where he crumpled to the ground beneath me.

The surrounding Charges that had been lurking in the trees similarly ignited, their light adding to the searing brilliance as the explosion continued outward another three hundred feet. My ears rang with a piercing and shrieking in my ears, the force rushing past them, wind howling. The portal that the Collector had opened in order to pull Casey through suddenly slammed shut, and the sudden absence of the Hell door sucking the air from all around made me gasp in the resulting vacuum. I cringed against the prone form of Mateo as the pressure reversed, back towards the ignition point of the explosion, wind rushing past my body, and I covered my face with my hands.

Everything suddenly went dark.

However much longer later... I didn't quite know.

Everything lay quiet. No sounds rustled in the grass, no tree peepers sounding from their hidden perches, no owls calling in the dark. As I opened my eyes, I saw that the moon rode high in the sky, silent witness to the destruction that had occurred.

I still lay half sprawled against Mateo, and I was afraid to move, my eyes unseeing, only the brightness of the moon coming through. I was afraid I had broken every bone in my body. I was afraid that Mateo lay dead beneath me. I stared up at the heavens, and struggled to wrap my head around the last few seconds of consciousness I could remember.

The stars twinkled bravely, coming into my field of vision, resiliently shining above. I sat up, slowly, hesitantly, hand to my forehead, it felt wet and sticky. I wasn't sure where I had hit it. I looked around cautiously, waiting at any moment for the Charges to come back out from the woods, for the Tenders to swoop in and take me. I looked down at Mateo, barely visible in the moonlight. He wasn't moving, and I wasn't entirely certain he was breathing. I rested a hand on his chest, the firm weight of his bullet proof vest below his shirt unyielding beneath my palm.

Mateo shot upwards, abruptly sitting up, clutching at his throat, gasping deeply, I shrieked, fumbling backwards, horrified. His hand moved to his side, the only way I could tell was the glint of his watch in the dark, and he panted, wincing. I could just barely make out the whites of his eyes as he choked out,

"God, Addy, I think you broke a rib," he flopped backwards onto the grass, gulping at the air like a stranded fish.

I waited for my heartbeat to settle, pounding against my chest. I struggled to my feet, the ground feeling strange around me, something different, something changed. I stooped to touch it, and realized the blades of grass were disintegrating where I touched them. I raised my fingers to my face, smelling the powder that covered them, and realized what had happened. The grass had turned to ash, the blades collapsing as the wind brushed across them, scattering across the burnt out cemetery.

What the Hell had happened?

I turned, facing roughly where I had last seen Deke, Clara, and Levina, and headed in that direction, my knees weak and shaking, kicking up dust clouds, coughing on the still warm ashes. Everything flowed in slow motion, my ears still ringing, my stuttering steps holding me back from running towards the spot they had last occupied.

It was so, so dark, even in the cold glare of the moon, and I wasn't sure if it was the spots in my eyes left from the flash, or if the dark itself was pressing in deeper than it had before, shadows deepening.

The ground tipped to a steeper incline, pebbles and small twigs joining the sliding cascade of ash that rustled down from below my feet. I had to be there, almost, just a little farther. I tripped, foot connecting with something soft and heavy. I fell hard, my legs still weak, the soft ash puffing out around my hands, and I retched, spitting out a damp paste from breathing in the charred grass. I felt around for where I had tripped, to find out what I had tripped on, the moon passing behind a cloud, the punishing darkness deepening.

When you gathered together the pressure of the dark, and the thickness of the air, the impression was of drowning in the deep, and I struggled with overwhelming feelings of panic. Where was Deke? Where was Clara? After what had just happened, I would never care where Levina went.

I pushed her far from my mind, not wanting to think about our life of lies, her final moments of betrayal. I fumbled again for where I had tripped, there had to be someone here, anyone. They couldn't just be gone. I couldn't stand it.

A cold stretch of skin appeared under my grasping fingers, a wrist, and the worn sleeve of a sweater. I cried out, thanking God that whoever it was hadn't been completely obliterated in the preternatural explosion of light and sound.

I cried in the dark, tears no doubt leaving streams in the ash smearing down my face. They had to be alive, had to be. My fingers groped at the shirt, finding stomach, chest, and a dusty throat, the scratch of his unshaved face. Deke; it was Deke. I struggled forward, unzipping the sweater, the metal hot against my fingers. I put my ear to his chest, desperately hoping to hear something, anything.

After all we'd been through, all we'd seen, all we'd struggled through, the ominous presence of this moment threatened to crush me.

Mateo limped up behind me; I could hear him wheezing through the pain and the dust. He stayed a careful distance back, hesitant and unbending.

I called Deke's name, over and over, touching his face, his hair, trying so hard to see. I could hear Mateo saying my name, in the back of my head, over and over, gentle, unyielding, so quiet I couldn't tell if his lips were forming the words, or if he had entered into my head. I ignored him, ignored the ringing in my ears. Nothing else mattered at this very second than for Deke to open his eyes, to wake up. There was so much that needed to be explained, said, torn down to the beginning and fixed. There was too much too fix.

I rested my ear near his mouth, holding my breath, hoping to hear or feel anything, waiting for the tell-tale tickle, waiting for a faint wheeze to give me a sign. I hauled him up by his sweater, a dead weight in my arms, pulling him to sitting, clutching onto him, determined he would wake up.

I was determined he would crack another joke, that I'd hear him laugh again. That this wasn't all for nothing. The tears rolled down my face, mixing with the dust and grime that covered us both, dripping into his hair as I sobbed, his head lolling against my chest. I could feel Mateo's hands on my shoulders, his long fingers prying at mine, trying to pull Deke from my grasp.

I froze as I heard a shuddering gasp from a few feet away, and Mateo turned his attention to the crumpled heap we had overlooked, Casey, broken and bleeding in the dark. He coughed, hard, a wet sound, gurgling in his throat. Mateo gently untangled him from the heavy chain, looping it in both hands, hauling it off him as slowly and carefully as he could. He was a mess. Mateo knew that there was a slim chance he was getting off this dusty hill, let alone seeing daybreak.

"Hey, hey, let me, get, me, me," Casey stuttered, pointing slowly towards Deke, torn arm stretching out slowly, lungs struggling for air, bloody hand flopping, finger slowly uncurling.

Mateo looked at him doubtfully, gently trying to extract the rest of the chains from where they had cut into his body. Casey didn't even have it in him to scream, only a hoarse cry escaped his lips in the absence of any strength he had left.

Mateo pulled him to his knees, supporting him under a shoulder, half carrying, half dragging him across the charred earth, cringing as one of Casey's legs bent wrong against the ground, obviously broken in several places. Luckily for both of them, the distance to where I sat cradling Deke's prone form was only a few feet, and Casey stumbled to the ground, pulling himself stiffly from Mateo's grip, gurgling on the ashes next to me.

He reached a tentative hand up, slowly, wrapping his fingers in the collar of Deke's shirt, pulling at him, trying to pull him down to where he had laid his cheek in the dust. I gaped at him, vision blurring, looking up to Mateo, not knowing what to do.

With Mateo's help, I lowered Deke down towards Casey, not wanting to let him go. Not wanting to see them lying there, face to face, the brothers' dead or dying, side by side, waiting for the end to claim them. Mateo turned his head away, standing tall, hands on hips, and then slowly turned away, something catching his attention, heading farther down the hill.

Casey hesitantly touched Deke's face, staring at his closed eyes. The hoarse wheezing coming from Casey was quieting, time slowing. I remained motionless, holding my breath, knowing when this moment ended, everything would be different, and terrible, astonishingly resounding. Casey's voice, ragged and quiet and barely above a whisper poured from his lips,

"Tell him I forgave him,"

Casey's hand strayed down Deke's face, finding his chest, resting on his heart. I heard him muttering under his breath, realizing what he was doing. I couldn't stop him.

Time stood still, and I watched in the darkness as Casey's hand erupted into light, lightning scattering across his bleeding and broken fingers, vivid blue, clutching at Deke's chest in a tight spasm, until the brightness abruptly went out. Deke gasped, hard, a deep and rattling breath, his heart starting once more from the blast of electricity of Casey's dying gesture, the final word quiet on his lips, visibly deflating as his last breath left his body.

There would be no more Hell for Casey, on earth or beyond.

Deke lay there, gasping, clutching at his brother's hand that lay limp on his chest, crying out his name. I started crying again, and Deke finally realized I sat in the dust at his side, and he sat up, rising from the ashes to cling to me, blinking and gasping in the night. I couldn't let him go. I wouldn't, not now, not ever. Every moment leading up to now, whatever direction we had taken, the choices we made, were irrelevant in the face of death.

His cool hands found my face, his thumbs at my cheeks, fingertips gently in my hair, and pulled my mouth to his, kissing me deeply, passionately, the taste of ash and salt and sweat and tears mixing together into an overpowering blend of survival on our lips. I touched his face, his throat, feeling the warmth returning to his skin. He was alive; so very alive.

I took a deep breath, savoring the moment.

"Casey?" Deke breathed, the word slowly unraveling from his lips, eyes squeezed tight.

I shook my head in his hands, taking a shuddering breath, squeezing back the tears. The seconds ticked by in the chill of the night; infinite and eternal.

"Clara?" My heart stopped.

I untangled from Deke's arms, stumbling to my feet, pulling at Deke's hands, pulling him to standing, dragging him upward as he faltered, a sudden surge running through me. Clara, not Clara, not now, where was she?

I had barely gone a few steps when I realized Mateo stood at the bottom of the hill, staring up at me, the moon finally coming back out from behind the scuttling and swollen clouds, bathing everything in moonlight.

The dark spots had left my vision, I could finally see, properly, and wished forever from that moment onward that I couldn't.

Mateo stood, wavering, with the tired, cold, and dispassionate stance of someone who had seen far too much, something dark and heavy in his arms. The moonlight glistened off her long blond hair, trailing over his arm where he held her close to his broken chest.

Deke and I both whispered, simultaneously,

"No,"

Together, we ran, stumbling, catching our steps, clouds of ash glittering in the bright light of the overhead witness. Mateo stood silently; face stony, holding Clara so tightly.

"Clara, Clara, honey, honey, you need to wake up,"

I clutched at her face, her hands, but she lay limp in Mateo's arms, her skin cold, much too cold.

"Put her down, put her on the ground," Deke instructed, rolling up his sleeves, scars glinting in the dark. He placed his hand over her heart, lacing his fingers with his other hand, to begin CPR.

"Deke, I already, I already tried, it didn't, it didn't take, it's too late," Mateo ran his hands nervously through his hair, turning away from where Clara lay motionless on the ground.

I reached for Mateo's elbow, offering a comforting hand, my eyes dry, everything inch of me stunned, numb. This couldn't be happening.

Deke began muttering the words he knew so well, the ones that had cured an endless stream of cuts, slashes, stabs, the words that had saved him, so many times, for and against his will; the words that had restarted his stilled heart, uttered by his dying brother.

Nothing happened.

Not a single spark sprang from his hands, no electricity rippled down his arm; the hot embers that would have erupted from his finger tips and from the silver plated barbed wire running up and down his forearms stayed dark.

He stared at his hands, bloody in the moonlight.

He looked at me.

I covered my mouth with my hand, choking down a sob.

Mateo put a comforting arm around my shoulders, his other hand clutching at his ribs.

Time ticked onward, beat by beat.

Deke remained kneeling by Clara's prone form, staring at his hands.

Deke was no longer a Charge - the electricity was gone. They were all gone, evaporated into the night.

Clara, was no longer a Charge either, the spark of humanity extinguished, the warm glowing ember of light and personality gone from her body. The wind kicked up the ashes once more, sending them sparkling up and into the sky.

Chapter 24

The Spark That Left Us

We returned the next day, chilled, numb, to survey the area, to try to understand why it went so wrong for my sister, for Deke's brother. Why Reggie had sacrificed everything.

The area had been blasted clear of the ivy and blackberry vines that had covered the gravestones, jagged teeth remaining in the scorched earth, the overnight wind having washed the ground clean of all the ashes and soot. It appeared to the untrained observer that a magnificently large fire had been set, contained, and left to burn to embers in a five hundred foot radius around the hilltop. We stood silently, holding hands.

I would sneak glances at him, occasionally, the tears glistening in our eyes, tiny beads in his eyelashes, brightening the hazy blue of his eyes, the color of late August afternoon, a color I never thought I'd see.

Aside from the scars, the broad stroke of silver across his stomach, the silver tapestry of his hieroglyphic symbols, the barbed wire running up his arms, Deacon Masterson was himself once more.

We felt hollow inside, empty, and feeling that coming to this place was a mistake. The birds had returned, singing, fluttering about the clearing, their lives unchanged but for the difference in the underbrush. No other sign of the torn apart lives, families, or timelines rearing its ugly head from the trees. Mateo had personally escorted the bodies of Reggie, Casey and Clara away with the authorities, very late last night, only a few hours short of the dawn, and was now dealing with the aftermath.

Rick had been fine, mostly, a broken leg and collarbone keeping him away from his enthusiastic explorations for more than a little while.

We found out, through his stuttering and raving in pain, that he had shot Stella.

She had tried to confront him in the woods, tried to convince him he should go back to Levina, that they were doing something horribly wrong by ignoring their destinies.

He considered that completely unacceptable.

We had all agreed.

Connor had carried Julia, kicking and screaming from the forest, tiny and violent across his shoulder, away from where they had seen Reggie crumpled, discarded and broken.

Julia would never forgive him. But he was okay with that – he'd obeyed Reggie's last wish, and as long as Julia was alive, he would never regret it. He had smiled wryly when he'd pointed out his matching black eye from Julia, mirroring Reggie's.

Deke moved forward, limping slightly, slowly climbing the steep hill, pondering his steps, hesitating every few feet. I suspected he was more grievously injured than he admitted, perhaps ribs had been broken, bones fractured from his forceful fall.

Once Mateo sorted out everything with the authorities, we'd find him proper care. Maybe in a small town somewhere, where maybe they hadn't seen his face on the news.

I watched him go, watched him kneel where the grass underneath his prone form had remained protected from the blast. I watched him stare, unseeing, at the spot where he had died.

We shared that in common now, the love of our siblings transcending our deaths, rising us up from where no one should ever have been able to follow.

And one day, maybe not today, maybe in a few weeks or months from now, when the numbness has shifted to pins and needles, when we allowed ourselves to think, and to feel, and to try to carry on living the lives they gave everything for, we will appreciate what they did for us; we will understand why they felt we were worth so much more than themselves.

We will finally stop regretting that we were the ones who lived, survived, left with the task of carrying on without them.

Maybe then, the spark of wonder, and beauty, the spark of life will return to us, and ignite the fire in us that burned so brightly in them. Ignite the fire and will to live, the testament to the endurance they left behind.

Maybe then, we will be able to burn vibrant without them, for they were the spark that left us.

Made in the USA
Charleston, SC
27 January 2017